GW01071908

Chrissa Mills lives in Newmarket with her husband, and is the mother of three sons. She has always wanted to be a writer, and now she started the stories are tumbling onto the page! BONDED is her first novel.

Bonded

Chrissa Mills

PIATKUS

First published in Great Britain in 1998 by
Judy Piatkus (Publishers) Ltd of
5 Windmill Street, London W1P 1HF

This edition published 1999

The moral right of the author has been asserted

A catalogue record for this book is available from the British Library

ISBN 0 7499 3083 7

Printed & bound in Great Britain by
Mackays of Chatham PLC, Chatham, Kent

For Graham
lover, mentor, friend

1

1967

The parking area closest to the entrance of the Old Bridge Hotel in Huntingdon was packed with posh cars – at least that's how Brenda Tree would have described them. Except, of course, for one small Morris Minor, slightly battered around the sills but clean nonetheless, belonging to Brenda's Gordon. They'd been the first to arrive from the church and had parked just a few polite spaces back. The blue-grey Morris Minor looked sadly out of place later on, but neither Gordon nor Brenda really noticed. Until, that is, it was drawn to their attention.

The wedding reception had nearly run its course, when, with a glass of champagne clutched tightly in her hand, Nancy strutted over in her too-high heels and her too tightly fitting vermillion bouclé suit with silly matching hat perched on her head like a dustbin lid. Her face was as red as her attire as she pursed her lips.

'Something up, Nance?' asked Brenda from her seated position. They were sisters, Brenda and Nancy, but there any similarity ended. Brenda was never allowed to forget that Nancy had married well. Her husband, Peter Lewis, was the financial director of Fordham-Clarke Construction Company in Cambridge. And today was their daughter Clare's wedding day; she'd just married Roger, the eldest, and some would say cleverest, son of Joshua and Cynthia Fordham-Clarke.

Nancy brought the champagne glass to her once generous but now noticeably pinched lips and took a sip. Nervously she scratched her flushed neck with claw-like nails, leaving livid marks in their wake. 'It's just that the bride and groom will be leaving in about twenty minutes and photographs will be taken outside. . . .' She hesitated and glared at them as though she really should not need to explain any further. 'Your car, Brenda,' she mouthed quietly, looking at her sister rather than Gordon.

Brenda frowned. She hadn't a clue what Nancy was on about. 'What about our car'

Nancy shook her head as though her sister was quite stupid. 'It's parked in the way.'

Gordon nudged his wife as a wide smirk crossed his face. He'd grown to love these little skirmishes with Nancy; they'd kept him endlessly amused over the years. 'And you'd like us to move it, Nancy? Our *Morris*? Is that what you're saying?' He spoke loudly, only too aware of the fact that she would rather die than admit the Morris Minor belonged to a close member of her own family.

Nancy's head twisted frantically around and the colour in her cheeks heightened. Nobody was listening. 'It's in the way,' she repeated beneath her breath.

'Is it?' asked Brenda, genuinely perplexed.

Nancy waved her free hand about. 'For the photos, silly.'

Gordon stood up and plunged his hand into his trouser pocket. He took out his car keys, complete with Morris Minor logo tag, and threw them in the air. He caught them flamboyantly. 'And where shall I put my Morris Minor, Nancy, seeing's how there'll be no free spaces anywhere now? Would you like me to park it in one of the flower beds? That'd make a nice picture, don't you think?'

'Oh, very funny,' she scoffed, well used by now to Gordon Tree.

Brenda, feeling thoroughly flustered, also stood up and straightened her Marks and Spencer suit in fine grey wool. She looked lovely in it and Nancy couldn't help taking a second glance, sickened by her sister's slim figure. 'Well, I'm very sorry about all this, Nancy. I can assure you, the last thing Gordon and I wanted to do was to disgrace you on a day like this. Especially with Julia being a bridesmaid.'

Nancy clutched her sister's arm and tried to smile. 'Oh, you're not disgracing me, Brenda, I wasn't implying that, not at all. It's just that the pictures will look so nice, don't you think, with all the Mercedes and BMWs in the background? And, of course, Joshua's Bentley.'

'And your new Jaguar,' Gordon put in.

Nancy ignored him, something she had a habit of doing. 'I'm

sure you'll find a space somewhere. I mean, it's not very *big*, is it?'

Brenda picked up her hat which was lying on the table and clapped it on top of her head. It immediately fell into the perfect position, at just the right angle over her forehead, and the dusky pink set off her grey suit a treat. 'Come on, Gordon,' she said, and politely pushed her way past her sister. 'I don't want to miss the bride and groom leaving.'

Gordon also pushed past Nancy, but not so politely. 'Put on a bit of weight, haven't you, Nance?' He shook his head. 'All this fine living, you know. It's obviously not too good for your waistline.'

Nancy would have liked to hit him, and clenched her fist, but he looked her boldly in the eye and she was reminded of how intimidating he could be. Strange really when he was nothing, just a head lad for some trainer in Newmarket. He'd been a jockey once, years before, but never quite made it, even though he'd tried desperately hard. Gordon Tree was a little squirt of a man and Nancy looked down on him in every way, but still he intimidated her.

She stood for a moment, watching them both weave their way through the throng. Gordon hesitated, and whispered something in Brenda's ear. He turned, and looked back at Nancy.

He said loudly, '*Rumour* has it that this fine hotel was once a brothel, Nance! But I suppose you already knew that?' And he grinned, from ear to ear, showing excellent teeth.

Mortified, Nancy's eyes flashed around. She needn't have worried, the comment went unnoticed. Nearly everyone was high on the constant flow of Bollinger. She turned her attention back to Brenda and Gordon, just leaving the reception hall. She noticed how he paid constant attention to his wife, courteously allowing her to go ahead of him through the double doors, and how they joked and laughed with each other, so in tune, so in love, even though they'd been married for years and years and years. If only Peter treated her like that. But still, you couldn't have everything in life, and she had money and position. Then, with a start, she realised that Roberta, Brenda and Gordon's elder daughter, was still sitting at the table, looking up at her.

'And how are you, Roberta?' asked Nancy, not at all interested. The girl was so dull, so plain, compared to her younger sister Julia, who obviously took after Brenda and herself. Roberta was workaday, like her father, and not particularly bright either. She'd failed her eleven-plus, left school with no 'O' levels and gone on to do some half-baked secretarial course at Cambridge Tech. How ordinary, how *uninspiring*, thought Nancy. Not like her Clare who could easily have gone on to university and great things had she not been waylaid by Roger. And now, of course, she would never need to work.

'I'm fine thank you, Auntie Nancy.'

Nancy looked more closely at her niece. There was something different about her. Some sort of improvement, although she couldn't think what. She shrugged, not really interested. Nancy turned to the top table where Julia, looking dazzling in her bridesmaid's dress, sat talking in animated fashion to the groom, her hand resting lightly on his arm, as though waylaying him. 'Looks lovely, doesn't she?' Nancy remarked.

Roberta seethed at her aunt's tactless remark.

Nancy peered at her once more. 'Don't you think?'

Roberta decided that next to Julia, she disliked Nancy most in the world. She gulped, almost choking on her words. 'Yes, I suppose so.'

Nancy smirked. It was easy to recognise jealousy, especially when it wore such a sullen face. No wonder Clare hadn't wanted her as a bridesmaid. Of course, her daughter had had no real choice in the matter, but Nancy chose to forget that.

'Well, I'd better go and find Clare. She's changing in one of the more luxurious bedrooms.' Nancy smiled condescendingly at her niece. 'You should see her going away outfit. Quite magnificent!' She downed the rest of her champagne and put the glass on the table right in front of the girl. 'Still, no doubt you'll be out there getting a glimpse when the time comes.' She paused. 'How old are you now, Roberta?' she asked thoughtfully.

'Eighteen,' snapped Roberta.

'Hmmm.' Nancy pursed her lips and nodded her head. 'Well, 'bye for now, dear,' she said, and strutted off in regal fashion.

Roberta watched her go, thinking of how comical she looked, then turned away, pulling a dire face before glancing around the reception room looking for someone with whom she could possibly strike up a conversation. There was no one. Everyone but her was having a whale of a time. Roberta stood up and fingered the laquered fringe of her short dark crinkly hair. It had a will of its own, her hair, unlike Julia's soft, long dark curls. Life could be so unfair. Roberta pulled on her homemade beige tweed jacket and smoothed her mini skirt over her skinny thighs. She snatched up her new leather handbag, which had cost a week's wages, and made her way towards the double doors. Pushing through them, she stood looking around. There was so sign of her parents. She supposed they'd probably had to drive somewhere else to park their car.

The Old Bridge nestled close to the River Ouse and the car park had limited space. Roberta wandered outside and glanced back at the impressive ivy-clad, eighteenth-century building. Previous wedding receptions she'd attended had been held in village halls. Never had she set foot in such a fine place and she'd liked the experience, found it exciting. How thrilling it must be to be the bride on a day like today. Idly she tossed her bag over her shoulder and made her way down the wide, worn stone steps into the car park. It was November and chilly, so she wrapped her arms around herself.

Sitting on the bonnet of Joshua Fordham-Clarke's Bentley were his two younger sons. The middle one, Nick, was nonchalantly smoking a cigarette. Roberta stopped in her tracks when she saw them, embarrassed. She didn't smile or show any sign of recognition, just hastened away towards a path which wandered down to the river. She had no choice but to follow it and walked briskly to warm herself. The two boys watched her go, neither making any comment.

It wasn't long before Julia followed her sister outside, and what a different picture she presented! Full of gaiety and laughter, positively brimming over with confidence, she immediately ran down the steps and waltzed up to Nick and his younger brother Kit. Both grinned widely to see her.

'Wotcha, chaps! Has either of you got a fag? I'm gasping!'

Julia beamed at them both, showing flawless white teeth. Her almond-shaped brown eyes smouldered as they rested on Nick. She shook back her curls, threaded through with tiny white rosebuds, and swished the fine satin skirt of her bridesmaid's dress. 'Cor, it's nippy out here.'

As quick as a flash, eighteen-year-old Kit slipped off his morning coat and put it tenderly around Julia's shoulders. He didn't say anything, he was much too shy. She snuggled into it gratefully.

'Thanks,' she said, accepting a cigarette and a light from Nick.

'Isn't the bride ready to leave yet?' he asked impatiently. 'We've been told by Ma to wait outside here. Gotta get the best photos for the family album.' He grinned as he held up his father's expensive camera.

Julia puffed smoke from her cigarette in Kit's direction. 'Aren't they going to cine-film them?'

'Of course, but the photographer will do that.' Nick tapped the camera. 'These are just private family snaps.'

Julia smiled knowingly, but wondered what the difference was. 'Well, if you ask me, Clare'll be ages.' Her eyes sparkled. 'Can't think why, with a new husband like Roger. He's fab. Really fab.'

Kit chuckled, his chunky shoulders heaving unattractively. For a fleeting second Julia gave him her full attention, noticing the paunch threatening to burst the lower buttons of his shirt. Shame about those spots and awful red hair. Her eyes moved quickly back to Nick.

He quipped, 'I wouldn't mind being a fly on the wall in their bedroom tonight.' Kit chuckled again before going totally pink.

'Aren't you cold, Kit?' enquired Julia, concern written all over her face.

He shook his head adamantly, with the distinct feeling she wanted him to clear off.

'Fancy a walk?' asked Nick, boldly.

Julia drew on her cigarette, liking his directness. 'A walk? Bit cold for that.'

He shrugged. 'It'll warm you up a bit.'

Their eyes locked. Kit watched them both with interest. Julia thought about it. 'Okay,' she said after a moment and walked off in the same direction as her sister had. 'Come on then,' she called to Nick. As an afterthought she looked at Kit. 'You too, if you like?'

Embarrassed, he shook his head and glanced at his twenty-year-old brother, who winked at him. 'No, I'll stay here.'

'You'd better get inside the hotel or you'll catch cold,' suggested Nick, in brotherly fashion, and began to follow Julia. 'See you later.'

'Oh, I'm all right, I never feel the cold,' Kit called after them. 'And what about the photos? Ma wanted you to take them.'

Briefly, Nick looked back. 'You heard what Julia said, Clare'll be ages.'

Kit shivered and looked inside his father's car, remembering the waxed jacket on the back seat. He tried the door, and to his surprise it opened. He reached inside and grabbed the jacket, putting it on. Then he put the camera on the back seat and closed the door. He looked in the direction that Nick and Julia had taken, and decided to follow.

*   *   *

'Race you to those trees over there,' giggled Julia, nudging Nick.

'In that dress?'

She hoisted her skirt in a most unladylike fashion and set off at a surprising pace along the river bank. Nick watched her: the roses bobbing about in her hair, and Kit's morning coat flapping as she went. Her legs, encased in silky white stockings, were incredibly sexy, so long and shapely and without an ounce of fat. She was a stunning-looking girl and he decided there and then that he wanted her. Nick Fordham-Clarke, the best-looking of the trio of brothers, usually got what he wanted. He raced after her.

Roberta, from her position within a dense clump of trees and evergreen shrubs, saw all this. She was cold, her body so chilled that she'd taken refuge out of the icy November wind. She supposed she ought to go back to the hotel, but wanted to wait until she was sure the bride and groom had left for their honeymoon. That way, she wouldn't have to witness such beauty, wealth and happiness. She wasn't jealous, despite what Nancy clearly thought. Roberta was merely fed up with being ignored, and hurt that she hadn't been asked to be a bridesmaid. Even her mother had remarked that it had been tactless to exclude her, especially as Roberta and Julia were Clare's only two girl relatives. True, Roberta was not as beautiful as Julia, but she was by no means ugly. She shared the same almond-shaped brown eyes, fine creamy skin, and her nose and mouth were well shaped. Unfortunately her features didn't quite fit together in the same way as Julia's did, and her tendency to scowl didn't help.

'Gotcha!' roared Nick as he grabbed Julia's arm and swung her round. He pulled her roughly into his arms and kissed her full on the mouth. She responded ardently and Nick, already out of breath, gasped. What a girl! Without further ado, he ran his hand across the bodice of her bridesmaid's dress, beneath Kit's morning coat. Julia's breasts were firm and much larger than he would have supposed. Eagerly, his hand wandered down to her legs where her skirt was still scrunched up. He traced his fingers to her crotch. She made no attempt to stop him, so he went further and pushed his hand inside her knickers. She was moist and plump and Nick felt himself grow harder.

And all the time Roberta watched. Not because she wanted to, but because she couldn't leave, or not without them seeing her. She stood shivering and silently cursing her sister, wrapping her arms tightly around herself for warmth.

By this time, Nick was undoing his own trousers and Julia was helping him. They were laughing and giggling as though the whole thing was a joke. Roberta frowned in confusion and watched, fascinated, as Nick pushed Julia's knickers down to her thighs and with a somewhat accomplished action semi-lifted her on to himself, entering her completely. With faces now the picture of ecstasy, they jostled up and down, up and down, still in their standing position beneath the trees.

It seems to go on and on. 'Arhhh, arhhh ... arhhh,' Nick called out, reaching his climax. 'Arrrhhhh!!!'

Julia was noisy too, swearing and squealing and carrying on like a demented pig.

Roberta, a virgin, was both disgusted and bemused but also riveted by the scene. Then they stood motionless and hanging on to each other breathlessly, muttering words Roberta couldn't hear. Nick withdrew from her sister and deftly pulled up his trousers. He retrieved a handkerchief from his pocket and Julia took it and popped it between her legs. She pulled up her knickers and pulled down her skirt. They hugged and kissed in a friendly sort of way, and then turned to go back the way they'd come. It was as though they'd satisfied their hunger and now wanted to get out of the cold. Neither seemed to set too much store by what they'd just done.

Roberta, appalled, and with her legs almost numb with cold, moved. A branch crackled beneath her feet. She froze, but neither Nick nor Julia had heard. They just carried on, arm in arm, back to the hotel. Roberta cranked her chilled body into action. As she was leaving the wooded area she paused, looking down at her chisel-toed shoes. The beige patent leather was scuffed on both feet. She licked her thumb and bent down to rub off the marks. They came away easily, but as she raised herself she caught a glimpse of Kit, standing silently just ten yards or so away from her. They stared at each other, faces red with embarrassment, before he averted his eyes and hugged his father's waxed jacket around himself. He'd obviously watched as well.

Mortified, Roberta quickened her pace. Dragging his feet, Kit followed behind.

2

'You're only sixteen, Julia . . .'

'Nearly seventeen!' she rapidly interrupted.

The two girls' high-pitched voices rang out from the small flint-stone cottage which backed on to the Heath in Newmarket. A few doors away a neighbour, Mrs Grimes, was hanging out her washing. From her back yard, she craned her neck to eavesdrop.

'And you could be pregnant,' Roberta hissed, her scowl holding a hint of dread. 'What on earth were you thinking of? It was disgusting.'

'It wasn't.' Julia didn't bother to lower her voice and the neighbour smirked. Everyone along Heath Row knew about Julia Tree. Her *goings on* in the stables, where her own father worked, were legendary. 'How can something like that be disgusting? You don't know what you're talking about. You're just jealous.'

'*Jealous!*'

Nastily, Julia rounded on her sister. 'Yes, jealous. You've always been jealous of me, haven't you, Roberta? Jealous and sick at heart because you can't get a bloke even to look at you.' Roberta was speechless and Julia waded in. 'What's it to you anyway? If you tell Mum and Dad I shall just deny everything and it'll show what a lying little Peeping Tom you really are!'

Roberta gulped at her sister's vehemence. Outside the neighbour's eyes bulged in indignation. Mrs Grimes liked Roberta who was kind and helpful and would babysit at the drop of a hat. Not like her sister. No, nothing like. But Roberta knew better than to take on her sister. Julia's capacity for lying was only too familiar and besides she had no intention of telling her parents; it'd taken a week to pluck up courage to tackle Julia herself. She took a deep

9

breath and straightened her back. 'Do you know what you are, Julia Tree? You're *promiscuous*!'

The two wooden pegs in Mrs Grimes's mouth dropped to the ground. As she stooped to pick them up, she nodded in agreement.

'Ooooh, big word, big word. I don't suppose a thickie like you even knows what it means?'

Roberta seethed. 'I am *not* a thickie and I hope you *do* get pregnant. It will serve you right.'

'You little fool, of course I won't get pregnant. You really are thick, aren't you, Roberta?'

Roberta narrowed her eyes, wanting to turn away from her sister's knowing stare, but that would be admitting defeat. She reached out and grabbed the edge of Julia's kidney-shaped dressing table, trying to think of a tart reply. Julia, who'd been brushing her lustrous hair when Roberta challenged her, continued to do so smugly. Roberta didn't understand. How could she? In sexual matters she was a novice.

But then it all fell into place, the penny dropped. Lowering her voice, she breathed, 'You've done this before, haven't you? You've done this before? Loads of times. You're on the pill?'

Julia hooted with laughter, great guffaws of delight. '*On the pill! On the pill!*' she mimicked her sister. 'Yes, loads of time. I'm *on the pill!*'

Mrs Grimes tutted with disgust. She tossed the pegs into her clothes basket, picked it up and walked back into her cottage with a twisted smile on her face. Just wait till she saw Peggy next door.

Roberta had had enough. She turned stiffly and walked towards the door.

Julia screamed after her, 'And next time, mind your own business!'

Roberta turned to face her. 'Oh, don't worry, I intend to. From now on, Julia Tree, I shall have nothing whatever to do with you. Nothing, *do you hear*?'

'Good.'

Roberta opened the door, went out and slammed it shut.

3

Brenda Tree sat in the Cosy Corner cafe at her favourite table by the window. She peered out on the hustle and bustle of Trinity Street, smack bang in the heart of Cambridge. Just a stone's throw away along the charmingly narrow ancient street was Trinity College, and its chapel, and even closer Gonville and Caius College. Further along, where Trinity Street opened out spectacularly into King's Parade, stood King's, next to Queen's, tucked behind St Catherine's and so on to Corpus Christi, Pembroke, and Peterhouse. Students hurried by on foot or bicycle, laden down with books and muffled in college scarves against the fierce winter cold.

Brenda glanced down at her wristwatch. Ten-forty-five. Nancy was late as usual. She sighed. She didn't really mind; these days her time was pretty much her own, but why was it that her sister was always late? Like Brenda she didn't work, and appeared to have no hobbies. She didn't even do any housework as she had a daily to do all that, and as far as Brenda could glean Peter ate most of his meals out, on business. On top of all that, Brenda had to get into Cambridge from Newmarket on the bus while Nancy drove herself in from Godmanchester, near Huntingdon.

Brenda leant forward in her seat and scrutinised the passers-by. No sign of her. The young waitress was making for her again. It was no good, she'd have to order something. Brenda smiled. 'I'm afraid my sister still hasn't arrived but I'll have a coffee, please, and one of your chocolate eclairs.'

The girl nodded and wandered off. Relief washed over Brenda as Nancy came in at that minute clad in a beautiful camel hair coat, bustling towards her and waving.

'The traffic! I can't tell you how busy it is. I thought I was never

11

going to make it this morning. And the car parks ... Anybody would think it was Christmas already, not a whole month away.'

Brenda scraped back her chair and stood up. She reached over to her sister and kissed her flushed cheek. 'How nice to see you, Nance. Gosh, your cheek's cold'.

She flopped down opposite and slipped out of her coat, allowing it to rest on the back of the chair. 'It's freezing out there.' She loosened the scarf round her neck and removed her leather gloves, flapping them on to the table, then twisted imperiously in her chair. 'Now, where's that damned girl? I need a coffee to warm me up.' She snapped her fingers, drawing the attention of everybody in the cafe. 'Can't we get some service around here?'

There was a deathly hush but as if by magic the waitress re-appeared, carrying Brenda's coffee and chocolate eclair. Carefully, she placed them on the table in front of her.

'And we'll have another one of those, and another one of those' said Nancy, pointing to Brenda's eclair. No please. No smile.

The girl turned on her heel and Brenda called after her, 'Thank you, dear.' The waitress looked back and gave her a half-smile. Brenda faced her sister. 'Pays to be polite.'

Nancy glared at her. 'Oh, does it? And since when have I needed you to tell me how to behave?'

Brenda stifled a desire to hit back. Instead she shook her head. 'Oh, I wasn't telling you how to behave, Nance, not at all. I was just thinking of myself. It pays for *me* to be polite. I get better service that way.'

'Huh!' scoffed Nancy. 'In my experience, you get what you pay for.'

Yes, Brenda mused and bit into her eclair, her sister would think that. Some of the cream oozed out and attached itself to the side of Brenda's mouth. Deftly she licked it way. Nancy watched, fascinated. Now, if that had been her, it would have made a fine mess everywhere.

'New dress?' she enquired.

Brenda looked down at her British Home Stores navy woollen dress. It had cost nine and eleven off their bargain rack and she knew she looked good in it, especially with the choker of imitation pearls she'd borrowed from Roberta. 'Yes, it is. Do you like it?'

Nancy sniffed. 'It suits you. It's your sort of thing.'

Brenda bit into her eclair once more, reminding herself not to be rattled. Her sister didn't mean to be unkind, it was just her unfortunate manner. Underneath, she had a heart of gold.

The waitress reappeared and placed Nancy's coffee and chocolate eclair in front of her. 'Anything else, *Madam*?' she asked coldly.

'No, that'll be all.'

Once again, Brenda looked up at the girl and winked. 'Thank you.'

'And I suppose you think that's funny?' fumed Nancy as the girl walked away.

'Funny?'

'Winking like that?'

'No, I was just being friendly.'

'Oh, so *now* it's polite as well as friendly is it? Does that pay as well?'

Brenda sipped her coffee and eyed her younger sister keenly, taking careful note of her lined neck and pouchy cheeks, her bulbous eyes and tired-looking skin. There was no glow to Nancy anymore. Years ago her skin had shone and looked healthy; her fine clothes had made her outstanding. Now, she'd deteriorated and fattened out considerably. Brenda sighed, feeling sad. By comparison she hadn't deteriorated, just grown naturally older and unfortunately poorer! She replaced her coffee cup in its saucer. 'Actually, I think its called charm, Nance, and if I remember rightly, our mother always said, "The art of being charming is a gift from the Gods."'

Nancy puffed our her chest. 'I've always been charming. How else do you think I support Peter? Behind every successful man is a good woman you know, Brenda.'

There was a pause. Brenda forced a smile. 'And how's Clare? Enjoying married life? No babies yet?'

Nancy's eyes nearly popped out of her head. 'They've only just got married, and if you think there's anything fishy going on, you're wrong.'

Brenda threw back her head and laughed at her sister's indignation. She couldn't help herself. 'Of course I don't think that, Nance.' She frowned and put her head on one side. 'Where's your sense of humour these days? We don't seem to laugh anymore. I can remember a time when you and me never stopped laughing.'

Nancy gulped, as though found out. She pushed the last of her eclair into her mouth then took a long slurp of her coffee. 'I'm tired, that's all. Just tired.'

Brenda would have liked to say, 'You look it.' 'Well, you must be,' she sympathised instead. 'What with all the wedding preparations and everything. I must say, it all went off tremendously well. Didn't Clare look a picture?'

'She did, she really did.'

'You must be very proud of her, Nance.'

'Oh, I am.' Nancy dabbed her mouth with a paper napkin. 'And how are your girls? Julia still enjoying the Perse?'

Brenda frowned. It had been Nancy's idea to put Julia forward for a full scholarship into the sixth form of the Perse Girls' School in Cambridge, and, lo and behold, she had walked away with it. The uniform could have been tricky, but luckily Nancy had kept all Clare's and it had fitted Julia perfectly. 'She's doing all right, I think, although she complains about the travelling. It's a long old day for her, what with the bus journey and everything, and I think she feels some of the girls are overly snobby.'

'Well, they're likely to be, aren't they? They come from some of the finest families in Cambridge. They're doctors' and solicitors' and all sorts of professional people's daughters! You'll not get hoi-polloi in schools like that, you know.'

Brenda grimaced. 'But unfortunately we *are* hoi-polloi, whatever that means.'

'But *she* won't be, will she?'

'No, perhaps not, but it doesn't make it any easier for her now.'

'Oh, rubbish, she'll cope. Julia's got everything going for her.'

Brenda giggled, 'Well, in that case, perhaps she'll marry a Fordham-Clarke one day?'

Nancy looked astounded; she practically choked on the words. 'I should hardly think so, not with her background.'

'Oh, thank you very much!'

Momentarily Nancy was contrite. 'I'm sorry, Brenda, I didn't mean it like that. But even you have to admit the chance of one of your girls marrying a Fordham-Clarke is remote.'

Brenda's eyes flashed. 'Roberta's doing well, she's just been promoted.'

'Oh, has she?'

'She most certainly has. She's next in line for a secretary's job at Dolman's.'

'Huh!' Nancy leant closer to her sister, hiding a grin. 'You know what a secretary is, Brenda? A walking diary – and glorified coffee maker. You ask Peter.'

'Roberta works hard, and is good at her job. Personal secretary is a very responsible position. I'm proud of her for getting on so well.'

'Oh, sorry I spoke. If you can't take a joke. . . .' Nancy ran a hand across her forehead in an attention-seeking manner Brenda had grown accustomed to over the years.

'Is something wrong, Nancy? You're not ill, are you?'

'Oh, for goodness' sake!' Her sister sat upright again. 'No, of course there's nothing wrong. For your information life couldn't be better – apart from Mr Wilson devaluing the pound, that is. What sort of Prime Minister is he turning into, for goodness' sake? Peter's hopping mad about that. Mind you, he's still *insisting* on taking me away in the early spring, most probably to the Italian Riviera.'

'Well, lucky you. How nice.'

'It's no more than I deserve.'

'I'm sure.'

'And it'll be good to see more of my husband, I can tell you.' Fleetingly, Nancy looked morose. 'You have no idea how hard that poor man works, Brenda. Some nights he doesn't get home 'til the small hours. It's downright ridiculous, I can tell you. Since Joshua put Roger in charge, poor Peter has to help out in all sorts of ways. I'm not complaining, mind, I'm only too pleased that he can help Roger. Our son-in-law's a fine young man, the best, and he does a damned good job, but that's only because he's got Peter to fall back on all the time. But I don't complain, I never have.' She sighed. 'I just get frightfully bored . . . frightfully.'

'You should take up a hobby, Nance.'

She snorted.

'No truly, you should.'

'What would I be wanting a hobby for?'

'You could join one of those new slimming and exercise clubs, it would do you the world of good.'

Nancy narrowed her eyes at her sister's impudence. 'That's a stupid idea.'

'Is it?'

Nancy glared at her sister. 'I don't like exercise and I buy nearly all my food from Marks. What could be better than that?'

Brenda laughed. 'Just because it has St Michael on the label, doesn't make it nutritious or low in calories.'

'I don't each a lot of calories. I've never been one for big meals. I can't help it if I put on weight. It's my metabolism. I'm healthy enough.'

'Well, perhaps you should cut down on the gin?'

Nancy looked as though she'd been stung. She glared quickly out of the window and without taking her eyes off the passers-by, whispered, 'So, what else have you got planned for today?'

'Oh, I'm meeting Julia later on. She wants to show me round Purley's.'

Nancy perked up. 'Purley's? You mean the new leather shop?'

'Yes, that's the one. Julia's landed herself a Saturday job there. She loves it. Gets on like a house on fire with Anne Purley.'

'Anne Purley? Julia works for Anne Purley?'

'Yes, don't look so surprised.'

Her sister shrugged. 'Well, I am a bit. I didn't know *she* was running the shop. She's very rich, you know. Widowed. After her husband Benjamin died, she copped his fortune, lock, stock and barrell. You must know the Purley family, Brenda? Lived down Bury Road in Newmarket?' Nancy flapped her hand about, but Brenda continued to look blank. 'Huge house, very grand? Blood-stock agents ... made a fortune. And Anne and Benjamin have a son. Now, what's his name? Oh, yes, Nathan. That's it. In fact, I thought it was he who ran the shop. Fine stuff they sell, the best. There's no need for Anne Purley to work though, no need at all.'

'Well, I'm afraid I don't know anything about them other than that they sell coats and handbags and belts and things.'

Nancy mused, 'Well, working for Purley's won't do Julia any harm, so long as she doesn't let it interfere with her "A" levels.'

Brenda laughed. 'Well, there's no telling with Julia. She's a law unto herself.'

'But she must finish her education if she wants to make anything of herself.'

'Your Clare didn't.'

'But she's different.'

'How?'

'Well, she's married to Roger Fordham-Clarke for a start.'

Brenda was tempted to laugh, but decided against it. 'He's nice actually, isn't he? Very charming. Gordon and I were quite taken with him, and he's very interested in racing. Said he'd love to look round Gordon's yard sometime.'

Gordon's yard indeed. Nancy sniffed. 'Oh, did he?'

'They chatted for ages.' Brenda patted her sister's hand. 'She's a very lucky girl, your Clare, very lucky.'

Nancy smiled widely and for the first time that day Brenda was reminded of just how lovely she used to be.

4

It was a beautiful June afternoon with hardly a cloud in the azure sky and just the whisper of a breeze. Julia Tree walked purposefully along St Andrews Street. Stuffed in her school bag, slung over her shoulder, was her loathsome Perse blazer along with her uniform skirt and blouse. Behind the school wall she'd furtively slipped on a pair of white hipster jeans and a halter-neck top. She'd bunked off school again and knew she'd be in fearful trouble if found out, but she'd had no lessons after lunch and sitting in the library until hometime was an immense bore. She knew she should be studying, even she was finding the going tough, maybe because she was now surrounded by amazingly clever girls who daunted her slightly, but she just couldn't face it. She'd slipped out as soon as lessons recommenced after lunch and strode briskly into the middle of Cambridge with every intention of popping in to Purley's to see Anne. The very thought gave her a buzz and she knew she'd be made more than welcome.

Since the Christmas and Easter holidays, when she'd worked full-time at Purley's, the attraction of the shop down Petty Cury was hard to resist. Unbeknown to her as yet, Julia had found her vocation. She liked selling, hard selling. There was something about her persuasive nature that even the most discerning customer responded to. She turned into Lion Yard.

'Julia!'

Turning guiltily, she was very relieved to see her cousin Clare and instantly jealous of her spectacular gear: a short-sleeved, figure-hugging yellow, red and orange striped jumper tucked snugly into a Gina Fratini mini skirt. Around her waist was a wide white belt and on her feet chunky chisel-toed white patent sandals. Clare's straight honey-blonde hair had been cut bluntly around her shoulders, and covering her eyes was a pair of large, round, white-framed sunglasses. She raised these and her beguiling blue eyes searched Julia's face. 'No school?' she queried.

Julia had to drag her eyes away from her cousin's clothes. She waved a hand dismissively. 'Oh, I've no lessons this afternoon.' She looked down at her feet and then up again, 'I'm playing truant, actually.'

Clare's expression became mischievous 'You naughty girl!' She moved closer and hugged her cousin, kissing her on both cheeks. 'You naughty, naughty girl. But I'm so pleased to see you. You don't know how pleased. I'm bored out of my skull, Julia. Sick of my own bloody company. Please, come and have a coffee with me, or a hot dog or something. Anything you like, really.'

Julia opened her mouth to speak, then closed it again.

'Oh, don't look like that, Julia. Am I such a boring old fart?'

The word *fart* quite took Julia by surprise. She'd always supposed cousin Clare was above such vulgarity. 'Of course you're not boring, nor are you an old fart. It's just, well, I'm surprised, that's all.'

'By what?'

'You. Being sick of your own company.'

They started to walk in the direction that Julia had been going. 'You wouldn't be surprised if you lived my life. There's nothing for me to do. Roger's out all day working at the damned office, and half the fucking night as well if he can get away with it. And I'm supposed to twiddle my thumbs like a good little wife.'

Julia stopped and faced her cousin. 'Hey, Clare, what's with all this swearing?'

She laughed, joyously. 'I know. Insane, isn't it? But it makes me feel so wicked, and I'm so bored with playing the lady.'

'But you *are* a lady, and you're married to a great bloke, a real gentleman.' Julia, for a seventeen year old, was no fool and frankly envied Clare her position.

'Oh, yeah, so very la-de-dah. And Mummy *is* pleased her precious daughter married into such a frightfully, frightfully family. *Fucking* awful family if you ask me.'

'Clare!'

They carried on through the covered shopping precinct of Lion Yard, heading towards Petty Cury, an alleyway with more shops.

Clare pointed left towards Market Hill. 'How about over there?' Julia looked across the bustling market square to a trendy coffee bar nestled in one corner, and then to her immediate right where Purley's was situated along Petty Cury. She shrugged and followed her cousin.

Cambridge market, in full swing every day with its abundance of fresh flowers in buckets, assortments of carefully displayed fruit and veg, cheese and clothing, records and hardware, buzzed as the two young women passed by. Chattering animatedly, they reached the coffee bar and went inside.

'I'll treat you to a chocolate knickerbocker glory, how about that?'

Julia nodded and followed Clare to an empty table.

They were served immediately by a student waiter, falling over hemself to please two such beautiful young women. When her knickerbocker glory arrived, Julia realised how hungry she was. School meals never interested her and she'd avoid them if she could. Now she dipped her long-handled spoon eagerly into the deep sundae dish and scooped out a large dollop of lime jelly, glacé cherry and chocolate ice-cream. Her mouth watered and she devoured it with relish.

'Hmmmm! Delicious.'

'Told you,' agreed Clare, tucking in with equal enthusiasm.

Both girl were silent as they consumed their sundaes in record time, then looked at each other and smiled. 'Almost as good as sex,' said Julia with a smile, hoping Clare would open up a little about her sex life with Roger.

But she looked glum instead and pushed away her dish, pulling her coffee towards her. 'And what would you know about sex, Julia?'

Without answer she delved into her school bag and pulled out her cigarettes. She offered one to her cousin who took it. 'Didn't know you were a smoker, Clare?'

She shook her head with the cigarette between her lips. Endearingly, it wobbled in her mouth. 'I'm not.'

Julia lit the cigarette and held her cousin's gaze. 'And I'm not a virgin.'

Clare drew on the cigarette and blew out smoke. For a novice she looked pretty good. She slumped back in her chair and with the cigarette dangling elegantly between the first two fingers of her right hand surveyed her cousin. 'And you like it, do you? Sex?'

As these words were being spoken, Julia drew on her own cigarette and inhaled deeply. She choked and then coughed and then laughed. 'Don't you?'

'Don't answer a question with a question.'

Julia took a gulp of her coffee and peered over her cup. 'Of course I like it. I like it a lot. Can't get enough of it, in fact.' She narrowed her eyes. 'Wish I was like you, you lucky devil, going to bed with Roger Fordham-Clarke every night.' She decided to be bold. 'Do you do it every night?'

Clare smiled softly. 'So you fancy Roger, do you?'

'Don't answer a question with a question.'

With a tinkling laugh, Clare threw back her head, shaking her hair away from her shoulders. 'If you were married to Roger, Julia, I guarantee you'd be as bored as me within a month. He's no great shakes as a lover, you know.' She shrugged. 'But then again, neither am I.'

Julia sat with her mouth agape. She didn't understand. 'Well, isn't it something you get better at? With practice, I mean?'

Clare laughed again. 'I'm sure it is, with the right person.'

'And you're saying he's not right for you?'

Clare shook her head. 'I only married him because I was pushed into it by my stupid bloody mother.'

'Clare, that's a dreadful thing to say.'

'But it's the truth.' She stubbed out her cigarette and leant closer to her cousin. 'And I'm bored, Julia. Bored silly.'

Julia took stock. 'Well, perhaps you should get a job, and then you wouldn't be bored.'

'A job?'

It was Julia's turn to laugh now. 'Yes, isn't that what most bored people do?'

'Oh, no, I couldn't possibly get a job. If I have to get a bloody job, there'd be no point in being married to Roger at all.'

Julia was shocked, really shocked, by her cousin's honesty. 'Well, what are you going to do then?'

Clare sat back in her seat and tapped her fingers on the table. 'I'm thinking about it, Julia, I'm thinking about it.'

'Have a baby?'

'Certainly not. That's the last thing I'd want!'

'Auntie Nancy will be disappointed.'

'Well, let her. I really couldn't care less.' Clare grinned. 'At least that's one of the compensations of being married, I don't have to live with *her* anymore.'

By this time, Julia was getting used to Clare's frankness and grinned at the remark, until her conscience pricked her sharply. Auntie Nancy had been good to her, very good. 'She adores you, Clare. She'd be heartbroken if she heard you talking about her like that.'

Her cousin slithered forward in her seat. 'Well, who's going to tell her, Julia? Certainly not me.'

'Nor me.'

'Good.' She waved to the waiter and snapped her fingers. 'Can we have the bill, please?' She looked back at her cousin. 'We must do this again, Julia, I can't tell you how much I've enjoyed it.' She raised her hand and snapped her fingers again. 'No, better still, come and stay at our house?'

'Can I sleep with Roger, teach him a thing or two?' The wisecrack was out before Julia could bite it back.

Unperturbed, Clare smiled knowingly and slipped her cool hand across the table to squeeze her cousin's arm gently. 'Or even me, darling. I'm sure you could teach me a thing or two as well?'

Julia wrenched back her arm as though stung. 'What on earth do you mean?'

With a ribald laugh, Clare threw back her head. 'Oh, Julia, you should see your face. You're not the only one allowed to shock. I like to do it as well.'

Julia gathered her thoughts. 'Well, yes, maybe you do.'

'And I thought you were being serious about sleeping with *my* husband.'

Julia stubbed out her cigarette, thinking they'd both said too much. 'I've got to pop into Purley's, Clare, down Petty Cury. I work there, you see, at the weekends.'

She pouted like a child, 'Purley's?'

'It's been lovely, though, I've enjoyed it. Thanks for the ice-cream.'

'And we'll meet again. I'll ring, shall I?'

'That would be great, really great.' Julia gathered her things together as the waiter brought the bill. 'Must dash.' She bent forward and kissed her cousin's cheek. 'Thanks again.'

'I'll ring.'

Julia shoved her chair beneath the table and hastened towards the door. 'I'll look forward to it. 'Bye, Clare.'

With a gleam in her eyes, she watched her cousin go. ''Bye, Julia. I'll see you soon.'

5

Joshua and Cynthia Fordham-Clarke lived peacefully in a cul-de-sac off Trumpington Road, Cambridge. Their rare Elizabethan mansion with it's curving gables, decorative chimney stacks and captivating entrance porch, or 'frontispiece', was almost hidden from view behind a wealth of established trees and shrubs. They had almost an acre of land surrounding the house which, for a private property in the middle of Cambridge, was unusual.

Joshua seldom went into the office these days. He left all that to Roger, his capable eldest son, and the rest of his able staff. At sixty-five, Joshua suffered from a dicky heart, and apart from the odd game of golf and his infrequent trips abroad with his wife Cynthia, did little but sit about in the garden or in front of the telly. From someone who had previously been dynamic, he's turned into a virtual cabbage and it hadn't helped his dreadful temper. Only Cynthia could still his wicked tongue.

Kit, their youngest boy, was home for the weekend from Lanchester Polytechnic. This was not out of choice but because he'd forgotten to pack his dinner suit for the end of term ball and needed to collect it. He tended to avoid coming home, knowing he was Joshua's least favourite son. Undoubtedly, this had something to do with his increasing obesity and flaming red hair, a throwback from Joshua's own maternal grandfather, but was primarily due to the fact that he had struggled at Oundle, his public school, whereas his brothers before him had excelled in everything there, including rugby and cricket. Joshua only respected academic excellence; anything short of that simply wasn't good enough. Apart from his wife, who was no scholar but whom he adored, everybody else in his life was measured by their academic achievements and prowess on the playing field.

Sunday was Annie's day off, and consequently Cynthia hated Sundays. She hated cooking and, even worse, having to clear up after cooking. Not that you could call what she did cooking exactly. Annie left everything prepared, right down to the gravy or sauce. The Yorkshire puddings, roast potatoes and roast parsnips were all cooked to perfection beforehand and just needed reheating in the oven. Other vegetables, cut into neat slices, were waiting in several covered saucepans. But Cynthia still had to put the beef in the oven, baste it and make sure it didn't overcook, which it frequently did when left to her care. Wearing a grimace fit to spoil her beautiful face, a pinny of Annie's, and holding a wooden spoon in her hand, she was looking flustered.

Kit strolled into the kitchen. 'Ma? Can I get you anything? G and T perhaps?'

She indicated a glass standing on the worktop. 'I've already got one, darling. Couldn't possibly cope without it.' She waved the spoon about. 'Why on earth do we have to go through this ritual every damned Sunday? Why can't your father take us out somewhere? I hate cooking damned roast beef.'

Kit walked towards his mother and lovingly kissed her cheek. He was her favourite and savoured the fact. 'But it'll be splendid, Ma. Roger and Clare are coming, and I'm *starving*.'

She looked at his spotty face and turned away quickly. Poor Kit. Compared to her other two magnificent specimens, he was such an apology for a son but she loved him all the more for it. 'Well, that's as maybe, Kit, but I'm no damned cook and I've never professed to be.'

He hugged her. 'I think you're wonderful, whatever you do. And so does Pa.'

Cynthia snorted and peeked at the beef sizzling in the Aga. She looked at her wristwatch. 'They should be here soon, or at least I hope so. Can't have this beef overcooking. That *would* upset your father!'

'Get rid of him, Roger. Just get rid of him! In matters like this it's no good hanging fire, you have to act quickly.' Joshua, whose mouth was full of roast beef and Yorkshire pudding, spluttered out his words, spraying food across the table. 'Don't dilly-dally, boy. *Never dilly dally.*'

Roger looked across at Kit and raised his eyebrows. Conspiratorially, his brother smiled back. 'It's not quite as simple at that, Pa. David Lennox has been running this particular contract from the start. He's our piling expert and the clients like him. They'd be upset if we just got rid of him.' Roger gulped back some red wine. 'Anyway, you can't just sack him, Pa. He's a senior member of staff and has been with us for years. Besides, it's not all his fault. The contractors let him down, time and time again.'

With steely blue eyes, Joshua peered across at him. 'What does Peter say?'

Roger smiled sarcastically. When it came to the crunch, his father would rather listen to Peter Lewis's judgement than his. And the trouble was, his father-in-law was an accountant, and, like all accountants, always sought to cut costs. He never spared the rod. 'Peter entirely agrees with me, Pa. Entirely.'

Joshua grunted and chuntered a bit more, totally incoherently, and continued to mop his plate clean. Finally he put down his knife and fork. 'If you ask me, the world is going mad.' He wiped his mouth with his napkin and thumped his fist on the white damask tablecloth. The plates jumped and cutlery jingled. 'There's no control anymore! What we need is control!' Belligerently, he peered across at Roger, as though *he* should work miracles. 'And now the railways – this bloody work-to-rule. Cancelled! A thousand bloody trains!' Joshua was going pink. 'And Ford! Women demanding equal pay – *women*, I ask you. They should be in the home where they belong. Not taking bread from the men who're bred to feed them.

'And what are you smirking at, m'boy?' he challenged Kit. 'You can wipe that grin off your face straight away. Don't come home here from your daft l'il third-rate *poly* ... whatsit and snigger at me across my own table. Huh! Won't do, won't do at all.'

Dismayed and embarrassed, Kit looked to his mother for help. On numerous occasions in the past she'd stuck up for him, but Cynthia averted her eyes this time. 'I didn't mean any offence, Pa,' he stammered.

'No,' boomed the old man, 'don't suppose you did. You can't help your face, can you?'

'Joshua!' reprimanded Cynthia, looking across at her daughter-in-law who had said nothing until now. 'I'm really sorry about all this, Clare. What must you think? Joshua's only joking, you know.'

Totally unperturbed, Clare shook her lovely head. Her thoughts were elsewhere. She glanced across at her father-in-law. 'Oh, before I forget, Daddy wants to know if you're available for golf next weekend, at the Gogs? He thought perhaps Sunday and then you and Cynthia could be his guests for lunch at the clubhouse.'

Cynthia dived in quickly. 'Oh, that sounds nice. Sunday lunch out. What a treat.'

Joshua rubbed his chin and looked across at his daughter-in-law. 'Sunday's not a good day, y'know. What about during the week?'

'Pa, Peter works during the week,' put in Roger.

Irritably, Joshua waved his napkin about. 'Well, he could get a few hours off, couldn't he? For me. Surely he could?'

'We're very busy at the moment, Pa.'

'Well, I like my Sundays here.' Joshua glared at his wife. 'Y'know I do, m'dear. Y'know I do.'

'Yes, Joshua, I certainly do.' She scraped back her chair and started to clear away the tureens and empty plates from the table. She noticed Kit had eaten little. 'Not hungry, darling? That's not like you.'

He gave a wan smile, but before he could reply his father cut in, 'Won't do him any harm. Could live off his gut for a fortnight with no ill effects.'

'Joshua!' she admonished again, with a quick glance at Clare.

Kit rose from the table and started to help his mother. Roger looked at him and winked, but neither he nor Clare made any attempt to help. They just sat and picked up the threads of their conservation with Joshua.

Cynthia left the dining room and made her way to the kitchen with Kit following. She started to load plates on to the draining board. 'He's just a bad-tempered old man, Kit. A really bad-tempered old man.' She turned and took the dishes from her son and put them with the others. 'I'm so sorry, darling. He didn't mean what he said.'

'Of course he did, Ma, you know he did. I sometimes think he hates me.'

She cupped his face in her hands and lovingly kissed his cheek. He stared back at her. His mother was always so calm and so elegant. She was too damned good for his father.

'Don't you ever feel he's too old for you, Ma?'

Cynthia turned towards the Aga. 'He's just unwell today, that's all. He'll get better now that the weather's improved. Hmmm,

27

smells delicious, don't you think? Annie's raspberry tart. Put the custard on a low heat, will you, darling? Stir it, though, we don't want it to burn. That would be the final straw, wouldn't it?'

Kit sighed and stirred the custard, wishing he was safely back in Coventry.

6

Ed Matthews, Senior Structural Engineer at Dolman Engineering, peered over the top of his glasses. 'That shy one? You know, the one who wouldn't say boo to a goose. Get her, she did an excellent job last time.'

Angela Brown racked her brains. Since they'd landed an enormous site investigation contract near Riverside in Cambridge, Dolman's workforce had risen to about sixty people, twenty of whom shuffled paper around. Angela prided herself on her position as senior accounts clerk, in fact these days referred to herself as Financial Supervisor, and didn't bother too much with the junior staff. 'I can't think who you mean?' she mused, cursing his stupid secretary for taking so much time off.

Ed Matthews snapped his fingers. 'Roberta. That's it. Her name's Roberta.'

Angela still drew a blank. 'I'll go downstairs and find her then.'

'Well, be quick about it. The meeting's at ten. She'll need her pad and pencil and her coat. The meeting's on site.'

Angela, already making for the door, turned and looked at him. She was piqued. It really wasn't her job to organise Ed Matthews's secretarial staff for him. 'Bit unusual, isn't it? Taking secretaries with you to meetings on site?'

'No, not at all. I haven't the time to mess about with tape recorders, and the girl can do the job, I know she can.'

Angela shrugged and left his office. Ed started to rummage around on his desk for the necessary documents. He seethed at his own secretary's incompetence and reflected bitterly upon the number of times he'd caught her filing her nails.

At thirty-three, he was thoroughly businesslike and competent, if a little brusque. Although he was unmarried and had no partner to knock off some of his rough edges, he was unquestionably a good-looking man in a rugged sort of way, with his tawny hair and alert hazel eyes, but most people found him intimidating and he certainly didn't suffer fools gladly. Rather than put up with sloppiness and stupidity, he preferred to do the work himself.

As he was piling papers into his briefcase there was a knock on the door. 'Come in,' he called. Gingerly, Roberta poked her head around the door.

'Mr Matthews?'

'Yes, come in, come in.' He held out his hand, smiling warmly. Frowning, Roberta moved forward to shake it. She didn't normally shake hands with her superiors. To her at nineteen Mr Matthews seemed dauntingly old and sophisticated. 'Now,' he said, beckoning her to sit down, 'I have a meeting in twenty minutes on site, and my bloody secretary has let me down again. How's your shorthand? Though I needn't ask, I remember it was pretty good.'

Roberta gulped. It wasn't often she was asked to do shorthand. Most of her work was copy typing handwritten letters and reports. She looked across at this bear of a man and noticed the twinkle in his hazel eyes. She gulped again, trying to appear confident and thanking the Lord she'd put on her best suit today. With a sweet smile she told him, 'It's fine, I think. Well, it was the last time I used it.'

'Good. Now ...' he looked at her feet '... is that the only pair of shoes you've got?'

She glanced down at her new black patent shoes and nodded.

'You need wellies. We'll have to get you some on the way. Got your coat?' Roberta nodded again, 'Pad? Pencil? Great! Come on, Robbie, we'll be late!'

7

Kit Fordham-Clarke rolled over in bed and felt the sun warm on his face. His curtains had been left open from the night before; in fact, it was a wonder he'd made it into bed at all, he'd been so drunk after the ball. Half his clothes were still on and he was suffering. His head throbbed and his stomach churned. He reached across to his bedside clock and checked the time. Eleven-thirty. He sighed and rolled back beneath the sheets. Sunday morning. One more week and it would be the end of term. He'd be expected to leave this cosy, comfortable lodgings in Bulkington, Coventry, and head back to Cambridge. The thought filled him with horror. If only he could get a job for the summer and stay here, in this spotlessly clean council house with Mavis, Brian and Judy.

Brian was a jobbing gardener, a gracious sixty-year-old man. For years he'd worked at the Jaguar factory in Coventry but had opted for early retirement because of ill health. He'd given up building cars and settled for the more gentle pace of cutting lawns and trimming hedges. Over the years he'd built up quite a business; in fact, turned down more people than he worked for nowadays. His own south-facing garden was a picture, rich with vibrant colours the whole year round. With its beds and rockeries and fountain, Kit liked nothing better than to sit outside in it and study. The garden was not at all overlooked, considered the close proximity of the next-door neighbours, and for the first time in his life he understood what peacefulness meant.

Kit roused himself from bed and put his hand to his head. He wobbled out of his bedroom and along the landing to the bathroom. He went inside, locked the door, and put the plug in the deep white enamel bath. Behind the closed door was a mirror, a long one, half concealed by a towelling robe belonging to Mavis and Brian's daughter, Judy. Kit caught sight of his half-clothed body and writhed in disgust. Since moving to Coventry he'd put on at least another stone and his face looked horrible, all greasy and with more spots than ever.

'You ugly berk!' he said out loud. 'You ugly, fat berk!'

He turned away quickly and vigorously swished the bath water around. 'You ugly fat berk!' he said again and again. 'You ugly, ugly fat berk!' He was reminded of his father, who never missed an opportunity to make some comment about his son's size. Then there was last night's ball. He remembered the rebuffs and cruel sidelong glances from the more fanciable females. Thank God for Judy. She'd accompanied him quite happily as a friend.

Kit turned off the taps and stepped into the bath, plunging his body into its cramped confines. With his knees raised, his stomach seemed to protrude even further. He squeezed his eyes tightly shut and imagined himself slim. Reed slim. The joy of it, the supreme pleasure he'd feel in the presence of his father. He grabbed soap and shampoo and briskly started to wash his face, hair and body. He rinsed himself and dunked his head beneath the water, using both hands to remove the suds. Then he stood up, reached across to the towel rail and plucked off a large soft blue towel.

Kit pressed it against his face, enjoying the sweet scent of Mavis's fresh washing. Everything in this house was well kept up. She cooked magnificently, cleaned meticulously and was a cheery soul into the bargain. He may only be a lodger – they'd taken in students since their own son Ed had left home years before – but for the first time in his life, Kit felt he belonged.

Lunch was always served at one o'clock on the dot. Like Kit's father, Brian liked his Sunday roast and Mavis never failed to produce a succulent feast. Kit's headache was beginning to disperse and now he was hungry, really hungry.

'Dinner's ready,' called Judy.

He skipped down the stairs and walked through to the kitchen where a table was set rather snugly in one corner, complete with gingham table cloth, jug of iced water and tumblers. Even paper napkins were used on a Sunday. 'Smells good,' said Kit, grinning at Mavis.

'Missed your breakfast, did you, lad?' she remarked while placing dish after dish in the middle of the table. 'Sit yourself down then. You'll be feeling hungry, no doubt. Come on, Judy, get that gravy on the table, there's a good girl.'

Judy placed the gravy boat on the table and raised her eyebrows at Kit. Her mother still treated her like a five year old and she'd given up trying to stop her.

Brian arrived from the garden and shifted around the mayhem in the kitchen to wash his hands at the sink. 'Lovely day, Mave, we could have eaten outside. It's a real treat out there. Later on in the year there'll be insects and things around, but the air's as still as still today.'

'Oh, well, never mind, we're having it in here now,' she said curtly. She wasn't one to be messed about. 'Now, lad, will you be wanting water or shall I fetch you a beer?'

Kit shook his head and laughed. 'Oh, don't talk about beer, Mavis, I've drunk enough to last me a lifetime.' He looked across at Judy, who'd tucked away a fair bit herself the previous evening.

Brian placed the roast lamb on the table. Carving was his job, a family ritual. He set about sharpening the carving knife on a steel. Down, across, down, across. Even the clash of the metals whetted Kit's appetite. And then the well-worn knife was sliding through the juicy pink meat, precisely and with ease. Brian served Judy first, just two small slices, and then Mavis, just the one, and then Kit, six slices, all pink in the middle and caramelised to a succulent crisp on the outside. His plate looked full already. Brian served himself three moderate slices and Kit frowned. Funny how he'd never noticed how little they all ate.

And then the vegetables. Mavis started heaping five roast potatoes on to Kit's plate and an enormous spoonful of cauliflower cheese, then freshly dug carrots and the sweetest garden peas. He watched as his plate was piled high. When everything was served and Brian had removed the remains of the lamb from the table, Kit looked at everyone else's plate. No one's looked like his. He shrugged, ladled on gravy and tucked in.

He'd barely finished when Brian was moving across the kitchen towards the lamb. 'Another slice, lad?'

It was a moment of enlightenment for Kit.

'No, no more, thanks.'

Brian stopped midway and turned back with a smile. 'Not feeling well?'

It wasn't a sarcastic comment, but it hurt nonetheless. They think I'm a pig, thought Kit, they bloody think I'm a great fat honking pig! And I am. 'I'm actually feeling fine,' he said lightheartedly, 'and the lamb was delicious, but I've had enough.'

Mavis patted his shoulder and stood up to clear. 'It's Pavlova for afters, so you can save yourself for that.'

It was teatime. Kit often had snacks between meals, especially on a Sunday. Mavis baked biscuits and cakes and all sorts of tempting treats. But he'd sat in the garden, soaking up the sun and steeled himself from nibbling. At lunchtime he'd asked for a moderate slice of Pavlova and had made a point of eating it slowly. He'd drunk three glasses of water and, at the time, felt full. By five o'clock he was ravenous.

Normally Mavis made sandwiches. They would be left on the kitchen table, with various other delights, and Kit would eat as the fancy took him, knowing full well he could always come back for more. And more, and more. But he wasn't going to do that anymore. He'd have a round of sandwiches and one piece of cake.

She was late, very late. Anxiously he looked at his watch. A quarter to six; his stomach rumbled. Even the sun had gone in, so he stirred himself from his position in the garden and wandered back towards the kitchen. No sounds, nothing; no Mavis either. Kit left the kitchen and walked into the hallway leading to the stairs. He peered into the homely sitting-cum-dining room, which was empty, and then out of the window which looked on to the front garden. No car, so they'd obviously all gone out. He must have dropped off to sleep, and they'd all left.

He walked back into the kitchen and across to the pantry. He opened the door. Standing temptingly on a shelf was a chocolate cake, uncut but oozing with butter cream and topped with chocolate icing. Kit moved forward and, with both hands, lifted the cake off the shelf and shuffled backwards out of the pantry, never taking his eyes off the glossy delight. Already he was imagining its taste in his mouth.

'Kit! What're you doing?'

The sound of his own name took him totally by surprise. He jumped and the plate slipped and slithered down the front of his shirt, splattering like a cowpat on the floor near his feet. The plate cracked cleanly down the middle. Kit's hands flew to his face as he turned to Judy. In horror, she looked down at the mess.

'Oh, Christ, I'm sorry,' he gasped, wiping his hands on his chocolate-smeared shirt.

Judy grinned. 'Oh, Kit, you should see your face. It's all right, I hate chocolate cake.' She bent down to pick up the broken plate. 'You'd better get some kitchen roll before Mum sees this mess.'

'Do you?' he asked, as he grabbed the kitchen roll.

'What?'

'Hate chocolate cake?'

She looked at him and smiled. 'I do. In fact, I rarely eat cake at all.'

Kit looked genuinely surprised. 'Don't you?'

She chuckled and thumped him on his arm. 'Clear it up, you fool, you're acting like an idiot.'

Kit started to scoop the mess into the kitchen paper. He stuffed it in the bin and then wiped the floor clean.

'I'll get the mop,' said Judy.

'Where are your parents?' he called after her.

'They'll be back in a minute. They went for a ride, I think, to some garden centre.' Judy looked at her watch as she started to mop the floor. 'Mum was worried about your tea, but I said you wouldn't mind waiting.'

Kit shook his head. 'No, of course not.' He looked down at the clean floor. 'It's just . . . I am rather hungry.'

Judy rinsed the mop in the sink. 'In that case, I'll make you a sandwich. That's what I came down to do.'

'No, I can make one, I'm not entirely helpless.'

'Okay, suit yourself.'

He turned around, wondering where to start. 'Judy?' He sighed. 'Would you help me?'

She grinned, 'Go on, off with you, I'll make the sandwich.'

'No, I don't mean that. I mean, will you help me get slim?' Awkwardly, he ran a hand through his hair. 'It's just – I'm so bloody fat and I hate it! Really hate it. Will you help me to diet? I haven't a clue where to start.'

'Well, you certainly made a good start with that, didn't you? A horribly gooey cake laden with calories – and you smashed it on the floor!'

He smiled. 'Seriously, though?'

Judy walked up to him and tweaked his face. 'It's easier than you think. Think fit, not fat. Eat less of what you like.'

Relief washed over Kit. He'd been doing that all day. 'Even chocolate cake?'

Judy folded her arms and slowly shook her head. 'Lay off the chocolate cake for the time being.'

He thought of the cake splodged on the floor – looking so unappetising. He beamed and grabbed her, kissing her firmly on the cheek. 'I think I can do this, with your help. Do you know, Judy, I think I love you!'

8

Nancy Lewis sat irritably in the Cosy Corner. She looked at her wristwatch and muttered beneath her breath. It was one thing for her to be late, but quite another for Brenda. Nancy, at forty-three, considered herself above being kept waiting. The only person she'd wait for, without complaining, was Peter, and even with him it was wearing a bit thin.

She looked down at her empty plate. She'd eaten an enormous chocolate eclair when she'd planned on eating nothing because of her new diet, but she was bored with waiting for Brenda.

Breathlessly, her sister appeared. 'Nance, I'm *so* sorry.' She was wearing a soft, sleeveless, button-through dress and strappy shoes. Her gently tanned skin seemed to gleam with good health and her normally greying dark hair had been cut short and tinted a lighter shade. She looked fetching with carefully applied make-up, and Nancy couldn't help but stare. Brenda slipped easily into the seat opposite and reached for her sister's hand. 'Have you been waiting long? I was hoping you'd be late as well.'

Nancy snatched her hand away. 'Long enough.' She shoved her plate to one side. 'What kept you?'

Brenda leant back in her seat, smiled kindly and surveyed her sister. 'I've had another interview, in Newmarket, at Style & File.'

'Style & File?'

'Yes, the hairdresser's and manicurist in the High Street. It's a really popular place. People come from all over to get their hair and nails done there.'

Nancy pulled a face. 'You're going back into *hairdressing*, at your age? I'm surprised they'd want you.'

Brenda chuckled. 'So am I, but they do. They're even sending

37

me on a refresher course to London for two weeks. I'm so excited, I can't tell you.'

'But you're forty-six, for God's sake.'

'I know, I know. But they like the way I look, and they like the way I cut hair. I always was a good cutter. Nance, even you have to admit that. Anyway, I saw the job advertised and applied. Never thought I'd get it, not in a million years, but Michael, who's my age and owns the shop, took a fancy to me and said he was fed up with young girls who got pregnant as soon as he'd trained them up. He wanted someone who'd stay with him for at least five years and I promised I would.'

Nancy narrowed her eyes. 'And what does Gordon think?'

Brenda turned in her seat as the waitress arrived. 'Another coffee, Nance?' Her sister nodded. 'Two coffees, please, and two chocolate eclairs.' She looked at the empty plate in front of Nancy. 'Or have you had one?'

Nancy, feeling thoroughly depressed, waved her hand indifferently. 'Yes, but I'll have another. I didn't have time for breakfast because of you.'

The waitress, well used to Nancy by now, just smiled at Brenda and walked off.

'Gordon thinks it's a grand idea. He's always encouraged me to go back to work. It was me, not him, who thought nobody'd want me. And now, with Roberta and Julia off my hands, I've more time to please myself.'

'But hairdressing. Not exactly well paid, is it?'

'No, it's not, and of course Michael can only pay me what he'd pay a young girl, but I don't mind, I shall love it. It's not the money I'm interested in.'

Nancy stroked her chin and reflected upon her sister's nature. Brenda had never been interested in money, even when she was younger. She'd never pursued men with flashy cars and lots of lolly to spend. Her Peter had been one of those. Briefly, Brenda had been his girlfriend then. He'd really liked her. Really, *really* liked her. Been quite heartbroken when she'd dropped him for Gordon Tree. Nancy shook her head to force away such thoughts and proudly remembered that, at the end of the day, it was she who'd stepped in and married Peter within the year.

'And how's Clare?' Brenda enquired with interest.

Nancy narrowed her eyes. 'She's fine, I suppose. But you'll never guess what she's planning to do now, the silly girl?'

'No, what?'

'Go to university, of all things. Get a degree. In psychology no less!' Nancy rolled her eyes, 'What would you do with her, Brenda?'

She saw the flicker of despair in her sister's eyes. Obviously no babies on the horizon then, and Nancy so desperate to be a grandmother. 'But that's wonderful! I'm impressed.'

'Impressed?' snorted Nancy. 'Whatever next?'

'But she's young, barely twenty. She has a lifetime ahead of her, Nance.'

'Well, what did she get married for then?'

A snappy reply was on the tip of Brenda's tongue but she decided against it. 'What does Roger think?'

'Oh, he's all for it. Mind you, he'd agree to anything just to keep her happy. To be honest with you, Brenda, I never really know what she's up to. She tells me very little these days.' Nancy's eyes devoured the chocolate eclair put before her on the table. 'My own daughter has become a stranger to me now. Perhaps she thinks I'm beneath her?'

'Oh, Nance, what rubbish! What a silly thing to say.' Brenda nodded her thanks to the waitress. 'Clare's not like that, you know she's not.'

Nancy forced a smile. 'And what about your two? How are they getting on?'

Brenda didn't know whether she dare say that Julia was seeing more and more of Clare, not that her daughter ever told her any details. She quickly weighed up the situation and decided against it. No point rubbing salt into Nancy's wounds. 'For starters, Julia's loving working at Purley's, and, to be honest with you, Nance, she's been offered a full-time job.'

'*What?* Surely she's not going to leave the Perse?'

Brenda shrugged. 'Well, maybe.'

'But that's ridiculous. Quite ridiculous. You must stop her, Brenda, she'll ruin her life.'

Brenda's hackles started to rise. 'No, she won't. Of course she won't. The world doesn't revolve around "A" levels, you know!'

Nancy prodded her sharply in the arm. 'Well, that's where you're wrong. How do you think Clare would be able to go back to her studies if she didn't have "A" levels?'

Brenda squirmed at her sister's reasoning. There was no way she'd be able to get the better of her. Nancy had all the answers. 'Clare's Clare, Nance, and Julia is Julia.'

'And ne'er the twain shall meet!'

Brenda smiled. 'Well, perhaps it'll never happen, but she's warned us it may. She's thinking of joining Purley's full-time and not going back to the Perse next term.'

'Silly, silly girl!' Disdainfully, Nancy popped an enormous portion of chocolate eclair into her mouth. 'If you want my advice, Brenda, you'll not let her leave the Perse under any circumstances.'

Sadly, Brenda shook her head. She turned towards the waitress and gestured for the bill.

'Well, Nance, you think what you like, and I'll do the same.'

'Yes, I'm sure you will, but don't come crying to me when it's too late. I did all I could to help her, Brenda, and if it's not good enough, I shan't be offering anymore.'

Brenda rummaged in her handbag and withdrew her purse to pay the bill. 'Okay, Nancy, you've made your point. I'll make every effort to remember it in the future.'

As quick as a flash, Nancy picked up the bill. She usually did. 'I'll get this.'

'No, Nance, I really should pay my way.'

Patronisingly, her sister smiled. '*I'll pay.*'

Brenda looked at her. Nancy's generosity was real, but the Lady Bountiful bit was infuriating. 'Just once, I'd really like to pay.'

Nancy scraped back her chair. 'And one day, Brenda, I'll let you!'

9

Julia's eyes were out on stalks. Totally mesmerised, she followed Anne Purley through her large, sprawling warehouse in Chesterton on the outskirts of Cambridge city centre. Wrapped loosely in heavy cloth and stacked neatly on shelves were expertly preserved and dyed skins of leather, suede and sheepskin. Ann paused, reaching across to throw back a wrapping.

'You see, Julia, this is hide. Very strong and so ideal for coats and handbags.' She pulled the leather towards her and beckoned Julia closer. 'Smell it, isn't it divine? Our tanning process is the very, very best, and the deep, rich aroma proves it. All these leathers are treated with minerals and oils to preserve them, then dyed with top quality chemicals to produce the wonderful colours. Always remember, the cheaper the dye, the more unpleasant the smell.' Julia sniffed the hide leather and stroked it with both hands.

'And this over here is nappa leather from sheep. See? It's lighter, a much finer grain, softer and more pliable, used mainly for gloves. And then the suede over here – smell this. Isn't it just bliss? But we only use suede for coats. Suede handbags and gloves are just too difficult to look after. We don't want unnecessary complaints from our customers, we want to give them the best.'

Anne rewrapped the skins and moved on down the aisle. 'Over there are handbags and gloves, waiting to be dispatched. We have three shops now, in Kings Lynn, Norwich, and of course, Cambridge. Nathan looks after them all. He's a treasure, I can tell you, he manages the lot. We don't keep too much finished merchandise in the warehouse. It should all be out on the shelves, waiting to be sold.'

Breathing in the atmosphere, Julia's eyes darted everywhere.

Belts and handbags, gloves and hats, rolls of silk to make scarves and shawls. And then container upon container of wooden beads, semi-precious stones and chunks and clusters of silver glinting in the sunlight of this bright July day, all used to make Purley's own jewellery.

Anne pointed to a large room in the far corner. 'The tannery's over there. I'll show you round it later'. She started to climb the polished wooden stairs which led to a mezzanine floor where six women and four men worked expertly and meticulously. Purley's latest line was the jewellery, no sooner made than it was sold. Nathan Purley couldn't keep up with the demand. His two specialist silversmiths were treated like royalty.

The mezzanine floor was predominantly open plan, although each worker had his, or her, own space and equipment. The noise level was high, but not irritatingly so, and everyone cheerily raised their heads when Anne introduced Julia.

'Nathan's along here. He needs his own office, away from all the noise.' She walked through the busy scene to the far end where she knocked on a closed door and, without waiting, pushed it open. 'Nathan darling, I'd like you to meet my new recruit.' Anne turned towards Julia whose heart slowed to a halt as she saw the man who got to his feet to greet her.

She'd been excited by it all, already on a high, but that was nothing to what she felt now. She stumbled over her words and eventually muttered, 'Hallo,' moving forward to shake his outstretched hand. Nathan Purley was *gorgeous*, with a capital G. Medium height, about 5'10", with the most remarkable dark brown eyes and slightly lighter coloured hair, streaked naturally by the sun. He was perfection and as he smiled Julia felt her body grow weak. Nathan turned towards his mother, revealing his one tiny flaw – a slight gap between his front two teeth. Julia fell instantly in love.

'I've heard a lot about you. Welcome aboard.' His handshake was firm and Julia read far more into it than she should have. At twenty-four, Nathan Purley was a past master at remaining detached. Women fell like flies in hot pursuit of him, and he didn't give a damn. He let go of her hand but gently took her arm and pulled her into his office. Smiling, Anne looked on. He called out, 'Caroline? Be a love?'

Blonde and leggy Caroline came breathlessly through from an adjoining office. 'Yes?'

'Coffee?' He looked at Julia, his eyes focusing directly on hers, melting her very soul. 'Or would you prefer tea?'

'Oh . . . er, tea would be nice.'

Nathan turned back to Caroline, still holding on to Julia's arm, 'Three teas then, sweetie.' He let go of her, leaving the impression of his fingers still tingling on her flesh.

'Mother, please, sit down.' Nathan shifted some chairs and gestured to his mother to sit. 'Now, Julia, what do you think? I know for a fact my mother wants you to be impressed. She's got great plans for you, *great plans*.'

Julia looked briefly at Anne then straight back at Nathan.

'I'm impressed.' She tilted her head to one side, allowing her eyes to speak her thoughts.

Disappointment jabbed him. Another easy conquest. What a pity – she was some girl!

10

1968

Roger and Clare's newly built house was in the charming village of Madingley, just a few miles north of Cambridge. Julia, relaxed after an elegant supper and sipping chilled Chablis, slithered back in one of the two sumptuous tawny-coloured leather settees. Sitting cross-legged on the floor, Clare gently ran the fingers of one hand through the cream shag-pile carpet. Simon and Garfunkel's *Bookends* hummed softly on the stereo. Roger was making coffee.

'You might go off the idea by next year, Clare?'

Hastily, she replied, 'No chance. I'm determined.'

'But three years . . . it's a helluva long time. Are you sure Roger doesn't mind?'

Clare shook her head and sipped her wine. 'I wouldn't care if he did. It's my life, and I'll do what I please. He does! He doesn't consider me when he works late every night.'

'But that's different, don't you think?'

'No, it's not. How can you say that? It's not different at all.'

Julia shrugged. 'Well, he'll miss you, I'm sure.'

Clare pushed a thumb into her mouth, tapping the nail against her teeth. 'I just wish I'd been able to get in this October, I'm *so* fucking mad about that.' She reflected a bit. 'But I suppose it gives me a chance to bone up a bit; maybe do an "A" level in psychology.'

'God, what a drag!'

'Of course it's not a drag! I didn't say that about Purley's. I respected your decision. You left school to work in a shop – I want to study. I intend to be a psychologist, what's wrong with that?'

'But what gave you the idea in the first place? Why psychology?'

Clare thought for a while, pouting. She sipped her wine then placed the glass on the carpet. 'Nick, I suppose. Yes, he gave me the idea.'

'Nick? Roger's brother?'

'Yes. You met him, didn't you? At the wedding?' Julia nodded. 'A while ago he was home for the weekend from London and we were invited to lunch at Cynthia and Joshua's. He got talking to me and ... it was just so *interesting*, Julia, what he had to say. So interesting. He works in Camden, you see, as a social worker. The usual inner-city problems, of course, but he's becoming more and more involved with children, the problem ones, under-privileged mostly. It's fascinating stuff, just fascinating.'

'But you don't like children.'

Clare looked astounded. 'Of course I do. Whatever made you think that?'

Julia blushed in embarrassment, she hadn't meant to be rude. She'd just assumed. 'You said you didn't want any babies.'

'But that doesn't mean I don't like children.'

'No, of course it doesn't. Anyway, go on.'

'Well, that's it really. I decided, there and then, that it's what I'd like to do.' Clare's eyes sparkled. 'You know, something really useful.'

'But how did Nick get involved in all that? I thought he was studying engineering, the same as Roger?'

Clare gave her tinkling laugh. 'He was, he did, but he packed it all in. Hated it, in fact. Got a very junior job with the Social Services in Camden, and that's how he started. Nick's talents lie with people. He's a charmer through and through.'

You can say that again, reflected Julia. 'So he didn't finish his degree?'

Clare shook her head. 'No, he didn't, but don't mention that in front of Joshua. He goes puce at the thought.'

Julia chuckled and narrowed her eyes. 'I'm hardly likely to mention it to anyone. Least of all Joshua Fordham-Clarke.' Her thoughts flew to the wedding. What a day, what a bloke.

'But why would you want to get involved in all that misery? You're married, Clare, and rich as well.'

'Oh, Julia, don't you start. All this means nothing to me, nothing at all.' Clare screwed up her lovely face. '*You* should understand. You're doing what you want. I'm just the same.'

Julia's mounting respect for her cousin's new ambition was finely balanced against her own confusion over Roger. 'But what if you get pregnant?'

'Ha! There's no chance of that.'

'Doesn't he want to have children?'

Clare hesitated briefly and ran a hand through her lustrous hair. 'He does, but he'll do what I say.'

Julia giggled. 'Lucky you, I wish I had a man to do what I say.'

A wicked grin crossed Clare's face. 'Do you know what you are, cousin Julia? You're bloody sex-mad!'

'And I'll be the first to admit it. You *must* like it too?'

Clare threw back her head and sighed. 'It can be a chore, I tell you. A bloody chore all the time.'

Julia thought of Nathan Purley, to whom so far she hadn't been able to get close. Sex with him would *never* be a chore.

'Oh, Julia, do you have to go home tonight?'

She was tempted but had to refuse. 'I promised Dad. He'd be upset if I let him down.'

Clare protested, used to getting her own way. 'But he's got all those stable lads. What does he need you for?'

'It's Sunday tomorrow, Clare, and several of the lads are away. I promised I'd ride out. Anyway, I'm looking forward to it. It's ages since I rode on the Heath. Yonks.'

Persuasively, Clare shifted her self forward. 'Well, how about if we run you back early in the morning?'

Julia considered the idea, but shook her head. 'Dad will be worried if I'm not there. I really must go back tonight.' She took another sip of wine, wondering why it was so important for her to stay. 'You've got Roger, what on earth do you want me here for?'

Clare straightened her back and raised the glass to her lips. She looked staggeringly beautiful, with her sleek, straight hair glistening in the lamplight and her sparkling blue eyes mellow from the wine. She opened her cupid's bow mouth and ran her tongue along her lower lip. 'It's just more fun when you're around.'

Julia felt enormously flattered. 'Fun?'

Clare leant forward again. 'Yes, fun!'

Roger pushed open the sitting-room door and walked in, carrying a tray of coffee. He grinned at his wife. 'I hope this is all right, darling? We seem to have run out of our normal beans. I had to use some others.'

Clare rolled her eyes. 'Oh, for shame!'

Julia looked across at Roger, who perched himself close to Clare. He put the tray on a round white table and, as he did so, accidentally nudged her. She immediately shifted to one side. Julia was surprised. It was as though Clare wanted no contact with her husband at all.

'I'm impressed,' commented Julia, 'at home we use Nescafe.'

Clare scooted across the carpet and propped herself in front of Julia. 'And so do I normally. It's just Roger and his ideas.'

He smiled indulgently at his wife. 'You change your tune like the weather, darling. When we first got married, you insisted on Fortnum and Mason's freshly ground Arabica beans. I remember it well.'

Clare rounded on him sharply. 'Yes, well, I was a naive little girl then, wasn't I, Roger?'

He reached across and tapped her leg. 'And you still are, Clare, you still are.'

Embarrassed, Julia looked at her watch. 'Well, I must drink this and dash. My bus goes at ten.'

'Oh, don't be silly, Julia. We'll take you home, of course.' Clare reprimanded.

'You don't have to. I really don't want to put you to any trouble.'

Clare looked at her husband. 'It won't be any trouble, will it, Roger? You'll take Julia home. You don't mind?'

Lazily, he smiled. 'Of course not.'

Clare turned to her. 'That's settled then. See? There's no hurry at all.'

Approaching Newmarket on the Cambridge Road, near Stetchworth, was a left-hand turn which led to the National Stud and on to the July Racecourse. It could be easily missed by passing traffic except on race days in July when the traffic queued to turn in. Further along this turning and running parallel with the July Course was Devil's Dyke, a favourite haunt for tourists, walkers and dog lovers. Devil's Dyke, or Ditch as some people called it, separated the Rowley Mile from the July racecourse, and dated back to the Bronze Age. This earthwork ran across the Heath and right through the racing territory of Newmarket, boasting a well-trodden track all the way along the top. At night, the surrounding area was a secret place, ideal for lovers.

Roger Fordham-Clarke's new E-type Jaguar, in its muted shade of gold, was very noticeable in daylight, but on this particular September evening there was no moon and the night was as black as pitch. He'd parked the car just far enough along the track to be almost private. There were a couple of other cars dotted around, but this didn't bother Roger, and it certainly didn't bother Julia.

The front passenger seat had been lowered and pushed back as far as it would go. She half-lay with her legs splayed, gripping the edge of the seat with her bare feet. Roger, on his knees in the footwell, clutched the back of her seat and slowly and ecstatically withdrew and pushed, withdrew and pushed. He groaned in pleasure. Now and then she'd rise and force him deeper within herself, sighing and moaning and dragging her fingers through his hair. They were enveloped in their mutual pleasure, becoming high on the act.

It hadn't been planned, certainly not by Julia. She liked her cousin, and the possibility of Roger's being unfaithful to such a beautiful woman seemed bizarre. Until, that was, he'd talked about how tough it was being married to such a beautiful but untouchable lady. And then he'd stroked Julia's leg as he drove along and it had sent shivers through her body. She'd felt hot and wet, and writhed in her seat. And then he'd touched her face and run one finger across her mouth. She'd sucked on it hard. That was enough, nothing further needed to be said.

It was as though he'd been totally deprived. Neither of them wanted it to end. It wasn't some sordid little sex act, it had turned into something else. They luxuriated in each other's pleasure, wanting to please. Roger whispered her name and with gentle fingers caressed her face, her hair and her body. He'd called her erotic and said she'd driven him crazy with desire.

But when it was over, he'd dressed in silence. Julia didn't pry. She just allowed herself to be dropped off at her parents' cottage with a nod and a wave.

Guiltily, she stood on the pavement and watched him drive away. She had no doubt that Clare would be in touch, but how would she face her? More to the point, how would she be able to resist her husband again? Julia shook her head. She was tired and it was late, she decided not to think about it anymore. She unlocked the front door with her key and stepped inside. Guilty thoughts of Clare kept niggling at her. Julia reasoned with herself that it was simple; she'd just have to pretend, and play the game. She was good at playing the game, after all, and wasn't about to wreck their marriage. With a man like Roger, Clare was doing that all by herself.

11

1969

Roberta snatched up the phone and said politely, 'Mr Matthews's office, his secretary speaking. May I help?'

'I don't want his bloody secretary! Is *he* there?'

Taken aback, she looked at the phone, and composed herself. 'I'm sorry, to whom am I speaking?'

'*Lady*, just get me Matthews!'

Roberta gulped in astonishment. 'I'm sorry, but Mr Matthews isn't here.'

'Bullshit! Don't give me that, I *know* he's there!'

Roberta looked at her watch. Nine-thirty. Ed was due anytime. 'I'm expecting him shortly, Mr . . .?'

The line went dead. Roberta looked at it in surprise. 'Ignorant pig!'

Her tiny office adjoined Ed's and she swivelled off her chair, picking up the post as she did so. She walked through the connecting door and proceeded to put the mail in order of importance on his desk. She'd already opened, read and date-stamped it all.

In a flurry, Ed bustled in. His fierce expression mellowed at the sight of his secretary. 'Morning, Robbie, I see you're well ahead of me as usual. Everything all right?'

She raised her eyes as the giant of a man strode towards her. His face was rosy from the winter cold, his hair tousled, creating an aura of vulnerability and making him appear younger than his thirty-four years. 'Morning, Ed. I think so.'

Without removing his coat, he leafed through the mail. 'Christ! Not him again!'

'And he's just rung ... I think. He wouldn't leave a name, but I'm sure it was Simons.'

'What did he say?'

Roberta shrugged. 'Nothing. Just aggro because you weren't here.'

'Oh, shit!'

Roberta smiled. 'Coffee?' Ed didn't answer, just carried on reading his mail. 'Ed? Coffee?' From the start, he'd insisted on her calling him Ed. It had been difficult at first, but as time went by she'd grown used to it, and now liked it. Roberta liked *him*, a lot. He'd given her her new position and it had led to increased poise and confidence.

Ed looked up and smiled. 'Brilliant idea, I'm gasping.' His eyes wandered over her. She always looked good to him. From the start he'd fancied her, but her competence in the office and unflappable nature made him respect her as well. Within six months of Roberta's working for him, Ed Matthews had fallen in love. But she was only twenty, just a girl, and, deep down he was a gentleman. He'd never abuse the boss/secretary situation. 'You're looking good. New dress?'

Roberta looked down at her short tartan skirt and cream flouncy blouse. 'It's a skirt, Ed, and a blouse.' She chuckled because she'd worn them before, many times. 'They're not new, but thanks.'

'You always look good to me, Robbie.' He picked up a letter. 'You'd better get me Simons, straight away. I suppose I'll have to try and placate the old boy.' He threw the letter across the desk. 'How the hell am I supposed to do my job when this bloody place is crumbling round my ears?'

She picked up the letter and walked through to her room, immediately grabbing her phone to dial the number. 'Mr Simons, please.' There was a wait. 'Mr Simons? Mr Matthews for you.' Roberta buzzed Ed and put the call through. She then turned towards the kettle sitting on top of a filing cabinet in the corner of the office and set about making Ed's first coffee of the day. Strong, sweet, with hardly any milk. She opened a new packet of digestives and put two in his saucer. She walked back into his office and set the coffee before him.

'Well, that'll get us nowhere. If our claims haven't been met, we can't carry on, it's as simple as that.' Ed rolled his eyes at Roberta. 'I know, I know, so it wasn't in our original tender, but certain things can't be foreseen ... Yes, but you can't expect us to meet the extra cost ... Look, *Mr Simons*, that is not the way Dolman's do business ... Now come on, that's no way to talk. I am sorry, but ... *all right, have it your own fucking way*!' He slammed down the receiver.

Roberta raised her eyebrows, 'Oh, dear.'

Ed jabbed his fist on the table and the coffee spilled on to the biscuits. 'Oh, shit!'

Roberta grabbed his cup and saucer and whisked them away, returning quickly with two fresh biscuits and a wiped saucer.

'Sorry, Robbie.'

She shrugged and turned to leave. As quick as a flash, he grabbed her hand. 'You're an angel, Roberta, you know that, don't you?'

She half-giggled in embarrassment, and didn't know what else to say. He dropped her hand, and she left the room. He followed her through.

'It'll go down, you know, Dolman's. It's on its way. They can't keep doing this.'

Roberta frowned. 'You sound as though you're blaming Dolman's?'

'I am, because it's the likes of me that take the rap.' He sat on her desk and Roberta saw how lean and fit he was. For such a big man, Ed Matthews didn't appear to have an ounce of fat on him. She swallowed and looked up as he removed his glasses. Roberta liked his eyes, the way they were flecked with gold. 'If I told you the number of times I've been approached by clients, to work directly for them, cut out Dolman's completely, you'd never believe me. I could walk out of this place tomorrow and set up in business. But I stay, and where does my integrity get me in this bloody firm? I'm up against this shit every bloody day. They put in a low tender, get the job, and follow it through with a load of hefty claims. They claim for this, claim for that. Dolman's damned profits depend on it! But unfortunately, as the prices rocket through the roof, so does the client.' Defiantly, Ed pushed out his chin. 'Dolman's has *massive* overheads to contend with and at long last they're getting their comeuppance.'

'But it'll come right in the end, won't it?'

'It's too late, Robbie, it's too bloody late.'

She was surprised by his candour. More and more he was beginning to confide in her. 'So what're you going to do?'

'Leave. There's no other way. I can't waste anymore of my time placating clients.' He stared at her, his eyes holding hers. 'It's simple, I'll set up on my own.' He caught the interest in his secretary's eyes. 'Why don't you join me, Robbie? Come with me?'

She was abashed. 'You mean, work with you? But I'm no engineer.'

He grabbed her hand and squeezed it tightly. 'You're no engineer, but you're bloody good at what you do. Nobody's ever looked after me like you, Robbie. I'll need someone to answer the phone, be nice to the clients and generally keep me in check. Who better than you? I can't promise a pay-rise, I can't exactly promise any pay at all until I get my first client, but I'll look after you, of that you can be sure.'

Briefly, she allowed her hand to rest in his, aware of his touch, liking it. 'But where would we work from?'

'Well, I suppose I'd start in my flat, but I'll sell it and buy a house big enough to incorporate an office. All I need is a phone and a drawing board, and ... you?' Ed saw her gulp and panicked, getting quickly off her desk and waving his hand in the air. 'I'm a structural engineer, Robbie, and bloody good at what I do.' He lowered his hand and peered across the desk. 'I shouldn't have to sell myself to you. You trust me, don't you?'

'Can you use your contacts from Dolman's? Would you be allowed to do that?'

Nervously, he laughed. Good old Roberta, always so straight. But at least she wasn't saying no. He leant on the desk. 'Roberta, I can use what I want.'

'And you'd want me to work from your flat?'

Moving closer, he allowed himself a smile. 'It's nothing grand, but you'll improve the surroundings no end.' She smiled back. 'So, Miss Tree, is that a yes?'

She felt his hand cup her chin as he raised her face to his. 'If you really want me, then yes.'

'I want you, Roberta. I thought you already knew that?' He moved his hand to the back of her head, pulling her closer, and kissed her on the mouth.

12

Late July, 1969

The front door of the Cosy Corner stood wide open to catch any breeze. The weather was hot and sultry, and Brenda mopped her brow intermittently with a napkin as she looked out of the window. Standing before her on the table was a large glass of orange squash which she sipped from. Nancy was late, over half an hour late, and Brenda was angry. Her sister's timekeeping was becoming a joke, and as Monday was Brenda's only day off during the week, the last thing she wanted was to be twiddling her thumbs in a hot sticky cafe in the middle of Cambridge. She looked at her watch and sighed once more. She'd wait another five minutes and then she'd go. She'd got heaps to do, Julia to visit . . . As Brenda's thoughts raced, Nancy arrived.

'Brenda, my dear, I'm most awfully sorry!'

Nancy stood in the doorway, commanding attention as usual. Everyone stared, Nancy always made sure of that, but as she hastened towards her sister, Brenda involuntarily eyed her outfit: a beautifully cut, apple green sleeveless A-line dress, nipped into tucks around the waist and finishing just above the knee. This was set off with a single strand of real pearls, and as Brenda's eyes crept down to her sister's feet she noticed chunky-heeled white suede shoes. To top all this, her skin was tanned to a light golden brown and her hair had received a much younger cut. And . . . Nancy had lost weight.

Brenda swallowed her pique and forced a smile. 'You're here at last.'

Nancy sat down with all the usual palaver of parking her handbag and numerous carriers, arranging them on vacant chairs behind and around her. 'I couldn't get away – I just couldn't get away.'

'Why? Why couldn't you get away? You're half an hour late, Nance, I was just about to leave.'

Nancy turned towards the waitress and beckoned with her hand. 'Quickly now, quickly, I'm about to expire!' The waitress scuttled forward, obeying her command. Nancy had that effect on people. 'Something long and cold, with masses of ice.' She pondered a while, as the girl looked on. 'A lime cordial . . . yes, that's what I'd like.'

As the waitress turned to go, Brenda commented, 'You look well, Nance, really well. And I must say, I love your dress.'

Nancy swayed in her seat, delighted with her sister's comment. 'It's Jean Muir. She's the best. I *adore* Jean Muir! Peter bought it for me in London.' She sat back in her seat and fanned her face with her hand. 'What a month! I can't tell you how exciting it's been.'

But you're going to, thought Brenda. 'Well, you don't really need to, Nance, I can see for myself. It's written all over your face.'

Nancy lurched forward in her seat and grabbed her sister's hand. 'What about Apollo 11? Those men on the moon? Wasn't that exciting?'

Don't tell me you went there too, thought Brenda. 'It was, it was.'

'And did I tell you we had centre-court tickets for Wimbledon? It was such a piece of luck! Peter bought the tickets for one of his clients, he does that sort of thing to keep people sweet. Anyway, at the last minute the chap dropped out, so he took me. I saw the Ladies Final, Brenda. *I actually watched Ann Jones beat Billie-Jean King!*' In her excitement Nancy spilled some of her lime cordial on to her dress. 'Oh, no! Darn it!' She looked down at the mark and then rubbed it with napkin, making it worse. 'Oh really, what a nuisance.'

'Try a dab of cold water, Nance, that should do the trick.'

'But it's the finest rayon – it's dryclean only. If I put water on it, it'll mark.'

'But it's marked already, Nance.'

Nancy turned towards the waitress and snapped her fingers. 'Girl! Some water, please. A bowl of water and a cloth.'

They arrived quickly. Nancy attempted to sponge off the mark which grew and grew as the water seeped in. 'Oh, dear. I *have* made a mess.'

'It'll dry, Nance. I'd just forget it, if I was you.'

'Well, you're not me, are you?' The old Nancy had returned.

Brenda held her peace and eventually so did her sister. 'Have you lost weight, Nance?'

Her good humour was instantly restored. 'You noticed?'

'Yes, of course. Anyone would.'

Nancy snorted. 'Even your Gordon?'

Brenda narrowed her eyes, surveying her sister. What difference did Gordon's opinion make? 'I'm sure he would.'

'I haven't been dieting, that's not my style. But I've been a few times with Peter to various golf courses. I don't play, of course, just walk round with him, and it can be a very long walk. Apparently, Cynthia does it too. She goes regularly with Joshua. We meet up with them occasionally at the Gogs, have lunch with them every now and then. But she's really not my type.'

'What type is she?'

Dismissively, Nancy waved her hand. 'Oh, you know the sort. All giddy and girlish. She's never grown up. Never had to, with all her money. Mind you, Joshua adores her. And she ticks him off as much as she likes, which isn't a bad thing because he's a grumpy old so-and-so.'

'How does Clare get on with her?'

'Clare?'

'Yes, Clare. Cynthia *is* her mother-in-law.'

'Oh, yes, of course. I really don't know. She's never said. Have I told you about her house? No, I can't have done, can I? She's got a *wonderful* house. A treasure of a place.'

'Who has?'

'Clare, of course, a pied-à-terre in Chiswick. Lovely position, looks out across parkland and the cricket green. Absolutely splendid view.'

'Oh yes, of course. I was forgetting she had to move. So, when does she start her psychology course?'

Nancy's face glowed with pleasure. 'Late-September, I think. Roger's been an incredible support, you know. He's bent over backwards to make sure she'll be all right. Bought her a brand new MGB-GT, given her a special account so that she can furnish her house as she likes. He's a marvellous husband, Brenda, she's a very lucky girl.' Nancy prodded her sister's arm with a well-manicured forefinger. 'And guess what? Clare has told me that as soon as she gets her degree, she'll try for a baby!'

'Oh, a degree and a baby? Won't you be proud?'

'I will, I will! But it's not going to be easy, you know, she's going to have to work tremendously hard.'

'And will she come home every weekend?'

Nancy pouted and shook her head. 'I shouldn't think so, but I really can't be sure. Of course, if she doesn't come home, Roger'll go to Chiswick.'

'Which university did you say?' Brenda already knew. Julia had told her.

'Brunel, Uxbridge campus.' Nancy sniffed. 'Not exactly Oxbridge, but it's the course that counts.'

'Clever girl. She's done well.'

Nancy sighed. 'I just hope that Roger manages without her, poor lamb.'

'Well it's only for three years and that'll fly by.'

Nancy looked down at the stain on the dress, which had faded in the heat but left a water mark. 'There, I knew I shouldn't have put water on it.' She glared at her sister momentarily then softened. 'Oh, what must you think of me? I've been prattling on and on about *my* family all the time. What about yours? How is Julia getting on in her little shop?'

'Julia's fine, loving every minute. I told you Anne Purley made her manager of the Cambridge shop, didn't I?' Nancy nodded rather disdainfully. 'It's important that it's run by a trendy young person, that's what the customers like in Cambridge. A lot of the goods are sold to passing trade, you know, visitors and the like. Anyway, she's becoming more and more involved in the designs of the coats and handbags too.' Brenda grimaced. 'I have to confess, Julia would like to change things a bit. What with all the new fashions coming along, especially these boutiques, she'd like to transform the shop and buy in more young trendy stuff. You know, like the clothes they sell in Chelsea.'

'Typical! And downright stupid if you ask me. It's quality that counts, Brenda, every single time. High class goods will still be here tomorrow, not all this cheap tat you see around today.'

'Oh, no, I'm not talking about cheap tat, Nance. Julia's not after that at all. She wants the same quality, but she also wants the latest designs.' Brenda sighed. 'Anyway, it's not Anne that's the stick-in-the-mud, it's Nathan, her son.'

'Well, good for him, I say.'

Brenda took a deep breath. 'I think you're wrong, Nance. I think you're missing the point . . .'

Brenda was cut off in mid-stream. 'I most certainly am not! You can't sit there and talk to me about clothes, Brenda. I've spent years buying the best.'

She gulped and gave in. There was no point in trying to explain. She finished her orange squash and pushed her glass to one side.

'And Roberta? How's she? Still working in *that chap's flat*?'

Brenda bristled. There were times when she was tempted to be really spiteful back to her sister. She reflected upon Julia's close relationship with Clare and Roger, which Nancy knew nothing about. Maybe she ought to drop it into the conversation? But she wouldn't, because the fact that Julia saw more of her daughter and Roger than Nancy did would hurt. Brenda took a deep breath. 'His name is Ed Matthews, and he's trying desperately hard to get his business off the ground. It's called Matthews Structural Design, Nancy, and Roberta is a partner. There's no need to make it sound seedy.'

'Oh? So she's a partner now, is she?'

'Yes, she is. What's so strange about that?'

Nancy smirked. 'Nothing, nothing at all.'

'She's doing well, Nance, she's getting on with her life. She loves working for Ed. They've just landed an enormous contract on the outskirts of Bury St Edmunds – a huge complex for Iber-Mac. Ed's designing and constructing all the reinforced concrete and specialised steel frames for their farming equipment. It's a lucrative contract, Nance, and I'm proud of Roberta for having the courage to give up her job at Dolman's and go and work for Ed.'

'Well, she had to give up her job. Dolman's went bust.'

'But Ed and Roberta left before they went bust, Nance. You know that.'

'Dolman's never was any good. Couldn't touch Fordham-Clarke's.'

'Well, you're bound to say that, aren't you?'

Nancy straightened her back. 'There's no need to be so sarcastic, Brenda.'

'Sometimes you make me, Nance, you really do!'

'I can't think why. I was happy 'til I came here today.'

'Well, I'm sorry, I'm sure.'

There was a short, uncomfortable silence. Brenda averted her eyes, not wanting to see the expression on her sister's face. She was surprised to feel a small squeeze of her arm. 'Come on, Brenda, this is no way for us to behave.' Nancy grinned, and Brenda smiled back. 'I've come to depend on our meetings. Life wouldn't be the same without them, you know.' Brenda nodded, welcoming the admission.

And then the old patronising Nancy returned. 'So, tell me all about your little hairdressing shop. I suppose you're still there?'

13

September, 1969

Tucked away from all main roads, about six miles east of Newmarket on the Cambridgeshire-Suffolk border, nestled the tiny hamlet of Tongate. It comprised twenty or so fifteenth-century, oak-framed thatched cottages with dotted in between three or four brick-built dwellings. More prestigious properties graced the surrounding area, being part of two highly acclaimed stud farms. Originally all the cottages in Tongate – pronounced Tun*git* by the locals – were tied cottages but with the advent of cars, easy public transport and outside labour, some of the cottages were gradually sold off.

Built on high ground, Blackthorn Cottage wasn't part of Tongate's nucleus. It was off the beaten track, down a twisting lane, and even then almost hidden from view beneath climbing roses, ivy and virginia creeper. The large picturesque property was snuggled into an acre of overgrown flower beds and vegetable plots, and densely surrounded by blackthorn, hawthorn, sycamore and ash. In the middle of the garden was a magnificent oak tree with dotted around it several chestnuts, and if you struggled through the mass of shrubs and trees to the very perimeter of the plot, there were panoramic views of the surrounding countryside.

Painted Suffolk pink, like all the houses in Tongate, Blackthorn Cottage hadn't been inhabited for years, probably because of its size and isolated position. It was the usual oak-framed, plaster and lath construction indigenous to the area, and had originally been thatched but now boasted a peg-tile roof. It was all the more attractive because both sides of its upper storey jutted out, making it an artist's dream – and a builder's nightmare!

On first sight Roberta fell in love with it. Ed wasn't so sure.

He'd imagined buying a ready-to-move-into house and had only reluctantly agreed to view this place. Blackthorn Cottage would need an enormous amount of work, only part of it fit to live in as yet. Inside, all the exposed beams had been plastered over and wall-papered in typically late-fifties, early-sixties style. The kitchen had a chipped enamel sink with one tap, a pre-historic stove and an old mangle. The remaining rooms were bleak, with cracked linoleum or bits of mouldy carpet on the floors, and a sweet, musty smell pervaded the whole building. Undaunted, Roberta wandered around enthusing about what could be done, how it would look, and what a dream of place it really was.

'What on earth did you bring me here for, Robbie?' Ed complained. 'This place needs bulldozing!'

'*What?*' Roberta put her hands on her hips, a habit of hers when she was about to disagree. 'How can you say that? I've never seen anywhere so ... so ... poetic!'

He laughed. 'Poetic? You're mad!'

They were standing in the garden, with the late-September sun casting long shadows around them. The air was still, except for the occasional calling bird, and Roberta felt an odd sense of belonging here. She held the key tightly in her hand. The agent hadn't even bothered to accompany them to the cottage, so sure they'd take a quick peek and scuttle away hot foot. Nobody was interested in such delapidated old houses. Not in this day and age when modern was beautiful.

But it *was* poetic. In Roberta's mind's eye this could be *her* home. Home and security, with Ed to look after her and protect her in his special way. And *how* he protected her! One cross word from a client in her direction and Ed would come to her aid immediately. Since working from his flat their relationship had developed beyond even Roberta's imagining. She was comfortable with him now, and knew she wanted more. The odd kiss here and there was no longer enough, she was looking for a lover. In fact she spent a considerable amount of her time imagining how things could be between them.

She breathed in the clear air, deciding to convince him with facts. 'It's not far from Bury, and just think of its potential. There's masses of room.'

He shifted closer and looked into her eager face. 'You can't be serious about this? Would you really want to work from here?'

'Yes. Yes!'

'But it'd take forever to do this place up, and forever I haven't got. Time and money – I've a shortage of both.'

'You can't let this go, Ed! You just can't let it go. It feels so right, and it's a snip at that price – six thousand pounds, for God's sake. It'll be worth double when we've finished.'

He studied her closely. 'We?'

She laughed. 'OK, you, then. But I'll help.' She nudged his arm. 'I'll do the garden, how about that? And my dad'll help, and my mum! Dad's a brilliant gardener.'

Ed chuckled. 'So's mine, come to that. Perhaps I should get him over. He'd clear this in no time.'

'You'll buy it then?'

He held up his hands. 'Whoah! I didn't say that.' Earnestly, he ran a hand through his hair. 'Robbie, it's not the six thousand, although you can double that before you begin to think of living in this place. It's the time, and the organisation, all the sheer bloody hard work.'

She grabbed his arm and held it tightly. He was all too aware of her touch, and looked down at her hands. 'Just think how impressed your clients will be, Ed. Visiting you here will be like stepping back in time. So peaceful and . . . conducive to good business.'

He laughed. 'But it's the future I'm interested in, not the past.'

'But the future's always tied to the past, Ed, don't you see that?'

He closed his own hand over hers. 'You intend to stay then, Roberta? You intend to see this through?'

She pulled her hand away and took several steps forward, breathing in the atmosphere and allowing her imagination to work overtime. 'Since I was a little girl I've liked old places and everything about this is *perfection* to me.'

'Well, in that case, perhaps you'd better move in?'

She turned, very sharply. 'Sorry, what did you say?'

He reddened slightly and quickly cleared his throat. 'I didn't mean . . .' He hardly dared steal a look at the woman he adored. But when he did, she was staring straight back at him, expectantly, not angrily. Oh, hell, he thought, I may as well speak my mind. 'I said, move in. If you like it so much, move in permanently.'

Roberta was affronted. 'Ed! I'm not going to *live* with you!'

'No, not *live* with me, Roberta . . . *marry me*.'

The words had hardly left his mouth before Ed Matthews got the biggest surprise of his life. Roberta's face was transformed. She took one tiny step forward then flung herself into his arms, wrapping herself around him.

'Oh, Ed! Yes, yes! I thought you'd *never, ever* ask!'

14

'Where are my shoes?'

Roberta stomped around her bedroom, looking for her new red wedge-heeled shoes. Her tiny room had little cupboard space and she'd checked everywhere twice before realisation struck. She hastened towards the door.

'Julia!'

Not bothering to knock, Roberta just barged into her sister's bedroom. 'Julia, have you seen my new red shoes?'

Lounging on her bed reading about Barbara Hulanicki's fabulous new Kensington store Biba, in the *Daily Mirror*, Julia raised her eyes. 'Sorry?'

'My new shoes? The red ones? I bought them last week.'

Julia slid off the bed and flicked her hair off her shoulders. 'Oh, the red ones . . .' Sheepishly, she faced her sister. 'Yes, I remember now, I did borrow them, for work.'

'*For work?* How dare you?'

Julia smiled. 'Well, I'm sorry Roberta, but I did.'

'And?'

Julia shrugged. 'And what?'

'What do you mean, *and what*? Where are they? What have you done with them? And don't you dare borrow my things *without* asking again!'

'Okay, big sister. Don't blow a fuse. I'm sorry, but I'm afraid they're not here.'

Roberta was incensed. She swallowed hard and stared at her sister. This was typical. Julia always took what she wanted without asking. She turned on her heel to leave the room.

'Roberta?'

She stopped and looked back. 'Yes?'

'I am really sorry. I just forgot them.' Julia smiled. 'You look nice.'

Roberta's eyes widened. Julia seldom, if ever, paid her a compliment. 'Thank you,' she mumbled.

'Going somewhere nice?'

Roberta frowned. 'Yes.'

'Where?'

'What's it to you?'

Julia drifted to her dressing table and perched on the stool. She picked up a hairbrush and dreamily tidied her hair. Since Clare had left for university, Roberta had noticed that her sister was frequently at a loose end. 'I'm just interested, that's all. I heard you talking to Mum and Dad. It's Ed, isn't it? You're going out with him. Isn't he your boss?'

Roberta's heart sank. She stared at her sister, all the old grievances ready to re-emerge. She swallowed hard and narrowed her eyes. 'Correct on all counts.'

'Roberta!'

She halted on her way out of the room but didn't look back at her sister.

'Is he nice?'

She immediately recognised the appraising look in Julia's eyes. It was rare for her to ask for information direct, generally their parents kept them informed of each other's business. 'Yes, he is,' Roberta confirmed, reluctantly.

'Are you in love?'

The sheer audacity of it! Roberta was tempted to laugh until she noticed the glimmer of rivalry in her sister's eyes. Julia was on the scent of a man, about to worm her way into Ed's affections unless Roberta was very careful. Her face turned to stone. She turned briskly away. 'Of course I'm not in love, Julia. Whatever gave you that idea?'

She went back to her room, pushed the door firmly shut and leant her weight against it. 'No,' she muttered. 'Not again, please, no.' This was her worst nightmare.

Ed arrived punctually bringing a bouquet of flowers. Roberta rushed to the door and welcomed him warmly. When it looked as though he would kiss her, she glanced quickly around. That would show Julia. But she was nowhere in sight.

'You look gorgeous, Robbie.'

She stared into Ed's eyes. 'Really? You really think so?'

He chuckled. 'I do, I do.'

She tugged at his arm, 'Come through.' Ed followed her down the narrow hall towards the sitting room. Warmly ensconced in front of the television were Brenda and Gordon. Her father rose politely from his seat. Nervously, Roberta said, 'Mum, Dad, this is Ed.'

Gordon beamed at their visitor. 'Pleased to meet you. My, you're a biggun!'

Ed laughed and turned towards Brenda. 'And these are for you.' He offered her the flowers and her face broke into a huge smile.

'Oh, how nice.' She rose from her chair. 'I must put them in water. Can I offer you a drink, Ed? Coffee or tea? I'm afraid we haven't anything stronger, unless Gordon pops down to the off-licence.'

Roberta smiled. 'It's all right, Mum. We're going out in a minute. Haven't time for a drink.'

Very gently Ed stalled her. 'We certainly have got time, Mrs Tree. I'd welcome a cup of tea.'

Roberta felt apprehensive. She wanted to get away. Away from Julia.

And then the girl herself appeared. Nobody every heard Julia come into a room, she was always just there, looking breathtakingly beautiful. Today she wore a multi-coloured silk scarf tied around her head in a narrow band and her hair fell in glossy, loose curls around her shoulders and on to the ends of the scarf, creating a vulnerable effect. She wore a short yellow jersey dress which outlined her curvaceous figure, particularly her breasts. Subtle false eye-lashes enhanced her upper lids, and she'd painted more lashes beneath her eyes, producing a Bambi effect which made her look quite ravishing. She moved towards Ed. 'Oh,' she murmured breathlessly, 'at last we get to meet you. Roberta's told us *so* much about you.'

Roberta was on pins. She flashed a look at Ed, and then back at her sister. Meanwhile, he was warmly shaking Julia's hand, saying, 'And I've heard so much about all of you.'

Julia allowed her hand to linger in his. 'All good I hope?'

He laughed. 'Oh, definitely.'

And then everything seemed to go haywire as Gordon offered him a seat, and Brenda arrived back in the sitting room carrying a pot of tea and the best china cups and saucers on a tray. There was much laughing and joking and Roberta became confused. She noticed that Ed appeared totally at ease in her home. Julia had gone to sit on the floor at his feet, quizzing him continually, about his job, his opinion of Newmarket versus Cambridge, anything she could think of. And he sat enraptured, or so it seemed to Roberta. He was hanging on her sister's every word, answering her at length and hardly sparing a glance in Roberta's direction.

Finally, she had had enough. She got to her feet. 'Ed, we really ought to be going, don't you think?'

He looked up at her and frowned, then reached for her hand, gathered his tall frame and eased himself out of his seat. He stood up and faced Gordon. 'Mr Tree?'

Her father waved his hand, 'Please, Ed, call me Gordon.'

Ed nodded and smiled warmly. 'Gordon.' He turned to his hostess. 'And Brenda. I'm not one to stand on ceremony, so I'll be direct. Last week I asked your daughter to marry me.' There was a hush. Ed looked at Roberta and squeezed her hand. 'She very kindly said yes. Can't think why, an old man like me.' He laughed. 'Anyway, with your permission, Gordon and Brenda, we'd like to get married as soon as possible?' He shrugged. 'And that's about all, really.'

Gordon, Brenda and Julia sat with their mouths open. And then Gordon hastened out of his seat and vigorously shook Ed's hand, and Brenda grabbed Roberta and began hugging and kissing her as though she'd won the pools. Only Julia sat still, with no comment to make for once. Finally, she stood up.

'Congratulations, both of you.' She pecked Roberta on the cheek and then stood on tiptoe to do the same to Ed. He bent down to welcome her kiss, but Roberta noticed there was no hint of attraction in his eyes, nothing more than brotherly interest.

The only attraction she saw in his eyes on that particular evening was to her.

15

February, 1970

Perched prettily on a white Arkana mushroom chair, Clare chattered and giggled with her cousin, sitting opposite. Julia leant elegantly against the matching round table, allowing herself to take in every detail of her cousin's spacious kitchen in Park Road, Chiswick. It was knockout. Everywhere was painted soft purple, except for the muted pink ceiling. White French Aubeque pans and casserole dishes adorned the shelves, with similarly French kitchen utensils hanging in between. The split-level, stainless steel cooker looked as though it had never been used – probably hadn't, knowing Clare's hatred of cooking. A washing-machine and dishwasher were neatly plumbed in next to a vast larder fridge. In such a short space of time, this Victorian semi had been transformed. It must have cost a fortune, Julia surmised, all three storeys of it! *Some pied-à-terre!* It all exuded style from the attractive high ceilings, bold colour schemes and ultra-modern furniture to the luxurious wall-to-wall carpets. The whole house bore Clare's stamp. Julia was impressed.

They drank freshly ground coffee from Denby mugs and in between bursts of laughter chattered excitedly about their plans for the weekend. 'Chelsea's a must, particularly the King's Road. It positively buzzes, Julia! Makes you feel so alive, like stepping into the future'. Clare reached across and touched her cousin's hand. 'That's where you should be working, that's the place for you. Not some boring leather shop in Cambridge.'

Julia bristled slightly. She never found Purley's boring, but her eyes still glowed enthusiastically at the prospect of seeing Swinging London. 'I can't wait!' she enthused.

'And Biba down Kensington High Street. I bought all my satin sheets from there . . . '

'You lucky, lucky sod.' Julia bit her bottom lip. 'Do you ever realise how lucky you are, Clare?'

'Luck doesn't come into it. Careful planning does. So where shall we go tonight?' Clare's eyes lit up. 'I know, how about Soho? Raymond's Revuebar? We could eat in The Birdcage?'

'Clare, that's a striptease joint. We can't go there. At least, not on our own.'

'Of course we can, it'll be a scream. All those tits! We'll have a ball.'

Julia pulled a face. 'And what would Roger say?'

Clare pulled one too. 'Fuck Roger. Fuck them all!'

Julia sipped her coffee. 'Poor Roger, how can you be so uncaring?' She imagined him back home, pining for his wife, little realising she was having a whale of a time in London. Then Julia remembered a very different Roger. The one who'd driven her down a quiet little track near Newmarket, parked, and proceeded to kiss her frantically whilst dragging off her knickers. Although their first steamy encounter had been followed by several more, Julia realised that since Clare had moved to Chiswick she'd seen nothing of him. She shrugged to herself. So what if it had blown itself out?

'Julia, are you listening to me?' Clare insisted. 'He's been ill, my faithless husband, actually off work. 'Flu of all things. Hong Kong 'flu in fact.' She laughed as though it was incredibly funny.

'But that's awful. People are dying from it like flies.'

'Well, he didn't, worse luck.'

'Clare, how can you say such a thing?' Julia cupped her chin in her hands. 'And what do you mean, *faithless*?'

Clare flicked her hand, dismissively. 'Oh, I caught him at it. Didn't I tell you?' She slid out of her chair and walked over to the sink to dump her mug. 'Yes, I bloody well caught him red-handed!' She turned and leant back against the sink. 'Called in at the office one evening, when he was supposed to be working late. Thought it was all rather quiet, nobody around, not a sound anywhere. Walked up to his office on the top floor and opened his door – and there he was, fucking his secretary. Yeah, on his desk of all places'. Clare saw the look of horror on her cousin's face. 'That's given you a jolt, hasn't it cousin Julia? Mr Nice Guy Roger isn't so nice at all.'

Julia's face reddened and she quickly lowered her eyes. She didn't know which had hit her the hardest. The fact that Roger had been two-timing her as well as his wife, or sheer shame at the thought that Clare could well have walked in on *her* and Roger. On more than one occasion he and Julia had been quite daring in the spare bedroom at Madingley.

'I'm so sorry, Clare, I had no idea. It must have been ... quite awful.' She reached one hand towards her cousin. 'Poor you.'

Clare shrugged her shoulders 'Don't be daft, Julia. Not poor me at all. I don't give a *fuck* who he fucks. He can fuck every woman he meets, so long as it's not me!'

Shocked, Julia looked at her cousin in an entirely new light. 'Yes, that's it in a nutshell, isn't it, Clare? You're the only one he really wants to ...'

'... fuck? Yes, of course I am. And so long as that's the case, I can keep milking him dry. I'm not daft, Julia. I intend to get all I want out of him before I let him go.'

'Let him go?'

'Too true, I'll have to eventually. He bores me to tears.' She straightened up and ran both hands through her hair. 'Everybody in Cambridge bores me.' She looked sweetly across at her cousin. 'Except you, of course.'

Julia suddenly had a strong urge ro run out of this house and head straight back to Cambridge. She felt out of her depth in Clare's London home. She cast her eyes across to the percolator. 'Any more coffee? I'd love another cup. It's delicious, Clare.'

Clare moved towards the percolator. 'I'll make some more. It's those Arabica beans from Fortnum and Mason. They're an absolute must. Personally, I never drink anything else.'

In the end, Clare rang Nick and asked him to escort them that evening. He agreed, intrigued at the prospect of seeing Julia Tree again.

'And bring Harry,' instructed Clare. 'We can make it a foursome.'

She put down the receiver. Cautiously, Julia looked across at her cousin. 'Won't Nick tell Roger?'

Adamantly, Clare shook her head. 'Nick's *my* friend, not Roger's.' She shrugged. 'Who cares, anyway?'

'Oh, I see,' was all Julia could think of to say.

Nick arrived, wearing a bottle green velvet-cord jacket, bell-bottom trousers and a round-collared shirt complete with floral tie. With his shoulder-length hair, he looked very dashing. He also made a bee-line for Julia from the minute he walked through the door. His companion Harry, on the other hand, was a bit of a surprise. *She* certainly cut a dash, with an up-to-the-minute asymetrical haircut and a black velvet trouser suit seemingly worn with nothing underneath. Dusky and striking, Harry was older than either Nick or Clare, a senior social worker in Camden Town, and from the minute she walked through the door, it was obvious that Clare greatly admired her.

They ate at The Birdcage in Raymond's Revuebar and stayed on a while though Julia made it obvious it wasn't her scene. Dressed to kill in one of Clare's Ossie Clark flimsy pants suits, and with her hair piled in tousled ringlets on top of her head, she looked beautiful. Clare, wearing a calf-length, ethnic-style dress, typically Bill Gibb with its mixed geometrical and floral prints, had tied her hair back severely with a matching bow. The party of four turned heads wherever they went.

They ended up in Tramp, the nightclub in Mayfair. The atmosphere there was electric and immediately appealed to Julia. She entered the smoky depths of the dimly lit room and the crush of people and impassioned blues music instantly lifted her mood.

She lit a cigarette. 'This is divine, Clare, I don't ever want to leave.'

Clare sniffed disparagingly. 'Rich kids' playground.'

'What?'

'Personally, I prefer downmarket. Say, The Scene in Ham Yard, Klooks Klique or Cafe des Artistes.'

Julia frowned. 'Are they nightclubs?'

Clare nodded. 'For students or the less well-heeled.' She shrugged and glanced at their fine clothes. 'But no good if you're dressed up like a dog's dinner.'

Julia continued to puff on her cigarette. 'Is that what we are?'

Clare didn't answer, she just looked around. Nick and Harry were busy trying to order drinks. 'I know,' drawled Clare, 'we ought to have champagne. That'd cheer me up! I love champagne.'

Julia grinned, blowing out smoke. 'Champagne? How *downmarket* can you get? Still, I'm game if you are.'

'Great, I'll go and tell the others.' She wandered off, and Julia turned back towards the crush on the dance floor.

'*Julia?* It *is* Julia. What on earth are you doing here?'

On hearing her name, she jumped and turned round rapidly, finding herself face to face with Nathan. 'My God! What are *you* doing here?' Her knees turned to jelly as the man of her dreams smiled into her eyes. Nathan Purley, wearing a typically Savile Row suit, with the top button of his shirt left temptingly undone and his sombre tie askew, moved closer as a passer-by bumped into him.

'Sorry!' He grabbed Julia's arms and turned to scowl at the offender. 'I wondered where you'd got to today. I called in at the shop this morning and they said you'd taken the weekend off.' His eyes wandered appreciatively over her attire. 'I must say, you're looking rather gorgeous. Are you on your own?'

'No, I'm with friends.' But how Julia wished she wasn't. She gazed expectantly into his searching brown eyes. He leant closer, and she could smell his sweet breath, tinged with alcohol, upon her face. 'My cousin, actually, she lives in Chiswick, and a couple of other friends.'

'Females?'

Julia nodded with a smile. 'Mostly.'

Nathan moved in really close, his eyes within inches of hers. 'I'd have thought you'd be surrounded by males?'

She decided to be flippant. 'I usually am, Nathan, but not tonight. I thought I'd have a change.'

He smiled, showing the irresistible gap between his teeth. Julia drew on her cigarette and turned to blow away the smoke. 'Why do you do that?' he asked. 'It's a filthy habit.'

Her eyes flashed. 'No, it's not.'

He grinned. 'Okay, it's not. *You* can get away with anything.'

Julia decided to be serious. 'I don't want to get away with anything, Nathan. I just want to be me.' He laughed and once more she drew on her cigarette. 'Why did you call in at the shop?'

Wrapping one arm around her, he pushed her forward on to the dance floor. 'Forget about it. Let's dance.' She turned quickly to stub out her cigarette, and Nathan loosened his grip. Julia went straight back into his arms, not allowing the moment to pass. The music seemed to hot up, and the dancing became brisk. Nathan really surprised her, dancing in a funky, uninhibited way. His clothes belied his lack of inhibitions. Delighted, Julia copied his style and they both threw themselves into having fun. She didn't want it to end. But the music slowed down eventually and she was fearful he'd walk away. Instead Nathan gathered her into his arms and they began to smooch as close as they could get.

'You're driving me wild, Julia,' he whispered. '*Really* driving me wild.'

Her knees felt weak as he kissed the back of her neck, his fingers digging into her waist. Holding her tightly, Nathan moved his mouth to the line of her jaw, then gradually their lips met and she hungrily kissed him back. His tongue explored her mouth as his hands moved down her back to her buttocks. Finally he crushed her hard against him and Julia caught her breath. She was lost.

And then the music ended and he pulled away. Nathan straightened his jacket and ran both hands through his hair. He smiled into her eyes and then they were cruelly interrupted.

'There you are.' A flame-haired female, wearing a low-cut dress with enormous bell sleeves, was glaring at Nathan. 'I've been looking everywhere for you.'

'Maggie!' He draped one arm around her shoulders. 'Meet Julia. She works for me in Cambridge. Isn't it a coincidence that she's here?'

Maggie looked as though it was hardly a happy one. Julia stood frozen to the spot. Nathan patted her arm and, with his back to Maggie, mouthed, 'We must do it again.' All Julia could do was nod. Then he walked away, arm in arm with the other girl.

Julia didn't see him again. For her, all the fun had gone out of the evening.

Clare's drawing room glowed softly in the firelight. In fact the fireplace dominated the room with its cast-iron chimneypiece and grate, shiny brass fender and mahogany overmantel. Although it fitted in with the period of the house, it appeared incongruous next to her furnishings, but it had been cleaned and polished till it shone and the fire was regularly laid by her daily so that a match was all that was needed to produce warmth and light.

At either end of the open-plan room, covering the two large bay windows, geometrically patterned curtains in tangerine, slate blue and warm brown hung in magnificent folds. In the middle of the room a wide arch had replaced a previous wall and had been painted to match the blue of the curtains. The floor was covered with a donkey-brown wool carpet and on the walls were two David Hockney prints.

The Beatles' *Abbey Road* played softly in the background. The party of four sat in a circle on a rug in front of the fire, with crossed legs, talking desultorily as a joint was slowly passed round. Nick had rolled the grass, best skunk, and Julia watched in pleasurable anticipation as he licked and pressed three Rizla skins together, then produced from his top jacket pocket a tiny, round tin coated in filigree silver and colourful stones. He'd pulled out a small amount of the moist mixture and carefully crumbled it along the Rizla skins. Then he added the contents of one and a half cigarettes before rolling the paper to make a joint. Nick tore off a corner from the Rizla skins' soft cardboard outer sleeve and rolled it tightly between finger and thumb. He pushed this into the end of the joint to form a roach, or filter. From the first puff, Julia was a fan. All the trauma of the evening, her disappointment at seeing Nathan with another girl, just floated away like the breeze and became a distant picture in her mind.

'Beer, no gear,' quipped Clare, taking a puff. 'If I'm sick, I'll blame you, turtle-dove.'

'*I* haven't drunk any beer,' Nick remarked. 'Just one line of coke earlier on, and *one* glass of champagne.' He shook his head. 'This is best quality stuff. I swear there'll be no ill effects. You won't feel a thing except euphoric.'

Harry winked at Julia, recognising a novice, and took the joint between her fingers. Confidently, she put it to her mouth and pulled on it hard, rolling her head as she allowed the toke to fill her lungs. And then there was no stopping her as she started to talk about Camden Town and its problems. It wasn't long before Julia, like Clare beside her, fully empathised.

Harry's coal black eyes sparkled in the firelight. 'Those poor kids – you only have to look into their lost eyes to understand. It haunts you for days and days.'

Nick reached out and squeezed her hand. 'Not all of them, Harry. They don't *all* have lost eyes. As young as they are, some are past masters at manipulation and we're never going to be able to solve all the world's problems. This has been happening since *time immemorial*. Just think of Dickens. At least we're an improvement on that.'

Harry grinned and leaned closer to her friend and protégé. 'You can say that, dear heart, but *you* of all people, with your posh house down Camden Street, allow the kids to stay with you!' She nudged him hard. 'That's a no-no. You're breaking the social worker's very first rule.'

Nick shrugged. 'I have on occasions, but what else could I do? Poor unwanted little bastards!'

Clare touched Harry's hand. 'Do you think this new Abortion Act will improve things in the future?'

Getting high on the grass, Harry threw back her head. 'Hah! You would have thought so in a perfect world. But now they're handing out abortions like lollipops. One for you, and one for you. Oh, you've already had one? Well, never mind, that's *two* for you!' She leant towards Clare, with an exaggeratedly stern expression. 'What's it doing to our *bodies*, and what's it doing to our *minds*?' She waved her hand about. 'Oh, hell! Let's change the subject. I get enough of this shit at work.' Harry looked at Nick. 'How's that lovely brother of yours? The one I met last year. Now, what's his name . . .?'

'Kit?'

'Ah, yes. That's the one. What's he up to?'

In a haze of euphoria, Julia dimly remembered Kit. Fat and spotty with ghastly red hair. 'He surprised the whole bloody lot of us, did Kit. Got a first class honours degree in structural engineering. Pa couldn't believe it. Expects him to go home now and work for him.'

'Huh, like hell he should,' scoffed Clare.

'He won't of course. Never. Kit likes to be as far away from Cambridge as he can get.'

'Him and me both,' nodded Clare.

'So where is he now?' asked Julia.

'Still in Coventry,' answered Nick. 'Although he's looking to move. He's a bit of a lad, is our Kit. Doesn't hang about. He's not long back from Aberdeen, six weeks filling in for some chap on sick leave – this North Sea Oil caper. There's a lot of money to be made up there.'

'What was he doing?' asked Harry.

'Oh, contract work, designing steel platforms for drilling rigs out in the North Sea. Nick laughed. 'Just think, those poor guys out there drilling for oil in the murky depths are putting their lives in the hands of my kid brother, who couldn't tie his shoe-laces 'til he was ten.' Nick adopted a Scottish accent. 'Major stuff, you know. He even visited Nigg Bay, in the Cromarty Firth where some of the platforms are actually being made.' He grinned and drew on the joint. 'Bloody loved it, he did. The boy must be bonkers. Too bleak and uncivilised if you ask me.'

Harry chuckled. 'Well, I liked him, thought he was a *real* sweetie.'

'Oh, he is, he is. As gentle as a puppy-dog. Till you cross him. Then he'll show his teeth!' Nick growled at Julia, who fell back helplessly giggling.

Rather unsteadily, Clare stood up. 'Well, I don't know about you lot, but I'm *starving*!' She pouted, putting a pink finger-nail to her mouth. 'A bacon, tomato and pickle sandwich . . . how about that?'

Everyone groaned and guffawed until Harry stood up and wrapped one arm around her friend. 'I'll join you, darling. I've got a touch of the munchies myself.'

Arm in arm, Clare and Harry left the room. Admiringly, Julia watched them go. 'What a woman! No wonder Clare's impressed.'

Nick nodded. 'We're all impressed with Harry.' He leant closer to Julia. 'But let's talk about you now. Who was that James Bond figure you were dancing with earlier on? I was madly jealous. I thought he was going to eat you before I got the chance.'

Julia's face fell. She averted her eyes, disconcerted, and pulled at the chiffon material of her outfit. 'Oh, him. He was no one . . . Well, actually, he's my boss, or rather my boss's son.'

Nick ran his hand gently over her shoulders, allowing his fingers to brush her neck. 'And you like him? I can tell. Don't deny it.'

Her eyes flashed. 'Yes, I like him. But he obviously doesn't like me.'

Nick squeezed her shoulder. ' 'Course he does. He just likes himself more.'

Julia smiled and allowed herself to be pulled closer to him. 'I don't want to talk about Nathan. He's screwing me up enough as it is.'

'And has he?'

'Has he what?'

Nick grinned. 'Screwed you?'

She thumped him playfully. 'No, he hasn't. I don't sleep with everyone I meet.'

'Good, because he's not right for you, Julia. I've seen his sort before. He'll break your heart into a thousand little pieces. You should avoid him like the plague.'

'But I can't, you idiot. He's my boss.'

Nick pondered a while. 'Yes, recognise the syndrome now. Bet he's a mummy's boy? I'll bet that's what he is.'

Julia pulled herself away from Nick. 'Well, whatever he is, he's my boss. And, as I love my job, I can't keep away from him.'

Nick frowned. 'What do you do anyway?'

'I manage Purley's in Cambridge. It's a leather shop, mainly, but we also sell jewellery.'

Nick shuffled back on to Clare's vast white leather settee and beckoned Julia to join him. She did so and snuggled into his arms. Both faced the fire, its warmth bringing a deeper glow to their faces. 'Clare's talked about you once or twice, Julia. She says you're a really bright girl. Why don't you move down here to London? Take a lease on a shop? Leather's big news. Hot news.'

'Funny you should say that – it's exactly what I'd like to do. I want to persuade Nathan to open a shop somewhere like the King's Road in Chelsea. If we can get hold of the premises, that is.'

'*Nathan?* What a name.'

Julia grinned. 'No worse than Nick.'

He ignored the remark. 'What're you doing tomorrow? Why don't you come out with me? I'll take you down Brick Lane, introduce you to my friend Madhav.'

'Madhav? Who's he? And where the hell is Brick Lane?'

Nick tapped the side of his nose. 'Madhav is in the leather business, and Brick Lane, dear heart, is in the East End. It used to be Jewish territory but gradually it's been taken over by Pakistanis who work like the devil and whose dress-making prowess is second to none. Brick Lane runs from Whitechapel to Bethnal Green; it's all manufacturers, traders and importers, and there are several leather and sheepskin dealers around the Bethnal Green Road end. I had my own, rather superb leather coat made there – by Madhav. Cost a fraction of what it would in the West End.'

Julia's brain started ticking as she listened eagerly, enjoying her close proximity to Nick and the interest he was taking in her. 'I'd love to come with you tomorrow. It sounds *fascinating*. Her thoughts sped to Nathan. Maybe this would impress him? Make him think of her in a different light, and kindle his interest?

'Great, that's settled then.' Nick squeezed her tightly. 'I aim to please. Now, Miss Julia Tree, on to more important things . . .'

In truth, Nick Fordham-Clarke had no idea how to please Julia, or of the depth of her feelings for Nathan Purley. She'd no intention of leaving Purley's to set up on her own. For a start, she couldn't afford to. But she wouldn't let Nick know that, or at least not yet. It was good that he saw her as a high-powered businesswoman. After all, one day she might be.

16

March, 1970

'And then we went to see *The Mousetrap* at the Ambassadors.'
Nancy rolled her eyes in ecstasy. 'I've always wanted to see it and
it's been going for nearly twenty years. Can't tell you how good it
was, Brenda. Several times I nearly jumped out of my seat.'

She sat opposite her sister in the Cosy Corner and sipped her
coffee. They'd both eaten vanilla slices, chocolate eclairs were off
the menu today, and Nancy hadn't stopped talking about her *wonderful* weekend with Clare.

'Was Roger there?' Brenda had noticed that his name was rarely
mentioned.

Nancy shook her head and shuffled in her seat. 'No, he couldn't
make it last weekend. Some conference or other. Pity, really, it
would have been nice for Peter if he had been there, and of course
for poor Clare. She works *so* hard, Brenda, so very, very hard. She
was even studying while we were there.

'Oh, I nearly forgot – and how did *your* little wedding go?'

Brenda swallowed hard and gouged the surface of the table with
her thumbnail. So she hadn't been forgiven for not inviting Nancy
to Roberta's wedding? 'It went well, very well, although quiet, of
course. Only a handful of us there. But Roberta looked lovely,
Nance, and she and Ed are as happy as can be.'

'Didn't they want a proper wedding?'

'It *was* a proper wedding, Nancy. I told you before, they need
every spare penny for their house and the business.'

'But Gordon should have paid for the wedding.'

Brenda laughed at her sister's rudeness. It was either that or hit
her. 'We gave them money, Nancy, for their home. And we've been

helping with getting the garden straight, and painting, and anything else we can do. Ed's parents have been helping too. In fact, the place is looking a picture. And Roberta's thrilled because the builders moved out last week.'

'It's finished then?'

'Not quite, but they've gone as far as they can afford to at the moment. The kitchen's done, and the sitting room, and Ed's office. Upstairs they've got a couple of bedrooms done, and a lovely bathroom as well.'

Nancy glared at her sister. 'Well, it all sounds very nice, but I don't suppose I'll ever be invited to see it.'

Brenda was flustered. 'Of course you will, Nance, I'll make sure of that.' She gulped, realising what she'd said. 'As soon as it's all finished, and the business is on its feet.'

'I bet.' Nancy looked up and flapped her hand at the waitress. 'Can we have the bill?' She turned back to Brenda. 'So, how's the business going? Has Ed finished that big contract near Bury St Edmunds?'

Brenda chuckled. Nancy didn't forget a thing. 'No, but it's all underway and they've landed several other contracts since.' She tugged at her sister's arm. 'He keeps tendering and getting the jobs. And now he's got *too* much work on.'

'Huh! That's bad management.'

'No, it's not. Ed is very shrewd. Anyway, he's getting an assistant.'

'What sort of assistant? I thought Roberta was his assistant?'

'Well, she is, his partner in fact. But he needs another structural engineer.'

'Well, *he'll* be lucky, stuck out there in the middle of nowhere.'

'*Nancy!*' Brenda thumped her fist on the table until the cups rattled. 'Haven't you anything nice to say?'

Nancy jumped, and for a second looked contrite. Then her eyes flashed. 'Well, you'd be hurt if you hadn't been invited to your *own* neice's wedding!'

'I know, I know, and I'm really very sorry. But, Nance, it wasn't up to me, truly it wasn't. Roberta didn't want any fuss, and I couldn't argue with that. The last thing I wanted to do was offend you.'

The waitress arrived with the bill and Nancy snatched it off her. 'Here!' she said, putting a ten-shilling note in the girl's hand. 'Keep the change.'

The women gathered their things together and made their way out of the cafe. 'What have you got planned for the rest of the day?' queried Nancy, in a much friendlier tone.

'Oh, nothing much. I'll call in and see Julia then catch the bus home.'

'You're going to see Julia? Good, I'll come with you.' Nancy caught hold of her sister's arm and together they headed for Purley's.

17

Roberta sat in front of the mirror in her bedroom, staring at her reflection. She ran her hands through her newly shorn hair and leant her elbows on the built-in vanity unit to get a closer look. Just the same, no obvious changes. Her skin glowed healthily and there were roses in her cheeks, but nothing out of the ordinary. And then she noticed, there it was, in her dark brown, almond-shaped eyes. A twinkle, a definite twinkle. A twinkle of delight. She ran a finger along her lashes, and down her small straight nose; around her generous mouth, and down to her chin. She put both hands around her neck, dragging them down to her breasts, then further to her belly. She clasped the natural swell of her stomach, imagining how big the baby was now. Eight weeks, or ten, or maybe even twelve. With all the excitement of renovating the house and the wedding, she really didn't know. But a smile curved her mouth and she felt warm and strangely smug inside.

Ed had been gone all day, visiting his parents. His father was ill, they weren't sure why, and he had thought it serious enough to pay a call. Roberta couldn't go, someone had to man the office and answer the phone. These days it rang continually. She had spoken to Ed on the phone during the day but didn't want to tell him the results of the pregnancy test, not like that, even though she knew he'd be delighted. It'd have to wait until he got home although she was bursting to share the news.

At six o'clock Roberta ate a cheese sandwich. There would be no need to cook this evening, because his mother would have provided Ed with an enormous lunch. Roberta waited impatiently for her husband to return home. She walked around the cottage to distract herself, admiring all the changes. The exposed beams had been treated for woodworm and stained their natural oak colour. Everywhere had been rewired, damp-proofed and replastered, and the walls painted magnolia. The natural strip-wood floors had been treated, sanded and restored. Only the sitting room had the luxury of a wall-to-wall carpet. One day, perhaps, they would be able to afford more. The kitchen had been quarry-tiled and so, eventually, would the utility room, but at the moment it remained an uninhabitable shell.

Roberta lifted the black iron latch of the sitting-room door and strolled inside. She folded her arms and allowed her eyes to feast on the room's natural charm and cosiness. Everywhere timbers had been exposed, and a beautifully restored inglenook fireplace dominated one end of the room. Every penny Roberta had put aside for a car had gone. She'd used it instead to buy an oyster pink three-piece suite with deep feathered cushions. It was the sort of furniture you sank blissfully into.

Her ears pricked up and she hurried out of the sitting room towards the hall. She pulled back the heavy oak front door and peered outside. He was home. Ed was back. Her heart took a leap. She rushed outside as he climbed out of his Volvo Estate.

'Ed!'

'Robbie. Have I got a surpise for you!' He bent forward to kiss his wife, smiling excitedly. Then he walked round to the back of the car and lifted the hatch door. He put both hands into an old cardboard box and withdrew a bedraggled and rather grubby-looking mongrel puppy. Grinning, he held it aloft. 'For you. To frighten away all interlopers.' He plonked the dog in Roberta's arms. She stood for a second, with the puppy desperately trying to claw its way to safety, horror-stricken.

'What is it?' she croaked, and wrinkled up her nose. 'Pooh! He stinks, Ed! Where on earth did you get him from?' The puppy started to lick her hands.

'A farm near Coventry. Kit told me about him when I mentioned we were thinking of getting a dog. The owners were going to put him down. He's the only survivor of a litter of eight. They all died, God knows why, and nobody wanted this one. He's puny, I know, but he'll probably grow up to be great guard dog.'

The puppy looked at her from a sharp ugly face, two pleading brown eyes its only redeeming feature. Roberta stared back at him. 'He's so ugly, Ed. I wanted a labrador.'

'Well, he is. Partly anyway. He's got some alsatian in him too.'

Roberta looked at her husband and wanted to laugh. This was typical of Ed. He'd never quite got the hang of what made her tick. And then she looked down at the puppy as he snuffled in her arms, desperately trying to get close to her face so that he could lick her. Something inside her melted. Maybe Ed wasn't so off-beam after all.

'What's his name?'

'Well, Kit said he looked like Boris Karloff, so I've been calling him Boris.'

'*Boris Karloff*? And you *still* went and bought him?'

'I didn't *buy* him, Robbie, they *gave* him to me.'

'Oh, yes, they saw you coming all right.'

He moved closer to her. 'Don't be like that, Robbie. He's a lovely little chap really. Or he will be when you've cleaned him up.'

Through narrowed eyes, she glared at her husband. 'Well, I've got news for you, Ed Matthews, that's your job. *You* clean him up!' With that, she plumped the dog into his arms and walked briskly off.

With his fur bathed and brushed and his tummy full of scraps, the puppy finally fell asleep in front of the fire in the sitting room. Roberta had put an old blanket down, in case of any mishaps, but so far the dog had behaved.

'So, how's your dad?'

Ed snuggled up to his wife on the settee, a glass of whisky in his hand. 'The old boy's rallied, actually. Seemed as right as rain. But I'm glad I went, and he was pleased to see me. And I'm particularly glad I saw Kit today. I don't know if I mentioned it, but he's a structural engineer?'

'But who exactly *is* Kit?'

'He used to lodge with my parents. He was a student at Lancaster Poly. He only moved out about six months ago.'

'What's he like?'

'He's a great bloke. Judy gets on with him like a house on fire.'

Roberta chuckled. 'She would. I can't imagine Judy *not* getting on with anyone.'

'Actually, he comes from Cambridge. You've probably heard of his family? They're very well known – the Fordham-Clarkes? They own Fordham-Clarke Construction Company in Cambridge?' Ed looked at his wife, noticing the colour draining from her face. 'Robbie? You all right, darling?'

She swallowed, feeling suddenly sick. Visions of herself and a red-faced Kit Fordham-Clarke watching her sister and his brother jostling up and down in the trees near the River Ouse flooded back to her. 'And this Kit . . . you've offered him a job?' she said faintly.

'I have, and he's accepted. I've told him all the draw-backs, about where we live and everything, explained it all. And he's keen as mustard.'

'Ed! You might have asked me first.'

He frowned and looked at his wife. 'Why? What's the matter? You look as if you've seen a ghost. Do you know him?'

Vehemently, too vehemently, Roberta shook her head. Then slowly she nodded. 'Sort of. His brother is married to my cousin.'

'His *brother*?' Ed laughed. 'You mean, you're related? You never told me you had such grand people in your family?'

Roberta snarled, 'And what does "such grand people" mean?'

'Robbie, darling, don't get so upset. I was joking, sweetheart, just joking.'

She lowered her head into the crook of his arm. 'I don't like them, Ed. I don't like them at all. They're all snobs, the lot of them. I don't want him to come and work here.'

'But *he's* not a snob! He's nothing like a snob. And for your information, he doesn't get on with his father at all.'

Roberta shook her head. 'It doesn't matter, I don't want him to come here.'

Ed stared at her. 'Well, I'm very sorry, but he is. I've offered him the job, and he's coming here tomorrow.'

'What?'

'Oh, come on, you're being ridiculous. He's excellent at what he does.'

'But don't I have any say in it?'

'Of course you do, but this isn't about business, is it? This is about something else. Tell me . . . was he a boyfriend?'

Roberta looked at her husband as though he were quite mad. That red-faced, spotty, fat, idle, rich . . . Peeping Tom? She rounded on him furiously. 'No! How dare you say that? I'd never have had a boyfriend like him.' She pulled away from Ed. 'My opinion should count for something. You can't keep thrusting things upon me after *you've* made the decision. First it's that!' Roberta glared at the dog. 'And now it's bloody Kit Fordham-Clarke!' She stormed off, out of the sitting room and upstairs to their bedroom.

Ed sat in a daze, wondering what this was all about.

'Roberta? Darling?' He finally crept into the bedroom and walked over to the bed where his wife lay quite still on her side. On his knees, he fumbled his way across the bed towards her and put his hand on her shoulder. 'Robbie. I'm sorry. The last thing I wanted to do was upset you. I'd been pig-headed again, not considering you. I'll ring Kit in the morning and tell him not to come.'

She turned to face her husband, her face blotched with tears. 'No, I don't want you to do that, Ed. That's the last thing I want you to do.'

His brow creased in confusion. 'But, I thought . . .'

She reached out and touched her husband's face. 'Oh, Ed, I'm so sorry. I'm such a stupid female. Forgive me, please?'

He sighed. 'But what's to forgive? I don't understand. Tell me what this is all about?'

She shook her head as though she didn't want a memory to be disturbed. 'It was all such a long time ago. I behaved . . . stupidly, and I've never forgotten it. I'm ashamed of everything that happened that day.'

'What day? What are you talking about?'

'My cousin's wedding. I was only eighteen . . . that's where I met Kit. Well, I didn't exactly *meet* him, just saw him across a crowded room. He was with the others, the posh lot, and I was with the riff-raff – or at least that's how it seemed to me. It's certainly how Auntie Nancy made us feel.'

Ed laughed. 'And who is Auntie Nancy?'

Roberta licked dry lips. 'My mother's sister. They're actually very close. See each other every month, without fail. But Nancy doesn't like me, never has. She thinks I'm really thick because I didn't pass my eleven-plus.' Roberta saw the grin appear on his face. 'No, don't laugh, Ed, it's true. I heard her talking about me once, years ago. She said it was a shame I was so dim-witted and *plain!*'

'*What?* What are you talking about, woman? *What rubbish!* How could anybody describe you as plain?'

'It's not rubbish at all.' She shrugged. 'And I suppose I was plain, compared to Julia. Anyway, you haven't met my Auntie Nancy.'

'And I don't want to, by the sounds of her!' He pulled a face. 'So, why does this make you hate poor Kit?'

Roberta snapped, 'He's hardly "poor" Kit. Not a creep like him.' She lowered her eyes. 'After this wedding reception, I went for a walk. I was just so miserable, Ed. Nobody wanted to talk to me . . . Anyway, I walked down to the river, in Huntingdon this is, and who should come along but my sister. Julia was in her *bridesmaid's dress* and she had the other brother, Nick Fordham-Clarke, with her. Anyway, it was November and really chilly and I'd sheltered from the wind. They came in among the trees where I was sheltering, didn't realise I was there, and – well, they did it, there and then, in front of me!'

'Did what?'

'*Fucked* each other!'

Ed looked startled. He blinked, them grinned. 'Julia did? With this Nick?'

'Yes. She was only sixteen. And there's no need to look so interested.'

He tried to straighten his face. 'Darling, I don't mean to look interested, but I thought you were going to tell me something really *dire*, not about a childish – to use your word – fuck!'

Roberta felt stupid now and too embarrassed to look at him. 'I know, I know. I'm sorry.'

He kissed her tenderly on the mouth. 'You don't need to be sorry, Robbie, and I didn't mean to hurt your feelings. I do understand. But where does Kit fit into all this?'

'He was watching! He'd followed them there like some *disgusting* Peeping Tom! At least *I* hadn't followed them. I was just stuck there, mortified.'

Ed put a hand to his mouth and tried to control himself. But then he chuckled. 'And is that it?'

'Yes, it is. And he saw me, Ed. He must have thought I was peeping too.'

'And weren't you? And, for that matter, wouldn't *anybody* peep if they got the chance? Oh, come on, Robbie. You're making a mountain out of a molehill. It was a tiny incident in your adolescence. I bet Kit has forgotten all about it.'

'I bet he hasn't!'

Ed shrugged. 'Well, that's as maybe. But something like that isn't worth being so upset about. I love you, Roberta, with all of my heart. You're my most treasured possession, the light of my life. You've turned my dull, grey world into every shade of the rainbow.

And you're intelligent, and beautiful. The most beautiful woman in the world.'

She smiled. 'More beautiful than Julia?'

'Far more beautiful than Julia.'

Roberta sucked in her breath. 'There's something else I have to tell you. Something far more important . . .'

He narrowed his eyes, wondering what else was to come. 'What's that?'

'I'm pregnant.'

'Pregnant? Are you sure?' He sounded incredulous.

Roberta shifted towards him. 'Of course I'm sure. All day, Ed, all day I've been dying to tell you. Bursting with this news. I'm so happy.'

He gathered his young wife into his arms and buried his head against her breasts. 'My God, Roberta. I never believed this could happen to me. Am I really going to be a father?'

'You most certainly are.' And then she pulled away abruptly and looked into his face, her own creased into a wicked smile. 'Will you tell Boris or shall I?'

18

It was eleven-thirty and Kit was due to arrive by midday. Roberta dreaded it. Worse even than meeting him again, Ed had promised Kit could stay with them until he found alternative accommodation. Resentfully, she had spent most of the morning preparing a bed-room.

'Does he know who I am?' she asked now as Ed wandered through to the kitchen where she was baking an apple pie.

'Sorry? What do you mean?'

'Well, do you think Kit could possibly have realised who I am?'

Ed grinned. 'Hardly, Robbie. Even I didn't know who you were until yesterday.'

She stooped down and picked up Boris. 'And you are due to go outside.' She walked through the utility room area and opened the back door to put Boris on the grass. Immediately he obliged. 'Good boy! Good boy! Aren't you a good boy?' She picked him up again, kissed his sharp little face and fondled his lop-sided floppy ears. As she took him back inside his ears pricked up. At the sound of the car outside she would have liked to rush upstairs and hide.

Ed reached over and kissed her. 'That'll be Kit.' He left the kitchen, walked through a room which was designated as the dining room but hadn't been decorated or furnished, and into the hall where he opened the front door.

Kit Fordam-Clarke parked his brand new, chocolate brown Triumph Spitfire next to Ed's Volvo Estate. He climbed out and nervously pulled down his cream roll-necked jumper before striding purposefully over with hand outstretched. 'Well, made it, Ed. Didn't get lost once.'

Ed pumped his hand eagerly. 'Great to see you. You'd better come inside.'

Meanwhile, Roberta had decided to give Boris some water. She put a bowl on the floor, but after a couple of mouthfuls he decided to bark. It was only a baby bark, and she smiled to hear it. 'You're a bit late, Boris,' she chided as he tilted his head to one side. He turned, put one paw into the bowl, and the contents splashed everywhere. 'Damn!' cursed Roberta as the puppy toddled off. She rushed towards the cupboard beneath the sink and pulled out a floor cloth. She was so busy mopping up the spill that she was unaware of Ed and Kit's arrival in the kitchen.

'Roberta, meet Kit.'

From her crouched position on the floor she raised her eyes, and then, with a hand from Ed, stood up. 'It's Boris's fault,' she blurted out, 'he spilt his water.' She smiled and Kit smiled back.

'I think you two know each other?' said Ed, matter-of-factly. 'Robbie's cousin is married to your brother.'

Kit looked momentarily disconcerted. Then he smiled, an enchanting smile, and moved forward to take her hand. 'Yes,' he said simply. 'Of course.'

He'd changed beyond all recognition, and the touch of his hand on hers felt strangely exciting. Was that because of the past? She didn't know. Tall and slim, with longish, tousled hair – more gold than red now – he was a splendid figure of a man. Kit's grey eyes held hers but there was no disdain in them. In fact, she read something else altogether. He was looking at her appreciatively and quickly she looked away. 'Coffee? Let me make you some.' She turned to put the kettle on the Aga, and noticed her own trembling hands.

'That would be lovely, thank you.' Kit ran a hand through his hair. 'And what did you think of Boris? He must have been a bit of a surprise?'

Not as much as you, thought Roberta. Her colour heightened and her eyes flashed, making her look truly beautiful for once. 'He was a surprise,' she said rather harshly, not daring to look at her husband.

'This is very charming,' said Kit, and Roberta shot him another glance. 'This place – Blackthorn Cottage.' He scrutinised her face. 'Captivating, in fact.'

Ed stepped in. 'Well, we're biased, aren't we, Robbie? We fell in love with it from the start.' He put his arm aound his wife's waist and kissed her on the cheek. 'Of course, I had to convince you, didn't I, darling?'

She grimaced slightly. 'I think it was the other way round, actually.'

'What's that gorgeous smell?' asked Kit.

'Apple pie.'

'Don't tell me you can cook as well?' There was amusement in his eyes, and Roberta unwillingly warmed to it.

Ed chipped in. 'She can cook, and more importantly convince the most miserable client that he's getting the best service there is.'

Roberta wriggled away from her husband's grasp. 'You make me sound too good to be true, Ed.'

'I'm only speaking the truth.' He shifted towards Kit. 'Come on, I may as well show you the office. Is it sandwiches for lunch?' Roberta nodded. 'And you'll bring the coffee through?' She nodded again. Kit smiled in her direction. She didn't reciprocate.

A week later, Roberta's peace of mind was in shreds.

It was suppertime and the three of them sat around the scrubbed oak table in the kitchen. Ed had opened a bottle of red wine to celebrate because in a few short days they'd stormed ahead with their work.

'Try this,' he said, pouring a healthy measure into Kit's glass.

Immediately, Kit looked across at Roberta. He tasted the wine and wisely nodded his approval. 'As my pa would say, you can't beat sloping shoulders.'

Ed looked down at the bottle of Burgundy – Gévrey Chambertin, 1965. He grinned, poured himself a glass, and put the sloping shouldered bottle of wine on to the table. 'Well, on this occasion I have to agree with him.' He turned to his wife. 'And you, Robbie, are you going to have some?'

She stopped whisking her sauce and turned to him. 'A little would be nice.'

She opened the Aga door and pulled out a tray of moistly baked halibut. 'It's ready.' She put piping hot plates on the table before Ed, and the fish, baked in lemon and parsley, on a heatproof mat beyond. Using a fish slice, he served the delicious-looking fare.

She produced fried potatoes straight from the frying pan, and *al dente* Savoy cabbage and carrots tossed in a nugget of butter and sprinkled with freshly ground black pepper and nutmeg. The final touch was a smooth and shiny parsley and dill sauce. Roberta walked round the table with a jug. 'Sauce?'

'Yes, *please.*'

Her arm brushed Kit's and she jerked it away. Their eyes met. Abruptly Roberta tuned to Ed. 'Sauce?'

'Thanks, darling.'

It was as though Kit's eyes were compelled to follow Roberta as she sat down and served herself, pouring just a little of the rich, creamy sauce on to her own fish.

Ed served her with the remaining vegetables. He knew his wife well and gave her just enough. Kit dragged his eyes away. What was it about her that tugged at his heartstrings so? She wasn't even particularly nice to him, most of the time acting as though she'd prefer it if he weren't there.

Twice during the week Ed had been out on site, leaving the two of them alone. They'd sat together in the office, Kit doing his drawing and Roberta typing documents or doing accounts. The atmosphere had been strained, with neither of them daring to speak of anything other than business. Kit had put all his energy into his work. When their eyes had met, Roberta had found some excuse to rush away.

Kit's thoughts were dragged back to the present. Ed was worried about small areas of reinforced concrete cracking on the Bury site. Boris nudged his leg and Kit bent to stroke the dog.

'Don't feed him at the table, please.'

Kit looked across at Roberta. He'd had no intention of feeding Boris. 'I wasn't going to,' he said softly, then turned his attention to Ed. 'Presumably you've checked back on the condition of the reinforcing bars before concreting? It couldn't be spalling due to rust, could it?'

Ed shook his head. 'No. Site records are very good on that. It definitely doesn't seem to be the problem.'

Roberta was admonishing Boris, who, tail between his legs, crept under the table and curled into a ball. Kit's eyes flickered from Ed to Roberta, then back again to Ed. 'Well,' he said, clearing his throat, 'I've heard rumours about chemical reaction in some areas, between the concrete and reinforcement. Seems to depend on the actual materials used in the concrete.'

Ed pondered a while. 'Hmm. That's a thought. I'll check that with CIRIA and the Concrete Association.'

Roberta started to clear away the plates. Kit immediately stood up to help. 'Don't bother, Kit. I can do it.'

Ed stretched out and squeezed his wife's arm. 'He's only trying to help, Robbie. Don't snap the poor boy's head off!'

She lowered her eyes. 'I'm sorry. I didn't mean to snap your head off.'

Kit smiled, his eyes lingering a fraction too long on her face. She flashed him a look which started warning bells ringing in his head. He remembered a similar look along the banks of the River Ouse years ago. He sat down.

Roberta stacked the dishes on the draining board and picked up her oven gloves. She removed baked bananas from the Aga and set the oval dish on the table. Kit raised himself slightly in his seat and peered into the dish. The bananas were steeped in rum, with a little butter and melted brown sugar. They smelt divine. He smiled and leant back in his seat. 'I can see I'm going to have to run five miles in the morning instead of my usual three.'

Roberta looked across at him. 'You don't have to have any.' She turned to fetch a carton of double cream from the fridge.

Ed nudged Kit and grinned. 'But you will, won't you?'

Roberta put the cream on the table with three small dishes. She started to serve the dessert and put a banana in front of Ed first. With no trace of a smile, she raised her eyes to Kit expectantly.

He nodded. 'They look and smell wonderful, Robbie. I could eat them all!'

She passed a baked banana to him via Ed.

'What, no jug?' Ed held up the carton of double cream. 'Getting slack, aren't we, Roberta?'

She hastened out of her seat and snatched the carton from him. 'All right, I'll put it in a jug.'

'Robbie! Hey, Robbie, I was only joking, darling.' Ed grabbed her arm, all too aware of her condition and putting everything down to that. 'Sit down, sit down. We don't need a bloody jug.'

But she insisted. She walked over to the dresser behind Kit and plucked from the top shelf a cut-glass jug. She then walked back to the table and proceeded to pour the cream into it. It came barely a quarter of the way up the jug and looked mean. 'See, Ed? That's why I didn't use a jug. I haven't got a smaller one.' Roberta turned towards the wastebin and threw the empty cream carton into it, then walked past her husband towards the kitchen door.

'Robbie? Roberta? Where are you going?'

She turned back briefly. 'I'm tired. I think I'll go and have a bath.'

'But what about your banana?'

'Kit can have it, if he'd like?' And with that she left the room.

Embarrassed, Kit looked at Ed who raised his eyebrows. 'Women!' He shook his head and picked up the cut-glass jug, liberally pouring double cream over his banana. He passed the jug to Kit and tilted his head. 'But there again, where would we be without them?'

Kit likewise poured cream on to his banana. He stole a quick glance at Ed who was now tucking in with relish and felt a tug of guilt. What a thoroughly nice bloke he was. Working with Ed was already proving to be the best move Kit had made. But his wife was something else. She was the most desirable creature he'd ever met. Kit reflected on the past, by the River Ouse, and even now felt his cheeks grow hot with embarrassment. She'd been different then, except for those eyes of hers. They'd pierced into his guilty soul, in just the same was as they had this evening.

'You'll share this with me?' Ed picked up Roberta's dish and offered half of the banana to Kit.

'You're a very lucky man, Ed. Your wife is . . .'

He beamed. '*Extraordinary?*'

Kit grinned. 'Yes, she's certainly that.' He accepted the rest of the banana. 'And these are divine.'

19

Julia's breath caught in her throat. She actually felt faint. Rapidly, she returned her attention to her customer. 'Yes, madam, that's exactly right. All this jewellery is handmade to our specification. Nothing is duplicated.' She fingered the clasp on the chunky, colourful beaded necklace. 'See that sign – that curly P? That's the Purley's sign. It also means *premier* quality.'

Nathan, looking unfairly desirable, was leaning against the counter, arms folded, watching her sales pitch. Julia's customer, with her back to him, noticed the assistant's sudden smile and turned round. Her eyes widened on seeing such a sensational man. He gave her a radiant smile. 'I'll take it.' she said, passing the necklace back to Julia. 'And the earrings as well.' Just one look from Nathan Purley and her day was made.

Julia wrapped the jewellery and took the money from the customer. She paused and nodded at Nathan as she turned to leave the shop. Julia watched as he devoured her with his eyes. The woman went quite pink as Nathan ogled her all the way out of the shop.

'And what can I do for you?' Julia interrupted, piqued by his obvious interest in someone else.

He turned and put his elbows on the counter, smiling at her in much the same way as he'd smiled at the customer. Julia narrowed her eyes. She wasn't going to be taken in. 'I was passing,' he said, looking down at his watch. 'It's lunchtime so how about lunch?'

Julia's heart skipped a beat. She looked across at her assistant whose break was due. 'It's Susan's turn, not mine.'

Nathan peered in Susan's direction. He straightened himself and walked towards her. 'Susan, I wonder if you could do me a favour?'

She listened attentively. 'I need to speak to Julia about a few things. Would you very kindly hold the fort here for an hour or so, until we get back?' He smiled again, charmingly. Susan, who'd planned to meet her boyfriend, found herself agreeing.

Nathan turned back to Julia. 'That's settled then. Get your coat.'

They went to the Blue Boar in Trinity Street where Julia drank gin and lime and Nathan had beer. He also ordered ham sandwiches. 'I'm sorry I didn't get back to you earlier,' he said, tapping her hand, 'but we've been so busy in the warehouse. Things are certainly hotting up.'

Julia siezed her opportunity. 'They certainly are, Nathan.' She frowned, 'What did you do about the jacket designs?' He looked blank. 'The ones you were going to show to me, remember? You mentioned them in Tramp that night?'

Nathan's memory returned. 'Ah, yes.' He waved his hand. 'I sorted them. They'll be fine.'

Julia grabbed his hand. 'But, Nathan, we do need to talk. Fashion is changing all the time. These new boutiques ... I mean, Petty Cury will eventually be *all* boutiques.'

He closed his hand around hers. 'I'm quite aware of what's going on, Julia. I do keep my ear to the ground.'

It's not your ears, you idiot, it's your eyes! she thought. 'But I'd like to be involved in the design side, Nathan. I've spoken to Anne and she agrees. I've already done some sketches – you know, my own designs. I can show them to you, they're back at the shop. They'd look great, Nathan, I know they would. You have all these experts working for you but they keep producing the same stuff all the time. Leather is hot news, but *only* if we give the customer hot fashion. At least here in Cambridge anyway.'

He released Julia's hand and took a swig of his beer. She noticed his long fingers and meticulously clean nails. 'Okay, get involved. Come along to the warehouse, speak to my designers. Tell them what you think.'

Julia basked in the pleasure of his agreement. 'Thank you, Nathan.' She bit her lip. 'When I was last in London, I visited Brick Lane ...'

His brow furrowed. 'Brick Lane?' He nodded, as though recollecting something. 'Sweatshops!' he scoffed.

Julia blinked. 'Are they?'

He smiled lazily, shaking his head. 'I'm not interested in Brick

Lane, Julia, I'm after quality. The merchandise that's pumped out of places like that isn't the sort of thing I want to sell.'

'But it's not trash.'

'I never said it was.'

She frowned. 'But you implied it. Look, Nathan, I spent a whole morning there. I met this guy called Madhav and his family who run a business. The coats he showed me were *wonderful*! If you traded with him, as a sideline even, you'd turn the stock over in less than a week, I'm sure of it.'

Nathan tilted his head. 'I'm not interested in trading with – whatever his name is. But if you draw us their designs . . .'

'You couldn't make them at the same speed.'

Nathan grabbed her hand. 'See what I mean? You said it! They're sweatshops.'

'No, they're not.' Julia was indignant. 'They just work in a different way. Okay, so they work all day, and some of them all night. But it's their choice. They're not sweatshops.' Still allowing her hand to rest in his, aware of his touch, she pleaded, 'It's the colours, and the skins, and the way they put them together. Nathan, you ought to see them.'

He released her hand and picked up his glass. 'We have the expertise, Julia. Ours is the best.'

'But it's not! Don't you see?'

He moved his face very close to hers. 'Not in your fashion conscious eyes, Julia, maybe. But don't tell me our machinists aren't the best. Don't ever tell me that. We'll still be going long after all these boutiques have come and gone.'

She felt like a child, ticked off for being cheeky. She gulped and groped for her handbag. She needed a cigarette. And then she remembered, Nathan thought cigarettes were filthy. Julia hugged her handbag, deciding to adopt a different tack. 'What about waiting until premises become available in, say, the King's Road in Chelsea, then we lease them and open a boutique, a really *way-out*, trendy boutique, and use Madhav then?' Nathan's face clouded ominously. She grabbed his arm. 'Hear me out, Nathan. This'll have nothing to do with your other shops. I'll do it all – the organising, the running, everything. All you'll have to do is put up the cash. And, listen to me, I promise you, we'll make a killing. A real killing.'

Nathan lifted his glass and drained the contents in one go. He put the glass back on the table and ran his hand over his mouth, sizing

Julia up. She was *some* female. He smiled. What had he to lose?

'Do you like football?' he asked her unexpectedly.

'I'm sorry?'

'Football. Ever since I was a kid, I've loved football. I even dreamt of being a famous footballer once.' Nathan held out his hands like a goalie about a catch a ball. 'Stand aside, Georgie Best, here I come,' he laughed. 'Chelsea are my team. My mother's old man was born in Chelsea, took me to watch them when I was barely out of nappies. And now, in memory of my ole granddad, I subscribe – I have my own box at the ground so that I can watch my team in comfort.' He became more serious, remembering his beloved grandfather, and looked at her thoughtfully. 'I tell you what – if Chelsea win the cup this year, and I certainly hope they do, I'll give very careful consideration to this shop of yours . . . so long as it's in Chelsea.'

She looked at him as though he'd gone quite mad, then her brain clicked into gear. 'Do you go to all the home games?'

'Too true I do. I never miss a home game.'

'I like football, Nathan.'

'You do?'

'I certainly do.'

He smiled warmly. 'Well, Julia, you are full of surprises. Hmmm, we'll have to see what we can do about that, won't we?'

20

'Have you seen Boris?'

Kit looked up from his drawing board and shook his head. 'No, not recently.'

Roberta was looking anxious. 'It's just, well, he was here one minute and now he's gone. I've searched and searched, and I can't find the silly dog anywhere.'

Kit sat back in his seat. 'I'm sure he's around somewhere.'

She left the office in a haze of worry. Kit stuck his pencil in his mouth and rattled it against his teeth. Then he pushed his chair away from his drawing board and stood up.

Roberta was outside, frantically looking around. He wandered up to her. 'No joy?'

She shook her head. 'I should have kept my eye on him. He's only a puppy.' She faced Kit in embarrassment. 'It's just, well . . . I haven't been feeling very good this morning.' Roberta lowered her eyes and Kit waited. She looked up again shyly. 'I'm pregnant, you see.'

Eyes of the darkest shade of brown appealed for his understanding. 'I know,' he whispered.

She was shocked. 'You know? Ed told you?' They'd decided not to mention her pregnancy to anyone just yet.

Kit raised his hands to reassure her. 'No, no, he hasn't said anything. I just guessed.'

'You guessed?' She sounded astounded, gazing down at her perfectly flat stomach. Kit laughed.

'Not like that.'

'Well, how?'

He shook his head. 'I don't know. There's just something about you. I guessed straight away.'

She decided he was telling the truth then scanned the garden. Boris was still nowhere to be seen. 'Where can he be?' she fretted.

Kit plunged his hands into his pocket. 'Look, take my car, cruise around a bit. I'm sure he hasn't gone far.'

She looked at his keys. 'But I couldn't.'

'Go on, take them.' He grinned. 'You can drive, can't you?'

'Of course I can. But are you sure?'

'I'm sure.'

'I might . . . *prang* it or something!'

He touched her arm. 'You won't.'

Together they walked towards his car. Kit opened the door and Roberta stepped inside, making herself comfortable in his seat. She looked up at him. 'Thank you, Kit.'

'It's a pleasure. I'd better get back. The office beckons.'

She watched him go before putting the keys into the ignition. The sports car purred into action. Roberta adjusted the seat and reversed the Triumph Spitfire within the gravelled parking area. She then set off down the twisty lane, driving very slowly and looking for Boris.

She mused as she drove along, imagining Kit sitting in this very seat. His hands touched this steering wheel, he stared into this wing mirror . . . 'Where are you, you stupid dog!' she said aloud to collect here wandering thoughts.

After searching the whole village and surrounding area, she gave up. A small puppy couldn't possibly have gone that far. Roberta drove home feeling thoroughly depressed.

She parked Kit's car in the exact spot she'd taken it from and turned off the engine. No sooner had she closed the car door than she was met by a gleeful, yapping Boris. He bounded towards her, furiously wagging his tail. 'Boris! You naughty boy! Where have you been?' She crouched down and he licked her face with delight. Roberta scooped him up into her arms and walked back into the cottage.

Kit was making coffee. 'Look who I've found!' she said, walking into the kitchen.

He smiled at her. 'I know, he turned up pretty soon after you'd gone. I kept him in 'til I saw you'd parked.' He turned back towards the kettle. 'Coffee?'

'That would be lovely. Thank you, Kit. And thanks for lending me your car.'

'It was my pleasure.'

'Well, it wouldn't have been if I'd bent the bumper or something.'

He shook his head. 'It wouldn't have mattered. That car was a sweetener – a bribe. My twenty-first birthday present too. Otherwise it would have gone straight back.'

She frowned. 'Oh . . . why?'

The kettle boiled and he filled two mugs then topped them up with milk and handed one to Roberta. 'I don't exactly get on well with my father.' He hitched himself on to the edge of the kitchen table and sipped his coffee. 'But after I got my degree he changed his attitude towards me . . . slightly. Before that, he'd treated me like a cross he had to bear.'

'Did he?' Roberta sounded surprised.

Kit nodded. 'When I came out of Oundle – fat, spotty, and with three extremely low A-levels – Pa called me everything under the sun. He said I'd never be any good, and would never live up to the family name.' Kit chuckled at the memory. 'But the old bugger did me a good turn really. I decided then and there that he could stick his family name, and I'd prove him wrong. His hostile attitude was my springboard, though it hurt at the time. I decided I'd make more money than he could ever dream of.' Kit gulped his coffee and raised his eyes to Roberta. 'And I'd never take a single penny from the bastard, ever again!'

Her eyes widened in admiration. Kit wasn't at all the spoiled rich kid she'd imagined. She moved closer, put her mug on the table, and sat down with Boris on her knee. 'What about your brothers? How do they get on with your father?'

'Oh, quite well, I think. At least, Roger does. Nick I'm not so sure about. He copped out of university and is now a social worker in London. Pa's none too pleased about that, but there again, Nick's always been his golden boy. The *good-looking* one, you see.' Kit downed his coffee and put the mug back on the table. 'And, believe it or not, Nick was as bright as a button at school. Out of all of us, he should have got the best degree. But he just seemed to wind down as he got older, and he *hated* engineering.' Kit smiled. 'Takes after my mother, in fact.'

Roberta was intrigued. 'And how do you feel about her?'

A smile crept around his mouth. 'Ma and I get on like a house on fire. She's not at all like my father. We meet up regularly. She

101

used to come to Coventry when she could, and occasionally we meet up in London. But with Pa not being too well, it's a struggle for her to get away.' He pulled a face. 'I do go home sometimes, if I *have* to.'

There was silence. He felt he'd said too much. 'Sorry if I'm boring you.'

'Oh, you're not boring me. This is fascinating stuff, especially as I'd imagined anyone born with the name Fordham-Clarke must be deliriously happy.'

He guffawed. 'You're joking, aren't you? I had the most miserable childhood imaginable.'

Roberta immediately empathised with him. 'How strange. I did too.'

He reached over and touched her hand, and instead of yanking it away, she found his touch comforting and left it where it was. Kit hesitated, feeling he should move on to safer ground. He grinned. 'And how's that sister of yours?'

Roberta raised her eyebrows. 'Julia? She's fine, as far as I know. Mum keeps me up to date, I suppose, but Julia's a dark horse, always has been. She confides in no one.'

'What's she doing now?'

'Works in a shop. No ordinary shop, mind. But Julia's no ordinary girl! A leather shop in Cambridge. She's the manager. Purley's – have you heard of them?'

Kit screwed up his face. 'No.'

'Though, from what I've been told, she's anxious to up sticks and move to London. She's very friendly with Clare, your sister-in-law. Stays with her quite often, as a matter of fact.'

Kit nodded thoughtfully. 'So you're not particularly close to Julia?'

Adamantly, Roberta shook her head. Boris looked up at his mistress, disturbed by her vehemence. 'We rub along okay, but we're certainly not close,' Roberta confided.

'She's very . . .' Kit stopped in his tracks.

Here it comes, thought Roberta. 'Beautiful?'

He looked embarrassed. 'No, I wasn't going to say that.'

Roberta narrowed her eyes. 'What were you going to say? It doesn't matter, Kit, I know all about Julia.'

Kit cleared his throat. 'I was going to say, she's very different from you.'

Their eyes locked. Roberta lowered hers first. 'Yes, you're right. She's very different from me, Kit. Always has been.'

21

Early July 1970

'So, when exactly is the baby due?' With a withering look, Nancy peered across at her sister.

Brenda was having none of it. 'Say what you mean, Nancy. Don't hide behind gentility.'

Her sister puffed out her chest, her cheeks too, and went quite pink. 'Brenda!'

'Or shall I help you out? Yes, Nance, the baby's due in September, which means they *did it* before. And don't look at me like that! It's not exactly *unusual*, is it? You know darned well we both did it before we got married.'

Nancy gasped. She looked as though she was about to explode. 'Well, *you* might have done but *I* certainly didn't!'

'Oh, don't give me that, Nancy. I know for a fact you did it with Peter.'

'I most certainly did not!'

'Well, *I did*!'

The two sisters glared at each other. Nancy swallowed hard. 'Yes, well, we all know what Gordon Tree was like.'

Brenda sat back in her seat and laughed. 'I wasn't talking about Gordon, Nancy. I was talking about Peter.'

Her sister's eyes bulged in her head. 'Brenda! What's happening to you?' She frantically fanned herself with a paper napkin. 'I never heard such smut. Is this what working in that hairdresser's is doing for you? Because if it is, I suggest you leave.'

Brenda took a deep breath. She leant across the table and squeezed her sister's arm. 'It's nothing to do with the hairdresser's, Nance. This is to do with *us*. Roberta's expecting a baby, and we're all as pleased as can be. Don't turn that into something grubby, please.'

Nancy lowered her eyes. 'I never meant to turn it into something grubby.' She faced her sister. 'It's wonderful news.'

Brenda beamed. 'Oh, Nance, it is! I can't tell you how thrilled I am.'

'Has she only just told you?'

Quickly, Brenda weighed up the question. 'Last month.'

'You mean, you knew last time we met?'

'Only just.'

'Why didn't you tell me then?'

Brenda lowered her eyes. 'I suppose I forgot.'

Nancy tutted beneath her breath, aware of her sister's embarrassment. And she'd every reason to be embarrassed, her daughter was a regular scarlet woman. Charitably Nancy decided to change the subject. 'What about our new Prime Minister then? Heath did it, he beat them.'

Brenda nodded. Gordon hadn't been too pleased about the new Tory government.

'And now,' continued Nancy eagerly, 'perhaps *we'll* be able to sort these unions out.'

'I'm sure you will.' Brenda corrected herself immediately. 'I mean, I'm sure *they* will.'

'Oh, and Brenda, I *must* tell you ... only the other day I was talking to Cynthia. She was giving me some insight into this business with Kit.' Nancy looked furtively around, as though about to say something confidential. 'Fordham-Clarkes are planning to buy Matthews Structural Design.'

Brenda's eyes nearly popped out of her head. 'What?'

'It's true! Ed and Kit might be keeping it under their hats for the time being, but it's true.'

'Well, it might be true, but it certainly won't happen!'

'Of course it will, Brenda. Don't be so silly. Ed Matthews isn't going to turn down an offer like that. He'll most probably be a member of Fordham-Clarke's board if it goes through. What could be finer than that?'

How blinkered could you get? Brenda took a deep breath. 'Nancy, I think I know my own son-in-law better than you do.'

'But, Brenda, he won't let an opportunity like that pass him by. He'd be a *fool* to.'

She straightened her back. 'Ed's no fool, he's a really smart man, and so for that matter is Kit. He's a lovely boy. They've both worked their socks off just recently, and things are beginning to look good. They won't sell up. What would be the point?' She glared at her sister, who had never got over Kit Fordham-Clarke's working for Ed. 'Why go back to being a small cog in a big wheel?' she challenged.

'A small cog? Is that how you see it? Peter's no small cog.'

Brenda sighed. 'I'm not talking about Peter, Nancy, I'm talking about Ed.' She searched around and started to gather her things together. Her sister was getting right up her nose today.

'What're you doing?'

'I'm leaving or I'll miss my bus.'

'There's no need to get upset just because I know more about these things than you do, Brenda.'

That was the final straw. She stood up and strode towards the door. Nancy scurried after her, then frantically returned to the table, slapping down a ten-shilling note. 'Brenda! Brenda!'

She paused outside. It was a warm, sunny day and Brenda took great gulps of the fresh air. She turned back to her sister. 'I'll see you next month, Nancy. Can't stop, I've got to rush!' At a snappy pace she set off down Trinity Street. Nancy called after her but Brenda affected not to hear, just kept going.

'Now,' muttered Nancy, affronted, 'what on earth's got into her?'

22

Kit sat with his hands cupping his chin and his elbows resting on the kitchen table. The *Newmarket Journal* was spread open before him at the property pages. Excitedly, he looked up at Ed. 'This is it! See?' He pointed to a picture of a delapidated cottage. 'It's being auctioned next week, exactly what I want.'

Ed, engrossed in the *Telegraph*, peered at the picture, tutted, and shook his head. 'A lot of hard work, Kit.'

He smiled. 'Well, you should know. And I don't care about the hard work. I like hard work, and it'll be worth it in the end.' He glanced at the agent's name. 'Carter Jonas. I'll ring them this morning, view it straight away.'

Ed looked across at his wife, who was giving Boris his breakfast cornflakes. 'There you are, now don't make a mess.' She put his dish on the floor and Boris eagerly lapped up the cornflakes and milk.

Ed grinned. 'Take Robbie with you. She knows about these things – loves old property.' He noticed the startled look on her face. 'There you are, I'll give you both the morning off. Isn't that kind of me?'

Kit flashed Roberta a glance but she didn't reciprocate. She ran her hands over her swollen belly and sighed. 'I'm sure Kit doesn't want to drag me around with him.'

'I'd love you to come.'

Her eyes met his. His gaze was steady, and to the onlooker gave nothing away. 'I'm not sure,' she wavered.

'Go on, give yourself a treat. It'll do you good to get out, Robbie. Cooped up in that office all day.' Ed stood up and walked towards her, giving her a bear-hug. 'A woman in your condition shouldn't be working at all.'

She pushed him away. 'A woman in my condition is a perfectly normal human being. I feel exactly the same now as I did before.' It wasn't strictly true, though. Before Roberta's pregnancy, she hadn't known Kit.

'Please, Roberta, I'd love you to come.'

Ed prodded her arm. 'Go on, I insist.'

'OK, Kit. Thanks. It sounds like fun.'

There was no strain anymore between Kit and Roberta. She no longer rushed from the office when they were alone together. Instead they laughed about certain clients, and developed running jokes that even Ed was excluded from. When he was around, Kit and Roberta behaved quite differently. If she thought at all about her relationship with Kit, she'd describe it as *close*. A close friend, whom she liked a lot and with whom she endlessly discussed things, often laughing and joking as she poured out her most private thoughts. Kit confided in her too and she believed she knew more about him now than anyone else did.

Ash Cottage was situated in a small village nearby called Ousden. Like Blackthorn Cottage, it was slightly off the beaten track, surrounded by farmland and paddocks, and set in about half an acre of garden. It was similarly timber-framed with plaster and lath, but Ash Cottage had a pantiled roof. It was also much smaller than Blackthorn Cottage.

Kit turned the key and pushed open the creaking door, waiting for Roberta to go in first. She stepped over the threshold and breathed in the familiar musty odour. Kit stood beside her and breathed it in as well. At their feet, partially covering a flagstoned floor, was a traditional square of moth-eaten carpet, cut to shape. The plastered walls, hiding the beams, were wall-papered in Chinese picturescape, redolent of the fifties. Leading off to the right was a narrow winding staircase, partially handrailed and painted dark green. It seemed to disappear into the gloom. A worn stair carpet was centred in the middle, complete with tarnished brass rods. To either side of the carpet, the exposed wood was also painted dark green.

They looked at each other. 'What do you think?' Kit asked, holding his breath.

She gave a joyful laugh. 'I love it!'

He wanted to hug her, but didn't dare. Instead he stepped forward and opened his arms. 'What is it about these old properties? They make your heart swell and your toes curl, don't you agree?'

Enthusiastically, she did, her face glowing as she cast her eyes around. Kit watched her, fascinated. Wearing a simple sleeveless cotton smock and flat-heeled sandals she looked so pretty and wholesome. He realised that pregnancy suited her. Her face had come alive, and her skin, golden-brown from the sun, had a lustrous natural bloom. She became aware of his scrutiny. 'Would you move in with it like this? In this state?'

He turned his attention back to the delapidated cottage and chuckled. 'I'd give it a hoover first.'

She moved closer to him. 'There's no hurry, Kit. You could stay with us for the time being, and do it up gradually.'

Their eyes met. 'It's time I found a place of my own, Roberta. Don't you agree?'

She swallowed hard, only too aware that he was right. And perhaps, now that she'd filled out so much, he found her repulsive? She shook off the thought. 'Come on then, let's have a good look around.'

They explored the ground floor first, then mounted the twisting staircase. 'Careful!' Kit said as she nearly lost her footing. 'These rods are loose. Be careful, Roberta.'

Upstairs was much the same as downstairs. Everywhere wallpapered in awful colours, with drably painted woodwork. Roberta was undaunted, though. 'This could be transformed with a simple coat of white paint. Why did farm workers go for such dark, dreary colours?'

Kit laughed. 'Perhaps because they didn't show the dirt?'

'And who could blame them, with all the kids they used to have?' She took a deep breath. 'Well, Kit, I think you've got your work cut out, but if it goes for a decent price, I'd say you'd be getting something really special.'

He walked towards the stairs, ducking beneath the low ceiling. With an imploring look, he held out his hand. 'Roberta. I don't want you to slip.'

She took his hand and allowed herself to be helped down the treacherous staircase. When they reached the bottom he didn't let go but drew her towards him instead, running his hands around her back. With a pounding heart, Roberta allowed herself to be pulled very close. His eyes were within inches of hers and she could see the turmoil within. 'I love you,' he quickly said. 'I just wanted you to know. I need a place of my own ... because I love you *so much*.' And then, as quickly as he'd siezed her, he let go. Roberta felt as though she'd been dropped from a great height.

She lowered her eyes. 'I love you too, Kit. With all my heart.'

He groaned and instantly wrapped his arms around her again, his head resting on hers. She could hear his heart rapidly beating and the noise was a confirmation of his feelings. 'Can I kiss you?' he asked.

Roberta raised her eyes to his. 'We shouldn't, it wouldn't be right.'

But he brushed his lips over hers. It was like being caressed by a butterfly and she found herself standing on tiptoes, her hands creeping to his hair. Delicately, he ran his tongue around the outside of her mouth, savouring the taste and not wanting the moment to end. Clutching his head, Roberta eagerly pressed her mouth against his and kissed him as she wanted to be kissed. A little surprised, Kit responded.

Both were on the verge of something more when, in horror, she pulled away, hands flying to her flushed cheeks. 'What are we doing?'

Roberta rushed out of the cottage, her head still spinning with desire. She more or less fell over the uneven ground towards his car, relieved to find it unlocked as she tugged at the door. She got in and breathlessly laid her head against the head rest. What had she done? What had she said? She'd openly declared her love for Kit Fordham-Clarke. Roberta buried her head in her hands. Where did that leave Ed? Thoughts of the first time he'd made love to her returned to plague her. It had been nothing like this passionate encounter with Kit, and even now, for all Ed's caring and gentleness and untold patience, it still wasn't. Roberta was racked with guilt. She was married, committed to a kind, caring, protective man who adored her, and she was expecting his child. But she'd just tasted something else and it had made every nerve in her body tingle with desire.

Anxiously, Kit fumbled to lock the cottage door. He looked across at Roberta sitting stiffly in his car. With the colour still high in her cheeks, she was looking straight ahead but he could see the shame written all over her. What had he done? He felt like a heel. With heavy heart he walked towards his car. She turned and looked at him briefly before putting up her hand to shield her face. But he loved her, he had no doubt of that, and he had no doubt that she loved him. They'd simply spoken and acted how they truly felt. Kit climbed into his car and put his hand on hers. 'It's me that needs forgiveness, Roberta, but if you want me to say I'm sorry . . . I can't.'

'I do love Ed, Kit, in my way. I know you might find that hard to believe after . . .' She faced him, her face on fire. 'I would never want to hurt him.'

Kit squeezed her hand. 'And neither would I.' He let go and started up the engine. 'I'll take you home.'

23

August 1970

Three times Julia had visited the Chesterton warehouse, and three times Nathan had been absent, either visiting Kings Lynn, or Norwich, or his leather suppliers. As a lot of the beads they used were imported, Julia quite expected him to be abroad the fourth time!

But this time his secretary breathlessly informed her that Nathan was in and would see her – even though she did not have an appointment.

'You should ring, Julia, before you visit. I can't help it if my diary doesn't coincide with your surprise visits,' he reproved her.

She ignored the chair to which he showed her and instead hitched herself rather elegantly upon the edge of his desk. 'You know full well, Nathan, that I have to fit my visits in as and when I can.'

'Well, you spoke to our designers last time, didn't you? And they're trying their best to incorporate some of your ideas. Isn't that what you wanted? Why should you need me there too?' He moved just an inch or two closer, his eyes quizzing hers. 'As much as I love your company, Julia, I am a very busy man.'

She raised a hand to her face, tapping her forefinger against her jaw. She stretched out one bare tanned leg, almost touching his trouser leg. Momentarily, Nathan allowed his eyes to wander along it, and then he shifted back, rather abruptly. Julia slid off the desk and sat down in the seat. 'You made a promise to me, Nathan. You can't have forgotten it?'

He frowned and leant back in his seat, lifting his hands behind his head. Julia noticed damp patches beneath the arms of his pristine white shirt. She would have liked to reach out and touch them,

112

climb across the desk and rub her nose in them, scenting his sweat like an animal. Nathan lowered his arms and propped them on his desk. 'I never forget a promise.'

'Well, they won. Chelsea won the Cup!'

He really smiled then, and chuckled out loud. 'Oh, sweet, sweet, Julia. You are the light of my life.'

She pouted slightly. 'What did I say that was so funny?'

'It wasn't what you said, Julia, it was the way you said it.' He laughed again, screwing up his eyes. 'As though your life depended upon Chelsea winning the Cup.'

'Well, I can tell you quite honestly, I was pretty excited when they did!'

'And why would that be?'

'Oh, Nathan, stop playing games with me. You said, if Chelsea won the Cup you would give careful consideration to opening a shop down the King's Road.' She thumped her hand on his desk. 'You know you did.'

As quick as a flash, he sat forward and grabbed her hand. 'Did you actually watch the game, from beginning to end?'

'I watched *both* bloody games! You'll not catch me out like that, Nathan Purley. I watched them draw with Leeds, then win at the replay.'

'And what was the score?'

'2–1.'

'Good God, Julia, I'm impressed. When you said you liked football, I thought you were throwing me a line.'

Still with her hand in his, she glared at him. 'I thought *throwing a line* was your game, Nathan.'

He bristled and withdrew his hand. 'Okay, go ahead. Find premises down the King's Road. As soon as you've found the right place, give me a call. I can't be fairer than that.'

Her face lit into a wondrous smile. 'You mean it? I can go ahead?' She lowered her eyes, hesitating for a second or so. 'So if I told you . . . I've already got something lined up . . .'

'Down the King's Road?'

'Of course.'

'Where exactly?'

'In a superb position, opposite Paultons Square, not far from the Fire Station.'

'Hah! Well, that's all right then. At least I know if you catch fire it won't be a problem.'

'Ha, ha.'

He softened a little. 'Well done, anyway. I have to give you top marks for initiative.'

'So you'll come with me to see it?'

He pursed his mouth, hesitating, then nodded. 'Whenever you like.'

'You say, Nathan. I can fit in around you.'

He reached for his diary and flicked through a few pages. 'How about . . . this weekend? If you could get Saturday off, we could go up in the morning, view the property, have lunch and maybe catch a show?'

Julia couldn't believe her ears. 'Yes, I'd love that. I'm sure I can sort out Saturday.'

'We could even stay over, if you like?'

She gulped, aware of the way he was looking at her. But she wasn't going to be a pushover, deciding to temper her enthusiasm. 'Yes, that's an idea. I tell you what, we could stay with Clare, my cousin. She lives in Chiswick. Remember, I told you about her in Tramp?'

Nathan frowned, obviously not remembering. 'Wherever.'

'It's a lovely house, Nathan. And she'd be really pleased to see you . . . me . . . well, both of us.'

'Good. Sort it out then. Let me know the arrangements. I shall look forward to hearing from you.' He looked at his watch. 'Now, I really must get on.'

24

Although Nathan offered to pick Julia up in Newmarket, she decided against showing him where she lived. They met in Cambridge instead, at nine o'clock. He drew up in Market Hill, near Petty Cury, on the dot in a new silver/grey Aston Martin with the personal number plate NP 44. Julia could hardly believe her luck. She climbed swiftly into his vehicle, feeling as though life had just begun for her. Nathan, in smart beige gabardine trousers and an open-necked shirt, allowed his eyes to linger over her alluring white silk jumpsuit which fitted snugly around her waist and thighs but flared out into wide trousers over chunky platform-soled shoes. Around her neck she wore a Purley's multi-coloured necklace, and her long dark hair fell luxuriously in smooth waves down her back.

'Have you got the details?' he asked, as soon as they'd left Cambridge.

She fished into her jazzy tote-bag and withdrew the agent's literature. 'It's all here. They're meeting us there at eleven-thirty.'

'And the lease is for how long?'

'It's rent we'll be paying, Nathan. We'll be the sub-tenants'

He pulled a face. 'How much longer does their lease run, the lease-holders?'

Julia read the papers in front of her. 'Well, the original lease was for twenty-one years.' She looked at him. 'Another eighteen, it seems.'

'Yeah, and if you make an enormous success of this, the rent'll go sky-high!'

'No, it won't. We'll fix the rent for at least . . . five years.' She plucked the figure out of the top of her head.

'Make sure you do.'

'You'll be there, Nathan. You can make sure for yourself.'

He reached across and put a hand on her knee. 'Oh no, Julia. I'm strictly along for the ride. This is your baby. All I'm doing is putting up the cash, remember? You said you'd organise it *all by yourself*.'

She looked down at his hand and was tempted to put her own on top. 'You trust me, then?'

'I most certainly do.' He put his hand back on the steering wheel. 'I've seen how you work, Julia. I have every confidence in your sound business sense.'

She smiled. This was going to be some day. The sun was shining, her future seemed secured – and she was with Nathan.

The premises were grubby and the lease-holders late. Nathan was none too pleased. He walked around, frowning.

When the lease-holders finally did arrive, with profuse apologies, the atmosphere could have been sliced with a knife. And to make things worse, the rent they were demanding was far more than Julia had been led to believe. At the first opportunity, when they were out of earshot, she whispered, 'It's in a superb position, Nathan, surely you agree? And it only needs a coat of paint . . .'

'It needs a darnsight more than that!' he hissed back.

'I'll do it! I'll sort it! And it won't cost you a penny. Wait and see.'

He folded his arms. 'For this rent, you'd better.'

He walked off outside. Julia watched him go before turning back to the lease-holders, Mr and Mrs Denton-Smythe. She smiled disarmingly, mustering her wits to play her hand correctly. 'My partner is none too pleased about the decor.' She shrugged.

Mrs Denton-Smythe snapped, 'It's been empty for a while. All empty shops look like this.'

'But the one we viewed before . . .' Julia stopped in mid-sentence and quickly averted her eyes.

Mr Denton-Smythe waved his hand airily. 'It's only a coat of paint. I'm sure we could run to that.'

Julia sized him up. 'And the loo in the back there isn't very nice, it needs replacing. And these floorboards need seeing to . . . will you do that, too?'

He opened his mouth to speak. Mrs Denton-Smythe jumped in first. 'You're not the only ones interested in these premises, my dear. If you don't want them, just say so. We won't waste anymore of your time.'

'You're not wasting my time. These premises are exactly what I want. If you give the place a coat of paint – in canary yellow – *and* secure these loose floorboards, *and* replace the loo, I'll take it.'

'*Canary* yellow?'

'Yes! Canary yellow. Oh, and the rent . . . it's very *high*.' With matching frowns, Mr and Mrs Denton-Smythe both opened their mouths to speak. 'It must be fixed for five years?'

'Not likely!' Mrs Denton-Smythe replied.

Julia glared at her, then turned on her heel. 'In that case, I won't waste time.' She actually started to walk towards the door, her heart thumping in anticipation and dread. Nathan, outside, turned to greet her. He pulled open the shop door.

'Hang on! Hang on!' Mr Denton-Smythe called out. 'Okay, if you sign an agreement to stay for five years, we'll fix the rent for that time. And I hope you realise what a good deal you're getting? Premises like this are beginning to go like *hot cakes*!'

Julia turned back with a smile. She nodded and held out her hand to secure the deal, inwardly triumphant.

They ate a leisurely lunch at the Top of the Tower in Maple Street. The famous Post Office Tower's revolving restaurant was packed with attractive cosmopolitan people. Julia, already on an almighty high, looked out for miles across London and felt incredibly grown-up for her nineteen and a half years. Nathan seemed entranced by her. Having added a navy blazer and red-striped tie to his attire, he made a point of spoiling her, even ordering vintage champagne to celebrate her success.

'And tomorrow? Will you visit Brick Lane with me tomorrow? Please, Nathan.'

He smiled very slowly, devouring her with his eyes. 'I told you, Julia, it's up to you from now on. You've got your own designs, and your own ideas, so get your friend down Brick Lane working on them. I'm expecting you to fill this boutique with the stock you want to sell. I'll agree a limit, and of course I'd need to see all invoices, paperwork, etc, but apart from that you're on your own.'

'But I don't want to be entirely on my own. I shall need some help. I want you to come with me tomorrow, Nathan. I want you to meet Madhav and see the quality of his clothes.'

'I want! I want!' Nathan took her hand and squeezed it tenderly. 'But I don't want what you want, Julia. I can think of nothing I want less than to visit this Madhav and view his merchandise. The stuff *I* produce back home is what I want to trade in.' He hesitated, seeing the distress in her eyes, then raised her hand to his mouth and kissed the palm. 'You've got your wish, Julia, I'm doing this for you. I value your opinion and think you'll do very well.' He bit her little finger, sending shivers down her spine, then lowered her hand. 'But we're very different people, you and I, so if I take the time to understand you, you must be prepared to understand me. OK?'

A twinge of fear ran through her. She'd envisaged Nathan gradually becoming more and more involved. That was what she'd wanted, that was to be part of the fun. 'But don't entirely cast me out into the wilderness,' she whispered.

He laughed. 'Oh, rest assured, sweet Julia, I'd never do that.' He twined his finger through hers. 'Anyway, my mother ought to be involved more. It's time we brought her out of mothballs, and she'd certainly be interested in helping you. Don't ever underestimate her ability to spot a bargain, Julia. She may be getting on in years, but she's no fool. Get her up here next week. She'd love it. I know she would.'

'What do you think she's going to say about me leaving the Cambridge shop?'

Nathan fanned out his hand with Julia's fingers still entwined. 'My mother will miss you, and so will the Cambridge shop, but that's life.' He leant closer. 'She wants you to succeed, Julia. I think she sees herself in you, and knows darn well that if we don't back you in this, somebody else will.'

'Is that what she said?'

He shook his head. 'Not in so many words, but it's the truth, isn't it?'

Julia's brow puckered as she considered his words. She brightened as she said, 'It's no longer an option, so why worry about what isn't going to happen?'

Nathan had managed to get tickets for *Oh! Calcutta!* It was still playing its eight-week stint at the Round House near Euston, in a converted engine shed, before moving to the Royalty Theatre in the West End. Sitting three rows from the front, Julia kept her eyes riveted on the stage. Nathan, however, sat with his hand propping up his chin and sighed occasionally.

'But you knew what to expect,' Julia laughed during the interval.

He narrowed his eyes. 'I knew what to expect, Julia, and I'm past being shocked by tits, dicks and bums.' He gave a slow smile. 'It's the storyline that fails to impress me.'

She giggled and looked him in the eye. 'It doesn't turn you on, even a little bit?'

He looked at her over his glass. 'The girl on the left with the size thirty-eights made me think about crossing my legs, but in answer to your question . . . *no*.'

Julia nudged him and giggled. 'But it's shocking, nonetheless?'

He looked at her and frowned, as though looking at a schoolgirl. 'It isn't shocking at all, Julia. It's tacky, and . . . dull.'

She hastily gulped her wine. Why did Nathan always make her feel so silly? She averted her eyes. *Oh! Calcutta!* hadn't been her choice, anyway.

Nathan finished his drink and placed his glass on the table. 'Do you want to stay for Act Two?' he asked Julia.

Her eyes widened. 'Why, don't you?'

He shook his head and said quite adamantly, 'I can think of nothing I want less.'

Julia suddenly felt tired and her head ached. The day had been long and exciting, she didn't want it to end on a sour note. Where had the romantic Nathan gone? 'Let's go!' she said with a smile, and quickly finished her wine.

With a light touch, he took her arm and guided her out of the theatre. They walked the short distance to his Aston Martin and climbed in. Nathan put his keys in the ignition. 'Where to now? Are you hungry?'

She sighed, 'No, not after that lunch. Actually, I'm quite tired. Shall we go to Clare's?'

'Will she mind?'

Julia looked at her watch. Nine-thirty. 'Of course she won't. She might not even be there.' Julia plunged her hand into her tote-bag. 'But I've got a key!'

Nathan looked at it and raised his eyebrows. 'Do you stay with this Clare a lot?'

Julia shook her head. 'When I can, which isn't very often, but we're really great friends, as well as cousins.'

He started up the engine. 'Good. Then I shall look forward to meeting her.'

25

Clare was in, and so were a few others. Feeling increasingly tired, and a little the worse for wear, Julia was greeted by her cousin with an enormous hug and a kiss. Clare, wearing a white silk blouse beneath a beaded and braided tight black bolero, and black flared trousers over satin criss-cross almond-toed shoes, resembled an exotic dancer. With her straight blonde hair spectacularly framing her face, she was in exuberant form. Julia felt envious of her straight away.

'And this is Nathan.' Julia presented him proudly though he looked slightly out of place in his ultra-smart clothes.

Clare stepped forward and pecked him on the cheek. He stood quite still, as though shocked, and for a second Julia thought he was going to turn tail and run. This was obviously *not* his scene. Then he surprised her. He raised his hand to the spot where Clare had hastily planted her kiss and Julia saw him swallow hard and stumble over his words. 'Clare, how . . . nice to meet you.' He cleared his throat. 'Julia's told me so much about you.'

'Oh, has she?' giggled a slightly drunk Clare, and grabbed her cousin's arm. 'Well, I hope it's all been lies, I couldn't bear to think you told him the truth.'

She didn't wait for any reply, just turned and walked towards the drawing room. 'Come through, please. A few of my friends are here from college.'

'Clare?' Julia fumbled with her bag. 'Do you mind if I freshen up first?'

She stopped in her tracks and smiled at her cousin. 'Not at all. Use my room, Julia.' She grinned. 'I'm afraid we haven't got a lot of space, these guys are staying over, so I've put Nathan in the room next to mine and you can share with me.'

Julia flashed a look at Nathan, who didn't seem to be listening. She shrugged and wandered off, making her way up to Clare's bedroom. She glanced back as she mounted the stairs and saw him following her cousin into the drawing room.

Julia threw her bag on to the huge double bed and slumped down on the stool in front of Clare's dressing table. She peered at herself, and wondered what had happened to the day. Everything she could wish for and more, yet it had all gone flat somehow. She picked up Clare's hairbrush and vigorously brushed her hair before tipping out the contents of her tote-bag. She'd brought a floaty summer dress to wear the next day, a change of bra and pants, her make-up and wash-bag and nothing else. Julia started to unbutton her jumpsuit. She slipped out of it and wandered through to Clare's bathroom where she filled the basin with warm water. She gave herself a thorough wash and towelled herself dry. Feeling better, she wandered back into the bedroom and sprayed herself liberally with Clare's *Femme* perfume then searched through numerous closets to find something dressier to wear. In the end she chose a peasant-style dress and a pair of pink suede shoes. She put her hair up and tied a chiffon scarf securely around it. With the heat of the day, it had formed its own natural curls which now cascaded around her face. The new look transformed the way she felt. She redid her make-up and went downstairs.

Minus his jacket and tie, Nathan sat alone, drinking whisky, on Clare's vast white leather settee. Julia smiled to herself, remembering making love with Nick upon the same settee. 'You all right?' she whispered softly as she slid down beside him.

Nathan smiled. 'I'm fine.' He turned his attention back to Clare, over at the other side of the room, talking to a group of her friends. Unaware of his interest, she threw back her head and laughed delightedly. 'You look nice.' Nathan added, as an afterthought.

Julia's eyes followed his across the room. 'Thank you . . . So, what do you think to Clare?'

He looked at Julia again, and she noticed the light in his eyes. He frowned slightly and tilted his head at her. 'The truth? *Gorgeous.*' He took a swig of his drink. 'But then again, so are you.' He nudged her, slightly drunk. 'I'd love to meet your mums. I bet they're a couple of stunners.'

Involuntarily, Julia giggled. 'Well, mine certainly is. But I don't know whether you'd say the same about Auntie Nancy.'

Nathan's eyes panned back to Clare. 'And she's Clare's mother? Auntie Nancy, I mean?'

Julia nodded, her heart plummeting. 'You like Clare, don't you, Nathan? You like her a lot.'

He dropped his eyes to his drink then raised them slowly, this time looking straight at Julia. 'Do you mind?'

'Of course I bloody mind!' It was out before she could retract it. 'She's married for a start.'

Nathan lolled back on the settee. 'Well, where's her husband then?' he pointed across the room. 'Any man with a wife like that should know better than to let her out of his sight.'

Julia gulped and twisted away from him, staring across at her cousin who seemed oblivious of her misery. And, Julia could tell, Clare wasn't the slightest bit interested in Nathan. She turned once more to look at the man she adored. 'You're wasting your time, she's not available.' Julia got up and looked down at him. 'Clare's very choosy and she certainly wouldn't go for you.'

'Julia, darling! You're not going?' her cousin called across the room.

Julia shook her head. 'I'm really tired, Clare. I hope you don't mind?'

She came swiftly over. 'Of course not, sweetie. You go to bed.' She smiled. 'I'll try not to wake you when I come up.'

Julia swallowed her misery and disappointment. 'Oh, don't worry, I most probably won't be asleep.' She looked towards Nathan, whose eyes were on them both now.

Clare raised her eyebrows. 'Forget him Julia,' she mouthed. 'He's just another fucking bore.'

A small smile crossed Julia's face and she was temped to shout Clare's words across to Nathan. Instead she left them to it. 'See you in the morning, Clare.'

Julia did fall asleep, even with all the laughter going on downstairs. She snuggled up, wearing a silk nightdress of Clare's though it hadn't originally been her intention to wear anything in bed that night, then woke with a start. Clare was in the room. Julia screwed up her eyes to look at her wristwatch. It was three o'clock in the morning. Clare turned out the light and slid beneath the satin covered duvet. 'You all right, Julia?' she asked.

She turned to look at her cousin. 'I'm fine. Did you have a good time?'

Clare gave her tinkling laugh. 'The usual.'

'Do these people often stay with you?'

'Hmmm, I suppose.'

Julia turned on to her side, her back to Clare. 'Your life is one long party.'

Clare didn't reply to that, commenting only, 'I hear you got the shop.'

Julia twisted round quickly. 'Did Nathan tell you that?'

Clare raised one hand from beneath the duvet and squeezed her cousin's shoulder. 'Yes, he did, but I wasn't prying.'

Julia turned right round and moved closer to her. 'Oh, Clare, I know you weren't. It's just . . . well, it's all gone so wrong.' She peered hard in the gloomy light and suddenly felt a strong desire to talk. 'I've got this . . . thing, you see, for Nathan. I suppose you've guessed? I'm actually quite, well, crazy about him. And tonight, it was all going to happen . . . until he saw you. It was you he wanted, *you* not me.'

Clare was silent for a while. Still with her hand touching Julia's shoulder, she whispered, 'Are you sure? I didn't realise.'

Julia twisted on to her back and looked up at the ceiling. 'No, I don't suppose you did.'

'Why do you say that?'

Julia looked at her cousin. The whites of Clare's eyes were visible in the dark. 'I know you, and you don't seem at all interested in having affairs. Your life is about people in general, society, deprived children, and all that jazz.'

Clare laughed. 'And you. You're very important to me, Julia. You must know how much I care about you?'

'Oh, Clare.' She snuggled closer to her cousin, and was surprised to find her naked. She shifted away slightly. 'Your friendship is everything to me. I trust you so much. I knew you wouldn't go with Nathan tonight.'

Clare snorted softly. 'But only because I didn't want to, Julia. Don't go turning me into a saint.'

'I know you're no saint.' Julia smiled. 'But you're very . . . refined.'

Clare guffawed into the sheets. 'Rubbish! And I swear like a trooper! You're always telling me off for swearing.'

'Swearing's got nothing to do with it.'

'Oh, what has?'

'You, Clare! *You* and your . . . ways.'

'Which are?'

Julia hesitated. 'Exceptional, I suppose.'

Clare moved fractionally closer to her cousin. She raised herself slightly, and put a hand to Julia's face. Tenderly, she caressed her forehead and ran her fingers through her hair. The effect was stimulating and soothing, all at the same time. Shivers went through Julia's body. 'Would you like a massage?' Clare asked. 'To calm you down.'

'What do you mean?'

'Lie on your tummy and I'll massage your shoulders and neck. It's wonderful, Julia. It's about the only worthwhile thing Roger taught me.'

The thought of him made the whole thing seem all right. Julia did as she was told. She lowered the satin straps of her nightdress and turned on to her stomach, resting her arms on the pillow. Clare knelt beside her cousin and very gently brushed aside her hair. Her hands began to glide across Julia's back and shoulders and then up towards her neck and even futher into her scalp. The gentle massage continued for several minutes, gradually gathering strength as Clare pressed her palms and fingers into Julia's flesh, kneading and stoking and pummelling. Julia began to luxuriate in the sensation. It was as though the cares of the evening were about to drift away.

But just as consciousness began to leave her, it was rudely restored. Julia realised that her cousin was now massaging her with only one hand. The other hand was otherwise occupied elsewhere. Where became all too clear as Clare began to writhe upon the bed. Julia jerked her head up from the pillow and turned towards her cousin. Even in the dim light, she could see the rapture in her eyes. Repelled, she looked down at Clare's fingers working in circles between her own legs, stimulating herself.

'Clare!'

Instantly, her senses were restored. She moved her hand away from herself and put out both hands to cup Julia's face. She could smell her cousin and was sickened but felt unable to move a muscle. In slow motion, Clare lowered her face to Julia's and kissed her tenderly on the mouth, flicking her tongue between her lips. 'I want you, Julia. I've wanted you for so long.'

With all of her strength, Julia shoved her away and clambered off the bed. She stood and glared at her cousin, the nightdress bunched around her waist. Realising Clare was staring at her bare breasts, she pulled the top up to cover herself. *'How could you? How could you, Clare?'*

She closed her eyes and slumped into a heap, covering her face with her hands. 'Oh, fucking hell, Julia! I'm *so* sorry.' She looked up again. 'I really thought you . . . cared?'

'Cared? What's caring got to do with what *you* just did?'

'But I thought you knew?'

Julia screamed, *'Knew what?'* and then jumped as her cousin loudly shushed her with a forefinger to her mouth. *'Knew what?'* she hissed again. 'That you're *queer*? Is that what you thought I knew?'

Clare was practically pleading from the bed. 'No! Please, Julia, please! Don't look at me like that. I'm sorry, I'm sorry . . . I really thought you'd guessed about me. I *do* like women, but that doesn't necessarily make me queer because I like men as well. Julia, please, it won't happen again, I can promise you that . . . it'll never happen again.'

She turned and groped about for something to wrap herself in. She grabbed Clare's dressing gown and hastily put it on. Lowering her voice, she uttered, 'Too true it won't happen again. And for your information, Clare, I didn't guess anything. I didn't even have the vaguest suspicion, because if I had, there is *no way* I would have climbed into that bed with you tonight.' She walked to the door and opened it. Not looking back, she declared, 'I am not a lesbian, Clare, and I never have been.' Then slammed the door and went downstairs.

She walked into the sitting room and slumped on to the leather settee, curling up and wrapping her arms protectively around herself. The room smelt disgusting. Pot, stale cigarette smoke and alcohol fumes. Julia felt even sicker then she started to shiver in shock. She shuffled off the settee and over to the fireplace. Although it was August she suspected the fire would be laid. It was. She reached up on to the mantel piece and grabbed some matches. Within minutes the fire was blazing.

Julia huddled in front of it, allowing the heat to soothe her trembling body but not knowing quite what else to do. She thought of Nathan upstairs in the bedroom next to Clare's, and wondered if he'd heard anything. She supposed not. No doubt he'd drifted off into a deep sleep, bitterly upset because Clare hadn't succumbed to his charms. Julia hated him. It was all his fault this had happened.

Eventually, she curled up into a ball on the rug before the fire and fell asleep.

26

Julia woke with a start. The fire had gone out and she was cold, very cold. She looked at her wristwatch. Seven-thirty. Her head ached, throbbed in fact. She remembered the previous evening and tried to banish it from her mind, but memories pricked her like darts. The whites of Clare's eyes, the smell on her fingers. Her cousin, a *lesbian*! Now it all fitted. Her disdain of Roger, and no wonder Clare had always made such an enormous fuss of Julia. She wasn't interested in her *as a person*, not at all, just a body. A female body.

Julia eased herself from her position on the rug and stretched out. Her head cleared slightly. At least the shop was secured, just waiting for her to take control. And she needn't worry about Nathan fancying Clare anymore. She was a no-go area.

Julia left the drawing room and walked towards the stairs. She hesitated, pushing her hands through her dishevelled hair, then braced herself, deciding to go back to Clare's bedroom, take a shower, get dressed and leave. She wouldn't even bother to tell Nathan. Instead, she'd go and see Nick. He'd take her to Brick Lane. She could speak to Madhav, put in an order for the beginning of September, then inform Nathan on Monday of what she'd done. He didn't want to be involved, so from now on she'd make sure he wasn't.

With a heavy heart, she mounted the stairs. It was as she reached the very top that she thought she heard a small cry. Julia stopped in her tracks, her ears pricking. Nothing . . . she must have imagined it. She continued along the landing towards Clare's bedroom. The door was ajar. Almost timidly Julia walked in. But there was nobody there. The bed was empty. In fact, the room looked very much the same as it had the previous evening. The nightdress Julia had worn lay in the exact same spot on the floor. The satin bedding was pulled back untidily from the bed. Clare's outfit from the previous evening was slung over a chair. There was no sign of her.

And then Julia heard it. Unmistakably. The sound of a man groaning in pleasure. Nathan!

Compelled, she left Clare's bedroom and walked to the next room. The door was very firmly closed but Julia's hand moved instinctively to the door knob. She turned it and the door clicked and opened. Catching her breath, she stood quite still, waiting for some sort of objection or command. There was none. Just the obvious noises of a couple making love.

She pushed the door open and silently took a couple of paces forward. The single bed was directly in front of her, about six feet away, and Julia's eyes widened in disbelief. Nathan, face flushed and hair streaked with sweat, was vigorously thrusting himself into Clare. Julia's hands flew to her face and she gasped in horror.

Clare, hardly visible beneath the bedding and a naked Nathan, instantly turned towards her cousin. Her face crumpled. Nathan, halted at a crucial point in his love-making, screamed, '*Get out, Julia! For Christ's sake, get out!*'

Julia fled.

27

With her nose running and tears streaming down her wretched face, Julia pounded on the front door. 'You've got to be here, Nick! You've bloody got to be here!'

'All right! All right!' He shouted from inside. Weak with relief she unclenched her fists and ceased her pounding. Wearily, Julia leant against the heavy black-painted door of Nick's three-storey town house in Camden Street.

The simple task of opening his own front door seemed to take him forever. 'Julia?' he exclaimed finally. 'What on earth . . .?'

She didn't wait to be invited in but pushed her way past Nick and into his hallway. She dropped her bag on the floor and collapsed against the wall. 'Oh, Nick!' she exclaimed between sobs. 'Thank God you're here. Thank God you're here.' Then threw herself into his arms. A bemused Nick, clad only in a thin dressing gown, hugged her to him.

After a few seconds, he gently raised her face to his and smiled. 'Good Lord, Julia, you do look a sight.' He patted her cheek. 'Come on, sweetheart, through to the kitchen, I think you need a strong cup of tea.'

She allowed herself to be guided through to Nick's bachelor kitchen. It was at the back of the house, overlooking a compact walled garden. The early-morning sun streamed brightly through the window and immediately her mood lifted. Heaps of dirty crockery smothered the draining board and a long table positioned against the nearside wall was covered in more mugs and plates and packets of biscuits, cereal boxes, a half-empty bottle of milk, and several beer cans.

Nick pulled out a chair and shoved off Melvin, his blue Burmese cat. 'Sorry, Melve,' he said, pushing Julia into the seat instead. Drained, she sat down and Melvin sprang back on to her lap. Gratefully, she petted the animal, his loud purr soothing to her state of mind. With one arm, Nick shoved some of the debris further down the table. 'Excuse the mess,' he said. 'I haven't had a chance to clear up.'

Julia giggled, Nick always had that effect on her, but at the same time a sob caught in her throat. He ran his hand down the side of her face, leant forward and kissed the top of her head. 'I'll put the kettle on,' he said softly. She grabbed his hand in both of hers and held it tightly, looking up into his face. Nick knelt down. 'I'm always here for you, Julia. You know I'm your friend.'

She tugged at his hand. 'Well just at this moment, Nick, your friendship is what I need.' Even unshaven, and with his hair tousled from sleep, his handsome face was still arresting. He grinned and made for the kettle. 'Don't suppose you've got a cigarette?' she asked.

He pointed to the far end of the table. 'There's some there.'

Julia reached for them as though they were a lifeline. She hadn't had a cigarette all weekend because of Nathan. She lit up and inhaled deeply before twisting in her seat. 'Do you want one, Nick? I can't move because of the cat.'

He nodded, filled mugs with boiling water and tossed in two teabags. Then he put the mugs on the table and pulled out a chair next to her. Nick reached over to the half-empty bottle of milk, removed the silver top and sniffed the contents. He pulled a face but proceeded to tip some into both mugs. 'Sugar?' Julia shook her head. 'Now, fair maiden, who's been upsetting you?'

Julia sipped the scalding tea and drew heavily on her cigarette. 'I don't really know where to start,' she said softly. 'And I suppose you'll only tell me: *I told you so!*'

'Promise I won't.'

She smiled and swallowed hard. 'Did you know that Clare's a lesbian?' Nick blinked and looked surprised. Julia felt relieved. 'See? *You* didn't know either.'

'Hang on! Hang on!' He touched her hand. 'I didn't say I didn't know, I was just surprised by you asking the question.'

It was her turn to blink now. 'You mean, you *did* know?'

He gave a sort of half chuckle and waved his hand. 'You're making all this sound very cut and dried, Julia. Life isn't as simple

131

as that, and certainly Clare's sexuality isn't. I'd say she's finding her feet. At the moment, she's one confused lady.'

'So she might not even be a lesbian? It was just a try-out with me!' Julia's face began to pucker.

'Julia, sweetheart, come on, come on.' Nick wrapped his arm around her shoulders and squeezed her gently. 'I gather from this that Clare has made some sort of pass at you?'

Julia looked into his eyes. 'It was horrible, Nick. It was *disgusting*!'

'Disgusting?' He shook his head with a smile. 'No, Clare could never be disgusting. She didn't mean you any harm.'

Julia's eyes widened. 'You speak as though you know her very well, Nick. What exactly do you know?'

'Nothing.' he said firmly. 'We each live our own life. I let her get on with hers and she lets me get on with mine. That's how friendship works, Julia.'

'Except when a friend does something to offend.'

Nick shook his head. 'She wouldn't have meant to hurt you, Julia. Come on, *grow up*!'

'Grow up! Grow up?' Julia shoved the cat off her knee and stood up. 'I'll have you know, Nick bloody Fordham-Clarke, I've grown up all I ever want to over the last twelve hours. I've been seduced by Clare and then *coerced* into watching *her* fuck the man I love!'

Nick was on his feet in seconds with his hands on her shoulders. 'Julia, for God's sake, calm down. Nothing's as bad as it seems, sweetheart. Sit down, come on.' He pushed her towards the chair. Julia sat down again and Melvin looked up at her before jumping back on her knee.

'Just don't tell me to grow up, OK?'

'I'm sorry. I didn't mean it like that.' Still with his arm around her, Nick pushed his face against her hair. 'Sweetheart, you've had a shock. Why don't you start at the beginning and tell me the whole story?'

Julia did.

'But you must have had an inkling? I mean, she slept with Harry the night we went to Tramp.'

Julia looked astounded. 'Harry? Clare slept with Harry? You mean, Harry's a lesbian too?'

Nick drew on his cigarette and narrowed his eyes. 'Harry's like

Clare, just older and wiser. Like I said, Clare's finding her feet.'

'And it doesn't bother you?'

'Bother me? Why should it bother me?'

'Clare's married to your brother!'

Nick guffawed nastily. 'Well, *he* fucks around.'

Julia lowered her eyes, ashamed. 'And don't we?'

Nick stubbed out his cigarette and grabbed her hand. 'Well, if we do . . . don't complain about Clare.'

'I'm not complaining about her, I'm just surprised. Well, shocked.'

'I think you're more shocked because you found her in bed with the man you can't have.'

'Who says I can't have him?'

'You did.'

Julia smiled. Nick kissed her hand. 'He's a shit, I told you that before. He's not worthy of either of you. Forget him.' He sighed deeply. 'And as for Clare, she was upset because you rejected her, poor thing. She feels pain too. She can't help her genes. Imagine it, Julia, the desperation and the loneliness . . . I suspect she was paying you back.'

'Paying me back for something I didn't do?'

'No, paying you back because you rejected her.' He kissed her mouth. 'You're so lucky, Julia. You're so *absolute* in your sexuality. You know exactly what you want and how to get it. No man is left in any doubt.' He shrugged. 'And Clare – well, I don't suppose she's ever come close to what you've got. Do you?'

Julia was silent for a while. 'I thought she cared about me. I was wrong.'

'No, you weren't, you silly girl! She *does* care about you, she cares about you a lot. And she'll continue to care about you, if you let her. This is just a hitch in your friendship, don't let it destroy the whole thing.'

'But what about my plans? The shop? What shall I do now?'

'Go ahead. The deal hasn't been signed yet. Cut him out. Cut this *Nathan* chap right out.'

'But I'm under twenty-one, Nick, I can't sign the agreement.' She pulled her hand away from his. 'And anyway, you're missing one very important point. I haven't got any money. How can I go into business on my own?'

Nick reached across for his cigarettes. He opened the packet and offered another one to Julia. She took it. Nick lit both cigarettes and drew on his own. 'How much do you need?'

Julia gulped. 'Why?'

He gave her a sidelong smile. 'I'm not without means.'

She brightened for the first time that day. 'You mean, you'd help me? You'd be prepared to go in with me?'

He squeezed her shoulder. 'If the price is right. And we can come to some sort of business arrangement?' He winked.

Immediately she was on her mettle. 'What sort of business arrangement?'

'If I put up the money, we go for, say, a fifty-fifty split on all profits?'

It was more than Nathan had offered. Her brain clicked into gear. Who had told her: *Never negotiate a fifty-fifty deal*. She remembered – Nathan. 'You put up the money, *I do all the work*. How about sixty-forty?'

Nick grinned and kissed her cheek. 'Sixty-forty it is.'

For a Sunday morning, Brick Lane was buzzing. Nick parked his Ford Capri outside the Stick of Rock pub, down Bethnal Green Road, and together they walked back to Madhav's premises which weren't far down the ancient narrow road with its cramped and decaying buildings. Almost opposite Truman's Black Eagle Brewery, over blacked out windows you couldn't see through, a huge sign read *Madhav Ayasch & Co – International Importers & Suppliers, Top Quality Leather & Sheepskin Merchandise.*

Nick pushed open the shop door and allowed Julia to enter first. For such a bright summer's day, the inside was gloomy and the smell of leather immediately hit her nostrils. She remembered Anne's comment about the sweeter the smell, the better the tanning. The smell here was pungent! But it didn't matter, she was excited.

'Neek! Neek! My dear friend.' Madhav entered the room which was piled high with coats, boots and bags and countless cardboard boxes waiting to be shipped out. It appeared untidy and disorderly, but Julia suspected it wasn't. She'd had experience of people working this way before, and quite often their fingers knew exactly where to fly to find what they wanted. Madhav moved across the room, grinning like a short moustachioed Cheshire cat. 'And *Juulia.*' He held out his hand and welcomed her warmly. She was surprised he'd remembered her name. Madhav was clearly no fool.

'We're here to do business, Madhav. Big business ... with a promise of more.' Nick patted his friend's back. Julia jumped in quickly, anxious that Nick should not spoil things by acting in a superior fashion.

She took Madhav's arm and led him slightly away from Nick. 'I know exactly what I want, Madhav, but I need your expertise and guidance. Last time we met your daughter Sarayu. Is she here now?' Julia fished in her tote-bag and withdrew a pad of sketches she'd made. 'She showed me some coats in nappa leather with pin-tucks?' Julia pointed to one of her sketches. 'A bit like this? And tooled bags, not unlike this. And suede-fringed skirts . . .' Julia flicked over a page '. . . similar to this?'

Madhav looked with interest at her designs. She'd used the basic idea of what she'd seen here but given the designs some clever twists of her own. He was impressed. He'd never thought of cutting on the cross in such a way, especially with leather and suede stitched together. He raised one finger in the air. 'Sarayu? Yes, yes. You come through. I show you Sarayu and she show you what you want. Follow me, follow me.'

Madhav's premises seemed to stretch back forever. They finally reached a cramped room where four antiquated leather-sewing machines hummed away with members of Madhav's family concentrating diligently over them. Suede and leather garments in unusual colours adorned the work surfaces. Julia's eyes were riveted to the scene. Although it appeared Dickensian in some respects, it was also ahead of its time. She had never seen craftspeople work with leather like this and was fired with enthusiasm.

'Sarayu! Sarayu!' demanded Madhav. 'Come to speak. Come, come!' Madhav's beautiful daughter, wearing a pale yellow sari, left the cluttered table where she was cutting leather to perfect size and did as she was bidden. 'Mrs *Juu*-lia wishes to speak.'

'Miss, actually,' Julia said before smiling at the girl. 'Sarayu, I want to place a big order. I want you to make me lots of way out and wonderful clothes.' She thrust her sketch pad in front of Sarayu who flicked through it, her face lighting up with each new page. 'This is just the start, Sarayu, my head is full of ideas. I want *one* of everything, in assorted colours of course, but *nothing* must be duplicated.'

Sarayu beamed at Julia. 'I remember you.' She tapped her forehead. 'Chiswick? Chelsea? You from Chelsea, yeah? You got a shop down the King's Road?'

135

Her accent was strictly East End where her father's was Pakistani but they seemed equally astute when it came to remembering a face. 'Not yet. I think that might have been wishful thinking the last time we met. But I will have and I aim to use your stuff.' Julia saw the interest in the other girl's and her mind started to work overtime. Sarayu was a young Londoner, hip to the scene. 'Hey, you wouldn't fancy a job, would you?'

Sarayu's eyes nearly popped out. 'You serious?'

From nowhere, Madhav appeared. 'Sarayu work for me. Sorry and all that.'

Julia turned to Nick who gave her one of his winks. 'Come on, Madhav, it wouldn't hurt to have a member of the family where it's at.'

Sarayu's eyes were pleading. She implored her father who adamantly shook his head. Sarayu turned back to Julia. 'You'd want me? Really?'

'Only if your father agrees.' Julia moved closer to him. 'You can come and inspect my new shop, Madhav, and I'd pay Sarayu well.' She tapped his shoulder. 'And I have one other *major* request.'

His nostrils flared suspiciously. 'Yes?'

Julia realised how to handle him. Business before *everything*. 'I borrow her name.'

'My name?' Sarayu interrupted.

'Yes, *Sarayu*. To go above my shop in Chelsea.' Julia turned to Nick who grinned. 'It's great, don't you think?'

Madhav was flattered. He lowered his eyes and shook his head thoughtfully before looking up at her again and nodding vigorously. 'This shop? You just bought?'

Julia nodded too. 'Something like that.'

'We come in? We join you?'

Julia's eyes flashed to Nick for guidance. He pursed his lips and cupped his chin in his hand. With a smile, he opened his forefinger and thumb a fraction. 'A little bit, Madhav, you can come in a little bit. Say . . . ten percent?'

Madhav was a changed man. 'We do good business! The best! The very best! Sarayu, get your coat on this instant. We must see this new shop. Come on, girl, get moving. There is no time to waste.'

28

Things were moving fast. Madhav, who'd now extended his work-force, was busily churning out the merchandise: softest lined and unlined nappa leather coats and jackets with pintuck detail; several pert sheepskin jackets in pale pink, oatmeal and olive green; hide leather coats and jackets in every colour imaginable; fringed, studded or beaded belts, suede skirts and long waistcoats with deep pockets; snazzy suede or leather gloves; suede cowboy-type hats; leather or suede beaded head and wrist bands; tooled handbags; beaded and fringed handbags, tote-bags, swing bags; the softest, long, snug-fitting, suede or leather boots, imported from Pakistan; and umbrellas and silk scarves also imported from family connec-tions of Madhav's. Everything bore the same label: *Sarayu of Chel-sea*. And Sarayu herself was proving to be quite an asset. Like her family, she believed in working very, very hard.

Mr Denton-Smythe had kept his promise. The floorboards had been made good, a new loo had been fitted next to the staff room at the very rear of the building, and the whole shop had been painted canary yellow, along with the two fitting-rooms. Julia had arranged for a dark-brown hessian-covered board to be fitted against one of the walls. Accessories were displayed on this. Deep shelving and large mirrors were everywhere, in any available space, the mirrors making the shop seem twice its size.

By the time the merchandise started to arrive, and had been priced up and displayed, either on coat-hangers on various racks around the room or on shelves, Julia was exhausted. They were opening the following week and she still hadn't found anywhere to live.

Nick had offered her a bed for as long as she wanted, but being his friend and business partner was one thing, living with him quite another. He was slob, for a start. His house resembled a tip! Although he had a cleaner twice a week, keeping abreast of his mess was a full-time job in itself. As fond of him as Julia was, his way of life did not appeal.

'I just wish we could have stocked Purley's jewellery,' she moaned to Sarayu.

'Who's Purley's?'

'Oh, just a place I worked in Cambridge.' Julia was fond of Sarayu, but a confidant she was not.

'Well, ask them. They can only say no.'

Julia smiled. She already had. She'd very politely rung Nathan on the Monday after their disastrous weekend to hand in her notice. He'd been perfectly understanding, assuring her she needn't worry about working out her notice, and wishing her luck with the new shop. He'd even told her to stay in touch. But when she'd asked about the possibility of selling his jewellery, he'd said, very firmly. '*No!*' Unfortunately, she'd found nothing else to touch it, and she knew jewellery would be another way to lure customers into her shop. She intended to keep looking for another supplier.

It was six o'clock in the evening when Julia wandered outside with Sarayu. It was chilly, and she wrapped her arms around herself. Sarayu, out of her sari and into cotton trousers and a t-shirt, did the same. Strains of *Close to You*, by the Carpenters came from inside the shop where music played continually. Together they looked up at their new round sign, suspended on chains and hanging just above the shop door. With the paint still wet, in gold letters on a cream background, it read: *Sarayu Boutique*, with their address and phone number underneath. A shrill ringing came from inside the shop. Julia darted inside and raced across to the small oval counter at the back of the shop. She snatched up the phone. 'Sarayu! Julia speaking, can I help?'

There was a silence, and then a small cough. Julia recognised it at once. 'Clare . . . is that you?'

'Hallo, Julia.' Clare's voice sounded weak and hesitant. 'Yes, it's me. Er, Nick's been in touch . . . I hear the shop's looking good. I just wanted to say, good luck!'

Julia's heart was pounding fast. She'd done a lot of thinking about her cousin. Some very deep soul-searching. In a way, Clare had paid her back for her own indiscretions with Roger. But he hadn't broken Clare's heart, even though she'd caught him red-handed with his secretary. Nathan Purley had certainly broken Julia's. Even now, she couldn't forget the expression on his face as he'd made love to Clare. But Julia decided to sound nonchalant. 'Well, it's lovely to hear from you. I'm pleased you've rung.'

'Really? That's nice . . . You're not angry with me anymore?'

'Angry? . . . No, that's not how I'd describe my feelings for you.'

'Well, that's good, because I bloody miss you, Julia. Why don't you come round?'

She looked at her watch. 'When?'

'Whenever you like.'

'I could come now?'

Clare laughed, and Julia sensed a release of tension in the sound. 'Now would be great. I'm so looking forward to seeing you.'

'Fifteen minutes, OK?'

'I'll be here.'

Julia turned to Sarayu who was now standing just inside the shop. 'That was my cousin. Have I told you about her? Her name's Clare and she lives in Chiswick. I'm going round to see her now. We'd better lock up and turn the music off. I'll see you back here in the morning, Sarayu. You'll be bringing more stock?'

She nodded and said wistfully. 'I wish I lived in Chiswick.'

Julia smiled and tapped her on the shoulder. 'So do I, Sarayu. So do I.'

29

A very pale and wan-looking Clare opened the front door. Julia was surprised. She had never looked ill in the past. Julia followed her through to the kitchen.

'Coffee? Tea? Wine?'

Julia grinned. 'A glass of wine would be rather wonderful.'

Clare turned to the vast larder fridge. She pulled open the door and withdrew a bottle of Montrachet. The wine had been previously opened so she pulled out the cork and filled two glasses to the brim, handing one to Julia.

'To you, cousin. To your good health and success. You deserve to succeed.'

Julia raised her glass and clinked it against Clare's. 'Thank you, that's kind.'

Clare slumped down in a chair by the table. Julia sat down next to her. She put her hand on top of Clare's and deliberately kept it there, determined to bury the ghost between them. 'What's wrong? Aren't you feeling well?'

Clare looked at her cousin then shot up from her seat and raced across the kitchen to the sink where she retched and retched, her whole body heaving as she did so.

'Clare!' Julia hastened after her. 'What on earth is wrong?'

She turned on the tap and swilled away her vomit, then rinsed her own mouth. Wiping it on a tea-towel, she turned to face her cousin and grimaced. 'Can't you guess?' Then turned back again and retched once more. Julia put her hands very tenderly on Clare's shoulders. She collapsed on to her elbows with her head still in the sink. 'I suppose you're going to say this serves me *fucking* right!'

Julia dropped her hands to her sides, her mind spinning with this new revelation. Clare was pregnant with Nathan's baby. Was he always going to come between them? 'I would never say that, Clare. I care about you too much.'

She turned round sharply, wiping her mouth on the tea-towel again. 'Do you? Do you really?'

Julia wrapped her arms around her cousin because it seemed the right thing to do. She would bury the hatchet once and for all. Still holding her tightly, she leant back and grinned. 'We've come a long way, you and me. I understand you now, Clare, and I hope you understand me.' She lowered her eyes. 'Nick put me right about a lot of things. He told me to grow up. I didn't like it at first but, well, I have grown up in the last few weeks and I'm getting my priorities sorted. *You're* one of them.'

Clare shifted closer and put her tired head on Julia's shoulder. 'And you're not frightened of me anymore?'

'Oh, Clare! I've never been frightened of you. It was a misunderstanding. It won't happen again.'

'And you can't know how much I wish it had never happened in the first place. I'm bloody well paying for my mistake now!' She turned back to the sink as though to retch again. Julia decided to move back to the table where she took a sip of her wine.

Clare finally joined her, and with an ashen face sat down and sipped her own drink. 'I shouldn't really be having this, but it's about the only thing I can keep down.'

Julia laughed. 'Good old Clare, pregnant in style! Most people fancy pickled onions or rice pudding on toast. You fancy Montrachet.'

Clare managed a smile. 'Well, I can't help the way I'm made.'

There was silence while Julia struggled to find the right reply. 'You've no need to help the way you're made, Clare. I think you're fine as you are.'

'Do you? Do you really? After what I put you through?'

'You didn't put me through anything. It was all my own silly fault.' She touched her cousin's hand. 'This baby . . . I presume it's Nathan's?'

Clare closed her eyes and sighed deeply. 'Who else?' She chuckled. 'I don't make a habit of sleeping with strange *men*!'

'But how? Aren't you on the pill?'

Clare took another sip of wine. 'I was. Of course I was. But when I left Cambridge, there seemed no need anymore. I wasn't sleeping with Roger. I wasn't sleeping with anybody, or at least nobody who could impregnate me, so it seemed stupid to stay on the pill.'

'What will Roger say?'

Clare laughed cynically. 'Ah, well, as luck would have it, he came to see me about a month ago. The tongues had started to wag because I didn't go back to Cambridge for the summer holidays. Anyway, after a lot of mumbling and prevaricating, he suggested we get a divorce. Kind of him, don't you think? He says I can sue him for adultery and he'll make me a generous settlement. I can keep this house and my car and whatever money I have left in the bank, and he'll pay me another ten thousand.'

'All this and ten thousand? Cor, you lucky thing!'

Clare shook her head. 'No, not really, Julia. He's getting off lightly. He's loaded.'

Julia frowned. 'Why does he want a divorce? I mean, he adores you.'

Clare ran both hands through her hair. 'I think he's found somebody else. And I think she might be in the same predicament as me.'

Julia gave a nervous giggle. 'Will he find out about you? Being pregnant, I mean?'

Clare shrugged. 'He's bound to, in the end.'

'So . . . you're going to keep it?'

Clare blinked and frowned. 'Of course I'm keeping it. If it decides to keep me, that is.' She narrowed her eyes. 'I'm not into abortion, you know, Julia. I'm not that much of a hypocrite.'

She looked down at her feet. 'No, of course you're not.' She raised her eyes, her heart thumping madly. 'And Nathan? Does he know?'

Clare laughed. 'Not yet. But he soon will.'

Julia had to ask. 'Will you marry him?'

Clare laughed again, tersely. 'You're joking.' She peered at her cousin. 'I will *never* marry again, Julia. Like I say, I'm not that much of a hypocrite.'

'But Nathan might persuade you. He likes you a lot.'

'Rubbish! He liked what he saw.' Clare glared at her. 'He doesn't like *me*. Not the real me. He liked a vision, that's all.'

'Has he been in touch?'

Clare screwed up her face. 'Yes, he has. I soon put him off.' She took another sip of wine. 'But I'll tell you one thing, Julia, he was pretty pissed off about you.'

Her heart lurched. 'Was he? Was he really?'

'Oh, yes. He wanted to know all about Nick, and was pretty damned mad when I told him you'd gone into business together.'

'Serves him right.'

Clare laughed and nudged her cousin. 'Treating us like he did.'

Julia hesitated. 'So, when will you tell him? About the baby, I mean?'

Clare took a deep breath and looked at her cousin. 'When I need the first instalment, I suppose. He won't get off lightly, I can promise you that. He's rich, isn't he? I aim to make him pay for his mistake.'

Julia flinched, unsure of her feelings. Part of her wanted to see Nathan getting his comeuppance, and another part thought her cousin was being unfair. 'He's much wiser than you might think, Clare.'

'Oh, yes, Julia.' She grinned. 'But when he realises what a sweet little innocent he's got into trouble, whose husband has abandoned her for being a naughty girl, and who's about to live on a shoestring *with his baby*, he'll cough up, you can be sure.' She threw back her head and laughed.

Julia cringed at her cousin's opinion of the man she still loved. 'And college? What will you do about that?'

Clare's eyes glowed with determination now. 'Continue, of course. Oh, don't worry, Julia, I don't intend to give up my degree.' She thumped her fist on the table, making the wine swirl about in the glasses. 'I might have screwed up a lot of things, but I certainly won't screw up my work.' She looked rather smug. 'The college wants me to consider doing an MA when I finish, but I aim to get straight into work and on with my PhD. I figure I can do that in my spare time.' Clare took a swig of her wine and looked at her cousin. 'I shall be a doctor, Julia, that's my aim.' She rubbed her stomach. 'And this little bundle will just have to fit in with that!'

30

September, 1970

Roberta struggled to pull weeds from the heavy clay soil around Blackthorn Cottage. She bent forward, her enormous stomach getting in the way, and tugged at a dandelion. The leaves broke off in her hands and she fell backwards. 'Damn!'

'Robbie?'

She turned, seeing Ed walking towards her. He was home and she was glad. At least there'd be somebody to talk to poor Kit, stuck there in the office by himself. Roberta couldn't bear him to see her looking like this. She was huge and the baby was late, a full fourteen days, and now she waddled like a duck and felt as attractive as a rhinoceros! Not that Kit looked at her any differently, on the odd occasions when she allowed him a glimpse, but she certainly felt conspicuous and inclined to hide herself away.

'What are you doing, Robbie? You shouldn't be out here like this.'

She struggled to stand up and put her hand to the small of her back. 'I'm all right. I can't sit around all day doing nothing, Ed. And perhaps a little exercise will get this lazy baby on its way.'

'If it's exercise you want, you could help Kit in the office.'

'That's not exercise. And you know I hate him seeing me like this.'

'But you look beautiful. I've never seen you look so well.'

'Beautiful? Huh! Really, Ed, I shall never believe you again when you pay me a compliment.'

He hugged his wife, and ran his hand over her stomach. 'Oooh, I just felt him kick. It's a boy, y'know, obviously going to be a footballer.'

144

She rested her head against his broad shoulder, and allowed his hand to roam over her distended stomach. 'D'you fancy a cup of tea?'

'That sounds good, but I must go and see Kit first. Any chance of you bringing it through?'

'I'd rather you fetched it, Ed. It'll be ready in five minutes.'

He smiled at her understandingly and walked back towards the house.

'I think she finds her size embarrassing, Kit. I know it doesn't make any difference to you, but these women don't think the same way as us.' Ed shrugged. 'I'll go and get the tea, be back in a minute.'

Kit watched him leave the office and put his pencil in his mouth. He rattled it against his teeth, thinking that for the last couple of weeks he'd hardly spoken to Roberta. He missed her like crazy, and she was silly to think her size mattered a jot to him. But if that was the way she wanted to play it, then he was happy to stay out of her way.

Ed was back in seconds. 'I'm afraid you're going to have to make your own tea, Kit. It looks as though the gardening did the trick.' He winked. 'Wish us luck!'

Kit smiled back and wondered whether he should get up and go and see Roberta. He decided against it. Within seconds, Ed and Roberta were walking past the office door. ''Bye, Kit, see you soon.'

He walked to the door and watched Roberta being bundled out by a solicitous Ed. She didn't look back but called out, ''Bye, Kit. Look after Boris for me.'

'Of course, Roberta. Take care.'

Kit walked back to the office and sat down at his drawing board, felling strangely sad. He couldn't be part of this most important event in her life. Her first child. He swallowed hard and shrugged. He picked up his pencil once more but for the rest of the day found it impossible to work.

31

'Push, Roberta! Push!'

With her legs splayed out, and Ed tightly holding her hand, Roberta pushed for all she was worth. The midwife paused and ran a hand across her own sweaty forehead. She placed a small black tubular heart monitor on to Roberta's stomach and put her ear against its lip to listen to the baby's heartbeat. 'Come on, Roberta. With the next contraction, give a really big push. We've got to get baby born – baby's ready to be born.'

'I'm trying, I'm trying! I can't push anymore.'

Ed ran a hand over his wife's cheek. 'Yes, you can, Robbie. Just one more really big push.'

'Oh, no, it's coming again! Oh, no, I can't bear this!'

The midwife inserted her fingers into Roberta. 'Come on, Robbie. Now a few short pants, and push when I say so. Pant, keep panting . . . now *push*!'

Roberta tried and she tried for all she was worth. The midwife moved swiftly round the bed and listened to the baby's heartbeat once more. She squeezed Roberta's shoulder and raised her eyebrows at Ed. 'I'll be back in a minute, love. Do as the nurse says. When you feel the next contraction, you pant and then you push.'

The midwife nodded at the young nurse at the foot of the bed. 'Call me if you need me. I'm going to fetch Dr Emerson.'

Roberta looked up from her pillows, feeling another wave of contractions coming on. 'Why? Why is she . . . oh, no, Ed . . . *this is horrible*!'

She tried again, but in vain. Roberta was so tired, and the pain was just too much. Why didn't somebody put her out of her misery? 'Ed? What's happening? Where has the midwife gone?'

He looked down the bed at the nurse, who slowly nodded her head. With worry furrowing his brow, he kissed his wife on the cheek. 'She's gone to get the doctor, darling. I think he's going to help. There's nothing to worry about, it won't be much longer now.'

'It's not dead, is it, Ed? The baby's not dead?'

The nurse moved up from the foot of the bed. 'Of course baby's not dead, but his little heart is slowing down. He's tired, like you, so the doctor will help him to be born. There's nothing for you to worry about.'

It seemed forever, but eventually the doctor arrived, bustling in and listening to the baby's heartbeat.

'Right, Mrs Matthews . . . Roberta.' He smiled at her, then looked at Ed. 'And Mr Matthews. I'm taking your wife into theatre. It won't be long now.'

With that she was wheeled away, leaving a confused Ed behind, pulling of his mask.

She remembered the lights in the ceiling and having her ankles strapped up in stirrups. The doctor was now gowned up completely, with forceps in one hand and a scalpel in the other. 'I'm just going to help your baby be born, Roberta. Just a little cut here . . .'

She felt a sharp sting, and then cold metal being inserted, but she didn't care about the pain anymore. She felt enormous relief that at last it was all going to be over. And then she screamed, *'Oh, my God!'* It was as though her insides were being pulled away. She barely had the strength to grip the side of the bed. It seemed to take forever.

'It's a boy! Look at that. My goodness, what a big chap.'

Relieved beyond measure, with her ankles released but too weak to raise her head, Roberta watched as they took him over to the far corner of the room. They were wiping and sponging him and clipping off the placenta. Checking him out.

In a weak voice, she cried out, 'He is alive? He is all right?'

She heard her baby's first cry. Weak at first, but slowly gathering strength. 'He's fine, Roberta. And he's a whopper! He weighs nine and half pounds. Have you got a name?'

'Yes, James.' And then she was cradling him, wrapped in a white blanket, and he snuggled into her arms and blinked against the bright lights. Around his wrist was a plastic name tag, with his date of birth, weight and name written upon it. She fingered this as tears ran down her face and she looked for the first time at her son.

'Hallo, James. Hallo, darling. We made it . . . in the end. Wait 'til your daddy sees you.'

And then she counted his ten fingers and ten little toes.

32

The maternity ward in Newmarket General Hospital was packed. Roberta was at the far end of the room, her father peering lovingly into James's cot at the bottom of her bed.

'He's waking up, Rob. See? He's opening his eyes.' Gordon turned to look at his daughter, pleased as punch with his new grandson. 'Hallo, little chap, what'cha doing then? Are you gonna say hallo to your old grandpa?' He grinned at Roberta. 'He looks like you, Rob, look, see? His little nose and, hey, look at those eyes.'

'Thanks, Dad. I'm flattered you think I look like Winston Churchill.'

'Winston Churchill! Whoever told you that?'

'One of the nurses, actually. She said James was a cross between Winston Churchill and Hattie Jacques.'

'What?' Gordon allowed the baby to grab his finger. 'What an insult. If I were you, little Jamie, I'd tell that nurse where to go. One of these days, you'll have all the girls in Newmarket chasing after you, won't you?' Again, Gordon looked at his daughter. 'Can I pick him up? He's fully awake now.'

Roberta smiled. ' 'Course you can, Dad.'

Very carefully, Gordon picked up James from his cot. He cradled him lovingly and walked towards his daughter to sit down on the bed. She winced. 'Oh, sorry, love. You all right?'

'Yes, it's okay. It's just these stitches. They're starting to pinch.'

'Well, he was a big chap, wasn't he? Look at him, he looks three months old already.'

James started to whimper. Gordon frowned, then looked worried and his eyes wandered to his daughter. 'I think perhaps you'd better take him, Roberta. I can see he doesn't think too much of me.'

She laughed. 'Well, he will do when he's older and rides out with you on the Heath.'

Very gently, Gordon handed his grandson to Roberta. She allowed the baby to nuzzle into her neck. 'I think he wants feeding again.' She put her finger into his mouth and he sucked on it. 'He's so greedy.'

'He's a big chap. He's likely to be.' Gordon squeezed her shoulder. 'Would you like me to go?'

'No, of course not. I'm not going to feed him again just yet. I'll wait. He's all right, he enjoys sucking my finger.'

Gordon pondered a while, eyes glowing with pride. 'Do you know what I'd like, Roberta? What I'd like better than anything else in the world? I'd like to buy that little chap a pony one day, give him the one thing I know most about.'

Roberta held out her hand, and her father grabbed it. 'Oh, Dad. Just give him your love, that's all he could ever want.'

'That's all he'll ever get, I'm afraid. I sometimes think I've been rich in my family, so I can't expect to be rich in anything else.'

Roberta looked at him and felt a lump rise in her throat. Then her eyes wandered further down the ward, to the double doors leading out into the corridor. Standing with one thumb caught in his pocket was Kit. Her heart leapt.

Seeing the look in her eyes, Gordon turned. 'Oh, it's Kit.'

Roberta shifted herself slightly, and ran her hand across her hair. 'I must look a sight?'

Gordon looked at his daughter. 'You've never looked more beautiful, Roberta. And, if I know Kit, he won't argue with that.'

Self-consciously, Kit approached. He carried in his hand a small fluffy elephant. As he came nearer. Roberta felt tears prick the back of her eyes. 'Kit, how lovely to see you.' He bent down and kissed her on the cheek, breathing in her mother and baby aroma, then peered closely at James.

'Handsome chap.' Very tenderly, he pushed one finger into James's hand and the baby gripped it. 'His skin feels like velvet, Roberta.' With pride, she looked down at her son.

Kit turned to face Gordon, who'd moved to the other side of the bed. 'Hallo, Gordon, and what does it feel like to be a grandfather?'

He nodded, with a wide smile on his face. 'Wonderful, Kit. I can't tell you how proud I feel.'

Kit looked down at the baby again, and then allowed his eyes to wander over Roberta's face. At that precise moment, he loved her more than he could bear. He gulped and moved away slightly, looking out of the window. He still held the elephant in his hand.

Gordon quipped, 'Who's that for? Roberta or James?'

Kit turned round with a smile. 'You, actually, Gordon. I thought it'd make a change from horses.' He held up the bright blue elephant. 'I chose the colour with care.'

Gordon chuckled. He and Kit always had a bit of banter going. He looked at his daughter again. 'Well, I must be getting back. I'll pop in again this evening with your mum. Look after yourself, love.' He kissed Roberta's cheek, then the top of his grandson's head. 'You be good, now, James. None of this messing your mother about. You'll have me to answer to if you do.'

' 'Bye, Dad. And thanks for coming.'

Gordon moved to the end of the bed and pointed at his daughter. 'You try stopping me. I aim to watch my grandson grow, every inch of the way.'

Kit and Roberta watched him leaving the ward. Kit sat on the bed then, not noticing her wince. He took Roberta's hand. She looked furtively around, so he dropped it again. 'I love you, Roberta, in case you've forgotten.'

She gulped and looked down at her son. Then she raised her eyes. 'I have so much love in my heart at the moment, Kit.'

He looked hurt. 'And there's not exactly room for me?'

She shifted James slightly into a more comfortable position. 'My love for you is like a shadow, it follows me everywhere.'

He put the elephant on the bed and reached into the inside pocket of his blouson leather jacket. He pulled out a package and handed it to her. 'For you, with my love.'

She looked surprised. 'Oh, thanks, Kit. What is it?'

'Open it and see.'

'Well, I can't at the moment. You open it for me.'

Kit shifted off the bed and put his hands either side of the baby. 'No, I'll take James. You open your present.' With surprising adeptness, Kit lifted the baby away from Roberta then held him in exactly the same way as she had been doing, with James's head against his shoulder. 'Hallo, James, I'm Kit. You'll be seeing a lot of me in the future, so you'd better behave.' He put his finger into the baby's mouth and James, who so far hadn't made a peep, sucked on it.

Roberta tore away the wrapping from the rectangular box. 'Perfume. How lovely!'

Kit sat down on the bed again. 'You've no idea the trouble I went to to buy you that. I bought it in Cambridge, Joshua Taylor's, and described you to the girl. She ended up spraying every inch of both of my wrists and hands in different scents. I can't tell you the strange looks I got when I walked back to my car.' Roberta giggled and pulled the filigree gold-encased bottle from the box. 'Anyway, I chose that one because it was the nearest to your natural smell.'

'My natural smell? I didn't know I had a natural smell.'

Kit blushed slightly. 'Well, perhaps it's my nose, but I'm turned on by the way you smell.'

Roberta's eyes flickered but she ignored the remark and sprayed some of the scent on her wrist. She sniffed it. 'Hmmm, it's different.' She rubbed her wrist with her fingers, then smelt it again. 'Yes, Kit, I like this.' She looked at the name. 'Parure by Guerlain. I've never heard of it before.'

He smiled at her. 'Wear it and remember me.'

James started to whimper, and Kit handed him back to his mother. 'I won't need perfume to remember you, Kit. You'll be in my heart forever.'

33

November, 1970

Nancy seemed tetchy, definitely out of sorts. Brenda couldn't really understand why. She'd tried not to gloat too much about her eight-week-old grandson, Jamie. She'd mentioned him just once or twice, it was hard not to, he was such a lovely little chap. Being a grandmother was such an added bonus, it had taken Brenda quite by surprise. She couldn't wait to get round to Blackthorn Cottage and see him again. Roberta as well, of course, who was proving to be a marvellous mother. And Ed, who adored his son. Brenda even enjoyed seeing Kit, who always seemed to be somewhere in the background and doted on the baby.

'What's up, Nance? You seem upset?'

Nancy, still wearing her classic Burberry trenchcoat neatly buttoned up, sat stiffly. She tapped her red fingernails on the table and pushed aside her half-eaten chocolate eclair. 'Well, to be honest with you, Brenda, I am upset. Very.'

Brenda gulped. Why did she have the feeling this was going to have something to do with her? 'Not something I've done, I hope?'

Nancy sighed heavily. She pursed her lips together. Brenda dearly wanted to say, 'You shouldn't do that, Nance, it only makes the lines around your mouth deepen.'

'Not exactly.' her sister scoffed.

Brenda frowned. 'Well what, then?'

Nancy tapped her fingers louder. 'Julia.'

Brenda looked surprised. 'Julia?'

'Yes, *Julia*!'

There was a pause. 'Oh, you mean . . . because she's temporarily moved in with Clare?'

Nancy's eyes nearly popped out of her head. 'Has she? Since when?'

Oh, lummie! thought Brenda, and shrugged defensively. 'Oh, I don't know. She doesn't exactly keep me informed. But she's paying her way.'

Nancy leant across the table. 'And that's not *all* she's doing.'

Brenda frowned again. What was she on about? 'I really don't know what you're talking about, you're going to have to explain?'

'Well, if you let me get a word in edgeways, instead of rambling on and on about your precious grandson, I *will*!'

Nancy shifted in her seat and clasped her hands in front of her. She took a deep breath. 'My Clare has always been a shy girl. You know that, Brenda, she's a girl not used to the wicked ways of the world.' She lowered her eyes and hesitated, as though she really did believe her daughter was beyond reproach. 'Anyway, she married Roger when she was very young and, well, naive, I suppose. And she's still naive. Very!' Nancy's eyes stared at her sister, insisting her daughter's purity must never be doubted. 'But her naivity was surpassed by her brilliance. The poor lamb went to London to get a degree, and now her whole world has been turned upside down.'

Brenda swallowed hard. What on earth was Nancy on about? 'What's happened then?'

'She's getting a divorce, that's what's happened. It's already filed.' Nancy's face crumpled as though she was about to cry. 'She's divorcing that . . . that . . . *adulterous* man!'

Brenda snorted in disbelief. 'Adulterous? Roger? I find that hard to believe.'

Nancy anxiously shushed her sister, her eyes darting round the room. 'Well, it true. You can take my word for it. Clare told me, and she doesn't lie.'

Brenda shook her head. 'But how does that involve Julia?'

'*That* doesn't involve her. But what happened next certainly does!'

Relieved that Julia wasn't having an affair with Roger, Brenda remained confused. 'Go on?'

'Your daughter took that dreadful *Nathan Purley* to my Clare's house!' Nancy closed her eyes as though the memory was too much to bear. 'And he took a real shine to Clare, a really big shine. We all know how beautiful she is, and he obviously thought she was the cat's whiskers.' Nancy averted her eyes and flicked her hand as though Nathan Purley was the wickedest of men. She steeled herself and faced Brenda again. 'He *seduced* Clare, Brenda. He seduced her when she was at a desperately low ebb . . . upset about Roger. He seduced my little girl and now . . . now . . . she's . . .' Nancy couldn't bring herself to say it.

'Pregnant?'

'Ssshhh!!' Nancy glared at her sister.

Brenda was tempted to smile. Instead, she made a concentrated effort to keep her face straight. 'Poor Clare.'

Nancy stabbed her fingers to her forehead as though the shame couldn't be contained. She threw back her head and sighed bitterly. 'How am I going to face people at the golf club? How am I ever going to hold my head up high again?'

'But she could marry him? Nathan, I mean.'

Nancy looked horrified, as though her sister had uttered the most ridiculous of words. 'Marry him, Nathan Purley, a common shop keeper? Not likely.'

Brenda did smile now. She snorted as well. 'Oh, come on, Nancy. That must be the understatement of the year. Hardly a common shop keeper. Wasn't it you who told me about his wealthy family? Wasn't it you who told me what a fine business he runs?'

Nancy shook her head and flicked her hand again. 'Well, she's not going to marry him. She's no intention of marrying him, so that's that.'

Though you wish she was, thought Brenda shrewdly. 'Does he know?'

'Know what?'

'That Clare's pregnant?'

'Of course he knows. Of course. He's the father, there can't be any doubt.'

Brenda was really curious now. She'd often wondered why Julia left Purley's. This could have something to do with it. 'Well, how did he take it? Did he ask her to marry him?'

Nancy looked really put out. 'Why are you asking all these questions, Brenda? You must know they're like knives to my heart.' She slumped back in her seat and started to undo the buttons of her Burberry. The whole scene had brought her out in a sweat. She slipped her arms out of her coat and let it fall back on to her seat. Beneath the coat she wore a fetching peach-coloured Aquascutum wool dress with tie neck.

'You look lovely, Nance, as usual.'

She looked down at her dress. 'Hmmm, I bought this in London to cheer myself up. Peter's heartbroken, Brenda, I can't tell you how disappointed he is in Roger. The time he's spent guiding that boy, teaching him the basics of big business, and this is how he repays us. Dreadful, quite dreadful.'

'Well, I'm sorry. I think it's all very, very sad.' Brenda decided to be positive. 'But you know, Nance, a baby is a baby, however it's born. And when it arrives, you'll be thrilled.'

'Huh!' Nancy cut her off. 'I most certainly will not. I agree with Nathan, I think she'd be wise to get rid of it.' The words were out before she realised what she'd said. Nancy looked at her sister with just a tiny show of guilt.

Brenda decided to be blunt. 'An abortion, you mean?'

'Well, what would be the harm? And at least nobody need know. I mean, she's young, she's got all the time in the world to remarry and have more children. What does she want to go and spoil her life for with this one?'

'And Clare? What does she think?'

'Well, that's the silly thing, she's desperate to keep it. It's as though she thinks it's her last chance.' Nancy shook her head. 'Silly, silly girl. All this time when she could have respectably had a baby by Roger and didn't, and now she wants to have this one out of wedlock! I ask you, Brenda? What could be more stupid than that?'

She tapped her sister's hand. 'Well, do you know what I think? That Clare is very, very brave. I think what's happened to her is quite awful, with Roger and everything, but under the circumstances I think she's made the right decision. This baby might not have been planned, but when it does arrive it will be adored.' Brenda squeezed her sister's hand. 'And I promise you, Nance, you'll adore it too.'

'But the shame, Brenda, the shame!'

'There'll be none. Who's to know? She lives in London. It's nobody's business.'

Nancy nodded in agreement. 'Yes, Brenda, I had thought of that. Perhaps if we keep it quiet nobody will find out. I mean, she'll marry again one day, and that'll make the whole sorry tale respectable again, don't you agree?'

Brenda decided to be honest. 'There is no shame, Nance, unless you make it so. You don't have to lie, you don't have to pretend, because it's nobody else's business. But don't deny Clare's baby his proud grandparents, that would be a sin.'

'Sin, huh! The only sin here has been committed by that awful man.' Nancy tapped her forehead and corrected herself. 'Two awful men.'

Brenda watched as she finished her chocolate eclair and turned around to order another. She looked at her sister. 'Do you fancy another, Brenda? Oh, go on, say you will, just to keep me company, please?'

The last thing Brenda wanted was another chocolate eclair. She shook her head. 'I'm sorry, Nance, but I'll have another coffee.'

Nancy shouted the order across the room before turning her attention back to Brenda. 'And Julia? How's this new shop of hers? And I see she's getting herself tangled up with another of the Fordham-Clarkes? She wants to watch out. She might find herself in deep water too, if she's not careful.'

Brenda took a deep breath. 'Nick is Julia's business partner, Nance, nothing else.'

'Yes, well, and so was Nathan Purley. And look what he did to Clare!' Nancy's eclair arrived and immediately she took a large bit. With her mouth half full, she said, 'And Kit Fordham-Clarke? How is he getting on?'

'Kit's fine. Got his own place now. A lovely little cottage in Ousden, not far from Tongate, just down the road. He's a nice boy, Nance, a really nice boy.'

Her sister looked fierce. 'Well, I thought they were all nice boys until I found out the truth. To be honest with you, Brenda, I wash my hands of them all. I just wash my hands of them.'

34

Sir Malcolm Fogerty was very fussy about his racehorses. He was a stickler for certain care procedures and insisted on round the clock attention. Gordon Tree, as head lad at Lovell's yard, was responsible for providing this. Jack Lovell, the trainer, trusted him implicitly. Sir Malcolm trusted him too; he knew it was Gordon who tirelessly looked after all five of his horses. So far he'd had a winner every season. Gordon was proud of that fact, and Sir Malcolm showed his gratitude with the odd five-pound note.

It was seven o'clock in the morning, and promising to be a beautiful spring day. The sun already shone brightly and all the surrounding trees and hedgerows were fully in leaf and blossom. Gordon sniffed the air in the yard, feeling glad to be alive. He strode along in his navy jodhpurs, thick woollen sweater and ancient leather boots that'd been mended many, many times, and shouted orders to his lads who were all getting ready to ride out. Gordon was hoping to ride Brown Sugar, Sir Malcolm's favourite, but was doubtful about this. The day before the horse had shown signs of a pulled tendon.

The early-morning ritual of exercising the horses was something Gordon never missed or tired of. He might be knocking on in years, and suffer the odd twinge of arthritis in his knees and toes, but he'd no intention of giving up the saddle just yet. As he marched through the yard he had a jolly word for everyone, and everyone liked Gordon. He was that sort of man. He showed respect and gained it. A popular man.

Bobby, one of Gordon's youngest recruits, came out of Brown Sugar's stable, shaking his head. 'Her tendon's still swelled, Mr Tree. I think we need the vet.'

'Have you hosed her down?'

'Yeah, several times, but there's still a lot of heat.'

'All right, lad, all right. I'll take a look m'self.'

Gordon pulled back the sliding lock and walked briskly into Brown Sugar's stable. Her hind quarters were against the door and she agitatedly swished her tail. He gently patted her rump as he walked right round her. 'There, girl. What's all this then? What's all this? What've you been doing to yourself? Come on, Brown Sugar, let's take a look.' She shifted on her hooves.

Gordon bent down, running his hand along her leg until he detected the heat of her swollen tendon. She took a swift step back. 'Steady, girl!' Carefully, he moved to her forequarters and ran his hands slowly down both front legs.

As he bent down to feel her swollen tendon again, Gordon felt something beneath his foot. It was a hoof-pick. One of the lads must have left it on the floor. He twisted to pick it up, and as he did so turned his foot. A sharp twinge nipped his toes and Gordon sucked in his breath. Standing on one foot, he tried to ease the pain but, to make matters worse, his knee gave way and rather clumsily he toppled over. As he felt himself falling forward, he reached out and unfortunately grabbed Brown Sugar's swollen leg. She whinnied, danced about a little, and Gordon, wavering unsteadily, continued in his fall. And then she kicked out her back legs and her hoof caught his forehead as he stumbled to the ground. The sharp thud was the last sensation Gordon Tree felt.

Brown Sugar steadied herself and turned to look at the heap on the floor. She stepped back and nuzzled Gordon, but there was no sign of life.

35

'When's the funeral?' Ed was out on site, so Kit allowed himself to touch Roberta's face. 'I'd like to be there, Roberta.'

She raised her own hand to his and pressed it against her cheek. In her misery his touch was comforting. She swallowed hard and twisted away. 'Wednesday, Kit. It'll be on Wednesday afternoon.'

He shifted back and perched himself on the kitchen table. 'He was a fine man, Roberta. I liked him a lot.'

Tears sprang into her eyes. Frantically, she tried to blink them away. 'At least he saw Jamie, started to know his grandson.' She turned and filled the kettle with water for something to do. 'Coffee?'

Kit moved forward and put both hands on her shoulders. She twisted round and threw herself into his arms. He held her tightly as she tried not to cry. 'You can cry if you like, Roberta, I really won't mind.'

She lifted her face to his. 'But it doesn't do any good. It won't bring him back. He was my father, Kit, and . . . he's dead, and I loved him very much. He was such a special man and he'll never be replaced. You see, he always took care of us, even though we were really quite poor.' She shook her head. 'And my mother simply adored him, I just don't know what she'll do now.'

'Your mother's strong, she'll get over this in time.'

Roberta pulled away from him. 'Do we ever get over losing the people we love?'

'I think we do. At least, most of us.'

'What about the ones who don't?'

Kit shook his head. 'Your mother isn't one of those, and neither are you.'

She shrugged. 'The King is dead, long live the King?'

Kit took her hand. 'Shall I make the coffee?'

She turned quickly and grabbed two mugs. 'No, I'll do it. You go back to the office, I'll bring it through.'

Enjoying their intimacy, he touched her shoulder. 'Don't send me away. Ed's not here, Jamie's asleep . . . and you know I'd rather stay here with you.'

'Oh, Kit.' Roberta grabbed the worktop with both hands and lowered her head. 'Please don't. Don't make life any more difficult than it already is, please.'

He moved quickly off the table and started walking towards the door. 'I'm sorry, Roberta. Bad sense of timing. Sometimes I don't think I've got any brains.'

She swallowed hard, already regretting her harsh words, and started walking towards him. He held out his arms. Roberta went straight into them. 'I didn't mean to be unkind, Kit. I can't bear to see you sad.'

He sighed deeply, breathing in her special musky smell. 'You don't make me sad. You make me ecstatically happy. One smile from you is all I need to make the day worthwhile.'

She pulled away, half-laughing. 'But it's not enough, is it?' She watched him ponder a bit, and then reluctantly shake his head. 'What are we doing to each other, Kit?'

He shrugged. 'Coping, I suppose.' He grinned and widened his wonderful grey eyes. 'I take lots of cold showers.'

She raised her hands to his chest and pressed them there. 'But it's unbearable sometimes. It's absolutely *unbearable*!'

'Make love to me then?' He smiled in his special way. 'Or let me make love to you?'

'And would that make us feel better, is that what you think?'

He ran a hand through his hair. 'Well it would make *me* feel better. Sometimes I think I'm going to erupt.'

Roberta smiled and grabbed his hand, kissing the palm. He pulled her towards him. 'One kiss? Please? One small kiss?'

She tugged at his sleeve. 'But it wouldn't be one kiss, would it, Kit?'

He started to pull her closer, moving his face nearer hers. 'I promise it would.'

'I have a child upstairs, Kit. I have a husband as well. They are *always* going to be in my life.'

'Which means,' he said, with his face still close to hers, 'it's time for me to go.'

Roberta panicked. 'Go? Go where?'

'Leave. Go away. Get myself out of your lives. It's the only honourable thing to do, Roberta. You know that as well as I do.'

She clung to him. She'd just lost her beloved father, couldn't lose Kit as well. 'I don't want you to leave, Kit. I *never* want you to leave.'

His eyes were tortured. 'Well, make love to me then. Show me how much you care. I need to know, Roberta. I really need to know.'

'You know I can't do that. It wouldn't prove anything, and it wouldn't be just once. It would be every time Ed wasn't here. And gradually you'd hate me, lose all respect for me.'

He made her look at him. 'I'd never lose respect for you, Roberta. I love you far too much. For God's sake, I love you with all of my heart. What I'm asking for is a part of you. I'm not asking you to leave Ed, I'm not asking for that at all. You can carry on with your life in just the way it is. I want just one small part of you.'

'Well, you'd better find somebody else . . . I can't give you that one small part, Kit, because it's not one small part. It's all of me! It's *everything*. And when I give that away, the rest will be a shell.'

He looked at her, long and hard, before swallowing and turning away. He ran his hand through his hair again then walked towards the door.

'Oh, Kit.'

'Let me know what time the funeral is, Robbie . . . and I'm sorry for all that I've said.'

She moved closer and touched his arm. 'I do understand.'

His eyes consumed hers. 'Can I ask you something?'

'Yes.'

'And you'll give me an honest answer?'

'Yes.'

'Do you ever imagine what it would be like? You and me, I mean?'

She smiled. 'Often.'

'And is it good? In your mind's eye?'

Roberta gulped. 'It's not just good, Kit . . . it's wonderful!'

He took her hand and kissed it, then let it go. 'It is for me, too.' He looked into her eyes and smiled. 'Ed's one hell of a lucky man!'

36

The funeral passed off as well as could be expected. Brenda braved the event with a stoic heart, as did her daughters. Everyone who mattered to them gathered back at the tiny cottage, which didn't seem quite so tiny any more now that Brenda lived alone. She felt a chill come over her on entering her home after burying her beloved husband.

Roberta had come up trumps by preparing all the food for the funeral tea: small sausage rolls, cheese straws, tiny ham or watercress sandwiches, fairy cakes. Ed had brought some wine, which loosened people up a bit and made the whole occasion less of an ordeal. Brenda was heartened to see her sister who'd rushed back here from London after the birth of twin granddaughters.

'And how's Clare?' Brenda asked her.

Nancy's face glowed. 'She's radiant, Brenda. Absolutely radiant. You should see the little cherubs. The are *so* beautiful. Just like Clare.' She rolled her eyes. 'And Nathan ... well, I can't tell you how thrilled he is.' She beamed proudly. 'Did you know his grandfather was a twin? And Nathan *adored* his grandfather. So you see, Brenda, it just proves it all. Personally, I think he would marry Clare tomorrow if he got the chance ... which of course he won't!'

Brenda smiled. She was pleased it had all worked out, but at the same time saddened beyond measure. She listened to Nancy with a heavy heart. With her husband gone, she'd have nobody to talk to anymore about this. Nobody to relate all Nancy's funny little ways to. No Gordon to say, 'Well, Brenda, take no notice, she always was a silly tart.'

Feeling out of place, Kit shuffled around the crowded room, not really knowing anybody other than Ed, Roberta and Brenda, and as all three of them were busy, he was at a loose end. He looked at his wristwatch and wondered if he dare leave. He could go back to the office, he'd got a mountain of work to do. He decided to look for Ed, make his apologies and slip away. He eased his way into the tiny hall and saw Julia coming down the stairs. He'd noticed her in the church and at the crematorium. It had been impossible not to. Dressed in a sleek black suede coat and high-heeled platform shoes, she had cut a dramatic figure. Her hair was simply tied back with a black bow and her face nearly bare of make-up but she stood out, like a star. For once Kit didn't need to drag his eyes away from Roberta.

Later on, he'd watched Julia chatting to her mother, her animated face reminding him of Roberta's and yet they weren't at all alike really. To Kit's way of thinking, Roberta was beyond comparison, she was the unobtainable object in his life. But he realised he'd become obsessed with her, and since she'd made it patently clear that he was wasting his time, that she wouldn't give him *anything*, he'd been seriously thinking of quitting his job. Ed would be upset, but he didn't understand the situation. Kit was finding it increasingly difficult to keep his hands off his wife. If Ed had so much as an inkling of this, he'd most certainly be shown the door. As it was he already felt like a traitor.

And then, out of the blue, a friend from Aberdeen had rung and told him that Crosby-UK were looking for structural engineers with his sort of experience. They were involved with Aberdeen's infrastructure: new roads, developing industrial land and particularly the revamping of Aberdeen's Dyce Airport. A five-year contract with the sort of salary they'd be prepared to pay would properly set him up. It was hard to resist.

'Kit? It is Kit?' Without her coat, but wearing a simple mid-calf checked skirt beneath a see-through black blouse, Julia looked beautiful. He caught his breath.

'Julia?' He held out his hand. 'How nice to see you again . . . I mean . . .' He corrected himself. 'Under the circumstances I'm sorry, but it's still good to see you.'

She smiled and pouted. 'And it's good to see you, Kit.' She averted her eyes, then shifted slightly to pick an ash-tray off the window-sill. 'Do you mind if I smoke?' He quickly shook his head. Julia took a cigarette from a pack in her hand and offered him one. He declined, but gallantly took her lighter and used it to light the cigarette in her mouth. It was a simple gesture, but one that Julia liked. With her eyes fixed on him, she inhaled deeply and blew the smoke away. 'So,' she said, 'I hear you work for Roberta's husband?'

He nodded. 'And you're in Cambridge?'

She shook her head. 'You're slightly behind the times, Kit. I work in London now.' Once more she drew on her cigarette. 'I've a shop down the King's Road ... you know, Chelsea? Nick's in it with me. I'm surprised you didn't know.'

Kit frowned and felt stupid. His life had slowed down almost to a snail's pace since moving to Tongate and Ousden. Outside structural engineering he knew nothing. The truth was, he wasn't interested in family gossip. 'Er, well, actually I haven't seen Nick for a while. Is he OK?'

Julia nodded, sizing him up. She liked what she saw. He was dishy. And *very* sexy. In fact, he oozed sexuality, she decided. 'He's very well.' She narrowed her eyes. 'You've changed, Kit. Considerably. You used to be ...'

'Fat, ugly and spotty?'

She laughed. 'Something like that.'

'And now I'm incredibly gorgeous. Is that what you were going to say?'

She giggled infectiously. 'Actually, yes. That's exactly what I was going to say.'

He looked up in the air. 'And there goes another.'

Julia frowned. 'Another what?'

'Flying pig.'

She giggled again and tapped his arm. 'I say what I think. I always have.'

Kit's face reddened slightly. He was immensely flattered. 'So,' he cleared his throat, 'you see a lot of Nick?' A vision of his brother and Julia in the trees by the River Ouse flashed through his brain. Kit averted his eyes. Thank God, they hadn't known he was there.

She shook her head. 'No, not really. He's my business partner, nothing else.'

'Where do you live?'

She grinned. 'With Clare, although I'm just about to move. This Sunday actually. You know she had her babies, twins? Really exciting stuff. You did know?'

Kit frowned again. He didn't. He shook his head. 'Well, I knew she was divorced from Roger, Ma told me that, but, no, I didn't know she'd remarried.'

'She hasn't, you idiot!'

He blushed even more. 'Oh, hasn't she? I'm sorry.'

'No, no. No need to be sorry, Kit. Clare has no intention of ever remarrying. Anyway, she's just had twins and I figured it was time for me to move out. I'm not sure I could stand screeching babies at all hours of the day and night. Anyway, I've found a lovely house in Margaretta Terrace, near my shop in Chelsea. I move in on Sunday. Do you want to come and help me?' She laughed gleefully.

'Well, er, yes. I mean, if you'd like?' Kit ran a hand anxiously through his hair. His weekends were precious. They were the only spare time he had to work on his house.

Julia touched his arm. 'Oh, I would like that. I'd like it very, very much.'

He suddenly noticed Roberta standing at the far end of the hall. She was holding Jamie in her arms and looking directly at him. He blinked and smiled at her, but she didn't smile back. Their eyes locked together before she quickly turned away. He would have liked to go after her, ask what was wrong, but at that moment Ed appeared.

'Julia . . . Kit.' He gave a commiserating smile to Julia in deference to the occasion.

She beamed at him. 'Ed, I need to borrow Kit. I've just invited him to help me move into my new house on Sunday.'

Ed grinned. 'Have you now? Kit's weekends are nothing to do with me.' He nudged Kit. 'Are you game?'

Julia interrupted, 'He most certainly is.' She drew on her cigarette, surveying him through narrowed eyes. 'And I'm keeping you to it, Kit. You're not going to let me down?'

He glanced down the hallway again, but Roberta was nowhere to be seen. He looked back at Julia, whose eyes searched his. Kit smiled. 'No, I won't let you down.'

37

Julia hadn't been able to get Kit Fordham-Clarke out of her mind. Not since Nathan had she felt like this. Who'd have believed it? Such a funny-looking boy turning into such a sexy man. She didn't know how she would be able to keep her hands off him.

'Julia! Julia!' Auntie Nancy's shrill tones called from the kitchen, Julia left the bathroom and raced down the stairs, 'Yes, Auntie Nancy?'

'Ah, there you are, dear. I wonder if you could take this cup of tea up to Clare?' Nancy put a hand on Julia's arm. 'Now, if she's asleep, please don't wake her. She asked for the tea ages ago . . . and I forgot.' Nancy giggled like a schoolgirl. 'My babies have been keeping me too busy, the little tinkers.'

Julia looked nonplussed. 'But isn't the nanny looking after them?'

'Oh, yes, she is. But you know what these young girls are like. I had to put her right about a few things.' She leant closer to her niece. 'I don't know where these agencies find some of these girls, they don't seem to have the first clue about four-hourly feeds. If you don't insist on four-hourly feeds at this age, you just make life incredibly difficult for yourself in the future. It's commonsense, plain commonsense. You have to be firm. Do you know, Julia, that silly girl was giving them both another bottle only two hours after the last!'

She frowned. 'But I thought Clare condoned demand feeding? I remember her talking about it before the twins were born.'

'Demand feeding? Huh, I'll soon talk her out of that.' Nancy tapped Julia's arm again. 'The nanny's being paid to look after them, she'll just have to keep them amused between feeds. That's her job.'

Julia's and Nancy's ears pricked up as they once again heard the distinct wail of a newborn baby. Already the noise was getting on Julia's nerves. She shrugged and took the cup of tea from Nancy. 'I'll take this to Clare.'

Her aunt called after her, 'What time are you leaving?'

Julia stopped in her tracks. Nancy obviously couldn't wait for her to leave. 'As soon as Kit gets here. Then I'll be off.'

'Kit?'

Julia nodded. 'Yes, Kit Fordham-Clarke.'

Nancy rolled her eyes. 'Oh, I see.' She tutted. 'When will you girls ever learn?'

Julia didn't bother to reply, just carried on to Clare's bedroom. Softly she opened the door. 'Clare? Are you awake?'

She rolled over to face Julia. 'Oh, thank God it's you. I thought for one awful moment you were my mother.'

Julia smiled and moved towards the bed. 'Cup of tea?' Clare eased herself into a sitting position and gratefully accepted the tea. 'How are you feeling? Still sore?'

'Too damned right I'm sore! So would you be if you had umpteen stitches where it most hurts.'

'Oh, don't, Clare, you'll put me off childbirth forever.'

Clare took a sip of her tea. 'Oh, I wouldn't want to do that, but believe me, it's no picnic.'

They both turned as Nancy bustled her way into the bedroom. 'Clare darling, I really must insist! This nanny of yours, she hasn't a clue. Where did you find her?'

'Mother, she's a Norland nanny, the very, very best. Trained for three years. And I didn't find her, Nathan did.'

Nancy exhaled noisily. 'Well, that explains it. I might have guessed.' She prodded Clare's arm with her forefinger. 'Fancy allowing *him* to choose a nanny. You'd have been far better off asking me.'

'But Nathan is paying for the f— nanny!' Clare's face reddened and she quickly took a swig of tea. She handed Julia the cup and turned to her mother. 'Please don't interfere. It's been hard enough getting him to hand over his whack as it is. And as he'll only pay for things *directly* linked to the girls, I was determined to ask for the best. And, Mother, I need a nanny. I intend to go back to college this week.'

'Clare! *You are not!* That's ridiculous. I will not allow it.'

'Mother – you have no say in the matter.'

Nancy looked at Julia. 'What do you think? Isn't that just ridiculous?'

She shrugged. 'Oh, please don't involve me.'

Clare jumped in. 'Julia agrees with me.'

Nancy sighed loudly. 'All right, I can see you're not going to budge, but I really must insist you tell this nanny to give the twins four-hourly feeds. All this demand feeding is asking for trouble.'

'Mother, please? Don't interfere!'

'You're making a rod for your own back, Clare. Don't come crying to me . . .'

'As if I would.'

Nancy grimaced. 'Well, you have done in the past.'

Clare seethed. 'Have I now?'

'You most certainly have. It's always *me* that picks up the pieces, and I don't mind telling you, Clare, this last adventure of yours has knocked the stuffing out of me. I thought I'd never be able to hold my head up again, ever.'

'Well, I'm sorry about that, Mother. It certainly won't happen again.'

Nancy fidgeted a bit then stuck out her chest. 'The thing is, don't let one mistake lead to a lot more.'

'What do you mean?'

'Start off as you mean to go on. Sort this nanny out now.'

Clare glared at her mother. 'But I don't want to. That isn't my way.'

'Clare, I insist!'

Clare's breathing was coming fast and furious. Julia cringed as she saw her cousin's eyes flash. 'Mother, if you can't allow me to bring up my babies the way I want . . . I suggest you *fuck off*!'

Nancy's mouth dropped open and her face went extremely red. She was shocked to the core and didn't move a muscle, as though the breath had been knocked right out of her. Her sweet little girl using such foul language! 'Well, I must say . . . I never thought I'd witness the day *my daughter* spoke to me like that.' She looked across at Julia. 'Is this what you've taught her?'

Julia suppressed a smile. Clare, sitting rigid in the bed, put her hands to either side of her head and made a wailing, screeching sound. It lasted a good few seconds and Julia looked alarmed. Nancy, however, remained resolute. Clare swallowed hard and

169

addressed her mother. 'I'm very sorry I swore, and I appreciate your concern, but I really do think it would be better if you went home to Daddy now.'

Nancy turned on her heel and walked out of the bedroom.

Clare slumped back on the pillows. 'Please God, somebody . . . give me strength!'

Julia squeezed her arm. 'It's all right. I'll go and make amends. Really, Clare, if she wants to believe I'm leading you into sinful ways, then so be it. I don't give a damn.'

'Well, I do.' Clare glared at her cousin then softened. 'Oh, Julia, I'm going to miss you so much.'

She bent forward and kissed Clare's cheek. ' 'Course you won't. I shall be popping in all the time. Wild horses wouldn't keep me away from those lovely little girls.'

Clare grabbed her hand. 'But you're not rushing off just yet, are you?'

Julia looked at her watch. 'Kit should be here soon, Clare. I'm packed, so I may as well be on my way.'

She pouted like a little girl. 'Oh, I was hoping you'd stay until Nathan arrives. I need someone here as a shield.' Clare laughed nervously. 'He'll soon put Mother right, and you do too in your way, but she makes bloody mincemeat of me.'

'What? You just told her to fuck off!'

'That was just temper. It's no way to handle my mother really.'

Julia hitched herself on to the bed and took Clare's hand. 'I don't really want to see Nathan, surely you understand that?'

Clare pouted again and lolled back on the pillows. 'I know, I know.' She raised her head slightly. 'And to tell you the truth, Julia, neither do I.'

Both women giggled and Julia said softly, 'He's been good to you, Clare, you know he has.'

'Only because he dotes on his precious offspring.'

'Well, it could be worse. He could refuse all contact with them, and you as well for that matter, and that wouldn't be very helpful to anyone, would it?'

Clare shook her head then grabbed Julia's hand. 'And you should see my mother with him, Julia, it's an absolute scream. She's a cross between a twitchy old maid and Uriah Heep! At least he's got the measure of her. There's no way she'll terrorise him with her sharp tongue.'

Julia slid off the bed and walked towards the bedroom window. She peered outside. 'It's a lovely day again. You ought to be outside, sitting in the sunshine.'

Clare groaned a little. 'I will, I will. It's just that with Mother around, my bedroom seems the only place of refuge.'

Julia turned and leant against the window-sill, folding her arms. 'Aren't you at least going to make yourself look glamorous for Nathan?'

Clare snorted in a most unladylike way. 'Certainly not!' She grinned and winked. 'But Harry's dropping in later. I intend to make myself look a bit special for *her*.'

Both women burst out laughing.

Kit turned off the M4 into Chiswick. It was a quarter to eleven, he was more or less on time and felt strangely nervous. The hood of his Spitfire was down to mark the beginning of summer and his hair was blown into a frenzy of long curls. Wearing blue denim jeans and a thick cream crew-necked sweater over a pale blue shirt, he looked casual and attractive. *Very* attractive.

Since meeting Julia at Gordon's funeral, Kit had done a lot of soul-searching and had finally decided it was time for him to move on. Roberta had been distinctly cool with him the two days following the funeral. She'd hardly spoken a word. This might have been due to the fact that Brenda was staying for a while, and so the atmosphere in the house was subdued, but he suspected it was more to do with Julia. But what was he supposed to do? Roberta herself had told him to find somebody else. Not that her sister was going to be that somebody else, but at least he was taking a positive step forward.

He found Park Road easily. Julia's instructions had been good. He drove slowly until he reached the right house and crossed the road to park. He was just climbing out of his Spitfire when an Aston Martin came roaring up behind, parking a few feet away. Kit paused and watched Nathan Purley step out on to the pavement. Although Kit hadn't a clue who it was, he nodded politely in his direction and then made his way to Clare's front door. He was surprised to find Nathan following him up the path. Kit turned to face him. 'This is where Clare lives?'

Nathan's handsome face tilted slightly to one side. He smiled. 'Yes. And you are?'

Kit shrugged, feeling out of place. 'Kit Fordham-Clarke. It's actually Julia I want.'

Nathan's eyes widened. 'Julia?' He gave a small chuckle and raised his eyebrows. 'A lot of us want Julia!' Kit frowned and knocked on the front door. Nathan continued unperturbed, 'Did you say Fordham-Clarke?' Kit nodded. 'You're related to Clare, then?'

'My brother was married to her, they're divorced now.'

Nathan nodded slowly. 'Ah, yes, of course.'

Nancy opened the front door. She peered at Kit and Nathan as though they were both grubby schoolboys, putting her finger to her mouth. 'Sshhh! We've only just got them off to sleep. For pity's sake, don't go and wake them.'

With a smile, Nathan pushed his way forward, hardly acknowledging her. Boldly, he walked straight through to Clare's drawing room where she lounged, looking fragile and pale, in a beautiful silk dressing gown. Nathan glanced around the room, actually looking for Julia, before he gave Clare his full attention. 'How are you now?'

Meanwhile, Kit floundered on the doorstep and Nancy hurriedly beckoned him in. She looked him up and down, surprised by how much he'd changed. 'And how are you, Kit?'

'I'm well, thank you.' He didn't know what to call her. Nancy seemed impolite. 'How are you?'

She ran a hand wearily across her forehead. 'Tired. It's an exhausting time for all of us.' She pointed towards the drawing room. 'You'd better go through.'

Clare held out her hand. 'Kit! How lovely to see you.'

He walked towards her and bent down to give her a kiss. 'You're looking well.'

'Julia will be down in a minute. She's packed and ready to go.'

Kit shrugged. 'I hope she hasn't got too much stuff. I've only got a small car.'

Nathan, who'd walked over to the front bay window, turned to ask, 'Where are you going?'

Kit frowned at this tall dark man, not sure that he liked him. His manner bordered on arrogance.

Clare came to his rescue. 'Julia's moving out. Kit, do you know Nathan?' She grinned wickedly. 'He's the twins' *father*.'

Kit blinked and smiled nervously. 'Oh, I see. And are they doing well? The twins, I mean?'

Before Clare could answer, Nathan cut in, 'Where are they? I'd quite like to see them.'

'They're asleep, Nathan. I'd rather you didn't disturb them just yet.'

Kit felt trapped between the two and was very relieved when Julia entered the room, but his mouth dropped open when he looked at her properly. Wearing a casual Yves St Laurent navy blazer with white trim, a skimpy knitted top and a white pleated skirt with navy high-heeled ankle strap shoes, she hardly looked to be dressed for moving house.

'You've changed!' said Clare in surprise and flashed her eyes at Nathan, whose own eyes feasted upon Julia.

Julia walked across to Kit. 'I felt crumby in my jeans.' She kissed his cheek and gave his hand a small squeeze.

Kit looked down at his own clothes and felt outclassed. He gulped. 'You look lovely, Julia.'

'Do I?' She gave him a dazzling smile.

'How's business?' Nathan moved closer to her. 'Doing well, I hope?'

Julia turned to him and their eyes locked. All this time she'd managed to avoid him, making sure that when he was around she was always out. All this time. And now her knees turned to jelly. He *still* did it to her. She tossed back her curls. 'It's going well, Nathan, incredibly well.' She laughed. 'Poor Madhav can't keep up!'

Nathan smiled reluctantly. 'And you coped all right with the new decimal currency? It didn't alter your profit margin?'

'Not a scrap!'

His eyes penetrated hers. 'Did you find some jewellery?'

Quickly, she looked across at Kit. 'Not yet, but I will.' Julia caught his hand. 'Come on, Kit. We'd better get loaded up.' She practically pulled him towards the drawing-room door.

'Julia, I haven't got a lot of room,' he started to say.

She looked at him, smiling. 'I haven't got a lot of gear.'

'Who are you trying to kid?' laughed Clare.

Nathan called out, 'Been to any good football matches lately, Julia?'

From the hallway, she replied, 'I never miss Chelsea at home.'

38

Kit's spirits lifted considerably as they drove away. The gorgeous girl in his passenger seat appeared to have not a care in the world, even though her hair was well and truly whipped by the wind. Following her directions, he turned off the King's Road into Oakley Street then first left into Margaretta Terrace, a small quaint cul-de-sac. Oakley Street was an extremely smart area of three-storey early-Victorian terraced houses with basements, and Julia's smaller white stucco-fronted house in Margaretta Terrace had a charm of its own. Kit liked it straight away.

'I'm only renting. The house is owned by a couple who've gone off for three years to make their fortune in the Emirates.'

Together they started to lift countless bags and carriers from the loaded car. 'Is it furnished?' Kit asked.

'Of course. In fact, it's beautifully furnished.'

He smiled. 'You didn't really need me, did you, Julia?'

'No, but I wanted you to come.'

He followed her to the front door. 'And I'm glad I did.'

Julia unlocked the door and they both struggled in with numerous bags. 'Just put them down here for the time being.' She pointed to a space in the narrow hallway. 'Let's get everything in first, and then I'll sort things out.' Kit went back to his car to retrieve more luggage.

Julia walked to the far end of the hall and pushed open a door on the right. It led into a spacious sitting room. She stood in the doorway and sucked in her breath with pleasure. The room was carpeted in thick blue Wilton with full-length yellow curtains framing deep windows overlooking a tiny town garden. The walls were cream-painted and adorned with good quality prints and paintings. A large gilt-framed mirror hung over a white marble chimneypiece inlaid with coloured marble. Standard lamps in blue and gold stood behind the two blue-upholstered settees.

Julia opened another door, walking into a streamlined white kitchen. Apart from the jazzy colourful saucepans, everything in it was white: white-tiled floor, white cupboards and a white split-level cooker. At the window, which also looked out on to the back garden, were white Venetian blinds. However, the blandness was broken with a few strategically placed exotic plants.

'This is all very smart.'

Kit's voice broke into Julia's reverie. 'Do you like it?' she asked.

'I do. You're a very lucky girl. Expensive, no doubt?'

Julia smiled. 'It is.' She turned to Kit. 'Too expensive, actually, but I'll manage.'

His grey eyes danced. 'Are you going to live here alone or do you intend sharing with someone?'

She held his gaze. 'Well . . . if you're offering?'

He shook his head. 'Oh, no. I've different plans.'

'Oh, what sort of plans?'

He stepped forward and peered out of the window. 'Plans that'll take me rather further afield than London.'

Julia was instantly disappointed. 'How far afield?'

'Aberdeen.'

'Aberdeen?' Julia was horrified, although she vaguely remembered hearing Nick talking about Kit working there previously.

He nodded. ''Fraid so. It's not the outer wastes of Mongolia, you know, Julia. Scotland has its charms. Anyway, I'm familiar with it. I stayed in Aberdeen straight from college for a short stint, and now I've been offered a five-year contract.'

'But what about Ed? Does he know about this?'

'Not yet, but he soon will.'

'When? When do you go?'

Kit shrugged. 'As soon as I've worked out my notice, I suppose.'

Julia looked at him, trying to weigh him up. He was like no one she'd ever met before, seeming to go totally his own way while at the same time totally desirable. 'Would you like to see my boutique? It's only round the corner,' she suggested.

Kit shoved his hands in his pockets. 'I'd love to see it.'

Julia held out her hand. 'Come on then, follow me.'

*　　　*　　　*

Hand in hand, and with the sun shining brightly, they walked along the King's Road. Kit sucked in the London air and felt a deep thrill at being somewhere new, with someone different. He stole a sidelong glance at Julia whose hair still tumbled around her shoulders in wind-blown tangles and realised how truly stunning she was. Since falling in love with Roberta, he hadn't really looked at any other females, but now he did look, he looked long and hard, and liked what he saw.

'Here we are!' Julia pushed her hand into her pocket and withdrew a key. She unlocked the boutique's front door and pushed it open. Kit followed her inside and the smell of leather immediately hit him. He looked around, amazed at all the stock. 'Goodness, this is *some* boutique!'

'It is, Kit. And I'm as thrilled with it now as I was when I started.'

'How long ago was that?'

Julia made a mental calculation. 'Seven months, give or take a week.'

Kit pushed his hands into his pockets again. 'And Nick's in it with you? What does he know about leather?'

Julia laughed. 'He knows nothing about leather, but the angel started me off. He put up the money to get me going.' She moved closer to Kit then closer still. 'And going it is. Business is brisk. I aim to make a killing.'

Kit was very aware of her closeness and liked the way she made him feel. Tall in her high-heeled shoes, Julia's mouth was level with his. She kissed him and quick as a flash shifted away.

'Stay there. Don't move. I'll be back in a minute.' She walked through to the back. Kit swallowed hard, still feeling the impression of her mouth on his.

She seemed to be gone for a while and he browsed around the shop, looking at all the way-out, trendy gear.

'Da-dah! What d'you think?' Kit jerked round as Julia came back into the shop with her arms held out. She was wearing the skimpiest pair of suede hot-pants with a bibbed and beaded front and looked outrageously attractive. She still wore her skimpy knitted top underneath, which was sleeveless and very cut away around the arms and shoulders, but was now bare-legged with nothing on her feet. Kit's eyes wandered appreciatively up and down her amazing legs.

'*Wow!*' he gulped.

She turned round and wiggled her bottom. Kit blushed and

pushed his hands into his pockets again.

And then she was gone, off into the depths of the shop once more. It crossed Kit's mind that she might return wearing something else. But she didn't. Julia returned in her white pleated skirt with her jacket carried over her arm. He couldn't help noticing, however, the well-defined outline of her breasts beneath the skimpy knitted top.

She looked at her watch. 'It's one o'clock. Are you hungry?' Kit didn't feel in the least bit hungry. He shrugged. 'There's a shop down the road, it's open all the time, sells all sorts of scrumptious food. Let's go and buy a load of nosh, and some champagne, and go back to the house and celebrate.'

'Celebrate?' Kit was a little surprised that Julia would want to celebrate when she'd only just buried her father.

'Yes. Celebrate my new home.'

'Oh, yes, of course. Excellent idea.'

Julia took his hand once more and led him out of the shop. He felt like putty in her fingers.

They ate rice with bacon and tinned smoked oysters in a sauce of mushrooms, onions and tomatoes and drank champagne. Kit realised straight away that Julia was no cook, but, giggling and laughing until their sides ached, they had thrown the meal together in the kitchen and he'd realised he hadn't enjoyed himself so much in ages.

By the time they'd both eaten enough and had drunk all the champange, it was six o'clock.

With the coffee table shoved aside, they sat opposite each other on the carpet in the sitting room, listening to *Just My Imagination* by the Temptations. As it finished Kit looked across at Julia. 'I really should be making tracks.' He glanced at his wristwatch and sighed, 'I've got things to do tonight.'

Panic clutched at her. He couldn't go yet. 'Can't your things wait? Stay a while longer?'

'Don't you want to unpack? You've got to work in the morning, when are you going to find time otherwise.'

She shrugged and stood up, holding out her hand. 'I'd like to dance. Hang on, I'll change the record.' Julia wandered over to the stereo and searched through her landlord's record selection. She chose *Make It With You* by Bread and placed it on the turn-table.

The music soon drifted round the room and she walked back to where Kit was sitting and once more held out her hand. 'Dance?'

He shook his head. 'I'm a lousy dancer, Julia. Two left feet.'

'I'll show you,' she insisted, 'just follow my lead.'

Rather clumsily, Kit stood up. He'd removed his shoes and sweater ages ago, and his shirt was hanging out. He looked vulnerable and yet very, very sexy. Julia wasted no time in threading her arms around him and pulling him as close as could be; the earthy smell of his skin heightened her desire. They both started to move to the slow strains of the music, and without her tall shoes she looked up at him. 'It's amazing what you can do if somebody shows you how, isn't it?' she teased.

Julia licked her lips provocatively and Kit lowered his mouth to hers. He kissed her, tenderly at first, until he felt her tongue flicking expertly around the inside of his mouth. His desire quickly mounted. Overtaken, out of control and just following her lead, what started with them standing up, ended with them on the floor. Kit couldn't remember how but suddenly he was naked and all of Julia's clothes were removed and thrown haphazardly across the carpet. Her hands were everywhere and Kit was struggling to retain some sort of command but instead found himself sliding into her as though it was the most natural thing in the world. All the previous months of suppresssed ardour found their release and Julia responded rapturously.

Kit rolled on to his back and looked up at the ceiling. 'Phew!'

She snuggled up against him 'Do you mind if I smoke?'

He looked into her eyes and smiled. 'I don't mind what you do, Julia.' He touched her face with his hand and ran a finger to her mouth.

'You don't think it's a filthy habit then?'

He snorted. 'I've never given it a thought. But I do think it's important to be free to do whatever you like.'

She shifted so that her face was very close to his. 'And did you like what we just did?'

He laughed and pulled her closer, kissing her mouth. 'What I remember about it. I certainly liked the bit at the end.'

Playfully, she thumped him. 'We always like the bit at the end, but it's the bit before that improves the bit at the end.'

'Well, can we take it slower next time, so I can remember the bit before?'

Julia wriggled away and went in search of her cigarettes. She called back from the kitchen, 'There is going to be a next time then?'

Kit looked at his watch. It was six-forty-five. Still naked, Julia returned with a lit cigarette. She slumped down next to him and blew out smoke. Very gently, Kit touched her tousled hair. 'I thought we'd give it half an hour or so ... if that's all right with you?'

She grinned gleefully and propped one arm across his waist. She looked at his face. 'Kit Fordham-Clarke, with you I could do it all night!'

39

It was five o'clock in the morning when Kit arrived home from Chelsea. Euphoric if exhausted he climbed into his bed for a couple of hours before rising early to meet Ed on site. He threw on yesterday's clothes, cleaned his teeth and dragged a brush through his hair. That would have to do. It was only sites they were looking at.

Roberta had seen Ed drive up the lane in his Volvo, with Kit following in his Spitfire. She left the office and walked through to the kitchen to put the kettle on. After trekking round sites all morning, she knew they'd be ready for a cup of coffee.

Brenda had gone home to face her lonely future. Roberta hated to see her go, but was relieved nonetheless. Jamie would be spoilt rotten if her mother continued to stay. He was asleep now, and Roberta had been relieved to be able to catch up on some work in the office.

'Robbie?' It was Ed, sounding anxious. She pushed the plug into the percolator and turned to face him.

'Ed, what on earth's the matter? You look dreadful.'

He walked around the kitchen table and put his hands on her shoulders. 'Kit told me this morning he's quitting.'

Roberta's legs suddenly felt too weak to support her. She gulped and looked up into her husband's face then looked behind him, expecting to see Kit standing there. 'No,' explained Ed, 'he's in the office. I think he feels as bad about this as I do.'

Roberta gulped again and found her voice. 'Why? Why is he quitting?'

Ed pulled out a chair and sat down. 'A career move. Nothing more.' He looked up at his wife with forlorn eyes. 'He's going to Aberdeen, Robbie, got a job with Crosby-UK. Huge construction company. Pretty fantastic prospects for him.'

'Aberdeen? But why? He has prospects here with you. You're doing wonderfully well, Ed. Why?'

He shook his head and briefly buried it in his hands. Then he sat up straight and took Roberta's hand. 'He's an amazing engineer, Robbie, brilliant, quite the best. I suppose it was too much to hope that he would stay with us. He's been totally honest, said he wants to set himself up so he can eventually run his own business. There's enormous potential for him in and around Aberdeen. He sees that, and he's grabbing his chance. Who can blame him?'

'After all we've done . . .'

Ed grabbed his wife's hand. 'Oh, no. Don't be like that, Robbie. That really isn't fair, not to Kit.'

'When's he going?'

'He's asked if he can leave at the end of the month. I said yes. What else could I say?'

He stood up and looked at his watch. 'Look, I have to go out again. Would you bring the coffee through? I'll drink it quickly and be on my way.' Ed walked to the door and turned back. 'Be nice to him, Robbie. Don't give him a hard time.'

She looked at her husband and forced herself to nod.

Kit's voice was strong and firm. 'You know why I'm going, Roberta. *You* of all people should know.'

'But you like Ed. The business is doing well. Why can't you stay until it's really on its feet and then leave?'

Kit sat at his drawing board, pencil in hand, and looked across at the woman he loved. He threw down the pencil. 'I can't stay, Roberta. This situation is driving me mad.'

Wearing a simple cotton dress, her skin lightly tanned from the sun, she grabbed the other side of his drawing board and glared at him. 'Well, you've managed up to now. Why, all of a sudden, have you decided to quit?'

Kit picked up his pencil again and rolled it between his fingers and thumb. 'It's not all of a sudden. It's been in my head for a while.'

She leant closer, her breath catching in her throat. 'Since I turned you down, I suppose? Is that what this is all about?'

He snapped the pencil and averted his eyes. 'I don't know, Roberta . . . I just don't know.'

She straightened herself, still clutching the drawing board. 'Well, you've made up for it, haven't you? You haven't wasted any time.'

His brow creased, but he knew what she was talking about. Kit swallowed hard. 'I haven't made up for anything, I'm just trying to get on with my life.'

'With *her*? With my *sister*? Is that what you call trying to get on with your life?'

Kit was annoyed. He threw the snapped pencil across the room. 'Well, what if it is? What's it to you, Roberta? What business is it of yours?'

She stepped back from him. 'I care about you, Kit. That's what business it is of mine.'

He looked at her as though she was quite insane. 'You care about me? You say you care about me. Well, if you *care about me*, why can't you be happy I'm with somebody else?'

Roberta opened her mouth to speak, but he scraped back his chair and stood up. They faced each other angrily. 'Have you any idea what it's been like watching you with Ed? Can you imagine how I've felt when he's touched you the way he does, and kissed your cheek, and made *everyone* know you're his? And you've enjoyed it all, you've luxuriated in his adoration. And I've watched! I've watched it for months! And guess what, Roberta? Guess what? It's made me love you more. Yes, it's bloody made me love you more!'

He walked towards the window and stared down the twisting lane. 'You told me to find somebody else. Why can't you be happy that I have?'

Eventually, she found her voice. 'Yes, I told you to find somebody else, Kit, and I do want you to be happy. But you'll never be happy with Julia. My sister isn't right for you.'

He rounded on her fiercely. 'You're just jealous, Roberta, that's what you are. Well, now you know what it feels like!'

Finding it increasingly difficult to fight back tears, she walked to the door. 'I've always known what it feels like, Kit. I've spent my life having Julia shoved down my throat.'

'I'm not shoving her down your throat. I haven't said a word about her.'

'No, you don't have to. It's written all across your face.'

Kit slumped back in his seat and dropped his head in his hands. 'For God's sake, Roberta, why are we arguing like this? I'm only seeing Julia, I haven't got a clue how it'll all work out.'

She lunged at him. 'Only *seeing* her? You *reek* of her!' She moved in closer. 'How long did it take you, Kit? An hour? Maybe two?'

He blinked and lowered his hands. 'It didn't take an hour, Roberta ... it wasn't like that at all.' He realised too late what he'd implied.

Roberta's eyes were blazing now. 'Hah! See! You had her, didn't you? Or should I say, she had you. I bet she couldn't wait to get her knickers off.'

Kit's heart was thumping wildly, and he knew he should defend Julia. It hadn't been like that. It'd been ... fantastic. 'She's a free spirit, Roberta. Perhaps *you* could learn something from her ways.'

She recoiled as if he'd struck her. 'I've already learnt a lot about Julia's ways, Kit, and for your information, she's always been a free spirit. Very free and ... *very easy*!'

She walked out and slammed the door.

Later, she stood in the kitchen and watched Kit's car go down the lane. She looked at her watch. It was four-thirty.

'Robbie? What have you said to him?'

She froze, and with her back to her husband struggled to reply.

'Roberta, answer me. He's left. Gone. He's not coming back.'

She turned towards Ed, her face quite red with embarrassment and misery. 'Nothing. I didn't really say anything.' She shrugged. 'Just, well, I might have said something about Julia ...'

Angrily, Ed moved towards his wife. 'Julia? What's she got to do with it?'

Something boiled up inside Roberta. 'Everything. Don't you see? Julia's got everything to do with it. He's leaving because of her.'

Ed shook his head at his wife's logic. 'Well, he might be now, but he certainly wasn't before.'

Roberta turned back to the sink and clutched the draining board. 'I'm sorry, Ed, I didn't mean to interfere.'

He softened his voice. 'Kit's private life has nothing to do with you, Robbie, even if he is having a relationship with your sister. You had no right to interfere.'

She turned quickly. 'Well, I care. Doesn't that give me rights? She'll make him miserable, Ed. She'll break his heart.'

'He's going to Aberdeen, Roberta. Julia lives in London.'

'It doesn't matter where he's going, she'll still be in his life.'

Ed leant across the table like an angry schoolmaster and wagged his forefinger at his wife. 'You've gone too far, Roberta, and you've totally missed the point.' He straightened himself and walked towards the kitchen door.

Confused, she called after him, 'How have I missed the point?'

He turned, briefly. 'For Christ's sake, Roberta. You only had to look at him to see what he was up to yesterday! She's giving him what he wants, and she'll continue to do that until he's had enough. But he's going to Aberdeen, Roberta, to further his career. And if anybody's heart is going to be broken, you can bet your life it won't be Kit's!'

Ed left the kitchen as Roberta burst into tears.

40

July, 1971

'I've bought it, Nance. I signed the contract.' Brenda's often strained face was now the picture of joy.

Nancy frowned. 'Is that wise?'

Brenda waved her hand dismissively. 'Wise or not, it's signed and sealed. Michael wanted rid, and it's put some direction into my life. That salon gives me something to focus on.'

Nancy pushed aside her ice-cream bowl. 'And you can afford all this?'

Brenda nodded. 'Thanks to Gordon.' She bit her lip and looked out of the window. 'He didn't make a lot of money during the lifetime, bless him, but he left me well provided for on his death. His insurance policy enabled me to buy the hairdressing salon, revamp it to incorporate beauty treatments and still have enough money left over to buy my cottage.' She laughed incredulously. 'And I didn't even know he'd got an insurance policy! He never told me, never mentioned it once.' She sighed. 'I suppose he didn't think he would die so young.'

Nancy snorted. 'None of us thinks we're going to die.' She leant back in her seat and Brenda noticed the buttons on her Frank Usher silk dress were strained to breaking point. 'So, who's going to run this beauty therapy whatsit?'

Brenda didn't hesitate. 'I am. I shall employ somebody to help me, of course, but as soon as the structural work is done on the salon, I shall go on one of these crash courses in London. It'll be money well spent. And accommodation there won't be a problem, I can stay with Julia.'

Nancy sniffed. 'Is there a call for a beauty salon in Newmarket?'

'Of course there is, Nance. All those trainers' wives?'

'Hmmm, I suppose. But personally, I don't see the point of facials and things.' She preened herself. 'Of course, I'm fortunate enough to have a good skin. I don't need any of that mullock.'

'Having a good skin is the best reason to look after it, Nance. And it's not mullock. The products I'll use will be the very best, I can assure you.' Brenda drank the remains of her orange squash. 'Anyway, it's massage I'm really interested in. Swedish massage.'

Nancy grimaced. 'You want to be careful, Brenda, people might get the wrong idea.'

'Of course they won't. Hardly down the High Street in Newmarket.' But Nancy wasn't convinced. Her eyebrows went up and then she yawned as though she was bored. Brenda immediately felt guilty for dominating the conversation. 'And how're things with you Nance? How's Clare?'

'She's fine, I suppose.' The twins are two months old now and really *beautiful*.' She clasped her hands before her. 'You should see Jennifer. She's obviously going to be the boss. A right little madam she is. Poor Vivien's always taking a back seat.' She whispered across the table, 'Nathan chose the names you know, I was most surprised. Quite classic, aren't they? And do you know, Brenda, Clare's taken Purley as a surname. To be honest with you, I don't think she could wait to get rid of Fordham-Clarke. Hmmm, Purley has quite a ring to it, though, don't you think? And it's a step in the right direction.' She sniffed. '*He's* having them this weekend ... the twins. He and his mother are going to look after them. I shall pop round, of course, to make sure everything's all right, but I'm really surprised at Clare. Fancy letting *him* take them when they're so young.'

'Why not? It's the best thing she can do. Bonding her daughters with their father. Sounds exactly right to me.'

Nancy nodded. 'And he's got Jennifer and Vivien down for St Paul's, you know. I must give him his due, he only wants the best for the twins.'

Brenda smiled. 'No state school education for your granddaughters then?'

Nancy puffed out her chest. 'Not likely! And I can't tell you how glad I am about that. That stupid Education Secretary! I wonder what the Tory Party is thinking of? Stopping free school milk, indeed.' Nancy sneered. 'I'm telling you, Brenda, that's the end of

Margaret Thatcher, you just wait and see.'

Brenda looked at her watch. 'I must be going, Nance, I've got things to do.'

'Well, that's nice, I must say.' Nancy pouted like a child. 'I come all this way into Cambridge and no sooner do we make ourselves comfortable than you're rushing off.'

'I have an appointment, Nance, with my solicitor. At twelve.'

Nancy started rummaging in her handbag. 'All right, all right. Don't mind me. I know when my company's not wanted.'

'Nancy, your company is wanted. It's wanted very much. But I genuinely do have an appointment with my solicitor. I don't get into Cambridge that often, so obviously I try to fit everything in.'

Nancy looked at the tattered ten-shilling note in her hand. 'Fifty pence, that's all this is worth. Look at it, a tatty piece of paper. Our ten-shilling note will soon be out of circulation altogether and once it bought a week's shopping.'

Brenda reached for her own handbag. 'Let me pay, please, Nance?'

Nancy stalled her with her hand. 'Don't be silly, Brenda. That's not what I meant at all. When you're a successful businesswoman I'll let you pay.'

Brenda sighed inwardly. She could read the expression on her sister's face and it clearly said: If I live to see the day. But she would, Brenda vowed to herself. One of these days she was going to rock Nancy on her heels, just see if she didn't.

41

It was late on Saturday evening when Kit drove back from Dyce Airport, Aberdeen, with Julia in the car beside him. He was delighted to have her company again. He parked outside his cramped digs in the Old Town area of Aberdeen and together they made their way up to his attic bedsit.

'And if you really look hard enough across the King's Links, you can just about see the sea.' Kit peered out of the small window into the darkness.

Julia forced a smile. Her eyes panned around the room, which in her opinion was grim. It was a depressing, badly decorated place with a kitchenette attached. All bathroom facilities were down a flight of stairs and along the first-floor landing below. The enormous granite Georgian house was owned by the McPhatters who, apparently, were big in fish and chips.

'Sometimes I get up really early in the morning and go down to the quay,' Kit enthused. The fishing boats are coming in and I watch them offload. You should see the fish, Julia. As fresh as you'll ever get. Do you fancy some fish and chips? We could get some later on.'

Her stomach heaved. Sitting on a cramped, smelly aeroplane was bad enough; fish and chips for supper was the last thing she fancied. She looked at Kit and managed a wan smile. He moved quickly to her side. 'Oh, I'm sorry. You look absolutely beat. Come on, let me make you comfortable, I know *exactly* what you'd like.'

She warmed to his attention and allowed herself to be led to his three-quarter-sized bed. Still wearing her fringed nappa jacket, she lay down on the ghastly grey and pink eiderdown. Kit snuggled up beside her and ran his hands through her hair and around her face.

He caressed her neck and, after removing her jacket, massaged her shoulders and fondled her breasts. Pleasurably, she sighed.

But Kit seemed eager to talk. 'I'd like to take you to Nigg Bay in the morning. Between Girdle Ness and Greg Ness, the beach is really sandy and you can see for miles. Of course, it's sandy here too, along the golf course. Typical East Coast. And we could go to Greyhope Bay near Girdle Ness ...' He kissed her mouth. 'Some people say it's depressing, but all these places have a charm of their own, don't you agree?'

Julia didn't reply and Kit continued to stroke her. She relaxed and eventually decided to speak her mind. 'You know, it's been a gruelling week. The boutique's going crazy, and I'm pretty well exhausted. All I want to do tomorrow is stay in bed all day. I have to go back at six o'clock. Can't we just take it easy?'

He shifted away from her a little, and looked sternly into her face. 'You're tired now, Julia, but you won't be in the morning.' And then he gently kissed her nose. 'Unless you keep me up all night.'

She grabbed his neck. 'That's what I want to do, Kit! I haven't seen you for over a week. I want to make love to you all night, and make up for lost time.'

He shifted back again. 'Julia, I do share this house with a family. I can't spend the whole weekend in bed with you. They'd think it very strange.' He grinned. 'They're typically Scottish, y'know. *No* hanky panky!'

She snapped, 'Well, what did you invite me here for?'

His eyes widened. 'Because I wanted to, Julia. Why else?'

'But I'm sharing your room, Kit. The McPhatters must have some idea of our relationship?'

'They have, of course. And ... they don't mind. I explained, Julia. But a little respect won't go amiss.'

'Respect? What does that mean? No *hanky panky* 'til it's dark?'

He laughed nervously. 'Yes, exactly.'

Julia sat up on the bed. 'How do you stand this, Kit? Living here like this? It's awful, bloody awful! And Aberdeen is awful too.'

He quickly put his arms around her and pulled her back on to the bed. 'I'm sorry. You've obviously tired and I've just rambled on.' He looked fondly into her eyes. 'It won't always be like this, Julia. I'm buying a new house in a smart area. It's being built at the moment. But the McPhatters have been good to me. I stayed with them before, when I came here straight from college.'

'You're buying a house? In Aberdeen? God, Kit! You make it sound as though you intend to stay up here forever.'

'No, not forever, but long enough to make some real money. If I get into new property now, I can sell when my contract's up. *Possibly* make a large profit.' He kissed Julia's forehead. 'Meanwhile, it's cheap here with the McPhatters, and they're very kind.'

'Why can't you get a normal job . . . in London?'

Kit was irritated. 'This *is* a normal job, Julia, with excellent prospects. I do know what I'm doing.'

She looked at him, long and hard. 'I'm sure you do, Kit. I'm just not certain I fit in with your scheme of things.' She desperately wanted him to say: *Of course you do, Julia!*

Instead, he rolled over on to his back and stared at the ceiling for a few seconds. And then, with a smile, he faced her again. In a fake Scottish accent, he said, 'Julia Tree, I've a bonny idea . . . Would'ya be wanting me to make *love* to you?'

He hadn't put her mind at rest, but she grinned. 'Kit Fordham-Clarke, that's exactly what I'd be wanting.'

He ran his hand up her skirt. Julia caught her breath. 'There is one snag, Kit.'

He moved down the bed and started to pull off her clothes. 'What's that?'

She sighed rapturously. 'I'm off the pill. The doctor said I needed a rest from it. Just for six months or so.' She manoeuvred herself off the bed and walked over to her hide leather overnight bag. 'I've got a diaphragm with me somewhere. This really is going to be fun!'

Kit propped himself on his elbow. 'It does work, this diaphragm?'

She turned on him sharply. 'Of course it does.' She withdrew the round pink plastic container from her bag. 'Is there somewhere I can put this in?'

He smiled. 'The bathroom's down the stairs and along the hall.'

She eased herself back on to the bed, pulling her skirt up as she did and handing him the container. 'Well, in that case, the job's all yours.'

Julia woke to rain thudding loudly on the bedsit window. She struggled within the close confines of Kit's bed to retrieve one arm and look at her wristwatch. It was eight o'clock. She snuggled back down against him momentarily then raised her head to look at him, remembering the night before. His face in repose was remarkably young looking. His tousled hair, beautifully shaped nose and Paul Newman mouth turned her on.

Kit's eyes opened and he looked startled for a few seconds. Then he whispered, 'Julia.'

'You've remembered my name then?'

He snuggled closer. 'How could I forget?'

She shifted away slightly. 'Well, you did last night.'

Kit frowned. 'Last night? What are you talking about?'

She looked at him coldly. 'You called me Robbie.' Kit flinched, and she couldn't mistake the pain in those expressive grey eyes. 'We were both half asleep, in the middle of the night, remember? We started to make love . . . and you definitely called me Robbie. I assume that's short for Roberta?'

Kit couldn't look at her.

'You know, your eyes really are the mirrors of your soul.' Very gently, Julia ran her fingers over his face. 'They reveal everything, so don't hide the truth. Did you have an affair with my sister? Tell me, I'd like to know.'

Kit wasn't going to hide the truth, nor was he going to pretend. 'I didn't have an affair with your sister, Julia, but I suppose you could say I was in love with her.'

Hurt overwhelmed her. Those words she'd longed to hear, but Kit had never spoken them to her. 'And Roberta?' she faltered. 'Do you suppose you could say she was in love with you?'

Kit hesitated. He didn't like all this questioning. His past was his business. He didn't quizz Julia about hers. And anyway, he'd never betray the woman he loved. He twisted himself out of bed and stood before her on the linoleum floor. 'I suppose you could say . . . she didn't want to know.' He grabbed his underpants and struggled to put them on, then thumped his way down the stairs to the bathroom below.

Bitterly stung, Julia started to see her sister in an entirely new light.

'I'm out of milk. Actually I'm out of everything. Come on, Julia, get up. We need to go shopping.'

She pulled herself out from under the sheets and peered across at a fully dressed Kit. 'But it's raining.'

'I know it's raining, but I can't even make a cup of coffee. Come on, the fresh air'll do you good. The shop's only round the block.'

Julia slumped back on the pillows. 'You go, Kit. I'll stay here.'

'Julia!'

She sat up sharply. 'I'd rather stay here, Kit, okay?'

'*Okay!*' He stomped out of the bedroom.

Kit decided to walk. He'd missed his early-morning run along the beach, and so needed the exercise. There was no way he would ever get fat again. These days he could eat what he liked as long as he took plenty of exercise. He quickened his pace to the shop five minutes away.

'Kit! How ya' doing, mate?'

He turned in the cramped confines of the small grocer's shop, arms laden with coffee, milk and bread. 'Andrew? Fancy seeing you here.'

Andrew was a friend from college and the one who'd found him his current job. Andrew's arms were similarly laden with shopping. 'Looks like we're doing the same thing.' He moved to the counter and put his goods down. 'How's it going, the new job?'

'It's going well . . . and you?'

Andrew worked for Wimpey. 'We're getting ready to construct the new graving dock at Nigg Bay. Helluva lotta work. Go ahead should be early next year. The largest single development yet.' The shop-keeper looked aghast. Andrew smiled at him. 'No, not this Nigg Bay . . . Cromarty Firth . . . the Highlands. Steel platform fabrication, for the North Sea.' The shop-keeper nodded more happily. Andrew turned back to Kit. 'Fancy a drink, mate? Got time for a quick one?'

Kit looked at his watch. What the hell!

Julia was beside herself with fury. She was dressed, and fully made-up; she'd paid particular attention to her hair and was wearing fine suede flared trousers with a thin ribbed sleeveless jumper. She looked out of the bedsit window on to the street below. Even the sun was shining now and there was still no sign of Kit. He'd been gone for well over an hour. What was supposed to take ten minutes had turned into a marathon.

Pacing the bedroom, Julia seethed. She wrapped her arms tightly around herself and raised her face to the grubby ceiling. 'Where are you, Kit? What the hell are you playing at?'

She heard laughter, female laughter, hastened to the window and again looked down on the street below. She breathed a sigh of relief. There stood a dishevelled Kit, arms laden with shopping, chatting to a pretty blonde. The girl threw back her head and guffawed in pleasure. Kit bent close towards her and seemed to be saying something amusing because the pretty blonde guffawed some more. Julia was incensed.

Finally he appeared, full of apologies, explaining to Julia about bumping into Andrew. He walked straight through to the kitchenette and dumped the shopping on the draining board then returned to the bedroom. He eyes wandered appreciatively over her. 'You look nice.'

Frostily, she turned towards the window. 'And so did the little blonde out there!'

He put his hands around her waist, pulling her towards him. 'Oh, that was just Oona. She lives here.'

Julia jerked away. 'Lives here?'

Kit looked startled. 'Yes – Oona McPhatter. She's the landlady's daughter.'

'Oh, she is, is she? Well, Kit, how very nice for you. How *convenient* having a nice little blonde down the stairs to dally with.'

Bemused, he leant back. 'Julia? Over-reacting a bit, aren't you?'

'And so would you be, if you'd been left in this dump all morning to twiddle your thumbs.'

'Hardly all morning, Julia. An hour at the most.'

'An hour too long.'

'In that case, I'm sorry!' Then he glared at her. 'Hell, Julia, I've already apologised. Look, I did ask you to come with me.'

'Oh, and you really think I'd want to go to some goddamn awful pub, do you? Well, I've got news for you, Kit Fordham-Clarke, that's not how I want to spend my only day off!'

His eyes widened. 'I'm getting the message, Julia. Loud and clear.'

She poked him in the shoulder. 'Good. About time too.'

He grabbed her hand. She squealed. 'Kit, you're hurting me!'

Instantly, he let go and walked back to the kitchenette. Julia followed. 'Well? Aren't you going to apologise again? You seem to think *sorry* solves everything.'

Kit turned towards her, throwing her a fathomless look. 'You really can be a cow when you like, can't you?'

'Well, if you don't like it, I suggest you go back to your little blonde down the hall.'

'I will, don't worry!'

'I'm sure you will. She looks very *accommodating*.' The jar of coffee in Kit's hands slipped. He caught it just in time. With a deep breath, he put it back on the draining board. Julia walked into the bedroom. After a few seconds Kit followed her.

'Look, I realise this hasn't been a particularly wonderful weekend for you and I'm s— well, I will make it up to you in the future. I know you don't like Aberdeen, and I'm ... '

' ... *sorry?*'

'*Julia!* For Christ's sake, what is the matter with you?'

She pointed down the stairs. '*Oona* for starters!'

In dismay, Kit shook his head. 'But she's just a friend.'

'Pretty *friendly* friend!' Julia watched as he shrugged again. 'Okay, without issuing any apologies, tell me honestly, how friendly are you with *Oona*?'

Helplessly, his eyes panned round the room. '*Honestly?* At this point in my life she is just a friend.'

Julia snorted and folded her arms resolutely. 'Oh, well, that tells me a lot, doesn't it? *At this point in your life.* And what about tomorrow or the next day? Or the day after that?'

'I didn't mean it like that! I wasn't talking about the future.' He scratched his head, realising he'd said too much. But it was too late. Julia glared at him, willing him to continue. Angrily, Kit weighed her up. She wanted the truth so she could have it. 'I was referring to the past.'

Julia's arms dropped to her sides and she balled her fists. 'Oh, the past. I see, I get it now. In the past you fucked the living daylights out of her, is that it? But now you're just good friends? Oh, yes, I'm really getting the jist of it all now. No wonder you wanted to come back to the McPhatters.'

Kit was struggling against anger now. He'd had enough. He turned and walked back into the kitchenette. Julia followed. 'I'm right, aren't I? Go on, tell me I'm right?'

'Yes. Julia! *You're right!* Satisfied.'

Not for the first time that weekend, she was stung. She stood wordlessly before Kit and her face finally crumpled. The floodgates opened and tears streamed down her cheeks, streaking her mascara to black rivulets. With her shoulders involuntarily heaving with sobs, she slumped against the kitchenette door.

Gently, Kit wrapped his arms around her and let her sob against his chest. He said her name over and over again, soothingly. She drew great comfort from this, and if he'd just said, *But I love you, Julia*, the whole miserable scene would have been forgotten, but he didn't come close to it.

Kit guided Julia back into the bedroom and they found their way to the bed. Tenderly, he cuddled and caressed and stroked her, but still he didn't say those three little words. In her heart, she knew he never would.

Enormous relief washed over Kit as he watched Julia walk into the departure lounge at Dyce. He waved and blew her a kiss then turned on his heel and walked back to his car.

He was almost home when he saw the small package on the passenger seat. A tiny box with a red bow around it. He'd only missed it because he'd slung his jacket over the seat. Kit picked up the box and entered the McPhatters' house, making his way up to his bedsit.

He sat on his bed and untied the box. Inside the box was a Yale key, sitting neatly on a wad of cotton wool. He picked out the key and read the tag attached. It said: *You already have the key to my heart, this is the key to everything else. What more can I give?*

Kit smiled and his heart melted. Julia had always said she'd never give anyone a key to her house. It was her castle.

Suddenly he felt a dreadful heel. Okay, so her own behaviour hadn't exactly been great this weekend, but Kit suddenly had an urge to race back to Dyce and get on the next plane to Heathrow. He had to make amends. Then and there he decided to ring the airport, find out flight times. He shifted off the bed to go downstairs to use the McPhatters' telephone. As he did so, the round pink plastic box containing Julie's diaphragm slipped to the floor. He picked it up and smiled, remembering the fun and games they'd had trying to get the damn' thing in!

He threw it back on the bed and went off to make his phone call. He could ask about flights the following evening. Get to Julia's as soon as possible, and return to Aberdeen early the following morning. He'd surprise her! Things would be different in her castle. Kit would show her that romance wasn't dead after all.

42

It was late-afternoon and following a ghastly weekend, Julia had had a ghastly Monday. There'd been two complaints. One woman complained about her unlined nappa jacket constantly leaving bits on her cashmere jumper and another young girl brought back a broken necklace. Julia was most upset about that. At long last she'd found a decent jeweller, or so she'd thought, someone to compare with Purley's.

'Would you like a replacement? Our selection is over there.'

'No, thank you. I only liked this necklace. Perhaps I could have a refund?'

Julia frowned, but it was her policy to keep the customer happy. 'Do you have your receipt?'

The girl shrugged. 'Sorry, I didn't think to keep it.'

Julia turned to Sarayu. 'Do you remember what this necklace cost?'

'Five pounds!' said the girl.

Julia smiled. 'We don't price our jewellery like that. It's more likely to have been three pounds ninety-nine.'

'Four ninety-nine then.'

'No. I'm sorry. After our three ninety-nine range, the price goes up to seven ninety-nine or over.'

'Seven ninety-nine then. Yes, that's right, I remember now. I paid with a ten-pound note.'

Julia's mouth twitched. 'You may well have paid with a ten-pound note, but this necklace was not priced at seven ninety-nine.' She walked to the till and withdrew a five-pound note. The girl snatched it away. 'I'm very sorry about the inconvenience,' said Julia politely.

The girl half-smiled and walked out of the shop. Julia sighed with relief. Sarayu clapped her hands. 'Cor, you 'andled that brilliantly.'

Julia sighed. 'Did I? I'm not so sure about that.'

Just as she was thinking of calling it a day and going home, Nick walked in. Seeing him was like a breath of fresh air. With his long hair shiny and clean, and wearing pin-stripe flared trousers and a red satin shirt with the sleeves rolled up, he looked outstandingly handsome. He walked towards Julia with outstretched arms. 'And how's my girl?'

She allowed herself to be embraced. With a huge smile, Sarayu looked on. Nick turned to her next. 'You're looking extremely gorgeous, Sarayu. Where *did* you get those leather hot pants?'

She put a hand to her mouth. 'Don't tell my ol' man. He'd do 'is nut!'

Julia laughed. 'Poor Sarayu. Every night she has to change before she goes home.'

Nick looked at his watch. 'Come on, Julia. Knock off early. I'm taking you out.'

'Oh, I can't. Not tonight, I'm too tired. All I want to do is go home, have a bath and crawl into bed. I've had a lousy weekend and a lousy day. Please, another time?'

Nick looked disappointed. He pursed his mouth. 'Okay, well, what say I come home with you and cook you a superb supper.' He winked at Sarayu. 'And I'll pay for all the food.` He tapped Julia's shoulder. 'I'll surprise you, how about that? A feast to delight and refresh you.'

Julia laughed. How could she refuse?

It was getting on for nine o'clock when Kit reached Julia's house in Chelsea. Immediately, he noticed Nick's Capri parked outside, and a smile crossed his face. It would be good to see his brother again. Without so much as an overnight bag, Kit fished in his pocket to retrieve the new key. He entered Julia's hall and quietly closed the door.

Strains of James Taylor's *You've Got A Friend* wafted gently from the sitting room as he peeked inside. No one there. He walked back across the hall to the kitchen. He went inside, but there was no one there either. Kit continued through to the dining room where the sleek ash table was laden with a half-finished curry, wine glasses and two empty bottles of claret. A Purchase and a Sales ledger, both open, displayed Julia's meticulous book-keeping. Kit frowned.

His heart was beating faster as he made his way to the stairs. Almost stealthily he started to climb them. Halfway up he paused at a familiar throaty cry. His face crumpled. The times he'd paced his lovemaking with Julia to wait for that sound. Like a cat he continued his journey until another recognisable cry of pleasure assailed his ears, Nick's voice mixing with Julia's cries of delight.

Kit pushed open the bedroom door and took a couple of steps inside, Nick lay face up on the bed with a naked Julia on top of him, legs astride, moving frenziedly.

She turned towards Kit, already in the throes of orgasm. Ecstasy turned to horror as his face hardened and he threw the pink plastic container on to the bed. 'You forgot this, Julia.'

He turned to his brother next, equally spent and guilty, and tossed over his new key. It came to rest within the tangles of Nick's long hair. 'You might like that, Nick. Or perhaps you've already got one of your own? I wonder what your tag said?'

To the sound of Julia's pleas for him to stay, Kit turned on his heel and walked quickly down the stairs. His legs were like jelly now and he stumbled at the bottom. He was about to open the front door when she caught him up, desperately hanging on to him and begging him to stop.

'*Kit!* For God's sake, don't go! *Please*, Kit, don't go! I'm sorry . . . It's not what you think . . . *Please*, Kit, it's not what you think!'

He turned briefly and looked down at her naked body. For once, he was repelled by her. 'Oh, but it is, Julia. Now please, *let go!*' Briefly, she did so and Kit put out his hand to open the door.

'Where are you going?'

He faced her. 'Where I never have to see your face again! Back to Aberdeen. Where do you think?'

She grabbed his arm, clutching it tightly. Disdainfully, Kit looked down at her hands. 'There's something you must know, Kit. Something you have to know!' Julia's sobs caught in her throat. She struggled to control her voice. 'I love you, Kit. *I love you!*'

He disentangled her fingers from his arm and shoved her away. She fell back against the wall. He leant forward, with his face close to hers. 'Don't kid yourself, Julia. You didn't come close.'

He opened the front door and was gone.

43

September, 1971

Roberta was surprised to be met at the front door by her mother. She entered the cottage down Heath Row in Newmarket and passed Jamie into Brenda's waiting arms.

Her mother rolled her eyes. 'Julia's here. She's in the sitting room. You go through and talk to her, Roberta, she needs us both very much at the moment.'

Roberta's brow furrowed. 'Since when had Julia ever needed her? She might need you, Mum, but I doubt she does me.'

Brenda, holding Jamie on her left hip, grabbed her daughter's arm with her other hand. 'She does, Roberta. Be kind to her. For me? Be extra 'specially kind.'

Roberta flicked her hair back from her face and turned to the front door. 'Is it all right if I bring Boris in? He hates being left in the car. He won't be any trouble.'

'Yes, of course. Bring him in. I like to see Boris.'

Roberta went back to Ed's Volvo and let the dog out of the back. Good as gold, he followed her into her mother's terraced cottage.

'Hallo, Boris, and how are you?' Brenda bent forward, still holding on tightly to her grandson.

Roberta held out her hands to Jamie and took him off her mother. 'Come on, let's show Grandma how clever you are.' She took her son and very gently stood him on the floor. 'Grandma's going to watch you walk, Jamie.'

'G-amma woch!' Little Jamie beamed at his grandmother then proudly toddled his way across the floor towards her. Tears sprang in Brenda's eyes as she scooped him into her arms once more. Boris, sitting patiently with his head cocked to one side, gave a little yip.

'Yes, Boris! Jamie is a clever boy.' Roberta squatted down and fondled the dog's ears. 'And you're a *good boy*, aren't you? And if you're extra-'specially good, Grandma might give you a biscuit.'

''Course I will,' Brenda looked urgently across at Roberta. 'Now please go through and speak to your sister.'

Roberta couldn't help pulling a face. 'Okay.' She tweaked Jamie's cheek. 'See you in a mînute, rascal.'

Brenda shooed her away with her hand. I'll amuse him for a while then I'll bring us all a nice cup of tea, how about that?'

Jullia sat in her father's old chair looking out of the window into the tiny back garden, and further out across the Heath. She turned to face her sister and Roberta noticed how wretched she looked, pale, drawn and thin. Julia gave her a wan smile and turned her gaze back to the window. 'Dad loved this view, didn't he? He never tired of the Heath. Do you remember how he'd sit here and chunter sometimes, especially if he saw someone mishandling a horse?'

Roberta smiled, remembering it well. 'I miss him too, Julia. Sometimes I think the pain will never go away.'

Julia allowed her eyes to linger on Roberta's face. Tanned, healthy-looking, with her hair slightly longer, Roberta was looking lovely, she realised with a slight sense of shock. Julia's breath caught in her throat. Up until now, she'd never thought of her sister as even remotely attractive. But still she detected an overwhelming sadness in Roberta's dark eyes. Julia lowered her own to her hands in her lap, where she twisted a paper handkerchief.

'I never really grieved, you know. For Dad, I mean. I was too busy enjoying myself.' She held up her head and looked out of the window once more. 'And now I'm paying the price.'

Roberta perched herself on the arm of Julia's chair and wrapped one arm around her. She didn't know why, it wasn't something she'd ever done before. Maybe it was because Julia seemed so genuinely unhappy. Roberta removed her arm after a while but it stayed on the arm of the chair close to her sister. 'Is Kit all right?' she asked softly, steeling herself to appear casual.

Julia turned sharply in the chair. 'Is that a joke?'

Instantly, Roberta moved away. 'No. What do you mean?'

'Well, Mum's told you. She must have done. You were chatting long enough in the kitchen.'

Roberta frowned. 'No, we weren't, or at least not about you. As a matter of fact I was demonstrating how well Jamie can walk.'

Tears pricked Julia's eyes. She gulped. 'I'm sorry, Roberta. Forgive me?'

'For what?'

'Being foul, as usual.'

'OK, I forgive you. I'm used to you being foul!'

Julia managed to chuckle, then sighed and allowed her head to fall against her sister's arm. 'She didn't tell you then?'

'Tell me what?'

'That I'm pregnant.' Roberta couldn't help herself – she shot off the chair and took an involuntary step towards the window. She turned and leant against the sill, clutching it with her fingers. Julia could see the whites of her knuckles and was tempted to say, '*Oh, don't worry, Robbie! It's not Kit's!*' but she wasn't going to be that generous. It was bad enough bearing the burden of carrying Nick's child herself, without having to suffer more shame by telling the truth. If only she hadn't weakened in the face of Nick's comforting charm, and if only Kit hadn't upset her so much in Aberdeen. 'I expect you're going to say it's no more than I deserve?'

Roberta swallowed hard and shook her head. 'No, I wouldn't dream of saying that. But what are you going to do? Get married?'

Julia laughed bitterly. 'No, Roberta, I'm not getting married. And in case you're wondering, I don't even see Kit anymore. He's up there in Aberdeen having a whale of a time, screwing Oona McPhatter!'

Roberta cringed. '*Julia!*'

'Well, why are you looking at me like that? It's true.'

Roberta shook her head again. 'You make him sound . . . so . . . base.'

Julia averted her eyes, feeling guilty. No, Kit could never be described as that. Nick maybe, never Kit. 'You wouldn't understand, Roberta, you don't really know what he's like.'

'Don't I?' The words came out too sharply.

Julia sized her sister up. 'Well, maybe you do.'

Roberta turned to look out of the window. 'If you're implying what I think you're implying, you were right the first time, Julia. I don't.'

Julia knew she was telling the truth. Roberta always did. 'He's in love with somebody else now. Isn't she a lucky girl?'

With a thudding heart, Roberta turned and faced her sister. 'Oona McPhatter?'

Julia laughed. 'You see, you've remembered her name.'

'Not exactly one you'd forget.'

'Nor the face either. Very *bonny*.'

Roberta took a deep breath. 'Does Kit know you're pregnant?'

Julia waved her hand. 'No. It wouldn't make any difference if he did.'

'But he has a right to know, Julia. It'll be *his* baby!'

'No, it won't! There isn't going to be any baby, Roberta. What sort of fool do you take me for? I haven't got Clare's nerve.'

'You mean, you'll have an abortion?'

'Of course I bloody will!' Tears pricked the back of Julia's eyes. Shame welled up in her heart again. Why couldn't she be brave and strong like Clare? But there was Nick to consider. She didn't want to marry him, and she was certain he wouldn't want to marry her. And the last thing he would want, in his job, was an illegitimate kid on the scene. He was her friend, and business colleague, and had been her bed-mate occasionally, but never more than that.

'Does Mum know?'

'She knows, and she agrees.'

'But are you sure, Julia? You might regret it one day.'

'I might do a lot of things one day, but just at this moment I can't face having a baby.' Julia's face crumpled and tears trickled down her cheeks. Roberta moved back to the arm of the chair and hugged her sister. 'You're so lucky, Roberta, you've got everything so cleverly sewn up. A husband who adores you, a beautiful baby and a lovely home, even if it is in the middle of the sticks . . . how can you understand how I feel?'

'But I do understand about heartache.'

'Do you really? Who's ever broken your heart?' Julia twisted to look at her sister's face. 'Kit, maybe?'

'Don't be silly.'

'Tell me you didn't fancy him? Go on, Roberta, tell me, then I'll know it's true.'

'There was nothing going on between me and Kit, Julia.'

'But you'd have liked there to be, wouldn't you?'

Roberta rounded on her sister. 'Why are you saying all this? Was it something he said?'

But there was no way that Julia would ever tell her sister he'd openly declared his love for her. She shook her head. 'No, of course he didn't. He didn't say anything. It's just me, Roberta. I think he's so sexy, the sort of bloke you can't help wanting to take to bed.' She looked at her sister. 'Just a little bit, don't you agree?'

Roberta smiled and managed a small nod. 'Was it good while it lasted?'

Julia saw the envy in her sister's eyes. Suddenly she felt smug. At least she had had him. And how! Julia widened her eyes. 'On a scale of nought to ten ... *amazing*!'

Involuntarily, Roberta laughed when actually she would have liked to cry. She was saved by her mother walking in with a tray of tea. Jamie crawled in behind her, followed by Boris.

Julia greeted him. 'Jamie! Hello, how's my very best nephew?' She slid off the chair and crawled on all fours across the floor, coming face to face with Jamie who giggled gleefully. 'You didn't know I could crawl, did you? Auntie Julia can crawl almost as fast as you.'

He sat back on his bottom and clapped his hands. 'Arny Yoolia cwall!' He turned to Boris behind him and banged him on top of the head. 'An Borry too!' Boris immediately went down on his haunches, looking very sorry for himself.

'Poor Boris! Don't smack him like that.' Julia leant forward and plucked her nephew off the carpet into her arms. She struggled to stand up, then walked over to the window. Clutching Jamie tightly, she looked outside. 'Your granddad used to love looking out of this window, Jamie.' She kissed her nephew's plump cheek, savouring the feel of his soft skin, 'And he loved you, too.' Swallowing hard, she pointed out of the window. 'Shall we see if we can see any *horses*?'

Jamie pointed out of he window too. 'Horsey! Horsey!'

Bonded in their grief, Julia, Roberta and Brenda laughed.

44

December, 1971

At twenty-seven years old, Nathan Purley still lived with his mother.
It was an arrangement that worked perfectly well. Apart from the
fact that they adored one another, Anne didn't interfere with his
personal life and he didn't interfere with hers. Their mock-Tudor
brick and pebble dash 1920s house sat rather splendidly down De
Freville Avenue in Cambridge, close to the river, with Midsummer
Common just opposite and the Chesterton warehouse a few miles
down the road.

Af fifty-nine, Anne considered herself completely retired. She'd
had enough of retailing and now left the running of Purley's in the
capable hands of her son. Her pursuits were more gentle. She played
golf, was an active member of a couple of Ladies' Circles and
regularly saw a few men friends. But, recently, since the birth of
Nathan's twins, her life had been turned upside down. Not that
she minded, Anne adored her granddaughters, but like Nancy she
wished Nathan would marry their mother!

But part of her knew he never would, although he hadn't surprised her in the least with his devotion to the girls. She knew her
son through and through. There were definitely three sides to
Nathan's character. The sharp professional one, the playboy, and
the affectionate protector. His mother was proud of all three. Mind
you, his business colleagues started to look at him in a slightly
different light. The ones with children found him far more approach-
able, and the ones without saw this as yet another of Nathan's
foibles. Some of his girlfriends found it extremely hard to come to
terms with being pushed into the background when the twins were
around. He wouldn't compromise then. Jennifer and Vivien had his

undivided attention, and any girl on the scene when they were around could like it or lump it. Nine times out of ten, it only made them want him more.

Clare allowed him custody of Jennifer and Vivien for a whole weekend every month. This worked rather well for her because Nathan's weekend always coincided with the nanny's time off. Consequently, Nathan and Anne never had the luxury of the nanny's assistance which they paid for. Not that Anne minded. For one weekend every month she devoted herself entirely to her granddaughters.

Nathan had long since given up shipping the twins' baby stuff to and fro between London and Cambridge. Permanently installed in Anne's house were high-chairs, play-chairs, swing-chairs, push-chairs, baby-bouncers, play-pens, and of course Jennifer and Vivien's own nursery with the finest cots and the most incredible assortment of toys. In fact, Nathan had surprised himself. Initially, he'd wanted Clare to get rid of his baby; marrying her had never even crossed his mind. Making love to her was one thing, living permanently with her quite another. But as the pregnancy wore on, and Clare's determination to keep the baby took hold, Nathan had a change of heart. He actually started to look forward to his child's birth; nobody knew then that Clare was expecting twins. Vivien had lain patiently behind Jennifer in the womb and her presence remained undetected until she was about to be born. When Nathan, who was not allowed anywhere near Clare at the time of the birth, found out that he was the father of twins, he was exultant. From then on, he was a devoted father.

At seven months old, Jennifer and Vivien Purley were talkative, agile and very able, already showing signs of great beauty. They could roll around on the floor, lifting themselves quite easily into a sitting position, and crawl like lightning. Jennifer was the most forward, but Vivien, for all her passivity, was not far behind.

'They'll be walking in a month or so, these two must qualify for the *Guinness Book of Records*!' boasted Anne.

It was lunchtime and Nathan was mopping up spills on the trays of their high-chairs. Sitting side by side, the girls were quite adept at feeding themselves although both were fussy about what they ate. 'Nah-na! Nah-na!' squealed Jennifer, squashing her sliced banana into the lip of her pelican bib. Jennifer liked squealing, she'd found out very early on that it was a sure-fire way of getting attention.

Vivien continued to push her slices of banana into her mouth, even though it was already full. Quite red-faced and finding it increasingly difficult to breathe, she blew hard through her mouth and spat it all out. Most of it landed in Nathan's hair.

'Yuk!' He picked out lumps of squashed banana then lunged at his daughter in a paternal way and tweaked her ears. '*You*, Vivien Purley, are a little minx!' She beamed in pleasure and blew noisy bubbles through her mouth. She loved her daddy.

'OK,' muttered Nathan, 'I think you've both had enough.' He bent forward to unclip Jennifer's bib, placing it on the high-chair tray. He lifted her out. 'God, you pong!' He turned and handed the baby to his mother.

'Pooh, you really are a smelly girl, aren't you?' chortled Anne.

Nathan then lifted Vivien out of her high-chair and kissed her on the cheek. 'I think it's nappy-changing time, don't you?' He tickled her tummy and she giggled in delight.

Nathan and Anne walked out of their splendid dining-room, with its priceless antiques, to make their way upstairs to the special baby bathroom. Nathan had insisted upon this. He disapproved of Clare's allowing the twins to be changed and fed in any old room. Nathan was a stickler for doing things correctly.

'Oh, no! Did you hear that?' Anne had heard tyres on the gravelled drive. She swore she could recognise *Nancy*'s tyres anywhere. 'The minge-bag has arrived!'

Nathan nudged his mother. 'I think you mean mingy old bag, Mother. You should be careful what you say.' He grinned.

Anne looked curiously at her son. 'Why is minge different from mingy?'

A slow smile crossed Nathan's face. He leant closer to his mother and Jennifer took the opportunity to pinch Vivien on the arm. Nathan tapped her hand. 'Don't do that, Jenny, that's naughty. But it just goes to show, Mother, you didn't waste all that money on my education after all. Minge is gypsy slang . . . for a sexy woman or even female genitalia.'

'Oh, good heavens! Well, I shall never call her that again.'

Nathan walked to the front door and turned back to his mother. 'No, I don't suppose you will. Or at least not in front of anybody else.' He pulled open the door and smiled warmly at Nancy.

'I just thought I'd pop by,' she said, bustling over the threshold already cooing joyously to her granddaughters.

'Actually, Nancy, you're just in time,' said Nathan, looking at Anne. 'Mother, why don't you give Jenny to Nancy, and you can go and make us all a nice cup of tea.'

Without further ado, Anne plonked a very smelly child into Nancy's waiting arms. Nathan watched as her nose wrinkled in distaste, her arms extended before her as she tried to hold Jennifer away from her. But the baby was too strong. She tugged at Nancy's coat with her sticky little fingers still covered in banana and black-currant juice. Her grandmother's new Harella wrap-over coat in winter white was very soft and touchable. Jennifer liked it. She pulled at the lapels and decided to have a good chew. Nancy was horrified.

'Nathan, she's ruining my coat!'

'Oh, Nancy, I'm so sorry. Here, give her to me.' He hitched Vivien on to one hip, and leant over to take Jennifer on to the other. Gratefully Nancy passed her over then frantically studied the marks on her coat.

'I've only just had this cleaned.'

Nathan was halfway up the stairs. 'Get it cleaned again, Nancy, and send me the bill.'

She started to follow him up the stairs. 'I'm no good at changing nappies, Nathan. I can't get used to these new-fangled disposable things, so I hope you're not expecting me to help with that?'

He turned briefly at the top of the stairs. 'I tell you what, you take the old ones off, give the girls a good swill, and I'll put the new ones on. How does that sound?'

He didn't wait for a reply, just continued his journey to the bath-room with an aghast Nancy following behind.

'You know, I didn't come all this way to change nappies,' she complained. 'I thought we paid a perfectly good nanny to do that.'

Nathan walked into the bathroom and sat Vivien on the floor. He lifted Jennifer on to the changing mat. 'We do, Nancy. Or at least *I* do. But it's Nanny's weekend off, so we all have to muck in.' With one hand securely on Jennifer, he held out Vivien to Nancy. 'She's all yours. I'm dying for a pee.'

'Well, I hope you're not going to do it in here!'

Nathan smiled, when he would really have liked to laugh. 'No, Nancy. Even I'm not that brave.'

She scowled at him. 'I hope you're not making fun of me?'

Nathan shrugged. 'Why should I do that?' He walked towards

the bathroom door. 'I'll close this, we don't want them crawling away. Won't be long.'

'Nathan! What about my coat?'

He opened the bathroom door again. 'What about it?'

'Well, can you take it from me, please? I can't do this with it on.'

He helped her to remove her coat. 'I'll put it downstairs. Back in a minute.'

'Make sure you are.' Her eyes darted to his hair. 'Oh, what's that, Nathan?'

He touched the top of his head, moved his hand around a bit and picked off a glob of banana. Grinning, he looked down at Vivien who was still sitting where he'd left her, chewing a rubber hammer. 'That little minx spat her banana out at me.'

Nancy looked down at Vivien, who was her favourite grand-daughter. 'You know, if you mashed the banana, Nathan, she'd find it so much easier to digest.'

He looked at Nancy, eyes focussing precisely on hers. 'Is that so? Well, I wonder why we never thought of that. I must go down and tell Mother.' He left, her coat slung over his arm.

Nancy frowned. He really was an odd character. She looked down at Jennifer and wrinkled her nose again. 'Really, you've made the most awful smell. Apart from *unripe* banana, whatever else have they given you to eat?'

45

Roberta hung her head over the lavatory pan and retched. Ed walked into the bathroom after her, concern written all over his face.

'Robbie, you all right, darling?'

She heaved some more, but there was nothing left. Roberta wiped her mouth with toilet paper and flushed the loo. She sat back on her heels. 'Oh, Ed, this is awful. I've never felt so ill.'

He frowned. 'You weren't like this with Jamie.'

With an ashen face, Roberta shook her head. 'It's a girl, that's why. You can bet your life on it . . . it's a girl.'

'Well, I'd rather *not* bet my life on it, but you're probably right.'

Roberta staggered to her feet and moved closer to her husband. For a few seconds he cradled her in his arms. 'Poor Robbie, and it's not going to be so easy this time with young Jamie demanding your attention. Will you be all right today? Would you like me to put off going?'

She shook her head. 'No, it's important that you see your dad. If he's as ill as they say, he needs you there.' She turned her head to look once more at the loo, wondering if she ought to move closer to it again. The wave of nausea passed. She turned back to Ed. 'John'll look after me, don't worry about me.'

John Clavell was Ed's new assistant. At thirty-five he was married with three young children, and fitted very well into Matthews Structural Design. It had taken a good few months to find him, during which time a very guilty Roberta had all but given up hope, but John had already proved to be an excellent find. Ed had even discussed with Roberta the possibility of making him a partner, and she'd heartily agreed. Good structural engineers were thin on the ground it seemed.

Roberta moved to the bathroom window and looked out on their wintry garden below, or what she could see of it at least. 'It's foggy, Ed. You will be careful?'

He squeezed her shoulder. 'Of course I will, don't you go worrying about me.'

Roberta had a lousy morning with James continually wanting her attention, and John needing her help with some paperwork.

'You look a bit peaky, Roberta. Are you sure you're all right?'

She smiled at him, and wondered whether to tell him she was pregnant but decided against it. Roberta was an extremely private person and as much as she liked John, the fact that she was two months pregnant was something to keep to herself, at least for the time being, she felt. 'Oh, just a bit under the weather, that's all.'

John touched her arm. 'Well, leave this. You go and have a rest. We can sort this lot out later, when you feel more up to it.'

Roberta was relieved. 'Thank you, John. But I'll make you a coffee first.'

'That would be great.'

She turned back as she was leaving the office. 'Have you heard from Ed?' John shook his head. Roberta frowned. 'Funny. I would have thought he'd have rung by now.'

John looked out of the window. 'With fog like this, the traffic could be very slow.'

Roberta shrugged, looking out at the thickening fog, before walking through to the kitchen to make him a cup of coffee. But the seeds of worry had been planted.

At two o'clock the phone rang. Roberta heard John pick it up in the office and walked through from the sitting room, something telling her it might be Ed. John handed the phone to her straight away.

'Hallo? Oh, Mavis, how are you?' There was a pause as what little colour there was in Roberta's face drained completely away. She swallowed hard and the tension in the office mounted as John kept his eyes fixed on her face. After a few placatory words and a promise to ring back if she received further news, Roberta replaced the receiver. She looked at him. 'I didn't want to worry her, John. She's got enough on her plate, what with Brian being so ill, but Ed hasn't arrived.' Roberta blinked, and put a trembling hand to her forehead. 'He should have been there ages ago.'

John reached out to comfort her. 'Anything could have happened, Roberta, I'm sure he's all right.'

She turned to leave the office. 'Yes, of course, he must be.'

It was two-thirty when she heard the car draw up outside. She knew it wasn't Ed because Boris started to bark. He never barked at Ed's car.

The doorbell went and John was up in a flash. He answered the door as Roberta sat like a block of ice before a huge fire in the sitting room. She'd lit it straight after her mother-in-law's call because she couldn't stop shaking. She had thought about ringing round hospitals and the like, but had held firmly on to the idea that no news is good news.

Sadly, not on this occasion. John walked through to the sitting room and came and stood before Roberta. He held out both his hands and she grabbed hold of him like a lifeline. 'Roberta, the police are here.' She stood up, although she didn't know how, her legs felt as though they were no longer attached to her body. She allowed John to guide her into the hall.

Two uniformed police officers stood before her, one male and one female, both with respectfully dour expressions on their faces. The policewoman spoke. 'Mrs Matthews?' Roberta nodded. The policewoman moved closer and put out her hand. 'Is there some-where we could go where you could sit down, Mrs Matthews?'

Roberta allowed herself to be led back into the sitting room where she sat down, this time next to the policewoman. The policeman stood close by. John stayed in the hall.

'We have some very bad news, Mrs Matthews. There is no easy way to tell you this . . .'

Roberta looked askance at her, eyes fixed on the policewoman's mouth. She didn't want that mouth to say anymore. She struggled out of her seat and, touching her forehead with one hand, moved swiftly across the room. If she got away, she wouldn't have to hear them tell her.

'I'm really sorry, Mrs Matthews, but this morning your husband was involved in a car accident. It was on the A45, near Ryton-on-Dunsmore . . .' The policewoman looked down. 'I'm very sorry to have to tell you this, Mrs Matthews, but Mr Matthews was very badly injured and later died on the way to hospital.' There was a dreadful silence and the woman added, 'Er ... the accident ... it wasn't his fault.'

Silence thickened in the room as Roberta allowed the words to seep into her fuddled brain. Still with her back to her visitors, she raised her other hand to her head, and with both hands now, tightly clutched her hair. And then she screamed and screamed for all she was worth before at last she slumped to the floor.

46

Roberta woke to her mother's touch. Very gently, Brenda ran a finger down the side of her daughter's hollow cheek. Roberta's eyes darted around the room, recognising familiar objects from her childhood yet not knowing why they were there. This wasn't home. This was her past. Her eyes focussed on her mother's worried face.

'Roberta, Julia's here. She's just arrived. She's downstairs. Shall I send her up?'

Roberta sat quickly upright in her old bedroom in her parents' house. 'Where's Jamie? Where is he? Why isn't he here?' Frantically she implored her mother, 'And Boris? Where's Boris? What's happened to them all?'

Fighting back tears, Brenda put her hands on her daughter's shoulders. 'They're all here, Roberta. They're safely here.' She moved closer and hugged her, wishing this dreadful conversation did not have to take place.

Roberta allowed herself to be pushed back on to the pillows. 'How did I get here, Mum? I can't remember . . . since . . . the police . . .' Then it all came crashing back, like waves on a stormy shore. She remembered John Clavell bringing her here. A tortured look crossed her face. 'Did John . . . did he identify . . .'

'He did, but try not to think about that now.'

'How awful for him, Mum, how *awful*!' Roberta swallowed hard. 'How long have I been here? Was it yesterday?'

Brenda nodded. 'The doctor gave you a sedative. It was the only way to get you to sleep.'

She shot up from the pillows again. 'But I'm pregnant, Mum! I shouldn't have taken a sedative.'

'Oh, Roberta, don't be so silly, love. One sedative isn't going to hurt you, even if you are pregnant.'

She implored her mother with her eyes. 'I *am* pregnant, Mum, and it might, and I just couldn't bear to lose Ed's little girl.'

With a sad face, Brenda kissed her daughter's cheek. 'You won't, love, you won't lose his little girl. Now, how about I send Julia up?'

Roberta refused to lie back. 'No. I must see Jamie and Boris. I'll come down. I want to come down.'

'Well, I think you should stay in bed.'

'No, Mum, I want to come down. I need to. I want to sit in Dad's chair. *Please?*' Tears started to roll down her cheeks. 'Just let me sit in Daddy's chair . . .'

Reluctantly, Brenda helped her daughter out of bed, wrapping a dressing gown around her shoulders. Roberta almost stumbled down the stairs, then stopped in her tracks. 'What about Ed's family? Do they know?'

'Get down the stairs, Roberta. We'll talk about it when you get to the bottom. Just be careful.'

'I need to know, Mum. I need to know now.'

Brenda grabbed her daughter's arm as Julia appeared at the bottom of the stairs with James. 'Yes, they know, love. Everybody knows. Now please take care.'

On unsteady feet, Roberta continued to the bottom of the stairs. She held out her arms for her son. 'No, I'll keep Jamie, Roberta, you go through to the sitting room. I'll bring him through.' Julia, shocked by her sister's appearance, held firmly on to her nephew.

Roberta tottered towards her father's chair in the sitting room. Brenda looked at Julia and both of them widened their eyes in worry.

'Where's Boris?'

'He's outside. He's all right, bless him. Look, there he is.' Brenda pointed to the dog who was rootling around in the garden.

James joined in too and pointed gleefully. 'Boris at-side.'

'Now, let me get you a nice cup of tea. How does that sound?'

Roberta shook her head. 'I don't want any.' Her head slumped back against the chair. 'I don't want any tea . . . *I just want Ed!*'

Julia looked at her mother, and gestured for her to go and make the tea. Brenda took James and headed off towards the kitchen.

Julia sat on the arm of their father's chair and put one arm lovingly around her sister. Softly, she said, 'I can't imagine how you must feel. For once in my life, Roberta, words fail me.'

'Don't say anything then!' she snapped, and tried to shrug her sister's arm away, but Julia held on steadfastly. 'When did you ever really care, anyway?'

She loosened her grip, and sat back. 'Roberta, your're entitled to think that, but if I didn't care before, I certainly do now. You, out of everybody I know, don't deserve this. This should never have happened to you.'

And then Roberta started to sob. Heart-rending sobs. Julia squeezed her eyes tightly shut, willing herself not to sob as well. Brenda had to steady herself against the sink in the kitchen. She too would have liked to join in.

And then Roberta cried: *'Oh my God, no!'*

She struggled frantically to get out of her father's seat. She pulled up her nightdress, borrowed from her mother, and saw the bright blood on her legs. 'Oh, Ed . . . Ed . . . I'm so sorry!'

Julia moved swiftly to her sister and pulled her closer, hugging her tightly and saying over and over again, 'You poor sweet thing, poor sweet thing.'

This time Roberta didn't push her away.

47

March, 1972

'I mean, she's all right, she'll manage, but she certainly won't be able to survive without finding some sort of work.' Brenda looked across at her sister. They hadn't managed to get their usual table by the window of the Cosy Corner and Nancy seemed more interested in watching the people who had than in listening to Roberta's plight.

'Hmm, well, of course, Peter has made sure that if anything ever happens to him, God forbid, I shall be very well off. I have to say, Brenda, I am rather surprised at Ed. I would have thought he'd have secured things a bit better for Roberta.'

'Oh, come on, Nance, that's hardly fair. He probably intended to, eventually. The poor chap was up to his ears in worry and hard work just before he died. And anyway, wasn't it you who once said nobody expects to die?'

'Well, I might have done,' sniffed Nancy, 'but anybody with any brains makes provision for the future.'

'Ed did. The house is Roberta's, and so is the business, and Ed's assistant John Clavell is very interested in buying that so she'll get something for it.'

Nancy screwed up her face. 'But the business can't be worth that much. Now, if Ed had gone in with Fordham-Clarke's, just think how secure Roberta would be.'

'But that's nonsense, Nancy, and you know it. If anything, she would be worse off. At least now she's got something to sell.'

For once Nancy was silent. She merely shrugged dismissively and Brenda felt hurt. She could stand her sister's pomposity most of the time, but not when it concerned poor Ed. Had the silly woman no humility, ever?

Nancy peered across at her sister. 'And how's your little business going? Anymore *rich* clients?'

Brenda bristled. Why did she always have to be so condescending? 'It's going quite well, actually. In fact, the salon's looking a treat. Perhaps you'd like to pop over sometime and have a free facial?'

Nancy looked aghast. 'All the way to Newmarket? You must be joking.'

'I thought you'd say that. That's why I offered,' Brenda retaliated. 'As Julia would say, offer freely what you know will be refused.'

Nancy's mouth dropped open. 'Well, I never heard such rubbish! And if that's the case with Julia, then we all know what to expect.'

Brenda donned a smug expression. 'You can expect away, Nance, but you'd be wrong because she's doing extremely well. They don't seem able to churn out her designs quick enough. No sooner are they in the boutique than they're sold. Sayrau is a hot name around London and she's making herself a nice big pile of money.'

'Oh, is she? Well, I hope she looks after it wisely.'

'Of course she will. Julia's not daft.'

'No, she's not, but she's a touch too sharp for my liking. So sharp she'll cut herself one day!'

'Nancy!' Brenda exclaimed. 'You are talking about my daughter. How would it be if I spoke about Clare like that?'

Nancy looked anxiously around the café. 'Keep your voice down, Brenda, we don't want everybody knowing our business.'

'But you just insulted my daughter.'

'No, I didn't. Well, I didn't mean to. Oh, come on, Brenda, you know me. I can't help being John Blunt.'

'John Blunt – is that what you call it? Well, sometimes you make me want to scream in frustration.'

Nancy lowered her eyes, remembering her own daughter screaming at something she'd inadvertently said. She looked towards the people at the window table, now preparing to move, and shook her head. 'I don't know, everyone's so precious these days, I can't say anything anymore without fear of offending you all.' She glared at her sister. 'I only speak the truth, you know, Brenda. It's always been my policy to speak the truth.' Nancy rose from her seat.

'Where are you going now?'

She pointed to the vacant table. 'Over there, where do you think?

Come on, we've got our table back. Make haste, Brenda, I haven't got all day.'

Exasperated, beyond measure, she followed her sister across the room.

48

August, 1972

Carefully driving her brand new Volvo Estate, Roberta turned right off Cheveley Road into Heath Road. It was a small private road, with just a few select houses overlooking Warren Hill, which was part of the Heath. In fact Heath Row, where her mother lived, was only a short distance away.

She drove slowly along Heath Road, with James in the back of the car in his child seat and Boris at the rear. Roberta passed a couple of smart detached houses and carried on until she came to a group of three Victorian town houses. She parked her car here and proceeded to take James out of his seat and stand him on the path. 'Boris come too,' he said pointing to the dog.

'No, James, Boris can stay in the back for a while.' She locked the car door and held out her hand. James held on to it. 'Come on, let's have a look at our new home.'

He let go of her hand and ran on ahead, his little legs speeding up as he went. 'Careful! You'll fall!' And he did, sprawled out on the pavement leading to the middle town house. 'Oh Jamie, you silly billy!' But, as quick as lightning, as he threatened to cry, pointing to his leg, 'Come on, darling, it's only a scratch.'

He looked down at the blood threatening to ooze from a tiny cut on his knee. 'Plas'er ... I want a plas'er. Mummy, it b'eeding, I need a plas'er.'

Roberta scooped up her son in her arms and kissed his cheek. 'You don't need a plaster on that. You're a big boy now. Big boys don't need plasters on little cuts like that.'

'But it's b'eeding, Mummy, it's b'eeding.'

'Is it bleeding? Oh, dear.'

Roberta fished in her pocket for the key to John Clavell's house. His wife was away, visiting her mother in York, and John had suggested that Roberta look round on her own without any interference. She was pleased about that. She didn't want any undue pressure from Mary Clavell. This idea of swapping homes seemed a good one, Roberta supposed it made good sense, and Heath Road did overlook the Heath with her mother only down the road . . . Yes, it definitely made sense. She turned the key and pushed open the door.

Covering the hall floor and sweeping up the stairs was a gold-coloured carpet. Roberta decided her first impression was favourable. She walked in and closed the door, putting James back on his feet. Roberta walked along the hall, with its attractive antique mahogany table and coat stand, towards the far end of the house and the kitchen overlooking the small back garden. The garden had been well looked after, and a wooden table with attached bench-seats stood in the middle upon a small patch of lawn. The kitchen was painted cream, and was light and airy with a split-level cooker and oatmeal-coloured units. But no Aga, no room for a big oak scrubbed table and chairs, and definitely no room for her lovely oak dresser. She sighed and wandered back across the hall to the sitting room opposite. James followed.

The room was rectangular-shaped and quite large. There would easily be room for her three-piece suite, and there was an enormous bay window looking out on to the garden. At least the room wasn't overlooked from the road. A wall-to-wall cream carpet covered the floor, and an uncomfortable-looking three-piece suite with shiny wooden legs and arms dominated the room. There was a set of flower prints on the wall, and a ghastly shag-pile rug in front of an obviously unused Adam-style fireplace. Roberta thought how clinical it all looked, too neat; no sign of children having a good time here. She sighed again, walking towards the dining room on the other side of the hall.

It was quite spacious, room for her oak refectory table and the high-backed leather chairs purchased just before Ed's death. It would be just the scrubbed oak kitchen table and dresser that would have to go. She sighed again, supposing that John and Mary Clavell would probably buy them off her. Or maybe she could exchange them for the mahogany hall table and coat-stand and the wooden table with bench-seat outside? She peeked into the downstairs cloakroom, and futher along into a tiny study.

She picked up James and started to mount the stairs. There were three bedrooms, two double and a single, and a fair-sized bathroom in pink. Roberta turned up her nose at the colour, but supposed she could live with it. She'd seen worse. There was another small flight of stairs leading to the attic. Tightly holding on to James, she wandered up. The attic room was quite charming, with its window set into the eaves, and she imagined her son having a lot of fun up there.

She went back down the two flights of stairs to the bottom and walked straight to the front door. 'Well, Jamie, what do you think?'

He looked at her as though he understood completely what she meant. 'Can Borry come too?'

Roberta kissed his cheek lovingly. 'Of course Borry can come too. You don't think we'd live anywhere without Boris, do you? Whatever next?'

They went outside, and she locked the door then put James back on to the ground. He held up his hand to his mother. 'Can I have a pla'ser now, p'ease, Mummy? I've been a big boy.'

She scooped him up into her arms again. 'I've got a better idea. Shall we go and see Grandma? Do you think she'll be home yet?'

'And will Gwamma give me a pla'ser?'

Roberta walked briskly to her car. 'I'm sure she will, especially as you've been such a big boy.'

James beamed, and then he saw Boris wagging his tail in the back of the car. 'And can Borry have a pla'ser too?'

49

It was Sunday afternoon, and after one of Brenda's splendid Sunday roasts Julia sat in her father's chair overlooking the Heath while Roberta stood by the window. James, exhausted, was fast asleep on the settee.

'But you loved your cottage. Why on earth are you giving it up?'

Roberta turned to face her. 'I can't afford it anymore. I can't afford the upkeep, and anyway it's far too big for just me and Jamie. With the money John will eventually pay me, I'll be able to send Jamie to a private school and live very nicely, thank you, with no worries about where the next penny is coming from.'

'Jamie at private school? I'm impressed.'

'It's the least I can do. Ed's son's going to have the best.'

'But you didn't need to leave your cottage. I could have helped you out.'

Roberta turned stubbornly away. 'I don't want your help, Julia. I want to do things for myself. I *need* to be independent.'

'But you had a perfectly good job, why ever would you want to give it up?'

Roberta swung round fiercely. 'Too many *memories*! Surely you see that?'

Her sister was contrite. 'I'm sorry.'

'No, *I'm* sorry, Julia. Sorry for snapping when you're only trying to help. But I've made up my mind. I've decided what I'm going to do.'

Julia studied her sister, who in her opinion was still far too thin. 'Join Mum, I suppose?'

Roberta snorted. 'No way! Independent, I said. Although I must admit it's great having her down the road. She'll be invaluable later for baby-sitting.'

Julia's eyes flashed. 'Baby-sitting?'

'Of course. I'm going into business, working for myself.'

'What sort of business?'

'Catering. I decided the other night.'

'*Catering?* That'll be hard work.'

'Well, isn't shop-keeping?'

Julia shrugged. 'I suppose it is. But not like catering. All that washing up!'

Roberta laughed, a welcome sound. 'I shan't be doing much washing up, Julia, and eventually I'll pay somebody else to do that. I aim to do lunches and dinners, private parties and the like. There's loads of trainers' wives around Newmarket who'll be happy to pay me to organise their dinner parties. I'm a damned good cook and cooking is what I like to do. I don't want to spend the rest of my life in an office. I want to be out and about, doing my own thing.'

'Well, good for you, Roberta. Well done. Full marks.'

'You mean it, Julia, really? You approve?'

She nodded enthusiastically. 'I not only approve, Roberta, but I'll help you in any way I can. I shall recommend you to everybody I meet from now on. It pays to put word round. You never know who might know somebody in this area who could use you. And I'm ace with book-keeping. Any problems on that score, I'll happily help.'

Roberta smiled. 'I did my fair share of accounts when Ed was alive, but thanks, Julia, I appreciate your offer. And likewise I shall recommend Sarayu's in Chelsea to all my future clients.'

Julia held out her hand. 'It's going to be all right now, Roberta, you'll see.'

She took her sister's hand. 'I hope so, Julia. For James's sake.'

50

January, 1973

Julia looked lovely. With her hair smartly back in a chignon, and wearing a natty camel-coloured sheepskin jacket over a red Biba roll-necked dress and matching leather boots, she turned heads wherever she went. It was noon on a Saturday and she had the whole day off. She took a taxi to Clare's where they'd arranged to have lunch, and her heart jumped into her mouth when she saw a silver-grey Aston Martin parked outside.

She knocked on the door. Nanny opened it and Julia walked straight in. 'How are you, Nanny? Jennifer and Vivien doing well?' This particular nanny, the second so far, insisted on being addressed in this fashion.

'They're doing very well.' She nodded in the direction of the drawing room. 'Their father is here. A fleeting visit, I understand.'

'I'll go through.'

With her heart beating faster, Julia walked through to Clare's drawing room. Nathan stood at the far window with Vivien in his arms, looking out on to the garden. He didn't notice Julia straight away, but when he eventually did his face lit up in a smile. 'Julia! How lovely to see you.'

'*Auntie Julia!*' squealed Vivien.

Nathan put her on the floor and she ran swiftly towards Julia, who gathered her into her arms and swung her round. 'Hallo, little Vivvy, and how are you today?' And then Jennifer appeared from nowhere, also squealing and shouting in delight, and had to be swung round as well.

Nathan stood patiently watching until Julia released Jennifer. Then he moved in and kissed the visitor on the cheek. He smelt of

Chanel aftershave. Julia would recognise the smell anywhere. She privately called it Nathan's smell. He grinned, showing that irresistible gap between his teeth.

'Let me guess, Julia, why you're looking so divine ... you're going to the football match?' He saw the blank expression on her face. 'You mean, you lied to me about never missing a Chelsea home game? They're playing Arsenal this afternoon. Should be a good match.'

'I didn't lie to you, Nathan, but you must know that Saturdays are usually spent in the boutique?'

He raised his hand to her face and ran two fingers down her cheek. 'I hear you're doing well?'

She moved away quickly. 'I am. Are you?'

He nodded with a slow smile. 'Of course, but I miss you.'

There he went again, turning on the charm. 'Do you? Do you really, Nathan?' She decided to change the subject. 'Where's Clare?'

Her cousin appeared, making a bee-line for Julia and hugging her warmly. 'You're looking wonderful, darling.'

'And so are you.' Julia stood back and appraised Clare, looking radiant in her black cord flares, with a short-sleeved black-and-white-striped skinny jumper worn over a white bell-sleeved blouse. Clare's straight glossy hair had grown considerably and was now halfway down her back.

She looked at Nathan. 'Are you staying for lunch?'

'Am I invited?'

Clare shrugged, as though she really couldn't care less. 'Well, the twins would certainly like it.'

He flashed a look at Julia. 'In that case, I will.'

They finished lunch, a delicious casserole bought from the food hall in Harrods, sitting snugly around the kitchen table. Jennifer and Vivien sat propped up on their booster seats and managed to flick food everywhere. Nathan continually admonished them, and once or twice so did Julia, but it was obvious that Clare didn't give a damn. Nanny didn't seem too bothered either. Julia's thoughts sped to her sister, who would never allow such behaviour from James.

By the end of lunch, she had had enough. She looked at her wristwatch, almost anxious to get away.

Clare moaned, 'You're not leaving us already, Julia? You've only just arrived.'

'I know, and I'm sorry, but it's not often I get a Saturday off. I wanted to do some browsing round the shops. Why don't you come with me?'

Clare pulled a face. 'I'm sorry, Julia, but I really don't think I can face the shops on a cold Saturday afternoon in January.'

Nathan pushed back his chair. 'Would you like a lift?'

Surprised, Julia looked up at him. 'I'm sorry?'

'I'm leaving as well. I told you, I'm going to watch Chelsea play Arsenal. The kick-off's in less than an hour.'

She gulped, and noticing Clare's raised eyebrows, stood up defiantly. 'Thanks, Nathan, that's very kind of you.'

Julia didn't know exactly how but found herself persuaded by Nathan to watch Chelsea play. At first it wasn't too bad, they sat in his box in the West Stand with a couple of his football cronies, but as the game wore on and it became obvious that Chelsea were going to lose, Nathan's charm disappeared. Every now and again he would turn to Julia and give vent to his anger. 'Did you see that? *Did you see it!* A foul if ever there was one!' He'd thump the front of the box before him and yell loudly across the stand, 'Come on, *Osgood*! What the hell do you think you're playing at?' Or, '*Hudson! Hudson!* To your right, you idiot, to your right!' And when Arsenal scored a goal, he yelled, 'For God's sake, any fool could have saved that!' Fans in the seats below their box would turn to see who was yelling so much. Julia found herself sinking further and further down into her seat. This was a side to Nathan she'd never seen before.

And to cap it all Chelsea didn't even score a goal. They lost 1–0.

Afterwards Nathan took Julia's arm and guided her through the throng. They reached his Aston Martin and he opened the passenger door. 'Have dinner with me tonight, Julia . . . please?'

For the second time that day, she could hardly believe what she was hearing. For some reason she hadn't expected him to invite her out. She'd thought he'd just drop her off and be quickly on his way.

Julia looked at her watch. 'It isn't dinnertime yet.'

'Well, in that case, you can invite me back to your place and show me this boutique.'

'Really, Nathan? You'd like to see my boutique?'

He grinned and looked at her, eyes devouring her. 'I can't wait.'

In the shop he browsed around, not saying much, but at least he didn't scowl or hurl abuse. Sarayu's eyes nearly popped out of her head. When he was out of earshot, she turned excitedly to Julia. 'Cor! He aint 'alf nice! Where'd you find 'im?' Julia just smiled and put a finger to the side of her nose. She was saying nothing.

Fortunately the boutique was busy, the two Saturday girls flat out, but Julia had a sudden desire to escape from her beloved shop. With Nathan by her side, she didn't want to waste time on business. He examined the jewellery range, spending quite a bit of time working the clasps and trying the pins on the brooches. 'Come on, Nathan, let's go. In case you've forgotten, this is my day off.' She smiled at him, but he turned instead to Sarayu, giving her one of his appraising looks. Her lovely skin tone deepened to a rosy hue. Then Nathan nodded in her direction, turned back to Julia, and followed her out of the boutique.

Nathan had managed to park his car outside but hesitated on the pavement.

'I live not far from here,' Julia encouraged, pointing in the direction of the house.

Nathan put a hand to his chin, looking around. 'Anywhere here sell alcohol?'

'Alcohol? Why?'

He grinned. 'Let's get some vodka and vermouth and olives, and I'll make you the best Martini you've every tasted.'

'But I've got vodka already, and I'm sure there's some vermouth in the back of the cupboard.'

He wagged his finger. 'It's probably an old bottle that's been opened for months. No, Julia, I want fresh vermouth and Smirnoff vodka.'

She pointed down the King's Road. 'Well, there's a shop down there, on the left. They sell most things.'

Nathan unlocked the passenger door of his car. 'Good. Hop in then, Julia. We'll stop on the way to your place.' She climbed in, amused at the way he effortlessly took charge. He climbed in next to her and put his hand on top of hers. 'Let's hit the town tonight, I'm in the mood.'

She looked at his beige roll-necked sweater and leather jacket. 'Hardly dressed for hitting the town, are you?'

He indicated a bag on the narrow rear seat. 'Oh, I always carry an overnight bag around with me . . . for emergencies.' He winked.

Julia frowned. 'Nathan, had you got all this planned?'

He shrugged and turned the key in the ignition. 'How could I, Julia? I hadn't a clue what you were up to these days.' He smiled at her once more. 'Had I?'

Nathan even produced a cocktail shaker from his overnight bag. He went to work on the vodka and vermouth as soon as they entered Julia's house, though complaining bitterly about the quality of the ice. 'You should make fresh ice every week, Julia, not keep the stuff for months!'

'Well, I'm sorry. But how was I to know I'd be entertaining a barman this weekend?'

He allowed her one of his tolerant smiles then shook the cocktail before pouring healthy measures into two Martini glasses. 'Are these yours?' he asked. She had to say no. Nothing in the house belonged to her, except her clothes. 'They're very fine,' he said, and put an olive in each. He handed Julia a glass. She took a sip and gasped.

'Nathan! How much vodka did you put in this?'

'A lot.'

'Well, how much vermouth?'

'A little, the merest hint.'

She took another sip, warming to the taste. 'You need to make a lot of cocktails then, to keep your vermouth fresh?'

He grinned. 'Shall we see if we can finish the bottle?'

She laughed. 'Then hit the town? Even I haven't that sort of stamina.'

Nathan refilled his own glass and took another long slurp. He narrowed his eyes, focussing them on her. 'Wear something slinky this evening, will you? I want to be seduced by you all night.'

She lowered her eyes, excitement coursing through her veins. She'd thought perhaps they'd make love before they went out; it was obviously not on Nathan's agenda. But if that was the way he wanted to play it, that was fine by her.

Nathan changed in the guest bedroom, and a bemused Julia sat on the bed in her own room. She hadn't got anything slinky. The nearest she came was a low-necked Horrocks dress in a bold flower print. It was hardly slinky. She drew a blank until she remembered something. At the back of the wardrobe, in a polythene cleaner's wrap, was an ancient Dior dress in the finest grey satin. Why her landlord's wife had left it she didn't know, but along with several other garments it still lurked among her own clothes. Julia slid off the bed and opened the wardrobe door. She pushed her hand in and withdrew the dress. It shimmered in the light and the supple fabric rippled. Julia undid the side zip and slipped it on. The satin felt wonderful against her skin, but the dress finished just below her knee – not a good length. She almost took it off again but decided to steal a quick look in the mirror first. Julia stood there and knew the length didn't matter a jot. The dress fitted her superbly, the neckline hanging low at the front and even lower at the back, falling in loose folds from thin shoulder straps. Definitely too low for her to wear a bra. She undid the zip, slipped out of the shoulder straps and flipped off her bra. She slid back in the dress, zipped it up, and took another good look, noticing the cut of the fabric, the way it clung flatteringly. She was bowled over by it. The dress could have been made for her. It was perfection. Julia adored it.

Nathan, elegant in a dark suit, white shirt and red floral tie, allowed his mouth to drop open at the sight of her. He could hardly believe his eyes. 'Wow, wow, wow!' He put down his Martini and with hands extended walked towards her. Julia placed her own hands in his. He spun her round, eyes widening in delight. '*Wow!*' He kissed her gently on the mouth. 'Julia, I'm going to be the proudest man alive tonight. I can't wait to show you off!'

'You don't look so bad yourself.'

He downed the rest of his drink and held out his arm. 'Your carriage awaits.'

She linked her arm through his and, grabbing a fur jacket also found at the back of the wardrobe, allowed herself to be led out of her home.

The Savoy Grill was packed, but that didn't stop the Maître d' paying obsequious attention to Nathan and Julia. He recognised a big tipper when he saw one and positioned them well away from the door.

'Is that mink, Julia?'

She watched as the fur jacket was carried away by a waiter. 'Oh, er . . .'

'Mink jacket, couture gown. You must be doing well?'

She smiled sweetly, spilling over with triumph inside. She waved aside the menu offered to her, saying, 'My companion will choose.'

He looked at the waiter. 'Two of your champagne cocktails to start with, please.' The waiter walked away and Nathan peered over the menu at Julia. 'Do you fancy steak? Tournedos Rossini? They use *pure* foie gras here and real truffles . . . and shall we go the whole hog and have oysters to start?'

Julia willingly agreed. She fingered the satin shoulder straps of her wonderful gown and thanked God for the good taste of her landlord's wife. For *beneath* the gown she was still ordinary Julia Tree.

The wine waiter brought their champagne cocktails and Nathan ordered a bottle of Chablis Premier Cru and a Pomerol Grand Cru.

'To us,' he smiled at Julia as he raised his glass in a toast.

'To us,' she replied.

Nathan leant across the table. 'Now tell me, fair maiden, are there anymore at home like you?'

For a fleeting second, Julia's eyes clouded over, remembering her sister. She cleared her throat. 'Well, actually there is. I do have a sister. Her name is Roberta.'

Nathan's eyebrows rose. 'Roberta? I like that.'

Julia gulped. 'But it's terribly sad. She's older than me, was married and has a child. Lovely kid called James, a credit to her really, but her husband died tragically. Got shunted off the road by some maniac in the fog, driving too fast. Ed had slowed down because of a lorry in front, and this other fool just rammed into him. Ed must have seen him coming because he steered off to the left and his car went into a ditch. He was thrown through the windscreen.'

Nathan took a long sip of his cocktail. 'That sounds awful. How old is she – Roberta?'

Julia pursed her lips. 'Well, I'm twenty-two so she must be twenty-four.'

'Married young?'

Julia shrugged. 'Yes, well, Roberta's not like me.' Julia pulled a face. 'She's more the shy and retiring sort, but a fabulous cook!'

'Is she now?'

'It's so sad and yet somehow inspiring, Nathan. They had this

230

wonderful house, an old cottage. I mean, it was way out in the sticks, too far out for me, miles from anywhere, but she loved it. Afterwards she had to sell it, and the business, and move into Newmarket. She was ill for months, but you should see her now! She's taken up catering, and she's running her own business. In such a short space of time, she's doing really well. Her name's getting about. And, Nathan, you haven't lived 'til you've tasted her food! She has this sort of knack of making everything seem so deliciously simple and yet it's really quite exquisite. D'you know what I mean?'

He nodded, looking quite sympathetic for him. 'How old is James?'

'He's two. Into everything now.' Julia sipped her cocktail. 'She's already teaching him to ride. Takes him down to the yard where my father worked, they've got a couple of old nags there. Roberta's determined Jamie's going to ride. He loves it.'

'Is she beautiful?'

The oysters arrived and Julia leant back in her seat. 'I didn't think so once, but as she's got older I've changed my mind. I suppose you could say she's beautiful inside, and that shines through . . . do you know what I mean?'

He weighed up her words. 'Sounds interesting. What sort of catering does she do? It's my mother's sixtieth birthday in a couple of weeks and I need someone to organise a rather special supper party for her. She doesn't want a big affair, nothing ostentatious, but we can't go out because it's our weekend with the twins. Could Roberta do that?'

Julia smiled at him, not a glimmer of presentiment in her brain. 'Oh, yes, Nathan. She'd love to. You're just the sort of person she'd like to meet. Shall I get her to give you a call?'

He reached across and squeezed her hand. 'I'd like that. You do it. I'll look forward to hearing from her. Now, how about these oysters?'

After leaving the Savoy, Nathan took Julia to Murray's nightclub in Beak Street where the floor show was just getting underway. They stayed a while then left, ending up at Annabel's. Julia was reminded of the evening in Tramp.

But this time she wasn't let out of Nathan's sight and they danced the night away. And he was different. He held her gently, quite formally, with his hand gripping hers. They smooched in each other's arms to the beat of the blues. Nobody disturbed them, although many gave them a second glance. To Julia it was heaven on earth, like a dream come true.

At three o'clock in the morning, the cold fresh air hit Nathan. When they arrived back at his Aston Martin, he handed Julia his keys. 'Can you drive?'

'A little. I mean, I've passed my test.'

Nathan, quite drunk, indicated his car. 'Can you manage it? It's quite receptive.'

Julia frowned. 'I'll try.'

She drove home to Margaretta Terrace, clipping the curb a few times, scaring the odd motorist out of his wits, and once going the wrong way round a keep-left sign, but the Aston Martin wasn't scratched. With a final bump of the curb, she managed to park.

'Ouch!'

'Sorry, I did my best.'

Sleepily, Nathan turned to her. 'You did good.'

As soon as they were inside, he wrapped his arms around her. 'Thank you for a won'ful *eve*ning. I shall – hic – *never* forget it.'

'Nathan, you're drunk!'

He looked at her indignantly. 'Me? I'm – *hic* – not drunk.' He gestured towards the kitchen. 'In fact, I was thinking of having another . . . have you any Remy Martin?'

'Find out for yourself! *I'm* going to bed.'

Thinking it was just her luck, Julia mounted the stairs. Contritely, he followed.

She walked into her bedroom and turned to face him. 'Perhaps you'd be more comfortable in the guest room?'

Sheepishly, he grinned at her. 'I'm not *that* drunk, Julia.'

She sat on the bed and he sat down beside her to give her a kiss. It was a gentle kiss, during which they both shifted further on to the bed and lay down. The kiss was prolonged and Julia's hands began to roam. This was Nathan. *The* Nathan! The man of her dreams. Suddenly, her excitement rocketed.

And then he grabbed her hand, stalling her. 'Julia, we're not running to catch a bloody bus.' Nathan propped himself on one elbow, and then slipped. He propped himself up once more as a smile lit Julia's face. 'Don't laugh at me . . . saucy lady.'

'But you're so funny when you're drunk.'

He kissed her again, and again Julia's hands were all over his body. 'Julia! For God's sake . . . let *me* make love to you! The *first* time a man likes to take control.' Nathan shifted himself into a sitting position and looked down at her. 'I want to take your dress off, and . . . don't you move an inch. *I* want to take it off.' He lifted her so that he could get his hands round the back of her dress. 'Where's the zip?'

Julia looked at him coolly. 'You want to take it off, Nathan. You find the zip.'

'You're a hard woman, Julia.' Then his hands found the side zip. Nathan pulled it down and the dress slipped luxuriously away from her shoulders and breasts. He signed with pleasure. 'God, you're gorgeous. You're bloody – hic – gorgeous, Julia.' He continued to trawl her dress down to her feet then tossed it on to the bedroom carpet. It fell like a pool, shimmering in the light. Nathan allowed his eyes to feast upon Julia's black suspender-belt and stockings, and teeny-tiny lace panties. 'Bloody gorgeous.'

He yanked off the lace panties and threw them across the room before leaning over to kiss her. His hand roamed idly down her body, coming to rest between her legs.

Delighting in the taste of his mouth, and savouring his tongue, Julia writhed and gasped as his fingers worked magic. '*What* . . . what on earth did you just do to me, Nathan?'

'Like it, did you?' His fingers worked some more. She writhed again, moaning in pleasure. 'Did you like that as well, Julia?' He moved as close as could be.

'I like it all, Nathan, but I'd like it better if you took off your clothes. I want to be able to feel your skin.'

Frowning, he looked down at himself and a slow smile crossed his face. 'Oh, yes, I forgot.'

As he shifted away from her, Julia quickly grabbed his hand. 'Can I ask you something, Nathan? Before we make love, can I ask you to give me something? Something really, really special? It'll cost you nothing, but it'll make me the happiest girl in Chelsea.'

Rather unsteadily, he kissed her mouth again. 'Tonight, Julia, I'd give you anything. Anything at all.'

'Even . . . permission to sell your jewellery in my boutique?' He shifted away, shaking his head. 'It can only be beneficial to you, Nathan. I have some pretty discriminating customers, they only want to buy the best . . . and yours is the best.'

He started to remove his clothes, flinging them untidily on the floor as he did so. Naked, he flopped down next to Julia. She couldn't help allowing her eyes to wander over his body, and liking what she saw.

He kissed her, and then raised himself to look down into her face. 'I'll send you a selection next week,' he promised.

Thrilled beyond measure, Julia gave herself to him.

She woke with a start, sitting up in bed to raise a hand to her throbbing head. And then she remembered the night before. How could she have forgotten? Urgently, she turned to Nathan's side of the bed. It was empty. Julia jumped out and hurried along to the bathroom. No Nathan there so she went downstairs. He was nowhere to be seen. Reluctantly, Julia went back upstairs and peeked out of the bedroom window. His Aston Martin was gone. She sped over to her wristwatch, lying on the table beside her bed. It was ten-thirty. Whatever time had he left?

Put out and a little hurt she folded her arms around her nakedness. Then, out of the corner of her eye, something caught her attention. She looked across the room to the large mirror over her vanity unit. She read. *'Business acu.: 10/10 – the jewellery's on its way! Sex: showed promise! N.P.'*

Julia raced across the room and stared at his message. The swine! Then she looked down at her favourite Lancôme lipstick now completely worn away. Infuriated, she picked it up. Worn to a stump. An involuntary smile crossed her face. 'Showed promise, indeed! You ain't seen nothing yet, N.P.'

51

With a heavily laden car, Roberta pulled into Anne and Nathan Purley's drive in De Freville Avenue. She parked as snugly as she could away from the front door. With guests arriving later on, there was nothing worse that staff dominating the prime positions. Roberta stepped out of her Volvo and walked over to ring the bell.

Almost straight away, Anne Purley opened the door, with Jennifer two paces behind her. 'Ah, you must be Julia's sister . . . Roberta?'

She nodded and smiled at Jennifer then gestured towards her car. 'Is is all right if I bring everything in?'

'Of course. Do you need some help?'

'That would be nice.'

'Hang on, I'll get Nathan.'

Roberta walked back to her car and opened the rear door. She picked up the essential goods first and started to walk back towards the house. As she stepped over the threshold, a dark-haired man appeared, looking casual in jeans and an open-necked checked shirt. 'You must be Roberta? Hallo, I'm Nathan. . . . I'll help you offload.' He hardly spared her a second glance, but as he walked past became aware of her perfume and actually stopped in his tracks for a moment as the scent assailed him. Reluctantly Nathan continued his journey to the car. Within seconds she was back again.

'Be careful with that, please.' She reached across, at the same time looking into Nathan's eyes. She smiled, and grabbed two dishes. 'I'll take these.' Then she was gone again, back into his house. This time he watched her go, something stirring inside him as he breathed in her scent.

When everything was laid out on the work tops in the well-equipped kitchen, Roberta turned her attention to Anne. 'Happy birthday.'

Anne was suddenly accosted by her granddaughters. 'Oh, thank you,' she said, bending down to give them a hug. 'And you two are going to be extra 'specially good this evening, aren't you? In bed by seven and no messing!'

Jennifer stuck her thumb in her mouth then pulled it out again and poked Vivien in the eye. Vivien burst into tears. 'Jenny! That's naughty!' Nathan squatted down and glared at his daughter. 'How many times have I told you not to poke Vivien?'

Contritely, Jenny put her thumb in her mouth again and looked up at Roberta. Roberta winked and Jenny giggled. From his crouched position, Nathan looked up and Roberta widened her eyes innocently before returning to the job in hand. 'I can't remember,' she said, facing them again 'did you want me to set the table?' She looked directly at Nathan, with whom she'd dealt over the phone.

'Yes,' he said softly, taking in her simple black dress and shoulder-length hair caught back in two gold slides, 'I think that's what we arranged.'

Delices Gruyère, roast fillet of beef with Madeira gravy and slices of crisp, light Yorkshire pudding, followed by individually baked Grand Marnier soufflés and a selection of French cheeses, were all served to perfection by Roberta. Finally she left the guests to sit and chat over coffee and petits fours.

She mounted the stairs to the first floor. The crying had started about ten minute before, an intermittent sound at first, gradually becoming insistent. She'd first heard it while loading up the dishwasher and clearing away the mess in the kitchen. Now her time was her own she could not ignore it.

She followed the sound of the crying, high-pitched and frantic by now, and pushed open the nursery door. With tears streaming down her face, Jennifer stood in her cot, red-faced and anxious, chubby little fingers gripping the cot rails. 'I . . .' she caught back a sob '. . . want . . . my dwink! Want my dwink!'

Roberta walked towards the child and scooped her up in her arms. 'You want your drink, do you, Jenny? Shall we find it?' Jennifer pointed to a table set against the far wall. Two baby beakers filled with juice stood on a tray. Securely holding the little girl, Roberta walked over to the tray and picked up one of the beakers. 'There we are, no more tears.'

Thirstily, Jennifer gulped the juice in one go and squealed for the other beaker. Roberta gently jigged her up and down in her arms. 'I think you've had enough, Jenny, we don't want you to be sick.' She kissed the child's hot cheek and turned to look in the other cot. Vivien still slept soundly. Roberta was amazed. With so much racket going on in the bedroom and the sound of raucous laughter downstairs, it was a wonder she wasn't screaming as well. Roberta looked around for a changing mat and some fresh nappies. She could see nothing. 'I think you need a fresh nappy, Jenny.'

'Baf'room,' she said, in between gnawing on the empty beaker.

'Bathroom?'

Jenny nodded and pointed to the door. 'Baf'room over d'er.'

Roberta walked to the door and along the landing until she found the bathroom. She put the light on and walked inside. 'Goodness me! It's all systems go in here, isn't it, Jenny?' She laid the child on the changing mat, pulled down her pyjama bottoms and slipped off the wet nappy. Roberta then proceeded to clean Jenny with cotton wool and baby lotion, gently smoothing on a dab of zinc and castor oil before she applied a fresh nappy. Happy with the attention, Jenny lay quite still while Roberta completed her task. 'Right, little girl, back to bed for you.' She picked Jennifer up and walked back to the nursery where she laid her carefully in her cot. Jennifer's face instantly crumpled.

'Me not want go s'eep. *Me not want go s'eep.*'

Roberta crouched down and pushed her hand through the cot rails. She squeezed Jennifer's arm. 'Shall I tell you a story then? Is that what you'd like? This is Jamie's story. It's about Jamie and his flying horse. Jamie is my little boy, he's a bit older than you, Jenny, and when he can't get to sleep, if he closes his eyes tightly a lovely white horse appears. The horse is called Phantom, and if Jamie is very, very good and keeps his eyes really tightly shut, Phantom will let him climb up on his back. And then he takes Jamie for a ride . . . way, way up into the sky . . .'

Roberta continued with her tale, completely holding the little girl's attention, and, unbeknown to her, Nathan's. He stood in the doorway, quite enthralled. Mesmerised, in fact.

'P'anton not d'er,' whimpered Jennifer.

'But he will be, Jenny, if you close your eyes, because he can be your horse as well. He's only ever there if you close your eyes and try to go to sleep. Phantom's a horse of the night, and he looks after all young children who can't go to sleep.'

Jennifer closed her eyes, tightly at first, then after a while she relaxed. Briefly she opened them again, until she was satisfied that Roberta was still there, then gradually Jennifer went to sleep.

Stiff from her crouching position, Roberta stood up and arched her back. She turned and jumped, one hand flying to her mouth. Had Nathan been watching her all the time? She was embarrassed. Telling fairy stories to his daughter was hardly the businesslike character she wanted to put across. She smiled and walked towards him. 'Jenny was thirsty and couldn't sleep. I gave her a drink and changed her nappy. She'll be all right now.'

Nathan's eyes didn't leave Roberta as his thoughts raced. This was the mother that *he'd* had as a child. This was the mother Clare could never be. This was the mother he wanted for his children. Roberta walked past him, out of the nursery, making her way to the stairs. Again he was aware of her perfume.

'Roberta?' he stalled her, swallowing hard. He moved after her. 'Would you have dinner with me sometime?'

She was already walking down the stairs. A faint blush came over her cheeks as she hesitated, looking up at him. 'Well, thank you, Nathan, that's really very kind but I don't get much time these days.' Nervously, she laughed. 'And when I do, I like to spend it with my son.' She continued down the stairs.

His mouth dropped open. He could hardly believe his ears. At twenty-eight years old, Nathan Purley had finally been refused by a woman. He licked his lips, and looked back at his sleeping daughters. It was no big deal, after all. Roberta wasn't that special.

And then, confused, he followed her scent through the house and back into the kitchen where he stayed helping her until it was time for his guests to leave.

About a week later, Nathan received Roberta's bill. He looked at it, noticing the artistic handwriting and remembering her face, her perfume, the food she had cooked. In fact she'd been niggling away at his thoughts ever since his mother's sixtieth birthday party. He couldn't quite understand why, except that she'd touched something deep inside him, then she'd rejected him, and he didn't know why. It was only dinner he'd been offering, nothing else, and she was no pin up, no Julia. And yet she'd stirred something within him, and he couldn't quite figure out what.

He tapped the bill with his hand and decided to take a trip over to Newmarket. He arrived at her door, bouquet of flowers in one hand and a cheque in the other. Very briefly, Roberta allowed him in, even made him a cup of tea and introduced him to James, but she was busy, baking and preparing food for another dinner party, and he was quickly shown the door. Again he asked her if she had a spare night available in the near future, to maybe have a quick drink? Very politely she said no.

That did it. He decided he'd never go near her again.

52

Nathan was busy, his workload far too heavy. He hadn't contacted Julia and was beginning to feel guilty. But he hadn't time to go to London, or at least not before his next weekend with the twins, and so dismissed her from his thoughts.

He'd called in at the Petty Cury shop, which he now regularly did, and was actually leaving when he caught a glimpse of Roberta striding by in the sunshine. She was wearing a fetching suit the colour of corn. He noticed how good her legs were in the shortish skirt, and how straight her back in the long double-breasted fitted jacket with its wide lapels. She stood out, and Nathan caught other men giving her a second glance. But Roberta was oblivious to it all. She strode on hurriedly and he had his work cut out to catch her up.

'Roberta?'

She stopped and flashed her eyes at him, brushing the hair from her face. 'Oh, Nathan, . . . I'm sorry, I didn't see you there. I'm afraid I'm in a hurry.' She averted her eyes. 'I've got one or two things to buy that I can't get in Newmarket.'

Nathan looked at her, totally lost for words. Each time she had this effect on him. He couldn't use his normal patter, knew she wouldn't fall for any of that in a million years. What, in the name of sanity, *would* she fall for?

'Which way are you walking?'

'Eden Lilley's and Joshua Taylor's.'

'I'm going that way too.'

Nathan fell into step with her, and she made no attempt to slow down. 'Are you always in such a hurry?' he asked, as they reached the Market Square.

She smiled, stopped, and looked at him. 'Come to think of it, I probably am these days.' She slowed her pace. 'Perhaps I should slow down a bit.'

He gave her one of his heart-stopping smiles. 'You're looking very smart.'

She threw him a look. 'I've just had a meeting, with Turner & Nugent. You know, the accountants? Prospective clients. They hold business lunches every second Thursday. I've just landed myself a trial run.'

'The job's yours then. When they taste your cooking, they won't believe their good fortune.'

'Thank you, that's kind.'

'It's the truth.' He stopped and touched her arm. 'Look, come and have a drink with me, please? It's lunchtime, just a quick one. Give yourself a break . . . nothing more.'

She hesitated very briefly then shrugged. 'Why not?'

Nathan breathed a sigh of relief and led her to the Blue Boar.

Much to his surprise, she asked for a Noilly Prat. He'd quite expected her to drink Britvic orange or something similarly non-alcoholic. He drank beer. They sat at the same table he'd once shared with Julia, tucked away in the corner. He noticed the glow on Roberta's cheeks, and watched as she unbuttoned her jacket and proceeded to remove it. She twisted round in her seat and, with his help, hung it on the back of her chair. In doing so, one of the buttons on her gold-coloured blouse popped open, right in the middle, revealing a glimpse of cleavage and white lacy bra. Nathan's eyes homed in on it straight away. Roberta didn't notice, and he was almost tempted to tell her, but she confounded him so much his normally easy charm escaped him. He drank his beer silently.

Roberta sipped her drink and idly fingered her silver necklace. He noticed her lovely nails, unpolished but well cared for, and then her necklace. One of his. He stretched out his hand, brushing hers in doing so, and touched the necklace with the curly Ps all the way round. 'Did you buy this?'

Roberta's eyes immediately moved down, and although she couldn't see the necklace she noticed the button. Hastily, she did it up, and raising her face locked eyes with his. Simultaneously, they noticed each other's dark brown eyes. Normally, Nathan would have quipped, 'Did you have to do that up? It looked rather fetching undone.' But the words stuck in his throat somehow.

'Julia bought it for me some time ago.'

Nathan's thoughts were abruptly brought back to the necklace. 'Ah, yes, Julia.'

Roberta fingered the necklace again. 'I wear it a lot, considering how intricate it is. It's so very comfortable.'

Nathan sat back in his seat. 'Well made, that's why.'

Roberta smiled. 'Which part of your business are you most interested in, Nathan? The leather or the jewellery?'

Slowly, he shook his head. 'Both. I wouldn't be able to choose.'

Roberta kept her eyes on his face, noticing how very good-looking he was. Extremely so in fact. She wondered about Julia. It was surprising her sister hadn't got her claws into him by now. 'Is it something you started up or a family concern?'

Roberta's eyes hardly left his face. He was disconcerted and flattered all at the same time. 'It was my mother's idea. After my father died, she wanted something to do. Years ago, before she married, she was involved in retail in London so she knew where to start. I left school and joined her straight away.'

'Did you go to school in Cambridge?'

'No, Ely. Kings.'

Roberta nodded. Another rich kid. 'I went to a secondary modern school in Newmarket. I'm afraid my education left a lot to be desired.'

He frowned. 'But I thought Julia went to the Perse?'

'Oh, she did. On a scholarship, though. She was a whizz at school, didn't take after me.' Roberta pulled a face which as far as Nathan was concerned just added to her attraction. She finished her drink. 'Look, thanks for this but I really must go.' She picked up her stone-coloured handbag which was lying on the table, and he noticed it was an Enny. Normally he would have spotted one a mile off for its high quality leather and superb workmanship. Purley's sold Enny bags in their shops.

Nathan panicked. He had to stall her. God, what was she doing to him? His heart was in his mouth. 'These business lunches, do they have to be hot?'

Roberta blinked then frowned. 'Sorry?'

He chuckled nervously. 'I've been thinking for some time that it would be an idea to offer lunch to certain business associates now and again. The only trouble is, I don't have any proper cooking facilities at the warehouse.'

'Best to take them out to lunch then.'

'No, that just disrupts things and takes far too much time. But could you provide, well, you know, sandwiches or something a bit superior?'

Roberta sighed. 'Yes, but you don't really need me to do that. Get your secretary to whip something up.'

Nathan flicked his hand dismissively. 'Oh, she'd be hopeless. Besides, I'd like *you* to do it.'

Roberta was amused. 'You want *me* to make sandwiches for a lunch at your warehouse?'

'No, not exactly. How about calling in at the warehouse to check out the situation? There must be other food you can serve cold?'

'Lots! Smoked salmon, quiches, assorted salads, prawns in flaky pastry . . . the list is endless.'

Nathan touched her arm, wholeheartedly agreeing with her suggestions, and she shifted out of her seat, brushing very close to him. He inhaled that perfume again and his head went into a spin. He had to fight a strong desire to pull her down on to his lap. Instead, he stood up and helped her on with her jacket, touching her hair which felt strong but silken. 'You'll call at the warehouse then?'

She nodded. 'I'll give you a ring. When exactly do you want this lunch?'

'Next week?'

Roberta raised her eyebrows. 'I'll have to make sure I can fit it in.'

Nathan shrugged. 'Whenever then, I'll have it to suit you.'

53

Even his work began to suffer. Nathan couldn't concentrate anymore. He couldn't think about anything else but Roberta. In all of
his life, he had never felt this way. And to top it all, he had to rack
his brains to think who to invite to this damned business lunch. His
bank manager, his accountant, his mother . . . the postman, maybe?

Roberta arrived at the warehouse two days before the lunch.
Nathan met her at the door and, taking his time, escorted her through
his precious building, explaining about his business. She was interested but not enthralled. Roberta just wanted to get on with her job
and go home. James was at kindergarten and she had a couple of
hours free. Time was precious to her.

She sat opposite him in his office while his secretary made them
both a cup of coffee. Roberta wore a smart red trouser suit with an
open-necked white blouse. Around her neck was a string of pearls,
superb quality, Ed's wedding present to her. Nathan recognised their
worth straight away.

The phone rang. He snatched it up, angry that his secretary had
put the call through. It was Julia.

'Help, Nathan, we've completely sold out! Sarayu and I have
spent the last couple of weeks watching your jewellery walk out of
this shop. It's hot stuff, please can you send up some more?'

He ran a finger round his collar and decided not to use her name
in front of Roberta. He didn't know why. 'Sure, sure. That's good.
I'll get another batch off to you today.'

Julia, at the other end of the line, was shocked by his brusqueness.
It had taken quite a bit of courage to ring Nathan up like this. She
could have ordered the jewellery through his warehouse manager
but had wanted to talk to him. After all, she hadn't seen or heard

from him since he'd climbed out of her bed. She was hurt, and not a little angry, and finally beginning to realise what an absolute shit he really was. 'Long time no see?'

Nathan sucked in his breath and allowed himself a quick look at Roberta who was tapping her pencil against her pad. 'I've been busy. You know what it's like.'

'You left your cocktail shaker. Oh, and I'm wild about your Martinis. In fact, I'm almost out of vermouth . . . and I make fresh ice every week.'

Nathan allowed himself to smile. She was trying to be jolly and indifferent, but the hurt came through, which only added to his feelings of guilt. But right now the last thing he needed, with Roberta sitting in his office, was to have to think about her sister. 'I'm sorry, Julia, I'm going . . .'

Roberta's ears pricked up. 'Is that Julia?' Reluctantly, he nodded. 'Say hallo from me.'

'Nathan? Who's that?' Julia's heart plummeted.

'Er, Roberta. She says hallo. She's doing a business lunch for me. We're organising it now.'

'A business lunch?' Julia frowned. This was all mighty strange. What was Nathan having business lunches for? And why was he acting so oddly? And then the truth hit her like a brick. She put two and two together and came up with five. She felt sick. This was the Kit Fordham-Clarke thing all over again. Finding out Kit loved Roberta was bad enough, but surely not *Nathan* as well? Roberta was *never* his type. 'So your mother's birthday supper went well?' There was an icy silence as Nathan fumbled for a reply. Julia cut in, 'Since when have you had business lunches?'

He bristled. Since when was he answerable to her? 'Since now. Call you back, Julia. Don't worry, I'll get that jewellery off today.'

She was tempted to say, 'Stuff your jewellery,' but her better judgement stopped her just in time.

Nathan put down the phone and looked across at Roberta, whose face was now animated. 'How is Julia? I haven't seen her in a while.'

Nathan shrugged. 'Fine, I think. She's selling our jewellery. It's going well.'

And then Roberta was leaving, he could stall her no longer. Nathan walked back with her to her car. 'How are your girls?' she asked.

Nathan caught the interest in her eyes. 'They're fine . . . just fine.' Suddenly he realised the way into Roberta's life. It was simple. It was through his own daughters. He seized his chance. 'It's my weekend with the twins in a couple of weeks. I'm thinking of taking them to Colchester Zoo, they love animals. Don't suppose you'd like to come along with your little boy?'

Roberta looked at him, something stirring within her. A faint blush came over her cheeks as at last she was flattered by his attention. He was very attractive, and when he saw her hesitate pushed his chance, smiling entreatingly. Little did he know but in that instant Nathan reignited a flame. It was quite a jolt to Roberta. How long had it been since she'd had any feelings like this? And he was a family man after all. She'd often thought about taking James to Colchester Zoo but didn't fancy going on her own, and her mother looked after him so much these days that it wasn't fair to keep asking her. What harm could there be in a trip to the zoo? 'Okay, that sounds good. I know James would like it very much.'

She unlocked her car door and climbed in. Nathan held on to the door. 'Roberta, do you mind if I ask you something . . . er . . . rather personal?'

She shook her head. 'No.'

'Your perfume, it's extraordinary . . . special. What is it?'

She smiled. 'Yes, it *is* special. It was bought for me by a very special person. I've only just started to wear it again.' She lowered her eyes. 'Been trying to eliminate certain memories from my life.' She cleared her throat and turned the key in the ignition. 'Guerlain, *Parure*.'

Nathan repeated the name to himself as he watched her drive away. He spoke good French. Parure: finery, *jewels*. How very, very apt. This woman was going to be the jewel in his life, of that he was sure.

54

May, 1973

Nancy, wearing a Linda Leigh trouser suit in Trevira, for the not-so-slim, looked very fetching. She dabbed her mouth with a paper napkin then pushed the rest of her chocolate eclair into it.

'Lovely waistcoat and trousers, Nance. Have you lost some weight?'

She chomped away then swallowed hard, giving a secretive smile. 'Well, I have to admit I've been trying to cut down a bit, Brenda, now that summer's on its way. I've lost half a stone just by sheer will-power . . . another half-stone and I'll be as slim as you.' *And the rest*, thought Brenda. 'Peter's tickled pink, says I look like a young girl!' Nancy dabbed her mouth again and took a sip of her coffee. She eyed Brenda's suit. 'And is that a *new* suit? Marks and Spencer?'

Brenda bristled. Nancy always assumed her top whack was St Michael. 'No, it's Alexon, actually.'

Nancy pulled a face. 'Alexon? Oooh, that's a bit of a change for you, isn't it?'

Narrowing her eyes, Brenda sipped her coffee, deciding not to retaliate. 'Do you think Princess Anne will get engaged soon? He looks a nice chap, doesn't he, Lieutenant Mark Phillips?'

'Oh, I hope so. We could all do with a royal wedding to cheer ourselves up because this government certainly isn't doing anything much!' Nancy shook her head as though the troubles of the country lay on her own plump shoulders. 'Edward Heath should crack the whip a bit more, sort out all of these ridiculous disputes. They're crippling our country! And what about these rumours of a three-day week? Whatever next!'

Rather absently, Brenda nodded. 'A royal wedding would be nice.' She grinned at her sister. 'No weddings in your family yet?' It was a deliberate attempt to antagonise Nancy.

She pinched her lips together. 'No, Brenda. You know jolly well Clare's too busy with her degree to want to settle down and get married.' She shook her head. 'But I do wish she'd stop seeing this Harriet woman . . .'

'Harriet? Who's she?'

'Oh, she's nice enough. Very clever, by all accounts. A bigwig in Camden Social Services . . . y'know, child abuse . . . so I can see where Clare's professional interest lies. But you only have to look at her to see she's a man-eater, and I don't want her leading poor Clare astray.'

Brenda suppressed a grin. 'Oh, I'm sure she's quite capable of looking after herself. Have you seen her lately?'

Nancy beamed. 'Well, as it happens we have. And do you know, she's already been offered a position at Guy's hospital . . . in August. It's assistant to some leading child psychologist, working in an out-patients' clinic, and it's a firm offer, even though she hasn't completed her degree. I mean, I'm not surprised. She's Brunel's star pupil. Brilliant, Brenda, she's quite brilliant.'

'I know she is, Nance, you must be very proud.'

'Oh, I am. And that's why I don't want this Harriet woman messing things up for her. She's always there, you know, with her men friends galore! My poor Clare. It's as plain as the nose on her face, she's just not able to cope.'

Privately Brenda doubted that very much but decided to change the subject.

'But you enjoyed your trip to town?'

'Oh, yes. And do you know, Peter took me to see *Hair*.'

'*Hair?* But isn't that supposed to be a really saucy show?'

'I know, I know. He got tickets, you see, for a client. I mean, Peter had no idea what the show was all about, he just asks his booking agent for the best show in town. Anyway, at the last minute his client couldn't go so he took me! It was a hoot, I can tell you.'

'Peter has a lot of trouble with his clients, doesn't he? Them always letting him down?'

Nancy glared at her sister. 'Well, their loss was my gain, Brenda. I must say, I did enjoy it. It was a lark. All those men, stripped naked, and some of them so very well hung.'

'I *beg* your pardon?'

Nancy tittered. 'Oh, don't look at me like that, Brenda. You see, the tables are turned. You think I'm a boring old so-and-so, don't you? Well, I'm not.' She leant closer to her sister. 'There was one chap in the show ...' Nancy tapped her chin '... now, what was his name? I looked it up 'specially in the programme.' She screwed up her face in contemplation.

'Oh, yes, I remember, an American chap ... *Richard Gere.* That's it. Yes, he was particularly so.'

Amazed, Brenda sat back in her seat. 'Nancy Lewis! I think this calls for a celebration.' She turned to the waitress standing close by. 'Would you mind, dear? Two more chocolate eclairs, please.'

Within seconds, the eclairs arrived. Smacking her lips, Nancy picked hers up and took an enormous bite.

55

Nathan's relationship with Roberta was developing slowly. In fact, never in his life had he taken things *so* slowly. He was frustrated beyond measure, because he wanted her so much, but cautious and gentlemanly because that's the way he had to handle her. But was it all a game? He was no longer sure. When he analysed his feelings, which he'd never bothered to do in the past, he couldn't imagine life without her, and yet she showed no commitment to him and in no way tried to tie him down. Quite the reverse, in fact. Nathan was the one doing all the chasing.

And then suddenly the pace changed, and the chemistry between them became highly charged. Even then, up to his neck in love with her, Nathan wasn't sure how to proceed. Roberta no longer rushed away at the end of their dates, but if the kissing and the petting got even slightly out of hand she'd quickly back off and he became scared he was reading the wrong signals. If he approached her too keenly, he might lose her for good.

His mother had watched with interest the dramatic change in Nathan, his weight loss, and the way his eyes blazed at the mention of Roberta's name. But Anne also picked up certain clues about Roberta, and so, at the first opportunity, took herself off on a golfing trip, suggesting in passing that he should use the opportunity to ask his new love interest to maybe stay?

He attempted as much, but it ended up as just a dinner invitation, with him preparing the meal. Fortunately, Roberta arranged for James to spend the night with Brenda. It was quite late into the evening, after they'd lingered over their meal, before Nathan finally decided to make a more positive move.

'Didn't know you could cook, Nathan? Why do you keep employing me?'

He didn't dare tell Roberta it was all courtesy of Fortnum and Mason, and his mother's parting gift. Instead, he pushed back his chair and took her hand, gently pulling her to her feet. 'Because nobody cooks like you. And in case you hadn't noticed, I just like having you around.'

Wearing a simple cream dress with high-heeled shoes, her hair falling loose around her face, Roberta smiled into his eyes. 'I've noticed.'

'You have?' Smiling broadly, Nathan came closer, folding her in his arms. 'Have you also noticed we're completely on our own?'

She raised her eyes teasingly to his. 'We've been on our own before, Nathan.'

'I know.' He buried his face in her neck. 'But not like this.'

She sighed, her whole body feeling weak with desire. 'What are you suggesting?'

'I'm not suggesting anything, but I know what I'd like to do.'

Aroused by Nathan's caresses, she responded to his pressure against her body and actually ran her hands around his waist and further down. Nathan breathed in quickly and Roberta sighed. 'I just needed time.'

Needed? Past tense. He looked into her eyes. 'And have you had enough time?'

'Yes, but I'm frightened.'

'Frightened of what?'

'I might be hopeless, and a big disappointment to you.'

He laughed. 'And so might I.'

'I doubt that.'

He kissed her mouth and Roberta really let go then and kissed him back, both of them only stopping to draw breath. Nathan began fervently kissing her neck and running his hands over her body. 'Let's go to bed?'

She blurted out, 'I'm not on the pill or anything, Nathan.' She felt foolish and rather naive. 'I wouldn't want to become pregnant.'

With a rapidly beating heart he stalled his lovemaking and smiled, gently holding her face in both hands. 'Roberta, don't worry, I'll take care of everything.'

She gulped, feeling both excited and ashamed, but took his hand, following him out of the dining room and up the stairs to his bed-

251

room, wondering whether to cross herself for her own salvation or quote Dickens' *A Tale of Two Cities*, out loud. '*It is a far, far better thing. . . .*'

He turned on one small lamp on the dressing table. It supplied just enough light and Roberta, feeling hot and guilty, sat on the bed. Nathan pulled off his tie and undid his top shirt button. He sat down beside her. 'Look, if you like, I'll buzz off and come back in five minutes?'

She grabbed his hand. 'No! I don't want you to go. Stay. It's just, well . . . shall I take my clothes off?'

Nathan put a hand to his forehead, suppressing a smile. 'Or I can?'

'No, I will.' Roberta kicked off her shoes and quick as a flash slipped out of her dress. She pulled down her tights, and whisked off her bra and pants. Like lightning she was in the bed. Nathan, who'd withdrawn to the other side of the room, hardly dared to watch. Instead, he opened the top drawer of his dressing table and rummaged about, withdrawing a packet of three Durex. He then proceeded to remove his own clothes, with his back to Roberta, all the time wondering if *she* was watching him.

He climbed into the bed. 'Would you like me to turn off the lamp?' She shook her head and he kissed her, this time savouring her mouth and allowing her time to respond. Roberta did respond, lustily, and he ran his hand between her legs, his own ardour taking an almighty leap. 'God, you're so *wet*.' Ashamed, she buried her head in his neck. Ecstatically, he sighed, 'You really want this, don't you?' He fingered her wantonly. 'You want this every bit as much as me?' And such was her urgency that she took him between her hands and eased herself under him.

Nathan moved quickly and grabbed a sheath from the bedside table, fumbling to put it on. Roberta watched then eagerly slid beneath him again and Nathan pushed himself inside. And then their passion really flared.

Finally, sweating from their exertions, they lay motionless yet still entwined. Nathan shifted slightly, and ran a finger across her damp forehead. 'Remind me, what was it you said?'

Roberta looked at him, recognising yet resenting his knowing smile. Her thoughts flickered elsewhere, to Ed, and she imagined him pointing a finger, saying, '*You were never so abandoned with me!*' And then she thought of Kit, the only man she had ever loved.

Would it have been like this with him? She shifted slightly away from Nathan and rolled on to her back. 'I'm sorry?'

'I said, "What was it you said?" ' He ran his tongue around her ear, sending shivers through her again. Nathan propped himself on one arm and looked down at her with a smile. 'About being hopeless and a disappointment?' He trailed his hand over her body and kissed her neck, whispering. 'You were *sen–sa*–tional.'

To his astonishment she got straight out of bed, leaving Nathan with his mouth open. She started to grab her clothes. He shot out of the bed to stand beside her. 'What are you doing?'

'Getting dressed.'

'Why?'

'It's late. I must go home.'

He grabbed her hands, stopping her as she was about to pull up her lace knickers. 'No, you mustn't! I want you to stay.'

'I can't stay here, Nathan. I must get home.'

'Why, for God's sake?'

She practically shoved him aside, pulling up her knickers and hastily shrugging on her bra.

Nathan stopped her, taking hold of both her shoulders. 'For Christ's sake, Roberta, what's the matter with you? We've just shared the most amazing experience, and now you're rushing off like a scalded cat!'

Aghast, she looked at him. 'My mother will be bringing James back early in the morning. Besides, the neighbours . . .'

'The *neighbours*! Who gives a *fuck* about the neighbours?'

Roberta rounded on him sharply. '*I do, Nathan.*'

He got dressed and drove her home.

They hardly spoke, all the way back to Newmarket from Cambridge, but at least it gave Roberta time to think and clear her head. Her own passion had taken her completely by surprise. It had been so easy with Nathan, he'd reawakened feelings that had lain dormant since Kit. Well, he wasn't around now but Roberta knew she wanted more. Her nerve ends still tingled with desire. Heaven forbid, she even thought she knew how Julia felt now. Lucky her if she'd had pleasure like this from the start.

Nathan parked outside Roberta's house and sadly turned off the ignition. She leant across and kissed his mouth. 'I'm sorry, I can't imagine what you must think of me. Would you like to come in?' He raised his eyebrows and his spirits rose. He followed her inside.

She led him straight upstairs into her bedroom then proceeded to help him out of his clothes, an act which ended in them both fervently peeling off each other's. They stumbled on to her bed. 'Oh, Christ!' Nathan moaned, 'I haven't . . .'

With a smile, Roberta moved off the bed and across to her handbag. She rummaged inside then eased her way back into his arms. They both looked down as she held up her hand holding the remaining two Durex. 'It seems *I* remembered this time.'

56

The weather had been blisteringly hot all week. Roberta, a keen gardener, had been continually watering all her plants in the small garden at the back of her house. Everywhere was a profusion of colour, but the more delicate flowers were drooping by the hour. She and James, and quite often Brenda too, ate outside at every opportunity. In fact, when she wasn't preparing and cooking food, she spent most of her time outside, either on the Heath with Boris and James or sunbathing in the garden. Her son had a sandpit there and would spend hours building and creating masterpieces with wet sand.

Nathan hadn't seen Roberta for a week, and when he did the deep golden colour of her skin quite took his breath away. Everything about her glowed, she looked so healthy and alive. He'd often reflected upon Julia's words that her sister was more beautiful on the inside. Nathan knew this was true, but that inner beauty certainly had an extraordinary effect on the outside, like an aura surrounding her.

Clad in white shorts and a suntop, with nothing on her feet, Roberta had prepared supper for him. Gazpacho soup, salmon with hollandaise sauce, and raspberries and cream. He'd brought some Sancerre, and quite late into this balmy Friday evening they sat outside.

Roberta was really content. She'd blossomed tremendously in the few short months she'd known Nathan. Her business was doing well, she'd established herself. In fact, there were only two people she now depended upon completely, her son and her mother. The rest she could live without.

Nathan surprised her by sliding something across the table top and Roberta's heart jumped into her mouth. She gulped and wanted to say, 'No, Nathan, don't spoil things.' Instead, she picked up the tiny red leather box. She opened it. Inside was a large solitaire diamond ring in an extraordinary setting of twisted white, pink and yellow gold. She caught her breath and looked across the table. 'Nathan?'

Straight away, he noticed the desperate expression in her eyes. 'Will you marry me, Roberta? You must know how I feel?' he pleaded.

She gulped again and bit her bottom lip. She put the box back on the table, without removing the ring and shook her head. 'I had no idea,' she murmured.

'Roberta! Come on, I love you. I've told you a thousand times. You love me too, you've said so . . . haven't you?'

She climbed off the bench-seat and continued to bite her bottom lip. 'I do love you, Nathan, yes, because . . . because you're a wonderful man. You've been so good to me . . . and, well, what else can I say?'

'What else is there to say? Marry me. It makes sense.'

'No, it doesn't.'

Nathan stood up and walked round the table. He grabbed her arm. 'Why?'

She pulled away. 'I live in Newmarket for a start.'

Nathan guffawed. 'So?'

'I don't want to live in Cambridge. I like it where I am. Jamie's going to Fairstead House School, it's just down the road . . . and I depend upon my mum.'

'Well, depend away, I don't want to change things. I'll move to Newmarket.'

'You can't. You're a Cambridge person, Nathan. You'd hate it here all the time.'

'And that's your reason for saying no? That's why you won't marry me?'

She swallowed hard and looked down at the ring on the table. 'It's just, I don't want to get married again . . . at least . . . not yet.'

He grabbed her again and looked into her eyes. 'If you don't want to marry me now, Roberta, I have a feeling you never will.'

She shrugged herself out of his grip and moved away from the table. 'Maybe you're right.'

'Why? Apart from where we live, for God's sake, tell me why?'

She turned away from him. 'It's not easy to say why. Except maybe ...' She faced him.

'Yes?'

'... maybe I don't love you enough.'

'Enough? Because of your husband, I suppose?'

Roberta rounded on him fiercely. 'Ed has nothing to do with this, Nathan!'

'Okay, I'm sorry. But you can't spend the rest of your life regretting the past.'

'I don't regret the past. As a matter of fact, I cherish it.'

'You cherish it, do you? Well, what about me? Don't you cherish me? You seem to cherish me enough when we're in bed!'

Tears sprang to Roberta's eyes and she willed them to go away. Fearful of her neighbours listening, she walked towards the kitchen, Nathan hot on her heels. They went inside and Roberta closed the kitchen door. 'That's not fair, Nathan. Sex is different.'

'Oh, so it's sex now, is it? Not *making love*, just sex!'

'Well, of course we make love, but it's still sex, Nathan. It still ... satisfies.'

'And do I? Satisfy you?'

'You know you do.'

'Well, marry me then. *Please?*'

She started to walk out of the kitchen. 'I think you should go, Nathan. If we're not careful, we'll wake James.'

He twisted her round to face him and glared at her. 'Oh, and we can't wake your precious Jamie, can we?'

'No, we bloody can't!' Roberta shrugged aside his hand and walked further along the hall towards the front door. 'Please, just go.'

She looked distraught. He touched her face. 'If I walk out of that door, Roberta, I shall never come back.'

'I know.'

'And that's what you want? You really want me to go?'

'I don't want you to go ... but I don't want to marry you.'

'They're one and the same thing, Roberta.' Nathan opened the front door and paused. 'Sell the ring, I don't want it back. Give the money to charity or something.'

With that, he left.

But Roberta did return the ring, the very next day. She drove over to Cambridge in the morning and, thankful that Nathan was not in, put it safely into Anne Purley's hands.

By four o'clock that afternoon a motorbike courier had arrived at her house with a package. She signed for it, then after the courier left ripped open the manilla envelope. Inside was the ring, with a short letter from Nathan.

Dear Roberta,

You may not want me, but I want you to have this ring. It was made for you. The diamond is flawless and the setting unique. That says it all!

It's worth a lot of money, Roberta. It could buy young Jamie a pony, a stable, all the tack he needs, and a paddock as well! But remember, if you sell it, you'll receive a fraction of its true value. So keep it, from me.

Nathan

Roberta walked back into her kitchen, clutching the red leather box, and sat down with her head into her hands. She wept. Tears that had been held in check since the death of Ed spilled down her cheeks, hot and salty, stinging her cheeks. It was as though she was weeping away the past few months, all the shame, all the love, all the passion, and all the new feelings she'd acquired. By the time she'd wiped away the very last tear, Nathan Purley might as well have been a figment of her imagination because she knew he was gone for good. Even if she asked him to come back, she knew he never would. Roberta shivered and wrapped her arms around herself, wondering if she'd done the right thing. But as her father used to say to her, on countless occasions when she'd failed as a child, 'Don't look back, girl, or you might miss what's in front.'

Just thinking of Gordon made Roberta feel better. If only he was still here! But the person he'd loved best in the world still was. And then it became clear to her. Roberta couldn't keep the ring, whatever Nathan said. But she knew who could. The one person who deserved such a gift. The one person who'd never been given an expensive piece of jewellery in her life. The one person who wore only a simple gold wedding band because her future husband couldn't afford an engagement ring and afterwards they'd needed too many things to spend money on one. The one person who'd put Roberta back on to the road to recovery after the death of her husband.

Her mother.

57

April, 1977

Nancy sat tapping her fuchsia pink fingernails on the window table in the Cosy Corner. Brenda was late again. Nancy looked down at her empty cup of coffee, and empty plate. She was steaming inside, trying hard to take long, deep breaths to calm herself. It was important she didn't show her wrath to her sister. These days, Nancy lived in fear of Brenda just walking away from her.

Relief washed over her as her sister arrived, to be quickly followed by jealousy. On this bright spring day, fifty-five-year-old Brenda could easily have passed for a woman in her early-forties. Her hair was now honey blonde, her figure still sleek, and her skin like peaches and cream. Today she wore a Jaeger drop-shouldered jersey dress. As smooth as you like, she slipped into the seat opposite Nancy, apologising profusely for being so late, and the ring she always wore on her wedding finger caught the light and flashed like a beacon, declaring its value.

'I called in at the salon, I know I shouldn't have. I just couldn't get away . . .'

Nancy sucked in her breath. 'Yes, well, never mind, you're here now. I've had a coffee already, *waiting* for you, and an eclair, but I'll have the same again.'

Brenda beckoned the waitress and ordered two coffees and two chocolate eclairs.

The waitress pointed to Nancy. 'I'm sorry, dear, but your friend here had the last one.'

Brenda looked at her sister, then back at the waitress. 'Oh, well, never mind. Just two coffees, please.'

'No, wait.' Nancy leant forward in her seat. 'Have you any vanilla slices? The fresh cream ones, not those synthetic things you some-times serve.'

The waitress raised her eyebrows but nodded. She smiled at Brenda. 'You too?'

She didn't really want anything, but she knew Nancy wouldn't like it if she refused. She agreed, and the waitress walked away. Brenda faced her sister, noting her bloated face and bulbous eyes. 'And how are you, Nance?' She decided to lie. 'You're looking well.'

Brenda shifted in her seat, and her diamond ring reflected the bright April sun through the window. It sent a shaft of light into Nancy's eyes. She shielded them, and reached over brusquely to move Brenda's hand out of the way. She didn't mention the ring. Never had. For nearly three years she'd wondered where it came from, and at first had thought it couldn't possibly be real. But it had kept its lustre, and the gold had stayed fine, and from the way the diamond glinted and sparkled it was no fake.

'I'm not too well, as it happens. Had a frightful cold,' Nancy complained.

'Oh, I'm sorry to hear that. Hmm, now you come to mention it, you do look a bit peaky.'

With her normal affectation, Nancy brushed one hand across her forehead. 'It's been such a gloomy month, what with one thing and another.' She looked up at the waitress. 'Thank you, dear.' Nancy took the top half off the cream slice and bit into it straight away. With her mouth full, she continued the conversation.

'Fordham-Clarkes have made sixty people redundant. Peter doesn't know which way to turn. He already works all the hours God sends. And, as if that's not bad enough, that Roger Fordham-Clarke is getting divorced again! His poor children, one five and the other only three. Cynthia Fordham-Clarke's quite washed her hands of him, I can tell you.'

Nancy looked across at her sister, as though about to confide something not many people knew. 'Mind you, she's no angel. Do you know, since Joshua died, Cynthia's changed completely. She's no reason to feel proud of herself, gadding about like a young girl. Peter doesn't approve, he's lost all respect for her. I mean, she's no spring chicken, must be nearly sixty!' Nancy didn't notice her sister averting her eyes but rambled on, 'And now Princess Margaret . . . I mean, whatever next? Divorce in the royal family, with all the money they've got.'

'What difference does money make when divorce is on the cards?'

Indignantly, Nancy puffed out her cheeks. 'Well, status then, position. You know what I mean. It's downright disgraceful.'

'But that's rubbish, Nancy. Your own daughter got divorced.'

'But that's different, Clare was the innocent party.'

'Well, how do you know Princess Margaret isn't?'

'What? With that Roddy chap? Hardly.' Nancy sniffed, and finished the top half of her vanilla slice. 'And poor Mr Wilson *resigning*, he's obviously in bad health. Mind you, *I* wouldn't want to be Leader of the Labour Party either. But I have to confess, I quite liked Harold. He was a genuine sort of a chap.'

Brenda nibbled at her vanilla slice. 'Are you still going to Montreal in July?'

Nancy's nostrils flared. 'Well, actually ... *no*. Peter's going to the Olympics by himself this time. I mean, I didn't really enjoy the last Games and he's quite desperate to go, so we've agreed I'll stay home. It'll be easier if he hasn't got me to think about all the time. And anyway, I can pop over and see Clare, give her a bit of a break from the girls. They're a handful now Nanny's gone.'

'Oh, she's gone, has she?'

'Yes. Didn't I tell you? Now that the girls are at pre-prep, they've got an au-pair. A lot cheaper, I can tell you.'

'But no doubt doing the same work?'

Nancy glared at her sister. 'If you choose to go into that sort of work, Brenda, you must be prepared to do the job.' She started on the lower portion of her vanilla slice, munched away for a moment and sighed. 'And Clare's so busy all the time. Mind you, she's almost finished her thesis now. She'll have her doctorate before long.'

Brenda nodded, reflecting upon her niece. 'What did you say it was on?'

'Young children's behavioural problems. Under tens that is. Non-classic difficulties created by verbal abuse, physical abuse and self-inflicted abuse. How to overcome them. A tricky subject, but Clare's handled it *brilliantly*!'

'You've read the thesis then?'

Nancy looked at her sister as though she was quite stupid. 'Brenda, it's this thick!' She held out her arms the width of the table. 'But I know it'll be a distinguished piece of work. Anything

Clare does always is.' In her excitement a piece of vanilla slice lodged in her throat and she choked, her face going quite red. For a minute, Brenda was alarmed. Finally her sister slumped back in her seat, one hand clutching her chest. 'Sorry about that. It's this cold I've had. It's left my throat in a quite dreadful state. Anyway, did I tell you that Clare now runs her own children's clinic? Twice a week.'

Brenda nodded her head. 'Yes, I believe you did, Nance. Last time we met.'

'Hmm. And what have you been doing with yourself? The girls all right? Any new boyfriends?'

Brenda narrowed her eyes and smiled. 'Yes, they've both got men friends ... nice sort of chaps. And I've been busy as well.' She leant across the table and squeezed her sister's hand. 'And guess what? I've taken up golf.'

Nancy was astounded. 'Golf? You? Whatever for?'

'Exercise, of course.'

'With your life? I'm surprised you find time.'

Brenda laughed. 'Yes, well, there are some compensations for not having a husband to look after.'

Nancy was aghast. 'Brenda!'

'Now don't take that the wrong way, Nance. You know how much I loved Gordon. But, well, since he died my life has changed. I've got Roberta down the road with Jamie, regular trips to Chelsea to see Julia, my salon which is going crazy, and a darn'sight more money to spend that I ever thought possible. And Gordon wouldn't want me to be unhappy, I know he wouldn't.'

Nancy sniffed. 'But golf?'

Brenda lowered her eyes. 'Yes, well, it wasn't exactly my idea, more ... a friend's.'

'A friend's?'

Brenda raised her eyes. 'Yes.' She blushed a deep red.

Nancy sniffed again. 'Oh, I see. A man friend?'

'No, don't talk daft. A woman friend. She's a regular client. Has a facial every month, and a full body massage. In fact, she's one of my best clients, and we get on tremendously well.'

Not for the first time that day, Nancy was consumed with jealousy. Brenda was her sister, she wasn't entitled to have friends. After all, Nancy hadn't got any. 'Do I know her?'

'As a matter of fact, you do. You were talking about her earlier on.'

Nancy racked her brain. 'You don't mean ... not ... Cynthia Fordham-Clarke?'

Brenda gave a short involuntary laugh. 'Don't look like that, Nance. Cynthia's very nice.'

'Very nice? With a son like hers? Personally I think the woman's a disgrace!'

Brenda bristled. 'She's not a disgrace, Nancy. She's very upset about Roger and his wife, and she doesn't gad about. In fact she spends a good deal of her time with me, in my poky little cottage in Newmarket.'

'And you expect me to believe that?'

'You can believe what you like, it's true. We go to the Bedford Lodge for supper quite often, or the Rutland now and again, and of course we play golf. Newmarket Golf Club, Cynthia prefers it to the Gogs. It's less pretentious. And, of course, occasionally we babysit for Roberta. And ... actually we're going on holiday together later in the year. To Cap d'Antibes.'

'*You're* going on holiday with Cynthia Fordham-Clarke?'

Brenda laughed. 'Yes, would you like to come?'

'*No, I would not!* Huh! You wouldn't catch me within a mile of that woman.'

Brenda knew her sister well. If for one second she'd thought Nancy would say yes, she'd never have issued her invitation. 'Well, don't say I didn't ask.'

'What does Roberta think?'

'She's quite thrilled. Which reminds me.' Brenda bent down and carefully picked up a carrier bag she'd brought with her. She withdrew a cardboard cake box and placed it on the table in front of her sister. 'From Roberta, with love.'

Nancy sniffed. 'What is it?'

'It's one of her best lines. A liqueur mocha cheesecake. Open the box and see.'

Nancy pulled up the lid and peeked inside at what appeared to be a frothy display of chocolate curls, but a wonderful aroma of rich, creamy chocolate combined with Brandy and Tia Maria soon pervaded her nostrils. Even after two cream cakes, her mouth watered. 'Hmmm ... looks quite nice.'

'It's divine. It's a properly baked cheesecake, so it'll keep for some time. You'll only need the tiniest portion, it's very, very rich.'

Nancy put the lid back down and read *RM Caterers*. 'And is that what she calls herself, RM Caterers?'

'Yes, and she's doing extremely well too. She employs two people now, to help her in her home, and out and about. She bakes and cooks and clients now collect food from her. I mean, she still does the odd dinner party, and quite a few business lunches, but she's stopped doing big parties and weddings. Too much trouble. Like I said, most people take their dishes round to her house and she prepares the food ready for them to reheat or just serve from their own kitchens. It means she spends more time at home with Jamie.'

'And it's profitable, all this?'

'Profitable enough. As I said, she's doing very well.'

'Well, thank her very much. Now how much do I owe you?'

'*Nothing*. It's a gift.'

'Hmm, well, I can see what we'll be eating for the next few days.' Nancy looked across at her sister's nibbled but uneaten vanilla slice. 'Aren't you going to eat that?'

Brenda shook her head. 'I'm afraid I can't.'

'Pass it over here then.'

'Ought you, Nance? What about your diet?'

She snorted. 'Well, as *I'm* not going to Cap d'Antibes, or anywhere else for that matter, I suppose it doesn't matter. And I do so *hate* to see things wasted, you know I do.'

Brenda smiled to herself, and watched her sister devour the rest of her vanilla slice. Roberta's box sat beside Nancy, she'd laid claim to it already in her way, and Brenda knew that the contents would be devoured within a very short while. She smiled to herself, and yet felt sorry. Poor Nancy. She had nothing else.

58

May, 1976

Where Bridge Street becomes Magdalene Street, just along from the Round Church in Cambridge and tucked away opposite St John's College, stands Portugal Place. Situated a short distance from Magdalene Bridge, the Place consists of three narrow paths meeting in the middle to form a Y-shape. Quaint old buildings nestle within the Y and to either side. The paths, or alley-ways, are typically Cambridge, cramped yet full of charm.

Kit Fordham-Clarke had always liked this end of town, and when he found out that the building in the primary position facing towards Bridge Street was for sale, he snapped it up. It was an ancient narrow building, three storeys high with an enormous basement, in need of some restoration but bang in the middle of the Place. After all these years of firmly believing he'd never work in Cambridge, Kit had had a complete change of heart. It would mean driving in every day from Ash Cottage but that was no journey at all. Now that his father was dead Portugal Place fitted the bill and Kit knew he wouldn't be too close to Matthews Structural Design either. Setting up in competition against a man he respected so much was not on Kit's agenda.

After nearly five years in Aberdeen, Kit Fordham-Clarke was a changed man. For a start, his demeanour was no longer that of a vulnerable post-graduate finding his feet. Kit had well and truly found his feet in Aberdeen, and made a tidy sum of money into the bargain. Early in 1972, during the course of his work, he'd come across an enormous, delapidated, early-nineteenth-century building in desperate need of either restoration or pulling down. Nobody was interested in the monstrous eye-sore but Kit knew it was bang on the outskirts of a proposed industrial site so joined forces with his friend Andrew and bought the place and the surrounding land for a pittance. He then invested a considerable amount of time and borrowed money on renovating and extending it into a surprisingly attractive office block. This had taken about twelve months or so to do, with Kit and Andrew overseeing and helping with most of the work. Then they'd rented it out. At first they'd struggled to find any takers, but as the vast area around the office block gradually grew up so did the interest in Kit and Andrew's block. By the time Kit was ready to leave Aberdeen, he and Andrew were able to sell. Because of the booming North Sea Oil industry, the site was snapped up straight away and the profit each made was enormous.

Kit had wasted no time during the three weeks he'd been home. His feet had hardly touched the ground. With the proceeds from the office block and his house in Aberdeen he'd bought an acre of land near the river in Cambridge. Although he'd only been back twice during his time in Aberdeen, the first Christmas and then again for his father's funeral, he'd kept his ear to the ground. Times were hard and even Fordham-Clarke Construction was in deep trouble so Kit had been able to snap up the land for a fairly reasonable price. He'd also been able to acquire several redundant staff members from his father's firm. An excellent site engineer for one, a structural engineer and two draughtsmen/detailers. Both engineers were in their late-fifties and so fearful of never finding decent work again, but Kit knew they would be worth their weight in gold. The two draughtsmen/detailers were young and keen and also fitted Kit's bill. The acre of land was to be transformed into an apartment block. A luxurious apartment block. Plans were already being drawn up by a local architect.

Wearing his navy blue city suit, and looking every bit the successful businessman, Kit leant back against the railings in Portugal Place, folded his arms and admired his new office building. It had been bought with his father's money. Joshua Fordham-Clarke left all three of his sons a hefty sum of money in his will. At first Kit had refused to claim his, until, that was, his mother had pointed out how churlish he was being. 'If you don't want it, darling,' she'd said very curtly, 'at least put it in a bank account somewhere for your own children.' Kit had quite liked that idea, and then expanded upon it. Such a large sum of money would be better invested in order that it could *really* grow. So Portugal Place was his legacy to children as yet unborn.

He'd already instructed builders to commence work the following week. They'd promised to have the place finished within six weeks, and meanwhile he and his new members of staff, plus a secretary, would have to manage in the one just about inhabitable office at the top floor. Kit wouldn't be spending much time there anyway. He intended to be out and about for the next few months, finding more structural design work.

In a few short years Kit Fordham-Clarke had realised his dream, and now through his own endeavours was well on the way to being very, very rich. It had given an edge to his personality; he now possessed an eagle-eyed perceptiveness about his work. But every now and again, he had to pull himself up sharply. There were a lot of idiots in business, and some of them carried weight. The last thing he wanted to do was to turn into his father. But even in his personal life, he was no longer the old amiable Kit.

At twenty-seven, there was no permanent woman in Kit's life; there'd been plenty flitting through during his time in Aberdeen though not a day had gone by when he didn't think of Roberta. The final words they'd flung at each other still hurt, and he bitterly regretted the way such a happy period in his life had ended. But there was no going back, and to his way of thinking no gain in becoming a friend of her family. The pain was too deep, his feelings too raw. Kit Fordham-Clarke had buried them all, along with that disastrous liaison with Julia, in the deepest recesses of his mind. But Roberta . . . *her* face, the smell of *her* skin, the feel of *her*, he couldn't bury. Every so often something triggered his memory and he'd indulge himself in thoughts of her. But that was all, he'd steeled himself against anything else long ago.

59

'And it just seems a logical move. I mean, what do I want with a house this size anymore? I rattle about like a lost soul, and now that Roger's moved in, I really feel it's time I moved out.' Cynthia looked across at her adored younger son and reached out one hand. He clasped it within his own. 'Roger needs his privacy, when he entertains and when his children come round, and what better place than here, his family home? Oh, Kit, I'd love to be nearer you, too, and in Newmarket the pace of life is much easier than it is in Cambridge. I'm getting too old for all this student stuff, I need a bit of tranquillity in my old age.'

'Well, I wouldn't exactly describe Newmarket as tranquil. It's a busy market town, with a lot going on.'

'I know, darling, I know. But Brenda's there.' Cynthia saw his raised eyebrows. 'You remember Brenda? Roberta's mum. We have such fun together, playing golf and the like. My life has changed dramatically since I met up with Brenda Tree. And I've seen *just* the house I'd like, except her daughter Roberta's living in it!' Cynthia giggled, not noticing the look on her son's face. 'It's a perfect house, quite big really but ideal for a single person, and Heath Road is a private road. Roberta manages the garden beautifully, and I know I could manage a garden that size as well.' Cynthia giggled again. 'But I don't think she's quite ready to move out just yet, although I get the feeling it won't be too long.'

Kit had turned to stone. Cynthia paused, watching the colour drain from her son's handsome face. His keen grey eyes now held something she didn't quite recognise, except that it was akin to horror and disbelief. 'Kit?'

He put a hand to his head, propping his elbow on the settee in his mother's sitting room. *Was Roberta no longer with Ed?* 'Why did she . . . they . . . move?'

Cynthia shrugged and frowned. 'Well, I wasn't exactly on the scene then, Kit, but Brenda said she couldn't manage in that old cottage. I think it was too big, and held too many sad memories for the poor girl so she did a swop with the chap who bought the business.'

'What chap? You mean *Ed's* business?'

Realisation dawned on Cynthia. 'You mean, you didn't know, Kit? About Ed?'

'What about him? Know what?'

It was Cynthia's turn to look horrified now. 'Oh, my goodness. You didn't. I'm so sorry, Kit, I should have told you but I just assumed you already knew . . . Ed died. He was killed several years ago in a car crash.' She squeezed her son's limp hand. 'I didn't know about it myself until I met up with Brenda again. But I just assumed you knew, darling.'

He pulled his cold hand away from his mother's and slumped back in his seat ashen-faced. He swallowed hard. 'But I was only reading about Matthews Structural Design in a trade mag a few months ago. About some contract they'd landed, how well they're doing.' He shifted forward again. 'Are you sure about this, Ma?'

'Oh, Kit, of course I'm sure. I see Roberta all the time.'

He closed his eyes and was aware of a pounding in his chest. 'You mean . . . she's *completely* on her own?'

'Yes, darling, except for Jamie of course, and Boris her dog.' Cynthia widened her eyes. 'Jamie's a lovely child, a real credit to her, and she adores that dog, it's like another human being.' Cynthia pulled one of Kit's hands away from his face. 'Don't look so upset, darling. Anybody would think it was your fault. It happened after you left Ed. You weren't to know. There was nothing you could have done.'

Kit shook his head quickly. 'No, it's not that, Ma. It's just . . . Roberta, *on her own.*'

'But she manages remarkably well. In fact, she's a very capable girl. Runs her own business now, catering, and is an absolutely wonderful cook.'

Kit sagged back against the settee. 'And I suppose you're going to tell me now that she's getting married again in the near future?'

Cynthia saw the desolate look in her son's eyes. 'Kit? Darling,

I've never seen you so upset. Tell me to mind my own business, if you like, but . . . you weren't in love with her, were you?'

He shifted forward in his seat, putting his head between his hands. 'Of course not, Ma, whatever gave you that idea?'

'It's just that you seem so incredibly upset.'

'Well, of course I'm upset. I lived with them for months! It's like losing a member of my own family. Ed was a fantastic bloke, I liked him a lot.'

'Well, if you liked him that much, why didn't you stay in touch?'

Kit turned to stare at his mother, noticing her questioning eyes. 'Have you been talking about me . . . to Brenda?'

Embarrassment suffused Cynthia's face. 'Well, naturally we talk about this and that. We discuss everything, Brenda and I.'

Kit was interested. 'And what has she said about me?'

Cynthia shrugged. 'She hasn't actually said anything about you, Kit. She's not likely to, you're my son, remember? But I know you were involved for a while with Julia.'

'Huh! And what a mistake that was.'

'Kit! That's not very kind.'

'She doesn't bloody deserve kindness.' He turned urgently towards his mother. 'You didn't answer my question, Ma? Is there anybody else in Roberta's life?'

'You did love her, didn't you, Kit? It's written all over your face.'

He implored his mother, 'Just answer me, please?'

Cynthia inclined her head slightly. 'Well, I'm not exactly sure but she does see this trainer chap now and again.'

'Trainer chap? What trainer chap?'

'Oh, I don't know. Why are you so angry, Kit? He's a trainer in Newmarket. A lot older than her, Brenda says. Widowed, like her. She's in catering, I told you, and does lunches and dinners for a lot of the trainers . . .'

Kit butted in, 'And she's seeing him? They're together? Is that what you're saying?'

'Well, how should I know if they're *together*?' His mother shrugged. 'But I suppose they are. Brenda's not too keen on him, mind. Says he's much too old for her.'

Kit stood up and strode towards the window. 'Why didn't she get in touch with me, Ma? Why didn't she tell me about Ed? She could have found me in Aberdeen or got in touch with you.' Kit turned to face his mother once more, his face red with anger. 'She should have let me know, Ma!'

Cynthia stood up and walked over to her son. She took both his hands in hers. 'Kit, darling, you're being very, very hard. You mustn't talk about Roberta like this, not after what she's been through. Brenda told me that she was *extremely* ill after Ed died. And to make things worse, she had a miscarriage. Brenda and Julia were just so relieved when she finally got herself together again. Don't blame her for not letting you know. That's quite ridiculous, Kit. She's a lovely, lovely girl.'

He twisted his hands out of his mother's grip. 'I'm sorry. Forget everything I've just said.'

Cynthia touched him on the shoulder. 'If you feel so strongly about it, go and see her. You have every right.'

'Oh, no, I don't, Ma. I don't have any bloody rights at all. I gave those up!'

Cynthia swallowed hard. This was new ground for her. Something she knew nothing about. 'Well, whatever went on in the past, Kit, it shouldn't stop you going to see Roberta now and paying your respects, especially as you didn't know about Ed.'

He gripped the window-sill. 'But you don't understand, Ma. I can't.' He faced his mother again. 'I can't just walk back into her life, and not . . .' Kit shook his head and looked down at the floor. 'Just leave it, Ma. Forget everything I've said. Don't mention me to them at all. Please?'

'Don't be silly, Kit. Brenda already knows you're home.'

'Well, don't mention this! Promise me? You've got to promise me, Ma?' Kit's eyes beseeched his mother.

'All right, I promise. But I don't know what else you're expecting me to say to them?'

'Just say I've got a girlfriend in Aberdeen. OK?'

'And have you, Kit? Is that the truth?'

In a gravelly voice he said, 'It's true enough, Ma, and it's all they need to know.'

60

'Julia!'

With Boris by her side, Roberta stood open-mouthed at her front door. She brought one hand to her face and beamed delightedly. 'Wow! Did Mum do that?'

Haltingly, Julia touched her shorn head, still not used to being without her long hair. 'No, it wasn't Mum, I had it done in Chelsea. You don't like it either, do you?'

Roberta hesitated, choosing her words carefully. 'I do like it, Julia. You look – well, stunning!'

'Stunningly awful! I shall grow it back straight away.'

'No, I really, really like it, Julia. It just takes some getting used to. But why did you colour it? A bit drastic, don't you think?'

Again, Julia fingered her honey-blonde layered hair. 'Because I needed a change. I'm fed up with my life, and I suppose I was dumping it, and its colour, in the bin along with my hair!'

Roberta moved closer to her sister and kissed her cheek. 'Oh, dear, you'd better tell me all about it. Come on, come through to the garden. I've prepared lunch. As it's such a lovely day, I thought we'd eat outside.'

Noting the gorgeous scent Roberta always wore these days, Julia followed her along the hall. Boris, wagging his tail, trailed along behind them both. Julia allowed her eyes to wander over Roberta's hair which now fell in luxurious curls and waves down her back. She'd flicked out the sides, around her face, making her look even more attractive, especially with her carefully applied make-up and light summer tan.

'You're looking good, Roberta. Have you put on a bit of weight?'

Julia followed her into her kitchen where her sister grabbed two glasses and a bottle of white wine. They made their way into the small garden and sat down at the wooden table. 'It suits you, you know, a bit more weight. You were much too thin before.'

Roberta shrugged. 'I don't know, I never weigh myself. My clothes still fit, so I can't have put on that much.'

'Well, maybe it's just that you look so fit and healthy. It must be because you're always in the fresh air.' Julia watched as her sister pulled out the cork of the chilled Pouilly Fuissé. Roberta poured healthy measures into both glasses, and immediately took a sip of hers.

She licked her lips. 'Mmm, I adore this wine.'

Julia looked at the label, then tasted it for herself. 'Yes, it is rather delicious. Who introduced you to this, then?'

Roberta put her glass on the table, and looked towards the kitchen. 'Oh, someone, years ago. I'll get the lunch. Salad and Quiche Lorraine, all right?'

'Sounds wonderful.' Julia watched as her sister, clad in shorts and a bikini top, with nothing on her feet, wandered back into her kitchen. Even her walk was graceful and at ease. She soon returned with an enormous tray.

Two linen mats and napkins, together with knives and forks, were carefully placed on the wooden table, and a huge bowl of French-dressed salad deposited in the middle, together with warm home-made Quiche Lorraine. 'I'll get the French bread.' Roberta wandered off again, returning in seconds. 'It's warm, I prefer it that way.'

Julie looked at the small feast before her. Everything so simple yet tempting. 'So, business is good, Roberta?'

She nodded, serving her sister with salad. 'It is. I'm busy, but I don't allow myself to become too busy. I only do selected lunch and dinner parties these days and farm the rest out to Sarah and Jo who work with me.' She shrugged and sipped her wine. 'It all fits in very well.'

'How's Jamie?'

'He's fine. Getting on very well at school.'

'Does he like it?'

Roberta nodded. 'I think so, her certainly never complains.'

'That's good. Poor Vivien hates school. She cries and cries every Monday morning. Jennifer doesn't seem to mind too much, but

Vivien can't understand why she has to go at all.'

Reminded of her sister's close contact with their cousin and Nathan's daughters, whom Roberta hadn't seen for nearly two years, she looked across the table 'You still see a lot of the twins, do you? And Clare?'

'Quite a lot.'

'And Nathan? Do you sometimes see him at Clare's?' Roberta knew nothing of her sister's feelings for him.

Julie shook her head. 'No, I never see Nathan.' What she didn't say was, 'If N.P.'s at Clare's, I make sure I'm not.'

'But aren't you in business with him?'

'Yes, but only for the jewellery, and I order that through his warehouse manager.'

Roberta shrugged. 'Oh, I thought maybe you and he were friends?'

'Well, you thought wrong.'

Roberta widened her eyes. 'Sorry.'

'No need to be. What about you? Do you still see him? After all, you were a lot closer to him than I ever was.'

Roberta's face went slightly pink and she quickly sliced two portions from the quiche, serving Julia with one. 'I never see him now, not anymore.'

'Why did you fall out? I mean, I know he gave you that ring, the one Mum wears?'

Roberta's eyes flashed. 'I'm surprised she hasn't told you. We fell out because of that ring.' Roberta served herself with quiche. 'He asked me to marry him.' Julia had always guessed the truth, but her sharp intake of breath stalled the conversation and allowed her true feelings to register with Roberta. She looked into her sister's eyes, recognising the pain there, and her mind flew back, remembering a brusque phone conversation in Nathan's office between him and Julia, years ago. She'd thought it strange then, Nathan's discomfiture. Maybe they were having a relationship even then, while he was pursuing Roberta? After all, it had been Julia who had put him on to her in the first place. If that were so, her poor sister! Once again, the tables had turned. 'I wasn't ready to marry again, Julia, so he left me. But he refused to take back the ring.' Roberta shook her head. 'I wouldn't have felt right wearing it, but I didn't want to hide away something so beautiful and Mum deserved something special.'

Confusion stabbed at Julia's brain. 'Didn't you love him?'

Roberta leant back in her seat. 'What is all this, Julia? We're supposed to be talking about you.' She broke off a chunk of bread and put it on her plate. 'I'm dying to hear all about your boutique?'

'You didn't love him in the same way as you loved Kit, is that it?'

Roberta's face immediately went pink. '*Julia!*'

She reached across the table. 'It's all right, you can tell me. I won't shout it across the rooftops, you know that.'

Roberta swallowed hard. 'He's back, Kit is. Did you know?'

Julia frowned. 'Yes, Mum did mention it. Or, at least, she warned me he was back.'

'Will you see him?'

She smiled at her sister. 'You're very clever, aren't you, Roberta? You haven't answered any of my questions, and now you've subtly turned this conversation round to me.'

'Sorry.'

'No need. And the answer to your question is, even if you won't answer mine, no. Definitely not. Will you?'

Roberta blinked and sipped her wine. 'I thought he might get in touch, but Mum says he's extremely busy. He works in Cambridge now and she says Cynthia's very cagey about mentioning him at all. *But*, she did mention a girlfriend in Aberdeen, so it looks as though you were right, Julia. It looks as though Oona McPhatter got him in the end.'

Julia lowered her eyes in shame. Poor Roberta, she'd actually believed all that stuff about Oona. It briefly crossed Julia's mind to admit that Kit had once openly declared his love for Roberta. She raised her eyes again and decided against it. Who knew what the situation was now? 'If you ever do see Kit again, Roberta, will you promise me something, please?'

'Of course.'

'Don't tell him about me – the abortion, I mean. I really would rather he didn't know.'

'If ever I see Kit Fordham-Clarke again, Julia, I certainly won't mention that. What do you take me for?'

'It's just . . . well, a period in my life I'd much rather forget.'

Roberta squeezed her sister's hand. 'Of course. It must have been awful.'

Julia snorted and tossed back her head. 'It was.' She pinched her mouth together. 'And I bitterly regret it, Roberta. Do you know, he'd be four now. My baby would be four.'

'Oh, Julia! You'll make up for it all in time. You'll have lots more babies.'

'Will I? I'm not so sure. Look at me. I'm burnt out, Roberta, burnt out at twenty-five. My life's a mess, I'm going nowhere, and there's nowhere I want to go.'

'Julia?'

'I'm sorry, I don't want to burden you with all my problems. Come on, let's eat this gorgeous lunch.'

'No, tell me, I want to know. Tell me, Julia?'

She put her head on one side. 'Where do I start? The landlords of my house are due back from the Emirates in a couple of months, so I have to move out. I suppose I should think myself lucky that they stayed an extra couple of years, but it seems like *my* home now and I love it and don't want to live anywhere else. And to cap it all the lease-holders of the shop are threatening to double the rent in September unless we negotiate to buy the lease. I don't *want* to buy the lease. I don't *want* to spend the rest of my life in a shop in Chelsea. I'm tired of leather, can't get excited about it anymore.'

Julia took a long gulp of her wine, and Roberta refilled both glasses. 'These days, Sarayu has more ideas than me. If it wasn't for her, the boutique would've gone the same way as some of the others down the King's Road. To be honest with you, I'm thinking of giving it all up and letting Sarayu negotiate for the lease. She's big with Nick now, you know. They've been together for some time.'

'Really? How interesting. Will they marry?'

Julia smiled. 'If Nick has his way, they will. He's really in love with her, and Sarayu sorts him out in a way nobody else ever could. She's definitely the boss. But I'm not sure Madhav's very keen. Still, it's not my worry, thank God.'

'But if you gave up the shop, what would you do? Where would you go?'

Julia smiled secretly. 'I think I'd come back here.' She took a mouthful of quiche. 'Mmm, this is superb. Seriously, though, I do envy Clare. You know, she's doing amazingly well. Doctor bloody Clare Purley! *And she's got her little girls.* Really in her element, she is. You should see some of the eggheads she invites back to her house!' Julia laughed. 'But she deserves it, she's worked hard, and

277

I think maybe I should take a leaf out of her book. Go back to school, get myself a degree.'

'What? But that'd take ages. What do you want to do that for?'

Julia shrugged. 'Something to do.'

'Well, I think that's going off at a tangent. If you gave everything up, you could regret it later on.'

Julia weighed up her sister's words. 'You may be right. I suppose I need something to get me interested in work again.' She giggled. 'Or it could be that I need a good man.'

'You haven't got one then?'

'Oh, I've got loads of men, but no *good* ones!'

'You'll find one in the end.'

'Have you? Mum said you're going out with some wealthy trainer, is that right?'

Roberta laughed with some embarrassment. 'Oh, Mum, she just likes to talk.'

'It's not true then?'

'He's a friend, just a friend.'

'Like Nathan was, I suppose?'

Roberta saw the hard look on her sister's face. 'No, not like Nathan. Nothing like him. Nathan was *cataclysmic* in my life. I changed after him.'

Julia pondered her sister's words. 'I suppose it's no good asking you how?'

Roberta shrugged, going slightly pink again. 'My confidence grew. He gave me a certain confidence, made me feel good about myself in certain ways.'

'And this trainer? Does he? Make you feel good in *certain ways*?'

Roberta smiled, then laughed. 'I'm beginning to think, Julia, that we understand each other too well.'

'Oh, I understand you all right, but I'm not sure you understand me! You've got everything neat and tidy in your life, Roberta, your priorities in the right place. Men just fall hopelessly in love with you and want to marry you because you're so . . . damned pure.'

'I'm not pure! I'm not pure at all.'

'Aren't you? I think you are, Roberta. Not like me.'

'But that's not fair. You've lived your life exactly the way you want to, and there were times, Julia, years in fact, when I just followed miserably in your wake. Don't accuse me of being something I'm not just because it makes you feel better about yourself.'

'I don't feel better about myself, Roberta. *Bitter* more like.'

'And I suppose you think I don't? I'm bitter too, Julia. Bitter because I lost the father of my son. Bitter because I lost my own father when he was still young. Bitter because I lost the home I adored and had worked my fingers to the bone to restore. Bitter because the one bloody man I ever *really, really* loved walked off into the damned sunset with *you* and ... and ... has never given me a second thought!'

Julia gulped at her sister's vehemence. 'I'm sorry. I say some bloody stupid things sometimes. I'm sorry, Roberta, I never thought.'

'No, none of you think. But it hurts just the same.'

Silence ensued. Both sisters tried to eat their lunch. Roberta gulped back some more wine and replenished both glasses. And then, together, they pushed their plates away. Julia spoke first. 'I'm sorry, Roberta. The food's lovely but I can't eat anymore.'

'It's OK. I'm not hungry either.'

Julia grabbed her handbag and withdrew her cigarettes. 'Do you mind?' Roberta shook her heard. Julia lit up, inhaled and blew out smoke. 'Let's talk about now, not the past. Tell me about this trainer? Do you love him, at least a little bit?'

Roberta smiled uneasily and tossed her hair away from her shoulders. She radiated well-being, and that, combined with her mature beauty, made Julia envious. She fingered her own scant hair. Roberta propped her chin on her hand. 'Yes, I suppose I love him a bit. He's kind, and he makes me laugh. He's good to Jamie, and takes me racing, and to posh places. I meet some incredibly interesting people.' She winked at her sister. 'You should see my racing outfits, I've even got a couple of hats.'

'Has he asked you to marry him?'

'Yes. Loads of times. But I always say no.'

Julia sized her sister up and boldly asked. 'Is he good in bed?'

Roberta tutted at her sister's audacity before allowing a smile to creep around her mouth. 'It's not like that, Julia. Not really. As I said before, he's a friend. But if you want the truth ... the answer's no. For someone so knowledgeable about the anatomy of a horse, he'd benefit enormously from a few lessons in the anatomy of women.'

Julia went into peals of laughter. 'Lawn-mower job, eh?'

'*Julia!*'

279

'Well, you'll never admit it but I bet it's true!'

Roberta gulped back some more wine. 'Do you fancy another bottle?'

'Why not? I'm certainly enjoying this.'

'We'll be squiffy. I have to pick up James at quarter past three.'

'Oh, I'll pick him up, Fairstead House is only down the road. At least all those well-heeled folk'll think I'm the drunken slob, not you!'

Roberta touched her sister's arm. 'Nobody would ever think of you like that, Julia. As we're being so honest with each other, shall I tell what I really think of you?'

'As long as it's nice. Just at this moment, I couldn't stand anything that wasn't.'

'It's not nice. It's the truth. This is how I see you, Julia Tree. How I've always seen you. My looks don't match yours, not really, they never have. Your beauty is rare, and if you stood back a little more and allowed life to come to you, instead of rushing forward all the time, grabbing everything with both hands, I think you'd gain a lot more respect and . . . maybe . . . start to benefit from the more important things around you that at the moment you miss.'

Julia gulped and finished her wine. 'You'd better get the other bottle, Roberta, before I run away and hide.'

'I'm sorry. I must sound like a prig.' She quickly turned away and Julia enviously watched her older and wiser sister pad briskly across the lawn towards the kitchen, hair flowing down her back, faithful Boris by her side.

61

August, 1976

L'Hôtel du Cap, on the tip of Cap D'Antibes, is small and select with its own private beach. Surrounded by irrigated, manicured lawns, palm trees, assorted sun-loving shrubs and creeping Bougain-villaea, the sprawling stuccoed building dates back to the early-eighteenth century. Painted cream, with panoramic views of the sur-rounding area, the hotel is packed from one season to the next and famous for its delicious cuisine.

Cynthia Fordham-Clarke, still remarkably trim in a fuchsia pink swimsuit, put down her *Daily Mail* and looked over the top of her large, square-framed, white sunglasses. 'We paid all this money, Brenda, and it's boiling hot back home.'

Sitting upright on her sunbed, beneath an enormous sunshade, Brenda wrapped her arms around her knees. With the sea sparkling in the late-afternoon sun, and a spotless beach stretching before her, she savoured the view. 'But it wouldn't be like this, Cynthia. I don't give a damn how hot it is back home. This is the first time I've been abroad, and I'm just so happy to be here.' She stretched back, in her white shorts and navy boob-tube, luxuriating in doing nothing but sipping her *Kir*.

'Oh, look, there's the waiter.' Cynthia nudged her. 'Quick, Brenda, attract his attention. *Vite, vite!*'

Amused, she looked askance at her friend. 'Not again, Cynthia. I haven't finished this one yet.'

'Oh, pooh, he's gone again.' Cynthia slumped back on her sunbed.

Brenda, used to her friend by now, took charge and raised her arm. The waiter, with eyes in the back of his head, appeared from nowhere. '*Vous desirez, madame?*' Brenda, whose French was limited, pointed to Cynthia.

'*Encor un Kir, s'il vous plaît. Un grand Kir.*'

'*Oui. Et pour vous?*' The waiter looked at Brenda.

'*Rien, merci.*'

With tray in hand, the waiter in the crisp white jacket bowed to them and left. Cynthia turned to her friend. 'If I'm not careful, I shall put on stones on this holiday. This swimsuit is already too tight. But what I could really fancy now is a dish of ice-cream with strawberries and that chocolate stuff on top.'

'Cynthia! It'll be dinnertime before long. You're as bad as Nancy.'

'Oh, crumbs, I hope not.' She covered her still lovely face with her hands. 'I'd shoot myself first.'

'That's my sister you're talking about, and you know full well, Cynthia Fordham-Clarke, I won't hear a word said against her.'

Playfully, she poked out her tongue at her friend and looked ahead at the shimmering Mediterranean. 'I wonder what poor old Nancy is doing now?'

'Oh, goodness knows. Getting fat on chocolate cake most probably.'

'Now who's being unkind?'

'Hmm.' Brenda reflected upon her sister back home. 'Well, I always wonder what Peter really thinks of her. I mean, he must love her because they've been married for so long, and putting up with Nancy for years and years is a feat in itself! You know, Cynthia, I only ever see him at the odd party but must admit, he's still an extremely handsome man. Clare definitely takes after him. And he was such a good-time chap in his younger days, and Nancy is so . . . so *staid.*'

Cynthia frowned. 'Yes. Makes you wonder what he ever saw in her. Was she always like that?'

'What, staid?' Cynthia nodded, and Brenda pursed her lips. 'She was very pretty when she was younger, much prettier than me, but she was always interested in money . . . *and position* . . . and how she was perceived, whereas I couldn't give a damn. Do you think it's possible to be born a snob? And if that's the case, why wasn't I? We came from the same parents, and they were relatively poor.' Brenda pushed back her sunhat. 'When Peter came along, with his high ideas and wads of money, she was like a cat on heat.'

282

'He asked me out, you know, it was rather embarrassing.'

Brenda raised her sunglasses and looked at her friend. 'Who asked you out?'

'Peter. After Josh's death. He asked me out to dinner, said Nancy wouldn't mind.'

Brenda turned on to her side. 'Really? *Peter* asked you out to dinner?'

'Oh, come on, Brenda. Everybody knows about Peter and his lady friends.'

Brenda's eyebrows shot up. 'Well, I certainly don't!'

'You can tell me to shut up if you want to but he carried on with his secretary for years. She was married, the same as him, had two kids I think, but they used to go *everywhere* together. Until she left the firm, that is.'

Brenda gulped and turned on to her back. 'Poor Nancy.'

Cynthia looked at her friend. 'I wonder if she's ever suspected?'

Brenda sat up again. 'Here comes your drink.'

Gratefully, Cynthia signed for the *Kir* and took it from the waiter's tray. '*Merci bien.*'

'*Je vous en prie.*' The waiter nodded, bowed and left.

'That's what I like,' quipped Cynthia, 'a grovelling male.'

Brenda watched him walk away. 'He's not bad, actually. Nice bottom.'

Cynthia's head turned swiftly. 'Hmm, I prefer a bit more meat, myself.' Both women grinned at each other. 'You haven't answered my question. Do you think Nancy's ever suspected anything?'

Brenda narrowed her eyes, and finished her own *Kir*. 'I shouldn't think so, she's too wrapped up in herself. But, if she has, she'd never admit it. Never!'

Cynthia grinned at her friend. 'Shall we change the subject? We're getting maudlin.'

'What a good idea.'

'How's Roberta? No wedding bells yet?'

Brenda sat up straight. 'Didn't I tell you? She's finished with him for good!'

Cynthia's face was a picture, suddenly suffused with real pleasure. 'Honestly? Are you telling me the truth? Roberta's finished with her trainer chap?'

'He does have a name, Cynthia,' Brenda reprimanded, 'John Chapman, and yes, she has. In fact it was a bit *déja vu*. He wanted her to marry him, said he was getting too old to be messed about, so Roberta said goodbye. It was the Nathan thing all over again.'

'The Nathan thing? What on earth was that?'

Brenda shook her head. 'Oh, nothing. She wouldn't like it if she thought I was discussing her like this.'

Cynthia eyed her friend keenly. 'Hmm, they're funny our kids, aren't they?'

Brenda smiled. 'What do you mean?

'Well, Kit's the same.' Cynthia looked out to sea. 'He's sworn me to secrecy.'

'Kit has? About what?'

'Roberta.'

'Roberta?'

'Hmmm.' Cynthia looked cryptically at her friend.

Brenda raised her sunglasses. '*Nothing* went on. I'm sure of that.'

Cynthia blinked, and looked surprised. 'I didn't say it did!'

Brenda touched her friend's arm. 'Gordon and I always suspected they had strong feelings for each other, but that's all. I'm convinced it was nothing more.'

Cynthia shook her head. 'Oh, Brenda, it's such a relief to be able to talk to you about Kit. He's so in love with Roberta. He asks me about her all the time – whether she's getting married, and when, and what she's doing, and how? And I've been sworn to secrecy, been told not to say a word. I keep telling him to go and see her but he won't, says he can't. Brenda, she would see him, wouldn't she? She must have some feelings for him still?'

Brenda swallowed hard and looked ahead. 'What about his girl-friend in Aberdeen?'

'I don't think there is one.'

'Well, there was! Oona McPhatter. See, I even know her name.' Brenda looked at her friend. 'And it's not that simple, Cynthia. There's Julia to consider too.'

'Yes, I know. What happened with Julia? He was so angry about her.'

'*Kit* was angry! Huh, that's rich!'

'Why? Tell me what happened? I'd really like to know.'

Brenda shook her head and lowered her eyes. 'I can't, Cynthia. I really can't. As much as I'd like to, certain confidences can't be broken.'

Cynthia grabbed her arm. 'You know it's Roberta he loves.'

Brenda looked at her friend. 'Everybody loves Roberta, Cynthia, in case you hadn't noticed. But it's Julia I feel sorry for.'

The two friends fell silent, and Cynthia, contrite, sipped her drink. Brenda decided to break the mood. 'Well, I don't know about you, but I think we should go for a walk.'

'A walk? You must be joking! I don't go for walks on holiday. Anyway, we're going to Monte Carlo tomorrow, we'll be walking all day.'

Brenda looked at her friend. 'You are a lazy so-and-so, Cynthia Fordham-Clarke. You don't deserve to be beautiful and svelte, do you know that?'

Cynthia giggled then her attention was taken by two swarthy gentlemen, in their early-forties, walking towards them. 'Hey, look over there! It's those chaps we saw last night.'

Both women looked across the beach towards the two handsome men, in bathing trunks, walking towards them. Brenda could hardly believe her eyes. 'They're making a bee-line for us, the same as they did last night. Good Lord, we're old enough to be their mothers!'

'Rubbish, they just look young.' Cynthia winked at her friend. 'How about it, Brenda? Will you if I will?'

She was astounded. 'Will I what?'

'You know . . . do it, while we're on holiday. After all, nobody'll know.'

'Oh, yes, and go back home with something ghastly!'

'Not if we're careful. Or make sure they are.'

'Cynthia, you never cease to amaze me!'

'Good, I like to keep you on your toes. Quick, they're getting closer. Will you? I won't if you won't.'

Brenda gulped. 'But they're not going to fancy us.'

'Oh, yes, they are. And I can tell you, Brenda, for certain, I might be sixty-one but I'm not ready to shut up shop down there just yet.' Cynthia giggled. 'We're on holiday, let's give ourselves an instant face-lift!'

Brenda laughed at her friend's wit, and as the two men drew closer, quickly sized them up. 'One condition, Cynthia.' She poked her friend in the arm. 'And it's a must.'

'Anything!'

'We don't fall in love . . . and I have the one on the left.'

62

Nancy Lewis topped up her gin. She narrowed her eyes and took a long swig. The phone rang, and she practically tripped herself in her eagerness to answer it. 'Hallo?'

'Nancy darling?' Peter's familiar voice startled her.

'Oh, Peter, where are you? I really thought you'd be home by now.'

'I know, I know. I'm so sorry, my darling. Got held up again, you know how it is?'

'Oh, Peter, this really isn't fair.' Disappointment washed over Nancy. She wasn't going to let him off lightly. 'You spent two whole weeks at the Olympics, and you're still away. It's just not fair! I haven't seen you for nearly the whole of August. This is Friday night, the weekend, and I'm fed up with being on my own.'

'I know, darling, it must be awful, and I wouldn't do it if there was any way I could get out of it.'

'Out of what?'

'This conference lark. I'm Chairman of this damned financial liaison committee, you know I have to be here. And I'm afraid it looks like it's going to go on for the whole bloody weekend.' He looked across his hotel room at the young blonde sitting on his bed. 'Why don't you pack your bag, Nance, and get straight over here? You could jump in your car and be here in a couple of hours.' He knew it was a dead certainty she'd refuse.

'Oh, yes! Typical of you. Expecting me to come all the way across London to see you. Why can't you jump in your car and come home to me?'

'Things to do, darling. Papers to go through. You know Roger leaves it all to me.'

'But I thought the firm was hard up for work? Why do you need a financial liaison committee?'

'Because, sweetie, it's the way to get back in the black. They're all merchant bankers here, with money to lend. I've been away, Nance, I've got to make up for lost time.'

'So when are you going to be home?'

'Monday evening. And I tell you what, my darling, why don't you pop into the travel agent's tomorrow and book us a quick trip to this Cap d'Antibes, or whatever the place is, that you so desperately want us to go to?'

Nancy jumped with glee. 'Seriously? For when?'

'As soon as poss, darling, as soon as poss. Damn the firm, I say. I deserve a double break. We could have a long weekend, just you and me. Be quite like old times.'

'Well, I'm not sure we'd get in at the Hôtel du Cap ... but I suppose I could try.'

'Tell you what, darling, I'll pull a few strings. Get my secretary on to it straight away. Don't you worry your sweet head about anything, Nance, I'll get us into this Hôtel du Cap.'

'Oh, Peter, will you? That would be nice.'

'How's the diet going, darling? You'll have to look good for that French beach.'

'Oh, I will. Won't it be fun?'

'Look, old girl, gotta go. Work beckons and all that. Speak to you soon. Love you.'

'Love you ...' Nancy's voice trailed off as Peter put down the phone.

She replaced the receiver and clapped her hands together, then picked up her glass of gin. Exultantly she took another long sip and beamed. That'd show Brenda and Cynthia Fordham-Clarke! Nancy's brain rapidly ran ahead as she staged a scene in the Cosy Corner. Brenda would be sitting there, telling Nancy all about her wonderful holiday, and very casually she would reply, 'Oh, did you say L'Hôtel du Cap? Well, fancy that. What a coincidence. Peter and I popped over there last weekend. It was a complete surprise to me, Brenda, I can tell you. Mind you, we wouldn't go again, not quite up to our standard!' That'd show her. Put her in her place once more. Brenda was getting far too big for her boots these days, far too big.

Nancy turned and looked at the enormous sandwich she'd made.

Chicken, ham, egg, cheese, mayonnaise, tomato, and a lettuce leaf of course. Nancy was very health conscious these days. She looked at the sandwich and then reflected on her figure. There was no way she'd be able to squeeze into any of her countless bathing suits at the moment, and there wasn't time to lose any weight. Nancy chuckled to herself. She could visit Clare, tomorrow, then pop along to Knightsbridge. She might even call in and see Peter, surprise him. That cheered her up considerably.

And then she sighed and muttered out loud, 'I do wish you'd slow down, Peter. It's just not fair. You should be here with me, not gadding about all over the place finding finance for that stupid, stupid firm!' She finished her drink and actually had to grab the worktop in her kitchen to steady herself. 'Oooh, better eat something quick.' She bit into the sandwich and rapturously chewed away. 'Mmm,' she murmured, 'this mayonnaise from Marks & Spenny's is divine!'

Nancy poured more gin into her glass and topped it up with a dash of tonic. Taking another huge bite from her sandwich, she crossed over to the fridge, running a hand over her sweaty forehead. 'Phew, it's hot,' she mumbled with her mouth full. 'If only it would rain and break this stifling heat.' She withdrew a tray of ice from the freezer compartment and plopped two cubes into her gin. She swallowed hard on her mouthful of sandwich, coughing as she did so, and put a hand to her chest. 'And the Mediterranean sun will do a power of good to my poor old tubes. Oh, I do hope you get us into the Hôtel du Cap, Peter, I shall be so disappointed if you don't.'

Nancy calmed herself. Leave it to Peter and his secretary. They'd worked wonders in the past, and he'd be pulling out all the stops on this one because he owed Nancy a few favours. She picked up her plate and her drink and walked out of the kitchen. She decided to have a bath, to cool down. She started to mount the stairs but by the time she reached the top was uncomfortably sweaty. She wandered through to her bedroom, which was also hot and clammy. Nancy put down her plate and drink on the bedside table and walked over to the window. She opened it wide, not that it made any difference, outside was worse if anything, and there were thunder flies everywhere. 'Damn the things,' she moaned, swiping some of them off the windowsill.

She slumped on to her bed and pushed off her high-heeled shoes then started to unbutton her summer dress. With a bit of huffing and puffing she managed to slip right out of it without standing up. But she was still hot. She looked up at the window. Their enormous house wasn't overlooked. Nancy undid her deep-line bra, which took some time with all the hooks and eyes, and finally tossed it off the bed on to the floor. And then, with great difficulty, she pulled down her Playtex panty-girdle with the firming, flattening panels in the front. She finally yanked the darn thing off and tossed that on the floor as well. She wasn't wearing tights, even Nancy had given up tights in this hot weather, so stretched out crossways on the bed, completely naked now.

Lethargically, she pulled herself up again and took a long sip of her gin, picking out an ice-cube and rubbing it over her forehead and down to her enormous breasts. She trailed the ice to her stomach and along both arms. By the time she'd rubbed it everywhere, it had completely melted. Nancy sat up again and took another huge bite of her sandwich. Rather heavily, she slumped back on to the bed, with her head against the pillows this time, munching away until she started to choke.

She sat up, a little alarmed, and put a hand to her neck. She'd got some of the sandwich stuck in her throat and couldn't cough it up. With strangled rasps she rapidly shifted back up the bed towards the headboard, almost squatting and fighting for air. She was panicking now, and put her fingers into her mouth to prise away what food she could, trying again to cough. She was heaving, and straining, and desperately striving for breath. With one last supreme effort her eyes flickered as she raised her face, trying to gasp in air. In vain. Nancy slumped back, unconscious, banging her head on the headboard.

63

Peter Lewis swung his blue metallic Jaguar into his wide gravelled drive in Godmanchester. Immediately his eyes alighted upon Nancy's car and he breathed a sigh of relief. Where the hell had she been? He'd rung her about ten times and she'd not answered. He'd even rung his daughter, but Clare wasn't there either. Perhaps they were together? Peter had been worried, and even considered cutting his weekend short. He would have done had not his new secretary taken him completely by surprise. Twenty-five, and a mere slip of a thing, she'd performed in a way he'd only dreamt of in the past. He'd never had so much fun. Some of the antics they'd got up to simply blew away his mind. Peter grinned. What a girl. What a *ball*.

He parked his car next to Nancy's and reflected upon his wife. She'd never liked sex, and he supposed he must be partly to blame. Peter remembered the young pretty virgin he'd married; Nancy had insisted on being a virgin on their wedding day, and he grimaced to remember their disastrous wedding night. Peter turned off the ignition. He looked at the time. It was seven-thirty. He was hungry, not that Nancy would have prepared supper, but he could take her out, make a fuss of her. They could eat at the Old Bridge, she'd like that, then he could break it to her gently that L'Hôtel du Cap was fully booked and he wouldn't be able to take anymore days off anyway. She'd moan and complain but he'd soon buy her off.

Peter grabbed his briefcase and overnight bag from the back seat of his car, and made his way to the front door. The first thing he noticed was the milk on the doorstep, and the newspaper stuffed into the letter box. They only had a bottle of milk on Sundays, and a couple during the week. Peter frowned.

290

Using his key, he unlocked the front door and stepped over the newspaper-ridden threshold. The smell hit him straight away. Peter's nostrils wrinkled in distaste.

He called out, rather feebly, 'Nance? Nance?' There was no reply.

He put his briefcase and bag on the floor and, not bothering to close the front door, walked towards the drawing room. With his hand covering his nose and mouth, he pushed open the door. No one inside. He stood in the hallway and looked up the stairs.

As he mounted them his heart was beating fast. Involuntarily, he kept sniffing and the smell was so vile he thought he was going to be sick.

Peter stood at the top of the stairs. The bedroom he shared with Nancy was further down the hall. Still covering his mouth with his hand, he walked forward until he reached the doorway. There he paused. Terrified, Peter looked towards the open window, with the curtains flapping slightly in a sluggish breeze. He took two paces forward and turned towards the bed. Then, with blood-curdling intensity, he opened his mouth and screamed.

A changed man, Peter Lewis tripped his way out of the bedroom, dragging himself along the landing and practically throwing himself down the stairs, screeching and wailing at the top of his voice. With outstretched hands he ran through the still open front door, along the gravelled drive and further into the street. Then stopped and stood still, fighting for breath, frantically looking around for help. Neighbours appeared from nowhere, obviously alerted by the racket he was making, and hastened towards him. Slumping to his knees, Peter pleaded with them to get help for his wife though he already knew it was too late for Nancy.

64

September, 1967

As Brenda and Cynthia arrived home from Cap D'Antibes on Monday morning, all hell was let loose. For a week or so Cynthia hardly saw Brenda at all. She was beside herself with grief and guilt and gave all her time to her brother-in-law, arranging the funeral and providing comfort to a broken man. He confessed everything to her, exorcising his own guilt and burdening Brenda in such a way that she couldn't sleep at night. If only she'd known of her sister's misery she could have helped in so many ways.

Brenda talked endlessly to both Roberta and Julia about Nancy's death, and as horrified as they both were, and saddened by their aunt's death, they were unable to allay her feelings of negligence. It was actually Clare, at the funeral, who finally put her mind at rest. She told Brenda that her mother had in fact been enormously happy and fulfilled in her own particular way. She said Nancy hadn't wanted a cosy marriage, but had preferred other mental stimulus to keep her spirits high. She even jokingly described her as a battering ram, aiming for certain ships' hulls. Brenda had smiled at this, remembering only too well that she had been the primary target for years. Of course, Brenda hadn't intended to mention her own father's infidelity to Clare, but it seemed she already knew.

Clare reflected upon her school days. 'I used to call in at the office sometimes, on my way home from school. Daddy would be sitting there, with his secretary, and I just knew. From very early on, I knew. So, you see, I was brought up to be very mistrustful of men.' She grabbed her aunt's arm. 'But honestly, Auntie Brenda, my mother adored my father, and he her in his way. And even if she did know about him screwing his secretaries, she wouldn't have wanted her life to be any different. If I'd told her my suspicions, she would have found some perfectly legitimate excuse for Daddy's behaviour.' Clare smiled. 'You see, we *Lewises* are above the mundane.'

Brenda had smiled, realising finally there was nothing she could have done. She already knew, in her heart of hearts, that her younger sister would never have thanked her for interfering. Instead she would have given Brenda short shrift and papered over any gaping cracks in her marriage as though they didn't exist.

Cynthia, meanwhile, hadn't wasted any of her spare time. She'd rung Kit on her return from holiday but there was no reply. So the following day she'd decided to call at his office, only to find that her son was in Aberdeen and would remain so for at least another week. Apparently, he'd got several loose ends to tie up there. Cynthia panicked, hoping that one of them wasn't Oona McPhatter.

She cast her eyes around, appraising Kit's smart offices. 'Hmm, very distinctive, I must say.'

His secretary leant forward over her desk. 'And we've just completed the basement. It's very swish down there.'

'Oooh, can I see?'

Mary Waits swivelled round on her chair and stood up. She was very attractive in a fluffy blonde sort of way. Cynthia followed her down the white spiral staircase to the basement below. Mary opened a door leading into a large room with an enormous oval table in walnut, intricately inlayed. There were also eight green leather-backed chairs. All around the room fitted cupboards were painted green and white. The floor was carpeted in pale green and the walls painted a much deeper shade with all doors and architraves painted white. Leading off from the boardroom-cum-dining-room was a small hallway with a cloakroom, and further along a galley kitchen, equipped in style.

'Is this where you have your lunch?' Cynthia asked, looking around the area.

The secretary smiled. 'We are allowed to use the kitchen, but the boardroom is out of bounds. Kit needs it for meetings.'

'Why do you call him Kit and not Mr Fordham-Clarke?' Cynthia wasn't averse to putting a young girl in her place.

Mary blushed slightly. 'Because he asked me to.'

Cynthia looked at the secretary in a different light. She obviously had designs on her son. 'So, he's into business lunches, is he?'

Mary nodded. 'Yes, we've got the first next week. Kit rang me this morning.' She rolled her eyes. 'It'll be a week on Friday, for five. I've got to organise it all, and I haven't a clue where to start.'

'In that case, you'd better leave it to me.'

'Sorry?'

'I know just the person. I'll speak to her.'

'Well, that's awfully kind of you, but I'd quite like to sort it out myself. If you could just give me a name?'

Cynthia weighed up Mary Waits. 'When does Kit get back?'

'A week on Thursday, but it'll be quite late. So you see, it'll all have to be arranged beforehand.'

'Look, Mary, I'll tell you what. If you tell me what food Kit would like, I'll sort it out ... and we'll pretend it was you who did it.'

'But I'd rather it *was* me.'

'I know, my dear, and in future it will be. But this caterer is pretty special, and if I don't talk to her straight away she might not agree to do the lunch. Now, if she *does* agree, I can assure you my son will be able to impress his clients beyond even *his* wildest dreams!'

Mary Wait, at twenty-two, knew when she was beaten and gave in gracefully.

65

Wearing her silver Purley's necklace, and a simple, calf-length black dress with a wide belt and high-heeled shoes, Roberta loaded up her car with the food she'd lovingly prepared. Her stomach was churning and her heart lurching; she'd hardly been able to sleep for over a week. After Cynthia had called to see her, and practically begged her to do this lunch, she'd thought of nothing else but Kit. Her thoughts had been analysed and sifted through, but however she looked at the past, whatever she imagined about the future, she knew she had to see him again. He might have changed, she certainly had, but Roberta couldn't help remembering the way he used to look at her, the way his grey eyes danced over her face, and even now the memory made her head spin. Of course, he might no longer look at her in that same way, but there was one thing for sure. *One look* and she'd know.

Even with dark circles beneath her eyes, she still looked lovely. Roberta had taken extra special care with her make-up and her hair, which picked up all manner of colour from any bright light, wisped around her face, escaping from its tumbling half-up and half-down style. Her skin, still tanned from a long hot summer, glowed with good health. She would have been happy and contented but for this elusive man who'd once floated in and out of her life.

It had been tricky off-loading her car, because she couldn't park outside Kit's offices, but she'd received help from one of his employees. As Roberta entered F-C Design for the very first time she sucked in her breath, expecting Kit to appear at any minute. But he didn't, not at all. He was apparently showing his guests around the new site of his proposed luxury flats.

Kit's secretary had specified chicken with orange sauce as a main course, and a light salad to start. Roberta had smiled, remembering Kit's favourite food only too well. She had chosen the lunch with care. A small dressed green salad to start, with slithers of melon and fried chopped proscuitto, sprinkled with curls of mozzarella. And to follow, chicken breasts lightly stuffed with a mirepoix of carrots, onions and mushrooms, served with a hot caramelised orange sauce, sauteed potatoes and spinach. No pudding, that had been the request, just cheese. All the food had been prepared and par-cooked beforehand, and just needed gentle reheating. Roberta laid everything out in the kitchen, ready for serving or re-heating, and prepared to set the table, having been previously informed by Cynthia of the dining-room's colour scheme.

Kit had certainly spared no expense. She found, in one of the cupboards, a huge canteen of the finest silver cutlery and countless cut crystal glasses. In another, Villeroy and Boch cups and saucers, and every size of plate in plain white with a dark green trim. But no table-cloth and no napkins, except for the paper ones his secretary had put on the table. Luckily, Roberta had brought along a large green table cloth and several white napkins. She set about laying the table, noticing the countless bottles of red wine standing on the side. There were more bottles of white in the larder fridge in the kitchen. She was tempted to open one and have a glass, she needed something to calm her nerves.

Finally she stood back and folded her arms, examining her good work. Even she thought the table looked impressive.

'How's it going?' asked Mary, bustling into the room. 'Oh, you've used a tablecloth.'

Roberta turned towards her. 'Yes, I normally do for business lunches.'

'Oh, but the table's quite beautiful. Didn't you notice? What a shame to cover it up. I hope Kit doesn't mind.' Unfazed, Roberta turned to walk out of the room. Mary touched her arm. 'By the way, he's back. He'll be down in a minute. I think he wants to see what food you've prepared.' Roberta flashed a look at Kit's secretary, hoping the girl couldn't guess how she felt. Mary Waits hadn't an inkling. She was too busy looking at the table. 'It's a pity you didn't put the serviettes in the glasses. I was going to do it with the paper ones I bought. You know, fan them out a bit, make them look pretty.'

Roberta took a deep breath. 'I don't think so.'

Mary moved forward and picked up one of Roberta's beautifully laundered linen napkins which had lain simply folded to the left of the place setting. She shook it out and proceeded to crease it in a concertina fashion before sticking it in a wine glass. It looked a bit like a cockerel's head and Roberta watched frantically as the girl proceeded with the next napkin.

But Mary stopped and turned towards the spiral staircase. 'Oh, here he comes.'

Roberta heard his footfall on the stairs and fled through the door to the kitchen, her heart beating so fast she thought she might faint. Bemused, Mary watched her go.

It was his voice she heard first. Clipped and to the point. 'For God's sake, Mary! What are you doing with those napkins?' Roberta smiled. 'Sorry ... er, the table looks great, but don't put the napkins in the glasses, this isn't the bistro down the road.'

Roberta stood in the kitchen and turned towards her salad bowl, covered in clingfilm and just waiting for the addition of an olive oil dressing before serving. She straightened the five salad plates for want of something to do with her hands, then checked the chicken slowly re-heating in the oven. Everything was ready, awaiting Kit's command. With her back to the door, she breathed deeply.

'Smells good,' she heard him say. His voice was so self-assured and to the point. 'Right, everything looks fine. I'll go through and see the cook.' He lowered his voice but Roberta, straining her ears, still heard. 'What's her name?' There was a pause. Mary had obviously forgotten. 'Never mind.'

He walked in briskly. Roberta, heart pounding madly, kept her back firmly to the door. With shaking hands she fiddled with the plates.

Looking cool and businesslike in a dark grey suit, Kit stood quite still in the kitchen doorway, frowning and catching his breath. It was as though the wind had been knocked clean out of him. He just stood and stared at the back of Roberta's head, anger welling within him, old memories raked up. '*Julia?*'

She froze, hardly daring to move, confused thoughts darting around in her head.

Kit took a few paces forward and rather brusquely stretched out an arm. Forcibly he turned her round, and then it was his turn to freeze. His eyes were on hers. He blinked, and immediately she knew all she needed to know. He was staring at her, really staring, and seemed totally lost for words. When he did speak, he first swallowed hard. 'Roberta?' he squeezed her arm. 'I . . . for one second . . . I thought you were Julia. I'm sorry.'

She quickly turned full circle back to her food, and his arm, inadvertently, brushed all the way across her breasts. There was silence. And then Kit touched her hair, making her whole body tingle. It was such a familiar thing for him to do. She felt both affronted and deeply grateful.

'I was so sorry about Ed.'

Roberta turned back and Kit's hand dropped to his side. 'So was I.'

Again he swallowed hard and averted his eyes, touching his forehead with his hand. 'I didn't know whether to get in touch.'

'It would have been nice.'

He looked at her again, drinking her in with his eyes. 'I've never seen you look so beautiful, Roberta.'

She allowed her own eyes to wander over him, appraising him, *wanting* him. 'Thank you.'

A pained smile crept around his mouth. 'I hear you might be getting married again?'

Roberta flashed her eyes at him. 'Sorry?'

Kit shrugged and looked glum. 'Ma told me about him.'

'Oh, did she? Which one?'

Kit's eyes widened. '*Which one?*'

Roberta smiled, rather sarcastically, remembering their parting words, or at least Kit's. 'I'm a free spirit now, Kit. Which one?'

He averted his eyes slightly, then locked them angrily back on hers. 'Some trainer, I believe?'

She shook her head. 'Oh, him. He's gone.'

'There've been others?'

'One or two.'

Kit frowned. 'I see.'

She held his gaze. 'And how's Oona?'

'Oona?'

'Oona McPhatter?'

Kit allowed himself to smile, 'You've been talking to Julia. Oona was a long time ago.'

'Weren't we all? A long time ago.'

Embarrassed, Kit's eyes darted round the kitchen. 'Look, I have to go. I needn't worry about the lunch anymore, it's obviously going to be splendid.' He stared at her again. 'But I do need to see you again, Roberta. When? When can I see you?'

She shrugged. 'When would you like?'

'Tonight? Can I take you out to dinner tonight?'

'No, I'm sorry, I'm busy tonight.'

He looked at her really angrily now. 'Tomorrow then? *Please?*'

She narrowed her eyes. 'It could be difficult unless . . . you come to mine? Do you know where I live?' He nodded. 'Come to dinner then. About eight?'

It was as though a weight had been lifted right off him. She could see him sagging with relief. He touched her arm again, squeezing it gently. 'I never stopped loving you, Roberta . . . I just couldn't forget you.'

And then he turned and walked away.

The pre-fried prosciutto was warming to perfection, ready to sprinkle over the dressed melon salad with mozzarella. Nervously, Roberta waited for the next instruction. She'd already removed the home-made bread rolls from the oven and they were standing in a small napkin-lined basket on the table. She had also replaced the two crumpled napkins with fresh ones. She waited, wishing someone had thought to offer her a glass of wine to quell her nerves. Never in all the time she'd been catering had she felt so apprehensive. This lunch was the most important meal she'd ever served.

At last she heard them arrive in the dining room. Roberta took a deep breath, expecting Mary to come through to the kitchen, but it wasn't her, it was Kit again. He strode into the kitchen and grabbed her arm. 'Come on, Roberta, I'd like you to meet my friends.'

Staggered, she allowed herself to be gently pulled into the dining room, with Kit clasping her hand. Four smartly dressed men stood before her. Goodness knows who they were, clients of some sort. Weakly, she smiled.

Kit let go of Roberta's hand, raising his to the small of her back. 'This is Roberta. Think yourselves lucky, you lot, that you're about to eat her food.' He looked down at her fondly. 'Roberta, meet Terry Leigh. Don't poison him because he's helping me finance the apartment building. And over there is George Benson, my bank manager, and Peter Green, my accountant. And last but not least my site engineer, Geoff Littlebury.' Roberta shook hands with them all, and they very graciously began asking her questions. She chatted for a while before catching Kit's eye. He nodded. 'Okay, ready when you are.'

Rather relieved she walked back into the kitchen and still Kit followed her. He removed two bottles of white wine from the fridge as Roberta finished off the salads. 'Would you like a glass, Roberta?' She nodded gratefully and he strode off to fetch a glass from the dining room. Roberta carried the five salads through to the dining room on a tray, bumping into Kit again as he walked back. She served the salads and went back into the kitchen. Kit was standing there with her glass of wine in his hand. He handed it to her, gazing into her eyes. 'Thank you for being here, Roberta.' She took the glass and their fingers touched. Kit leant forward and kissed her cheek, brushing his face against her sweet-smelling hair. 'I love you,' he whispered. 'And I'll never let you out of my sight again.' And then as quickly he walked back into the dining room.

Shaking like a leaf, Roberta gulped back the wine.

66

Kit parked his Porsche 924 as close to Roberta's house as he could. More casually dressed now, in navy trousers, an open-necked dark blue shirt and cream jacket, he fingered the tie in his pocket, not seeing any reason to wear it. He reached across to the passenger seat and picked up the wine, chocolates and flowers he'd bought then made his way to Roberta's front door.

He'd hardly rung the bell when he heard squeals of delight inside. Kit looked at his wristwatch. It was five past eight. He'd expected, rather hoped, that James would be in bed. It didn't really matter, he was looking forward to seeing the boy again. And nothing really mattered beside the prospect of seeing Roberta. The door opened and she stood before him, hair flowing around her shoulders and down her back. She looked enchanting in a very fitted flimsy white top tucked into a deep-pocketed, gathered floral skirt.

'Kit!' Roberta smiled and moved back, allowing him to step over the threshold.

'I bought you these.' He handed over the dozen red roses and the chocolates. He held on to the Pouilly Fuissé. 'And this. I seem to remember you liked this wine?'

She nodded, peering at the bottle. 'I still do.' Her arms full, she led the way into her sitting room. Kit followed, breathing in her familiar scent. She turned back to him. 'You remember Mavis, of course, and Judy? And this little rascal down here is James.'

With his mouth open, Kit's eyes panned around the room. Sitting on the well-remembered oyster pink settee was Mavis, how could he ever forget Mavis? And next to her, about to stand up, was Judy. She hadn't changed at all. And then he looked down at the small boy directly in front of him, with his hands on his hips, wearing pyjamas and a jockey's riding cap in scarlet. Roberta's eyes stared back at him from a face that was a younger version of Ed's. Kit warmed to him immediately. James wasn't so sure. 'Are you Kit?' he boldly asked.

'I most certainly am.'

James pouted, sizing him up. 'Would you like to see my dog?'

Kit's eyes darted to Roberta, smiling broadly. 'Is his name Boris?'

'Yes. I'll get him.' And with that, James ran off.

Taking a deep breath, Kit looked at Judy, now standing next to him. He took her hand, and kissed her cheek, 'Judy, how nice to see you.'

'Long time no see,' she said, letting go of his hand and giving him an old-fashioned look.

Roberta then moved across the sitting room towards Mavis, and placed the red roses very carefully in her arms. 'These are for you, Mavis, from Kit.' Mavis beamed in appreciation as Kit's face fell.

'Oh, thank you, Kit. It's a long while since anybody bought me red roses.'

Everybody's eyes were on Kit and he mumbled, 'Yes, of course.'

And then Roberta handed the chocolates to Judy. 'And these are for you, Judy. Kit used to love repeating the tale of you, and him, and the chocolate cake.'

Judy gave Kit a naughty, naughty look, and then grinned, accepting the chocolates. 'You kept the old weight off then, Kit?'

Before he had time to answer, James was squealing delightedly again as he dragged a forlorn-looking Boris into the sitting room with his rocking-horse's saddle tied tightly round his back.

'Oh, Jamie! Poor Boris,' laughed Roberta. 'How did you get that off the rocking horse? It was stuck on.'

James then cocked his leg over Boris, trying to ride him like a horse. The dog, not at all amused, slumped down on all fours.

'Poor Boris.' Roberta squatted down and patted her beloved dog. 'Take it off, James, that's not a nice thing to do to Boris. He doesn't like it. Come on, I insist you take it off.'

'Oh, Mummy, he *does* like it. He's my horse.'

'No, Jamie, Boris does not like it, and he is not your horse. Come on, be a good boy.'

Mavis, meanwhile, was reading the card on the red roses. It read, *'I never stopped thinking about you. Kit.'* She smiled across at him.

'That's nice, Kit. I never stopped thinking about you, too.'

He felt the colour rise in his face and his eyes darted to Roberta, busy releasing Boris from the saddle that James had put on. He felt thoroughly set up. With a half-smile, he looked again at Mavis. 'Where's Brian?'

There was a hush. 'He passed away, lad, years ago now. It was a happy release.

'*Oh my God*,' he muttered beneath his breath, then mumbled, 'I'm sorry, Mavis.' He looked at Judy and gave an apologetic smile. Kit then glared at Roberta, who was now standing up.

Defiantly, she looked back at him. 'Can I get you a drink?'

'Yes, what a good idea.'

He followed her out of the sitting-room and into her kitchen, liking what he saw. Everywhere looked warm and welcoming. 'What can I get you?'

Kit shrugged. 'A glass of poison for the condemned man?' He narrowed his eyes. 'Or perhaps I'll thwart you all and have a glass of red wine.' Roberta smiled and grabbed a bottle of Beaune, passing it over to Kit with a bottle opener. He proceeded to pull the cork. 'You might have warned me, Roberta.'

'You don't have to stay.'

He accepted the glass she handed him and filled it with red wine. He took a sip. 'I want to . . . so long as there are no more surprises waiting for me.'

'Well, there may be one or two.'

'One or two? What do you mean?' Surely not Julia as well?

'It was James's birthday last week. This evening has been arranged for some time, Kit. He had a party with his friends on the actual day, but I always try to get Mavis and Judy over here, near his birthday and Christmas.'

Kit nodded his approval. 'That's good, I'm pleased. Judy never married then?'

Roberta shook her head. 'But she will do, one day. And she's a wonderful aunt.'

'Aren't you drinking?' asked Kit.

Roberta turned to her white wine, which was standing on the side. She took a sip as the doorbell rang. 'Perhaps you'd like to answer that?'

Kit rolled his eyes. 'Why are you doing this to me, Roberta?'

'I'm not doing anything to you, Kit. This is my life. Take it or leave it.'

303

He allowed his eyes to linger on her face, before he left the kitchen and went to answer the front door.

'Kit! What a surprise!' Cynthia and Brenda stepped into Roberta's house carrying flowers and wine. Excitedly, Cynthia kissed her son on the cheek. 'I didn't expect to see *you* here, darling?'

Brenda was more reticent. 'Hallo, Kit. How are you?'

Kit looked at her, reading censure in her eyes. He gave a half-grimace, half-smile. 'I'm fine, thank you, Brenda. And yourself?'

'Fine.'

The two women joined Mavis, Judy and James in the sitting-room and Kit wandered back into the kitchen. 'How long are they all staying?'

Roberta smiled, 'Well, Mum and Cynthia will go home tonight, but Mavis and Judy are staying until tomorrow evening. Why?'

Kit shook his head, 'Nothing.' He walked back into the sitting room, and rather proudly Roberta watched him go.

'Come on, Jamie, it's time for bed.'

'But, Mummy! I'm playing with my Lego.' Jamie sat cross-legged on the floor, building with Lego bricks.

'No buts. You promised if I let you stay up to see everyone, you'd go straight to bed.'

Kit watched as Roberta prompted her son to say goodnight to everyone in the room. He was feeling more relaxed now, and sat chatting to Judy. 'Goodnight, Kit,' said James.

'Goodnight, James.'

Kit's eyes followed Roberta and her son out of the room. She turned. 'Supper's almost ready, but if you'd like to help yourselves to more drinks . . . I'll be back soon.'

Kit did the honours of refreshing everyone's drink then quietly made his way up the stairs. He finally found James's bedroom and peeked through the door. Roberta sat on the bed, talking to her son. 'And he worked for Daddy at the very start. Kit helped your daddy set up his business, James, and it was a very exciting time.'

'Is Kit a stuck-chal engineer?'

'He is, James, just like Daddy was.'

'I want to be stuck-chal engineer when I grow up.'

Roberta kissed her son's forehead. 'But now you must go to sleep.'

'Will Gran and Auntie Judy still be here in the morning?'

'Of course they will. You'll have all day with them tomorrow.'

James put his thumb in his mouth. 'Mmmm . . . goody.'

Roberta slid off her son's bed and squeezed his arm. 'Goodnight, darling. See you in the morning.'

'See you in a' morning.'

Roberta left the room, and jumped as she saw Kit standing at the top of the stairs.

'Sorry, I didn't mean to pry.' He'd removed his jacket downstairs, and now gripped it in his hands. 'When can I inflict my home on you?' he asked softly. 'I don't think you'd recognise Ash Cottage anymore.'

She shrugged. 'I'm not sure.'

'Tomorrow evening?'

Roberta shook her head. 'I'm sorry, Kit, I can't just leave James.'

'Your mother could babysit.'

'Tomorrow's *too* soon, Kit.'

'Monday?' Roberta laughed as he moved closer. She backed off slightly. He looked hurt. '*Don't* not let me in, Roberta, please?'

'I'm hardly not letting you in, Kit. In case you hadn't noticed, I've invited you back into my life.'

'Yes, with every defence around you. But I want to see you on your own.' She walked past him and started down the stairs. Kit grabbed her arm. 'When?'

'Next Friday I think I'm free.'

'Next Friday? But that's nearly a week away . . . Roberta, it has to be sooner.'

Roberta looked at the man she loved, the only man she'd ever loved, and wanted him more than ever. But she couldn't just forget the past, and he seemed so confident that she could. 'I'm not sure.'

'Monday, *please*?'

His touch was sending wild messages through her body, and how could she even think of stopping the inevitable? Roberta shrugged away his hand and nodded, continuing down the stairs. 'All right, Monday.'

67

Kit insisted on picking her up although she'd offered to drive herself to Ash Cottage. James was staying with Brenda, who'd given Roberta a warning look when she dropped him off.

'It's all right, Mum, I can take care of myself.'

Brenda touched her daughter's face. 'I wouldn't want to see you hurt, Roberta. It was bad enough with Julia.'

She considered her mother's words, and decided against saying anything. But they'd cast a cloud over any future she might have with Kit.

Roberta wore a new pale pink angora wool dress, with a grey belt and grey high-heeled shoes. She knew she looked good, and Kit practically devoured her with his eyes. She climbed into his car and listened to idle chatter about his life in Aberdeen all the way to Ash Cottage.

Kit parked in almost exactly the same spot they'd parked in years before, except the outlook was quite different now. It was positively smart. Together they looked at Ash Cottage. 'I was fortunate really, I rented the cottage out to a Colonel at the American air base in Mildenhall. You know Americans, how they love old English property. Anyway, he and his wife practically landscaped the garden and decorated the entire house. I think they used to entertain a lot. They've moved on now so I didn't have to throw them out or anything, which I would have found rather difficult to do, under the circumstances.'

Kit climbed out of his Porsche and hastened round to Roberta's side, opening the door. He helped her out of the car then didn't let go of her hand. They walked side by side towards Ash Cottage. He unlocked the front door and stood back for Roberta to enter. For her, it was like stepping back in time except that the place had been transformed.

'What a lovely wooden floor,' she remarked, looking down at the polished oak strips.

'Yes, too good to cover, don't you think?'

'Definitely. And I'm pleased to see you kept the staircase.'

'Well, actually, it's new, just in the same style as the old one which was rotten.'

Roberta breathed in the air around her, liking the smell of the place. This was all so familiar, and yet so poignant, she almost wanted to cry.

'Come on, come through. I think we need a drink.'

She followed Kit through to his kitchen, which had been well fitted out with oak cupboards, an Aga and quarry tiles on the floor. But there were no kitchen objects about, apart from a kettle, and no curtains at the window, just marks where a blind had obviously been. The whole room cried out for someone's personal touch. She smiled at him. 'I can't smell any food cooking?'

Swiftly, Kit moved to the fridge and removed two fillet steaks and a bowl of salad. 'And I thought about making some chips.'

Roberta's face lit up. 'My very favourite food.'

'Yes, I know. You see, I remembered.' He took a bottle of wine from the fridge. 'Would you like a glass of white? Red? Or something else?'

'White wine would be lovely.'

Kit opened the wine and filled two glasses. Tonight, he reflected, he was determined not to rush things; scared stiff, even now, that she might run away. 'To us,' he toasted her.

'To us.'

'The nights are turning so chilly,' Roberta remarked, shivering slightly and grateful that she'd worn a warm dress. They'd finished their meal in the sparsely furnished dining room; in fact everywhere was sparsely furnished she'd noticed. Roberta looked towards the window. 'It's pitch black outside.' Kit stood up, and walked over to close the floral chintz curtains which Roberta didn't particularly like.

He offered her his hand. 'Shall we have coffee in the sitting room?'

Roberta took his hand and stood up. 'What about the washing up?'

'Oh, you can do that later,' Kit joked and led her through to his sitting room, with its beautifully restored oak timbers and wide open fireplace crowned with a enormous oak beam. A welcoming log fire crackled in the enormous dog-leg grate.

'Oh, Kit, how lovely, a real fire. When did you light it?'

'A while ago. I thought you'd appreciate it.' Roberta looked around the room, carpeted in cream but with little furniture except for a small settee, an ancient armchair and a couple of small tables. Kit saw the expression on her face. 'I didn't want to rush out buying furniture, I thought I'd wait and give myself time.' Roberta reflected upon how different Kit's house was from his offices. Obviously, his energy had all been poured into his work.

'Was this a furnished let?' she asked.

Kit smiled. 'Hardly. I never got round to furnishing the place in the way I would have liked, nor could I have afforded to then. I think my tenants bought a lot of furniture while they were here. You know what these Americans are like. As soon as they come over here they can't wait to buy our quaint British stuff.' They sat down together on the tiny settee. Roberta was aware that this was the closest she'd been to him in a very long while. Kit looked at her. 'Brandy?'

She shook her head. 'Just coffee.' She shifted slightly. 'Would you like me to make it?'

Kit stalled her with his hand, and his face became serious. 'Can it wait, for just a while?'

Roberta was surprised by his sudden mood change. 'Of course.'

He continued to hold her hand then brought it to his mouth, slowly kissing the palm. Such a simple act, and yet it sent shivers down Roberta's spine. 'I think we need to discuss certain things, don't you?'

She was surprised. She'd actually thought he was about to kiss her. All evening she'd watched his mouth, remembering their one kiss. She'd wanted him to kiss her. 'Perhaps.'

'Perhaps? That sounds feeble.' Kit dropped her hand and repositioned himself so that he almost faced her. He came straight to the point. 'I saw the way your mother looked at me on Saturday. If looks could kill, I'd be a dead man.'

Roberta frowned, then touched her hair. 'Well, what else do you expect?'

Kit looked angry. 'I didn't expect anything . . . because I'm not sure what I'm supposed to have done? You were married when I left, Roberta, and I can't think that Brenda would blame me for leaving Ed?' His eyes questioned her.

'No, of course she doesn't.'

He picked up Roberta's hand again and examined it. 'So, in that case, everything points to Julia, although I can't think why.'

Roberta flashed him a look and snatched her hand away. 'You sound so casual, Kit. You do realise you broke her heart?'

Anger flared in his eyes and he stood up. He leant one hand on the fireplace and poked a log with his foot before turning to stare at Roberta. 'And what about what she did to me? In fact, so far as Julia is concerned, I'd rather I'd never met her.'

Roberta stared back at him. 'No doubt you would, Kit, but you still broke her heart.'

'No, I did not! If anything, she broke her own bloody heart!'

Roberta had never seen him quite so vehement. She gulped, and stood up as well. Even at the height of their quarrel, she noticed bits of angora fluff from her dress on his dark green shirt. She picked a bit off, and quite fiercely he grabbed her hand. 'And what about you? How's your free spirit today?'

Roberta was shocked, and again snatched her hand away. 'What's that supposed to mean?'

Kit glared at her then took a deep breath, calming himself. 'I'm using your own words, Roberta. You said you're a free spirit now.'

'Maybe I did, and can you blame me, after what I've been through?'

Kit's face hardened. 'For God's sake, I can't believe you could say such a thing?' He slumped back on to the settee and looked up at her fiercely. 'How many men have you had then? Go on, *tell me*?' Roberta sucked in her breath as Kit looked away from her almost in disgust. He leant forward in his seat, staring into the fire. 'Considering you wouldn't let *me* anywhere near you.'

She stepped closer and touched his shoulder, and swiftly he pulled her down next to him again. 'You were special, you were different. I can't bear to think of you with other men.'

Roberta's temper soared. 'Isn't that the pot calling the kettle black, Kit? What about you? You had Oona whatever-her-name-is while you were still with Julia, and I bet there've been a good few since?'

Kit glowered. 'I didn't have Oona while I was with Julia. Did *she* tell you that? See? That just shows what a liar she is.' He ran his hand through his hair. 'Oona was in my life way before I even met you, Roberta, and she's been nothing more than a friend ever since. And, yes, there have been other women, but what else do you expect?'

'Well, I happen to have feelings the same as you.'

Kit grabbed both of her hands. 'I'm not talking about feelings, Roberta, I'm talking about a free spirit. I'm talking about fidelity, and loyalty . . . and trust. I really thought that that was *you*!'

'Well, it *is* me. I don't understand what you're trying to say?'

His face hardened and he pushed her hands away, shifting forward in his seat again. He stood up and threw another log on the fire. 'I *mean* your sister screwing my brother when she was supposed to be with *me*!' Roberta gulped and looked up at him, things becoming clearer now. He faced her. 'Do you remember that bloody awful wedding day all those years ago, and us watching Nick *fucking* Julia? Oh, yes, it gave me one hell of a thrill then, I can tell you. But when I had to watch the second time, it didn't appeal to me in quite the same way.' Kit questioned Roberta with his eyes. 'But she obviously didn't tell you and Brenda about that, did she?'

Roberta took a deep breath. 'And is that why you split up?'

'Of course it bloody is! I came all the way back from Aberdeen to see her. Thought I'd surprise her, and I certainly did!' Roberta moved quickly off the settee and touched his arm as his eyes implored her. 'I couldn't *bear* for you to be like *her*.'

'I'm not like her, Kit. How could you even think it?'

'But *you* made me think it.' He thumped his forehead with the palm of his hand. 'I can't get your words out of my head.'

Roberta let go of his arm. Catching her breath, she turned slightly away. 'I've had three lovers, Kit, and one of those was Ed. If you really want to know, I'll tell you. I'll tell you everything if it will make you understand.' Her eyes searched his. 'Although the last one could hardly be called a lover, he was just a friend really.' Kit swallowed hard, waiting for her to continue, obviously wanting her to. 'Do you want me to go on?'

'Of course I bloody do! I want to know everything about you, Roberta.'

She half turned away from him. 'Well, the other one I met through Julia . . . his name was Nathan Purley.'

She'd hardly got the words out when Kit rounded on her in horror. *'Nathan Purley? The father of Clare's kids? You slept with him?'*

Roberta backed off defensively, and then glared at Kit. 'Well, what's wrong with that? What on earth have you got against Nathan Purley? He was kind, and he was caring, and he taught me a hell of a lot.'

Kit was beside himself. 'I'm sure he did! I can imagine it very well.'

'Well, you imagine what you like. Perhaps now you know how I felt when I had to imagine you with *Julia*!'

Kit turned and faced the fireplace, banging both fists on top of it. 'I regret Julia, Roberta. Do you regret Nathan?'

'No, I certainly do not.'

Rather nastily, he turned round. 'Why? Don't tell me you loved him too?'

'No, I didn't love him. If I had, I'd be married to him now.'

'Married to . . . *Nathan Purley*?'

'What's he ever done to you, Kit?'

'He's just a jumped up . . .'

'Actually, he's not. And believe it or not, Kit, he really cared about me, he looked after me in a very special way, so how can I regret somebody like that?'

Kit sneered at her. 'Oh, I see, I get it, *Ed* all over again.'

That did it. Roberta stepped forward and swiped him hard across the face. He reeled backwards, tasting blood in his mouth and touching it gingerly. Roberta's own hand stung from her action, which she regretted straight away. She hesitated, waiting for some response from Kit, but there was none, so she turned on her heel and started to walk towards the door.

He was beside her in a flash, clutching at her arm. 'Roberta! For God's sake, please don't go.'

She looked at him, seeing the misery in his grey eyes. 'I'm not *going*, Kit. In case you've forgotten. I haven't got a car.' She smiled weakly, holding up her red and burning hand. 'Actually, I'd like to go to the cloakroom and run this under the cold tap.'

Even Kit managed to smile at that. And then he entreated her with his eyes. 'I'm sorry. I'm sorry about everything I said, I'm just so jealous of any other man in your life.'

'There aren't any other men in my life, Kit. Apart from my son.

311

And I've only ever loved you. You've got it all wrong. There's no way I've been sleeping around.' She touched his mouth, wiping away blood from the corner. 'Shall I tell you what Nathan taught me? I think you ought to know.' Kit closed his eyes, not sure he wanted to hear anymore. 'He taught me that sex can have nothing to do with loving . . . and all those years with Ed I thought it had.'

Kit flinched and put both hands on her shoulders. 'And if you'd known that then, would you have let me in?'

'But sex with you would have been loving, Kit . . . and don't you see, that would have been the end of Ed and me?'

He groaned at her words and gathered her into his arms.

She looked up at him. 'Now can I go to the loo?'

Reluctant to let her out of his sight, Kit smiled. 'If you go upstairs, along the landing to the far end where the window is, my bedroom's off to the left. There's a bathroom in there.'

'Is that the only bathroom? Isn't there a cloakroom downstairs?'

Kit shook his head. 'It's not very nice, I haven't got round to sorting it out yet.'

Roberta had a feeling this wasn't true. 'You will stay here, please?'

Kit pushed out his bottom lip. 'Okay. But on the way back, look out of the window. There's a wonderful view of Ousden at night.'

Roberta smiled and left the sitting room, making her way up the stairs. She walked quickly along the landing to where the window was, lifted the latch on the bedroom door and took a step down into Kit's bedroom. It had a double bed, two nondescript bedside tables, plain fitted wardrobes, and little else. Just scrubbed wooden floors with a couple of rugs, and the same awful chintz curtains at the window. They must have been left by the Americans, she couldn't imagine Kit choosing them.

Roberta walked through to the bathroom, which was lovely, with a shower cubicle, bath, basin, bidet and loo, all in cream, with lovely old brass taps. There was also a huge mirror over the washhand basin, and Roberta caught sight of the high colour in her cheeks and noticed bits of fluff from her dress caught in her hair. She smiled. The dress hadn't been such a good idea after all.

She left the bathroom and bedroom, and paused to look out of the window. It was as black as black, and she really couldn't see a thing. Roberta stepped back slightly, wondering what Kit meant. Wonderful view of Ousden at night? She couldn't see anything.

Perhaps there was an outside light that hadn't been switched on. She leant forward again and peered through the window, then stopped in her tracks, trembling, as she felt Kit's hands stroking her hair. With a rapidly beating heart Roberta stood quite still, allowing him to caress her hair and kiss her neck.

'I can't see anything out of this window, Kit. Everywhere's so dark.'

He turned her round, and in the dim landing light she noticed a slight swelling around the corner of his mouth. Very gently he pushed her hair away from her face. 'I lied about the window.' He moved his face very close to hers. 'Roberta . . . I want you to know, I'm sorry for the hurt I've inflicted on you through Julia, and I don't care about Nathan or anybody else in your past. I was wrong to say all the things that I did, but they were all said out of jealousy and misunderstanding. I just want to love you from now on.' And then he wrapped his arms around her and kissed her on the mouth, not gently, but passionately and hard. Roberta responded ardently.

And then Kit was pushing open the bedroom door with his foot, and pulling a very willing Roberta inside. They both looked at the bed, and then, holding her face, he kissed her again. And then he let go, and began to remove his clothes while Roberta kicked off her shoes and frantically undid her belt, tugging her dress over her head. She ripped off her tights, tearing them in the process, and discarded the satin underwear she'd so carefully chosen earlier on. With one sock on, and the other yanked off, Kit drew Roberta on to his bed and urgently kissed her again, running his hands over her body while she ran hers over his. And then he entered her for the first time.

It was over within minutes, and he buried his face in her hair. With her knees still gripping him, Roberta cradled him in her arms. 'Will you marry me?' he whispered, looking into her eyes. She smiled and moved beneath him, and Kit shifted his weight to one side but didn't let her out of his arms. He ran his hand down the side of her face and kissed her cheek, and her forehead and then her mouth again, pushing his fingers through her tangled hair. He asked her again. 'Will you be my wife, Roberta? Marry me soon?'

She looked into the eyes of this man she'd waited so long for, and said, 'Yes.'

68

October, 1976

Roberta was welcomed into her mother's kitchen with, 'Julia's here!'

Her eyes widened. 'Oh, that's good.'

Brenda shook her head and put a finger to her mouth. 'I haven't said anything. I thought I'd leave it to you, Roberta. She's not too happy at the moment, so be careful how you handle things, won't you, dear?'

Roberta frowned, and looked down at the emerald and diamond engagement ring that Kit had bought her the day after they'd first made love. She twisted it lovingly on her finger and wondered whether to take it off. But her hand would look too bare, because she no longer wore Ed's wedding ring. That had been safely put away for James.

'Where's Boris?' asked Brenda.

'Oh, I left him at home.'

'Poor Boris.'

'Well, my car's loaded up with food.' Roberta looked down at her watch. 'And I'm doing a lunch in a couple of hours. Look, I'll go through and see Julia. A coffee would be lovely, Mum.'

Brenda nodded. 'I'll bring you one through.'

Julia was sitting in Gordon's old armchair, looking out across the Heath. Roberta was quite shocked by her appearance. Her hair, now dyed back to, supposedly, its normal shade, looked tatty and out of condition, in desperate need of a good cut. Her face was too harshly made-up, with too much eye make-up and bright orange lipstick. She wore beautiful suede trousers, a cashmere roll-necked sweater and expensive leather boots, but she was too thin and too pale.

'Julia?' Roberta walked towards her sister and bent to kiss her cheek. 'How nice to see you. Is this a fleeting visit or are you staying?'

Julia blinked and looked up at her, immediately noting the bloom in her cheeks and the shine on her hair. Roberta looked wonderful. She had never seen her sister look so ravishing and was envious beyond belief. 'Oh, hello. It's a fleeting visit. Mum's running me back to Cambridge station this afternoon.'

With her left hand hidden in a pocket of her gathered skirt, Roberta smiled down at her sister. 'I see you've changed your hair?'

Julia's hand flew to her head. 'Oh, don't talk to me about my hair. I've bloody ruined it, and don't dare disagree!' Her brow furrowed. 'I went to the hairdresser's again, and asked them to dye it back to my normal colour, and came out looking like this! Mum says I should just leave it now, and let it grow out naturally.'

'Couldn't you cut it, though, to give it a bit of shape?' Roberta could have bitten off her tongue as soon as she'd uttered her bold advice.

Julia snapped at her sister, 'I don't want to cut it, Roberta! I want it to grow . . . *right down to my feet!*'

She said, 'Sorry,' and averted her eyes. 'So, what's happening with you? What are you doing about the boutique?'

'Sold out! *Finis!*'

'Completely?'

'Yes. Sarayu and Nick have bought the lease. I would have liked to keep a small share but they weren't keen. Said if I'm not going to work there, they don't think it's fair for me to have a stake.'

'Well, that's not very nice, considering it was all your idea!'

'Yes, I know, but times are hard, Roberta. They've got their work cut out making the shop pay as it is.'

'Did they give you a fair price?'

'Oh, yes. Well . . . they will do, over a period of time. I'm not desperate. I've saved some money. Not a lot, considering what I've earnt, but I suppose I spent too much on rent.'

'You've left your Chelsea house, I hear?'

'Yes. Temporarily moved back in with Clare.' Julia pulled a face. 'Very temporarily, I can tell you!'

Roberta laughed. 'She hasn't changed then?'

'Oh, it's not Clare, it's those bloody daughters of hers. They are *so* naughty. They drive me up the wall.'

Roberta's thoughts swung to Nathan. 'Doesn't their father control them?'

Julia shook her head. 'I wouldn't know, I never see him. I make a point of not being there when Nathan's around. But it doesn't matter if he *does* control them, he only sees them about once a month. They're nice enough girls, they just need discipline.'

'Don't we all?'

Julia lolled back in her seat and eyed her sister keenly. 'So, what have you been doing with yourself?'

Roberta shrugged, thinking of Kit, hoping his effect on her wasn't emblazoned across her. 'Working as usual. Too much work, really, I'm continually having to turn it down, but I'm not complaining. And James is very well.'

Julia watched her sister's face, easily reading all the signs and wondering whether to ask or wait to see if Roberta would mention it herself. Julia knew she was back with Kit. She knew by her mother's odd behaviour and – well – the look in Roberta's eyes said it all.

Julia's former good humour was restored. She narrowed her eyes, wagged one finger at her sister. 'Okay, you asked me something once, Roberta, quite a long time ago. I'm going to ask you the same question. On a score of one to ten, what's Kit like with you?'

Roberta caught her breath and quickly looked down at her feet, feeling the blood rushing to her face. And then she considered the question, and Kit, and immediately her body softened with private thoughts of their lovemaking. Roberta took her left hand out of her pocket and put it under Julia's eyes. She examined the exquisite ring, then looked up, and Roberta saw her pain. She sat on the arm of the chair and gently folded her sister in her arms. 'I'm sorry to have to hurt you, Julia.'

'Oh, don't worry, I'm not hurt, not anymore. He was never the man for me.' She shifted in her seat. 'But let me have my bit of fun, Roberta. You're not wriggling your way out of this one. Please, give me an answer to my question . . . on a score of one to ten?'

Roberta laughed, saved by her mother walking into the room with the coffee. Julia nudged her sharply in the ribs. Roberta took the cup of coffee from her mother and gave Julia a sidelong look. 'Okay . . . *100!*'

Julia gave a brittle chuckle. 'I bet he bloody is!'

Both girls looked across at Brenda, who frowned. She sat down on the settee with her own cup of coffee. 'Do you have to swear, Julia? It doesn't sound at all nice. You've seen the ring then?'

'Yes, Mum, and it's lovely. And I'm sorry I swore but I'm madly, wildly jealous . . . but I will get over it.' She looked up at Roberta. 'When's the big day then?'

This wasn't for public knowledge, and that included Julia. 'Soon.'

'Soon? When's soon?'

Roberta shrugged and looked at her mother. Brenda wasn't averse to the odd white lie. 'Oh, they haven't quite made up their minds. But it does look as though you might be miles away by then, Julia.'

'Oh, I see. So that means I'm not invited.'

Roberta glared at her mother. Brenda stumbled over her next words. 'Oh, don't be silly, Julia. I just said, they haven't made up their minds.' She looked at Roberta. 'Have you, dear?'

Roberta shook her head. 'No, not yet.' She nudged her sister. 'Anyway, what's all this? Where are you off to?'

'I'm taking a sabbatical.' Do you know, I haven't had a proper holiday since bloody Ilfracombe!' She looked at her mother, putting a hand over her mouth. 'Sorry, Mum, I really am trying not to swear. It's Clare, she swears like a trooper, and it's so hard not to pick it up.'

Brenda tutted. 'Those poor little girls. Whatever would Nancy say?'

Roberta looked at her sister. 'I think that's a wonderful idea, Julia. Where are you going, and for how long?'

'Europe, I think, although I suppose it'll get cold with winter on its way. But I'm not worried about the weather because I really want to visit Italy. Their leather industry is second to none. And France, and Greece. Somebody told me they have wonderful silver jewellery in Greece. And maybe Germany and Spain.'

'Are you going alone?'

'Of course I am. I've nobody else to go with.'

'Oh, I'm sure that's not true.'

'Well, nobody I *want* to go with.'

Roberta smiled encouragingly. 'I think you're very brave.'

'Bravery doesn't come into it. I need to sort myself out. I want to take the time to look around and see how other people are leading their lives. I aim to travel light and live cheaply. Who knows? I may not come back at all.'

Roberta panicked. 'I want you to come back, Julia. We all do.'

She scowled. 'Even Kit?'

Roberta sucked in her breath. 'You're my sister, Julia, and he respects that.'

Julia stared at her. 'Did you discuss me?'

Uncomfortably, Roberta's eyes panned to her mother. 'What do you mean?'

'I suppose he told you about that disastrous weekend in Aberdeen?' Julia bent down to her handbag and pulled out her cigarettes. She lit one quickly, and drew on it heavily. 'I'm trying to give these up,' she said, breathing out smoke. 'But right now, they're the only friend I've got.' She sucked on the cigarette again, and narrowed her eyes at her sister. Brenda picked up the coffee cups and walked back into the kitchen. 'Did you discuss me, Roberta? Tell me, please?'

She lowered her eyes. 'Briefly.'

'And you told him about the abortion?'

'No, I did not!'

'Honestly? You didn't tell him? You're telling me the truth?'

'Of course I am! I promised you, remember?'

Julia tipped back her head and smiled. 'You're very trustworthy, Roberta. I respect you for that.' She lowered her head again. 'In fact, I respect you for everything, because you're everything I'd like to be.'

'That's rubbish and you know it, Julia! It's good you're going on holiday, because it's time you cleared your head. You wouldn't want my life, you'd be bored within a week.'

Julia smiled genuinely for the first time that morning. 'Yes, I suppose you're right.' She drew on her cigarette again. 'But, you see, everything I've ever wanted has eventually disintegrated in my hands. And I'm so afraid of the future. I mean, look at me. I'm such a bloody wreck.'

Roberta moved to her sister's side and put her arms around her neck. 'Maybe you're holding on too tightly, Julia. Perhaps, if you just let go, the future would take care of itself?'

'And if it doesn't?'

'Well, one way or another, I promise you it will.'

69

'Did you know Nick and Sarayu are getting married?' Clare looked across at her cousin, and saw the wounded look upon her face. She shrugged. 'I thought maybe Nick would have told you?'

Julia averted her eyes and looked out on to Clare's garden. 'I haven't seen either of them for a while.'

Clare moved closer to her and touched her arm. 'Just because you no longer work there, doesn't mean you can't visit. They'd love to see you, Julia, you must know that?'

She turned round quickly. 'But it hurts.'

'You wanted out.'

'I know I did, Clare, but I also wanted *in*.' Julia dragged her hands through her ragged hair. 'I suppose I wanted someone to make the decision for me, and they did. They wanted me to leave.'

'But only because of the circumstances.' Clare tugged at her arm and pulled her across to the enormous white leather settee, scattered now with cushions. Clare's sitting room had changed dramatically, only the luxurious settee remained the same. On the floor was an apricot-coloured carpet with a tiny blue flower motif. The walls had been fitted out with white shelves and filled with masses of books. Fine blue and apricot striped silk curtains hung at the windows, and the wall surrounding the fireplace was covered in expensive prints and paintings. Antique tables laden with lamps and books adorned the room. 'You know, you really must stop feeling sorry for yourself, darling.'

Julia was hurt. 'Is that what you think?'

'Well, not exactly, but I do know you're deeply depressed.'

Julia reached for her cigarettes, Clare's *darling* grating on her. She lit up. 'Well, you won't have to put up with me for much longer, will you?'

'Julia! Don't talk like that. You're the dearest person in my life.'
Clare pushed back her silky chin-length hair, tucking it behind both
ears. At twenty-eight, she was still extremely beautiful, although
maybe a little plumper.

Julia frowned, suddenly noticing the silence. 'Where are the
girls?' She'd been out shopping until the early afternoon, getting
ready for her departure to Athens the following Friday. Funny she
hadn't missed them before.

'They've gone with Nathan. Out somewhere ... I'm not sure
where.'

Julia shot out of her seat. 'Nathan? Is he here?'

'*Julia*, for God's sake! It's only fucking Nathan.'

'I don't care. I don't want to see him. What time is it?' Julia
looked at her watch. 'Oh, God, I bet he's gone to that bloody football match. It's Chelsea playing Charlton Athletic, I bet that's where
he's gone. He'll be back any minute.'

'Don't be stupid, Julia! He wouldn't take the twins to a football
match!'

'Wouldn't he?'

'Of course he wouldn't. At least, not without asking me first.'

'But it's not his weekend. Why is he here?'

Clare shrugged. 'How should I know? He often pops in.'

'Only if there's a football match, Clare.'

'Julia! What *is* the matter with you.'

'I don't want to see him!'

'Well, bugger off then.'

'I will!'

Poor Julia. With nowhere to go, she sat on her bed and felt this
must be her lowest ebb yet. And then she heard them returning.
Suddenly the noise reached fever pitch.

'Chel-*sea*! Chel-*sea*!' And that was only Jennifer.

Julia bolted off her bed and stood before the mirror in her bedroom. She knew she looked frightful, and absolutely loathed her
hair. She ran her fingers through it, and peered more closely into
the glass. She looked down at her simple blue jeans and tired old
shirt. Sod it! she thought. Why should I change? He's a shit anyway.

Taking her courage in both hands, she wandered down Clare's
staircase and into the racket going on below.

'*How dare you?* How bloody dare you?' Clare was thumping

Nathan in the chest. 'These are my girls, in case you've forgotten. First and foremost they belong to me! For Christ's sake, Nathan, they're only five years old. We're forever hearing about the disturbances and fights at damned football matches. And *you* . . . you subjected my darling babies to a load of fucking louts!'

'Don't swear in front of the girls, please, Clare.'

Julia noticed that Nathan's voice remained cool and controlled. Although she hated him, she definitely admired him for that.

Julia peered into the kitchen, seeing Nathan for the first time in ages, with his back to her and his hands on his hips. Clare, red-faced and furious, was baying for his blood. Julia carried on to the drawing room, where the girls had already turned on the TV.

Vivien turned round excitedly. 'Auntie Julia! Guess what? We've been to a football match. We watched Chelsea beat Charnton Afflepics. They beat them 2–1!'

'And Mummy's really *fu*-rious! She's giving Daddy a *dreadful* telling off.' Jennifer walked over to her aunt and as Julia sat down on the settee, sat down beside her, cuddling up really close. Julia and Jennifer got on very well. 'Daddy likes football,' she said, looking into Julia's eyes.

Vivien raised her arm. 'Chel-*sea*! Chel*sea*!'

Julia suppressed a smile, realising, for perhaps the first time, how much she was going to miss these spirited little girls. 'Was it a good game?'

'*Hex*-ellent!' eulogised Vivien, turning round excitedly to face Julia. 'Even Daddy said so!'

Julia raised her eyebrows. 'Well, in that case, it must have been good.'

She sat for a while, cuddling Jennifer and watching television, listening vaguely to the heated argument going on in the kitchen. She quite expected to hear the slamming of the door as Nathan left, but much to her surprise he eventually marched into the drawing room though he didn't give her a second glance.

'Vivvy? I'm off, see you next weekend. Give Daddy a kiss?'

Julia watched, fascinated, as he bent down over his daughter now glued to the television. And then, lovingly, Vivien turned and wrapped her arms around her father, giving him lots of sloppy wet kisses. Julia noticed that Nathan, in his fatherly capacity, looked slightly different, less of the man about town.

He turned, obviously expecting to see just Jennifer, and blinked at the sight of Julia. He raised himself to his full height and gazed down at her, staring for a good few seconds. 'Julia.'

'Hallo, Nathan.' She noticed the lines etched around his mouth and eyes. But they just added to his attraction.

'My God, what have you done to your hair?'

Jennifer shot to her defence. 'Mummy says you mustn't say that to Auntie Julia because she's very sad about her hair. And, anyway, she's going to grow it again all the way down to her feet, because she told me so.'

He smiled, showing the gap between his teeth. He moved towards his other young daughter and kissed her on the cheek. Jennifer, like her sister, wrapped her arms around her beloved father. And then he moved towards Julia, and quickly kissed her cheek as well. She reacted as if she'd been stung, immediately shifting off the settee.

'Julia?'

She scurried through to the kitchen, and took a bottle of white wine from the fridge. She filled a glass and took a long gulp. And then Nathan was standing in the doorway. Julia blurted out, 'Where's Clare?'

'Avoiding me, I think.'

She turned her back on him, hoping he'd just leave. But he walked towards her and touched her shoulder, and even after all this time it still made her legs feel like jelly.

'I didn't mean to offend you about your hair. It's so good to see you.' He felt her soften beneath his grip. 'Look . . . what are you doing tonight?'

And that did it! She turned round and glared at him. 'What did you just say?'

Nathan took two paces back and she noticed there was a sort a smile upon his face. He held up both hands. 'Hang on a minute, Julia. It was only a suggestion, there's no need to blow a fuse.'

'How dare you? How bloody dare you?'

'I only asked what you're doing tonight. What's wrong with that?'

Julia walked towards him, and punched his shoulder. 'I am not some daft little pick up, N. *bloody* P., and I wouldn't go out with you again if you were the last bloody person on *earth*!'

'Okay! Sorry I spoke. Message understood.'

'Good!'

Embarrassed, he looked around awkwardly then left.

Julia watched him go from the kitchen window. She watched him drive off in his new bronze-coloured Aston Martin, and told herself she didn't feel a thing.

70

November, 1976

It was seven twenty-five on a drizzly November morning. Roberta sat in Kit's car, with James on her lap and Boris in the footwell. They had just parked on the cramped gravelled drive of St Agnes church down Bury Road in Newmarket. To their left was the black timbered building of Mrs Lane's Nursery School, where James had once been a pupil. But today he wasn't going to school, and was looking extremely smart in a maroon suit with blue shirt and navy tie. Even Boris had a blue bow attached to his collar.

Roberta looked anxiously out of the front windscreen, in the direction of St Agnes, waiting for Kit. She looked wonderful, with a single red rose in her upswept hair and wearing a cream bouclé Chanel suit which Kit had bought for her in London the previous week. On her feet were high-heeled cream leather shoes.

Kit walked round the side of the church towards her, and she caught her breath. He looked so fine in his light grey suit, white shirt and dark grey and red spotted tie. He smiled widely at her, hastening towards the car. He climbed into the driver's seat and leant towards her, kissing her mouth. 'The vicar's not here yet, but I'm sure he won't be long.' He turned, and looked in the direction of Bury Road. 'No sign of Brenda and Ma, then?'

Roberta's voice was almost a whisper. 'They'll be here . . . you know your mother.'

Kit tweaked James's ear. 'And you, young man, have got to behave yourself while Mummy and I are away. Look after Boris, and Grandma, and my ma. Can you do that? Is it worth a big present?'

Roberta frowned at Kit and spoke to her son. 'You don't need presents to be a good boy, do you, James?'

He looked at Kit. 'When am I getting my pony?'

Kit smiled, and raised his eyebrows at Roberta. 'When I get the paddock sorted out, James. After Christmas.'

'But that's ages away.'

'James!' admonished Roberta.

And then he pointed out of the window. 'Oh, look! Here comes Grandma.'

'Hmm, all we need now is the vicar.' And then his car arrived and everybody piled out of their vehicles.

Very firmly, Roberta held on to Boris. She smiled in the direction of the Reverend Richard Chalmers, together with his warden, Eric Packer. The vicar, fully rigged out in cassock and gown, rubbed his hands together. 'Bit chilly this morning.' He looked up at the sky. 'Dismal too. Still, they say we'll have sunshine later on.' He looked down at Boris, who was sitting next to Roberta. 'You do know we can't allow dogs in the church, m'dear?'

Her face fell. 'Oh, please. It's only Boris. He'll behave himself, I'm sure.'

'Sorry, it's the rules, I'm afraid.'

Kit reached into his pocket and withdrew his cheque book. He tore out a cheque, that had previously been made out, and handed it over to the Reverend Chalmers who looked at it and raised his eyebrows.

'Well,' he said, 'I suppose we can make an exception on this auspicious occasion.'

'Thank you,' said Roberta, and flashed her eyes at Kit.

The vicar and his warden started to walk towards St Agnes, the tiny church down Bury Road that had been built in 1886 by the Duchess of Montrose, for her own private use. 'Now,' he said, looking over his shoulder towards the handful of people following in his wake, 'has the bride someone to give her away?'

Roberta shook her head. 'No. We'll all walk up the aisle together, if you don't mind?'

The vicar shook his head, and Kit squeezed Roberta's hand and quickly kissed her cheek, as they continued towards the church door. They all waited while the vicar unlocked the door then followed him inside. He turned to them all. 'If you give me a minute, Eric'll tell you when to come up to the altar.'

Roberta turned and looked at her mother, radiant in purple, but already in tears. She handed Boris's lead to Kit and hugged Brenda, and afterwards Cynthia. 'Pity about the weather,' said Kit's mother.

He looked at his bride. 'Oh, we don't care about the weather, do we, Roberta?'

And then the warden beckoned them down the aisle.

Roberta linked her right hand through Kit's arm and held James's hand with her left. All three of them walked up the aisle, followed by Brenda, holding firmly on to Boris's lead, and Cynthia. There was no music, just the sound of their heels clicking on the stone floor of this august church.

Beginning to enjoy this unusual occasion, the vicar smiled warmly at the group of people approaching him. He cleared his throat and announced: 'Dearly beloved, we are gathered together here in the sight of God, and in the face of this congregation to join together this man and this woman in holy Matrimony . . .'

Just a simple ceremony, but moving nonetheless. And then they couldn't get away! The vicar kept them talking in the vestry, regaling them with tales of the Duke and Duchess of Montrose, and how keen they had been on horseracing. He also mentioned how years ago one particular vicar had prayed earnestly for rain during a particularly parched summer, only to be ticked off after his sermon by the Duchess because her horses ran far better on hard ground!

There was no confetti, and no flowers. Roberta had asked for it that way. She just wanted to marry Kit in a church with nobody else around. It was her dearest wish, and he made sure it was granted. But they were given one unexpected gift. As they left the church, the rain had stopped and the sun broke through, brightening the dark November sky and making everything around, from the damp leaves on the evergreen trees and shrubs to the grass and pavement, simply sparkle.

Protocol was forgotten. The vicar and his warden left first, closely followed by Brenda, Cynthia, James and Boris. The bride and groom watched them all drive off down the Bury Road before they climbed into Kit's car.

He leant across and kissed her mouth. 'Well, Mrs Fordham-Clarke, have I told you lately how beautiful you are, and how proud I am to be your husband, and how much I really love you?'

She responded warmly to his kiss. 'I believe you did mention something along those lines a while ago. In fact,' she looked at her watch, 'about three hours ago, to be precise, when you woke me up . . . remember?'

His eyes searched her face. 'Oh, yes, so I did. It was a worthy way to start our wedding day, don't you think?'

She wrapped her arms around his neck. 'I don't know about worthy, but it was certainly very good.' And then she pulled away slightly. 'Will we always love each other this way, Kit?'

He put his finger on her lips. 'I'll always love you, Roberta. I think I was destined to love you.'

'Well, if you were destined to love me, I was certainly destined to love you.'

He ran his hand down to her stomach. 'And you're okay for this journey, still no morning sickness?'

She shook her head. 'No. No sickness. Not this time.'

He straightened himself in his seat and turned on the car's ignition. He looked briefly at his wife. 'Well, in that case, my darling, Venice here we come!'

71

March, 1977

Julia picked up the German Etienne Aigner handbag and examined it thoroughly. An unusual gathered shape, made in the softest hide leather, superbly stitched and dyed olive green with a tan trim. A small nugget of gold, enscribed with the maker's name, adorned the front of the handbag and the zipper section inside. She recognised its supreme quality straight away and her thoughts flew back to Purley's. She replaced the handbag on its stand at the Mipel Trade Fair in Milan and moved on. The sweet smell of leather pervaded the air everywhere, and to Julia it was like being transported back to yesteryear. She felt half-thrilled and half-scared because she'd come such a long way in a few short months, and now that she'd actually booked her ticket home, was beginning to be frightened.

She continued her browsing, noting the high fashion, bright colours and way-out styles of the many big-name traders at this prominent fair which had been running, spring and autumn, since the beginning of the sixties. Mipel took its name from Milan and *pelle*, Italian for leather. In Italy the rich changed their leather clothes and accessories with the season, and revelled in buying goods made from expensive skins like ostrich, lizard, snake and crocodile. All the merchandise at the Mipel Trade Fair was at least two years ahead of anything sold in London. Julia could pick up a lot of ideas for the future here.

She continued on amongst the throng of people, to the Friitala leather wear. She stroked one of their supple coats, of the finest leather, and remembered something Nathan had once said. 'The English put their wealth into their gardens, the French in their mouths, and the Italians on their backs!' She smiled; another one of Nathan's sweeping statements, but something stirred within her because this was where she wanted to be, back in the leather business. But how?

She flicked back her glossy hair, feeling confident in her new cut. The first thing she'd done, when she'd arrived in Milan was to book herself into a hairdressing salon. In the five months she'd been away, her hair had grown considerably but still hung in its untidy layers. Now, it had been bluntly bobbed to just below her chin, transforming her face with its thick easy curls. Julia looked relaxed and felt healthy, she'd put on about a stone in weight and was tanned a light golden brown from being out of doors in the early Italian sunshine.

She slipped off her dusky pink jacket and slipped on a blood red suede coat. Nobody was around, and she snuggled into the silken suede. She noticed a couple of men looking at her, smiling approvingly. She smiled back and slipped out of the coat, looking at her watch. It was nearly lunchtime. She was hungry and thirsty. She decided to get something to drink.

It was the usual thing at trade fairs. You queued relentlessly for a cup of cappuccino, then struggled to find a seat. But she did manage to squeeze herself between two enormous Italian ladies. Julia hadn't bothered with food, she'd eat like a king later. Instead, she lit up a cigarette, slumped back in her seat, and allowed her eyes to wander around the stands.

And then her thoughts slipped back a few weeks. *I wonder what you're doing now, my darling Nefris?* She looked at her watch again. The *gymnasio* where he taught finished at 1 p.m. so he'd be home, in his tiny little house on the hillside, looking out on to the Plaka. Julia's heart jumped into her mouth as her thoughts lurched back to Athens and her arrival at the Pension Acropolis House in the old Turkish quarter or Plaka. She drew on her cigarette, and watched as the two Italian ladies gabbled in their native tongue. Julia blew smoke into the air, and indulged herself in memories. *I did love you, Nefris, but I suppose I didn't love you enough.*

Her first week in Athens had been cold, miserable and damp. The Plaka, with its narrow labyrinthine streets nestling into the northeastern slope of the Acropolis, positively buzzed with tourists in the summer, but in early-November it had seemed dead, and when she'd walked out in the evening and taken her courage in both hands to enter a bar or a restaurant, she'd stuck out like a sore thumb. Groups of unsavoury men gawped at her. In fact, after three days, she gave careful consideration to going back home. She'd done the tourist bits, visited the Acropolis, the Parthenon, the Theatre of Herodes Atticus, and the Roman Stadium, to name but a few, but it wasn't much fun on her own. And she couldn't speak Greek, except please, *sas paraka-lo*, and thank you, *sas efhari-sto*, and yes, *ne*, or no, *o-hi*.

And then just as she thought she could bear it no longer, an extremely deep voice had asked, '*Apo pu i-ste?*'

At the tap on her shoulder, Julia turned in her seat and looked into a pair of smouldering dark eyes. 'I'm sorry?'

Nefris Patras smiled. 'I said, where are you from?' Immediately he moved from his table and pulled a chair out at hers. He sat down, bringing his glass of red wine to his lips. 'You look so sad, English lady, you've looked sad all week.' He touched her hand, and then confidently sat back in his chair, drawing on his cigarette. Julia was actually eating at the time, but the Greeks didn't bother about such things.

She stabbed at her *meze*. 'You speak good English?'

He leant closer. 'I teach at a *gymnasio*.' He pointed out of the restaurant. 'Over there.'

Julia smiled. 'Where's over there?'

'Koukaki. I teach twelve year olds English.'

She laughed. 'Well, that's a relief.'

He pointed to her. 'See, you laugh. I thought you'd never laugh.' Nefris pulled a dire face. 'I thought you always *so* sad.'

Julia averted her eyes and sipped her wine, sizing him up. Early-forties, very handsome but typically Greek. He obviously thought she was a pushover. Julia decided there and then she was going home *immediately*.

But she didn't go home. Instead she allowed Nefris Patras to become her friend. And that was when Ancient Athens came alive for her and she started to relish her sightseeing on the arm of her wise friend. Julia soon learnt that wisdom is like power, it's an aphrodisiac very hard to resist.

His house was so tiny, just two up and two down. The usual flat-roofed, flimsy-looking abode and painted bright blue. Julia's thoughts flew back to Aberdeen, and how she'd turned up her nose at Kit's bedsit. That was luxury, compared to Nefris's home. But it didn't matter, because this home wasn't meant to be a showpiece, although his numerous friends milled in and out. It was simply used for eating, and drinking, and washing, and eventually making love with Julia. And when Nefris went off early in the mornings, school beginning at 8 a.m., Julia would clean, and write letters home, and sometimes cook or even sketch. She'd do all the things she'd never found enough time to do before.

She stayed on. Straight after Christmas, Nefris took her to visit his ailing parents at Nafplion, tucked securely into the Argolic Gulf on the Peloponnese, a major port in Greece since way back in the Bronze Age. Nafplion, with his narrow streets, elegant Venetian houses and fine Neo-classical mansions, was originally the capital of Greece but now just a charming up-market seaside resort. They stayed for the Feast of St Basil, a church ceremony followed by much eating and rejoicing, and ate *vasilopitta*, or New Year pie, and in Julia's slice was a coin which was meant to herald a lucky year. It was also in the backstreets of Nafplion that she found the most wonderful silverware shop, specialising in handmade jewellery which was different from anything she'd ever seen. The way they worked and twisted the silver, often part-oxidised, or polished, or both, or even mixed with gold, grabbed her attention and sent her rushing for her sketch pad.

Before they returned to Athens, Nefris took her on a brief trip into Central Greece, to Delphi in Sterea Ellada. They travelled by train, and stayed for two nights at the Hotel Amalias to visit Ancient Delphi on a crisp, sunny, winter's day. Built on the slopes of Mount Parnassos and overlooking the Gulf of Corinth, even in its winter starkness it was breathtakingly beautiful. To wander through the ruins of such an amazing civilisation was like being transported back in time. Nefris explained to Julia how Ancient Delphi was once regarded as the navel of the world. According to mythology, Zeus released two eagles at opposite ends of the earth and they met there.

Then it was back to Athens, and Nefris returned to school. That was when Julia became restless, and by the beginning of February she'd booked an air-ticket for Rome. She knew she broke his heart when she left, and had a feeling they'd never meet again, but he didn't beg her to stay and she was grateful for that, amongst so many other things that he'd enriched her life with during their unforgettable time together.

After Rome, travelling mostly by bus, Julia visited Naples, then Sorrento and over to the island of Capri, then a train trip all the way back up to Perugia, and then Florence which she adored, and Rimini and Venice. Milan was her last port of call. She was flying home directly afterwards.

She had allowed herself just two days in Milan, staying at the Hotel Manzoni, and was grateful she hadn't decided on more. Milan might well be considered a commercial powerhouse, but she missed the laziness of the rest of Italy. She couldn't imagine Milan sleeping in the midday sun. But she enjoyed looking round the headquarters of Gucci, and bought herself a pair of shoes from Salvatore Ferragamo.

Julia's mind slipped back into gear. She stubbed out her cigarette and, picking up her ancient Enny hangbag, eased herself away from the two Italian ladies. She was tired and decided to take one last look around then head back to her hotel. She hitched her bag over her shoulder and headed for the Beltrami stand.

72

'Been to any good football matches lately?'

The voice was like velvet stroking her senses. Julia turned round quickly and saw Nathan standing behind her. He wasn't smiling, his eyes were searching hers, and Julia felt dizzy beneath their gaze. He was impeccably dressed as usual, the perfect embodiment of everything she'd ever loved back home. She suddenly felt stupid because all she wanted to do was cry.

'Nathan?' she whispered.

He took her arm and led her slightly away from the bustling crowds. 'What are you doing here?'

She shrugged. 'I'm actually on my way home. Milan is my last stop-over and I just happened to see the Mipel Trade Fair advertised. It was a pure coincidence, me being here the same time.' She looked into his eyes, and noticed they weren't mocking her anymore. His eyes had always mocked her in the past. Or perhaps that was just her interpretation. 'What are you doing here?'

He shrugged. 'Just thought I'd take a look.'

She smiled. 'Rather a long way from Cambridge to take a look?'

'Yes, well, you know me. If it's worth having, it's worth going a long way for.'

'And is it?' Julia looked around herself. 'Worth having?'

He laughed. 'Well, it's certainly worth nabbing a few of their ideas.' He eyed her keenly. 'How did you get in, Julia? Are you back in the trade?'

She shrugged. 'I'd like to be, Nathan, but no, I'm fancy free at the moment. Open to all offers.'

He half-smiled, half-frowned, 'I thought they were very strict here? Or did you slip in the back way?'

'No, Nathan, I did what you often do. I smiled sweetly and *I lied*.' He laughed, and stepped closer to her avoiding a group of people coming his way. He looked down into her eyes, and once more she basked in his charm. She steeled herself. 'Are you alone?'

'Yes. Are you?'

'Yes.'

He nodded thoughtfully. 'Good. Then let's be together.'

73

Nathan was staying at the luxurious Principe di Savoia, near the Stazione Centrale, and they took a taxi and ate *Agnolotti* for lunch in Doney's cafe there. After two bottles of Frecciarossa, Julia was feeling relaxed.

Nathan looked at her expectantly. 'What would you like to do now?'

She picked up her handbag and pushed back her seat. 'I'll like you to call me a taxi, please, Nathan. I'm tired and I'd like to go back to my hotel.'

He stood up quickly and moved rapidly to her side. 'Don't go.'

She looked into his eyes and was surprised to read panic. It reminded her of Nefris's expression when she'd told him she was leaving. It was a look that gave the observer strength. 'Why? What did you expect?'

Nathan floundered slightly. 'Nothing. I just don't want you to go. If it's rest you want, come up to my room. You can rest. I won't disturb you.'

She snorted unkindly. 'Oh, Nathan, I'm not *that* Julia anymore.'

He looked at her, quite sincerely. 'I know you're not.' He took a deep breath and looked around. Julia noticed the uncertainty in his behaviour and it was endearing, too endearing, so she gritted her teeth and turned on her heel. '*Julia!* Can I see you tonight?'

He was by her side again, breathing so hard she could smell the wine on his breath. She said flippantly, 'I don't see why not.'

'Okay. I'll call you a taxi, and pick you up at eight.'

Julia dressed very carefully in the only dress she'd packed. In fact, she hadn't packed one at all originally, but Nefris had bought this

335

particular one for her in Athens, in a sale, and even then had spent a whole month's salary on it. It was a semi-fitted Nina Ricci button-through grey silk dress. She looked at herself in the mirror and remembered the girl in the grey Dior gown, hungry for Nathan's attention and even hungrier for his loving. Then she remembered the hurt and the pain when he'd switched from her to Roberta, and knew she could never trust him again. But that didn't mean she couldn't enjoy his company and accept his hospitality here in Milan.

They ate at the famous Giannino's, with Nathan dancing attention on Julia. Again she allowed him to order for her, trusting this man to provide only the best. They drank Frascati and Sassella, and ate *Fritto misto*, a deep fried medley of assorted fish and shellfish, followed by *Bistecca alla fiorentina*, Florentine-style steaks grilled with olive oil, pepper, lemon juice, salt and parsley, and then *Granita*, a lemon-flavoured ice.

Nathan reached out to take her hand. 'You're more beautiful than I've ever seen you, Julia. And you seem so relaxed. A transformation from the last time.'

'Am I?'

'You know you are. What are your plans now?'

She shrugged. 'Something to do with leather and jewellery, I hope. I suppose I'll just have to find myself a job. I've made lots of sketches, gleaned so many ideas, and the most wonderful thing is that I feel alive again. I have my old drive back, and after all this time I still want to conquer the world! I'd forgotten what that felt like before I came away.'

'Where will you live?'

'In Cambridge. I've already got that planned. My brother-in-law is just completing some luxury flats near the river, I suppose you've seen them? Anyway one of them is reserved for me.' She watched Nathan's discomfiture and decided to rub salt into his wounds. 'You did know Roberta was married? She's expecting a baby in three months' time.'

He narrowed his eyes. 'I'd heard on the grapevine. I hope she's happy. She deserves to be.'

'And you, Nathan? Are you happy?'

He scoffed, 'I'd be a darn'sight happier if my sales suddenly shot up.'

'Bad?'

He inclined his head. 'Could be better. I think Jim Callaghan's on borrowed time.'

'But your business is rock solid, Nathan. If you didn't sell anything for a month, you wouldn't need to worry.'

'But that's where you're wrong, Julia. I'm surprised to hear you say that.'

She smiled. 'I suppose I just see you as very, very rich.'

He raised a hand to the waiter. '*Il conto, per favore.*' He looked again at Julia. 'Getting rich, and staying rich, are a world apart, Julia. Especially in business.'

'But haven't you got it all securely stashed away?'

He laughed. 'Is that what you think?'

She smiled wisely. 'Yes, I know how you operate, Nathan, from your head, not your hip.' She touched his hand. 'But as far as I'm concerned, I don't particularly want to be rich.'

'You will always be rich, Julia. It's built into your genes.'

The waiter arrived with the bill and Nathan paid with cash. '*Grazie.*'

'*Grazie, grazie. Buona notte, Signor, Signora.*' The waiter bustled off, very grateful for his enormous tip.

Nathan looked at Julia. 'Your hotel or mine?'

How could she pass up this opportunity? However much she distrusted him, she wanted him just the same. But she decided to make sure that this night wasn't the same. 'I think . . . yours.'

74

Flopping on to a soft peach brocade-covered settee, Julia gazed around at the magnificent Italian plasterwork of Nathan's opulent hotel sitting room. 'Trust you, Nathan, to have a whole suite.' Divested of his jacket and tie, he sat down next to her holding two goblets of cognac. He offered one to her. She took the goblet and sniffed the contents. 'What's this? Cognac?'

Nathan smiled. 'I'm happy to drink Italian wine, but don't expect me to drink their brandy.'

Julia sipped the cognac, knowing she'd already drunk far too much. She slipped off her shoes and tucked her feet beneath her. Nathan watched and ran one hand across her knee. 'Don't . . . please.'

He lifted his hand, and slumped back in his seat. 'So, you've told me about Athens, and Nafplion, and . . . where was it . . . Delphi? And I know you've seen a lot of Italy. But where else have you been?'

Julia pouted slightly and shuffled in her seat. 'Nowhere. Although I shall take lots of holidays in the future, I've promised myself that.'

Nathan frowned. 'How long did you spend in Greece?' She counted out her fingers and held up four. He folded his hand around them. 'Four weeks . . . or months?'

She pulled her hand away. 'Four months and five days to be precise.'

He looked at her quizzically. 'And now you know Greece pretty well?'

She shook her head. 'No. Well, I know Athens pretty well.'

'You spent all that time Athens?' Julia nodded. Nathan licked his bottom lip. 'Who with?'

She reached down to put her glass on the carpet. 'A friend I met, a rather special friend.'

'Oh, I see. So you fell in love?' Julia took Nathan's free hand again and brought it to her face, enjoying the feel of his skin against hers. She gently kissed its palm. Very quickly, he placed his brandy on the floor and moved closer. He kissed her cheek, and then her neck. 'Tell me?'

'Why?'

'Because I'd like to know.'

'Does it matter? It's past, Nathan.'

He moved away slightly to look into her eyes. 'Is it?'

'Oh, yes. Definitely.'

'But he changed you, didn't he? Made you happy?'

Lolling back on the settee, Julia chuckled and pulled him closer, enjoying his caresses. 'He certainly did, and he gave me back my confidence, and taught me how to enjoy my freedom.'

Nathan started to undo the small buttons down the front of her dress. 'Your freedom?'

Julia raised her head from the settee and ran her tongue over Nathan's bottom lip. He responded by flicking his over the soft inner part beneath her lips. But Julia just carried on talking. He smiled and looked into her animated face. 'Freedom to sit on a bus for hours and watch the landscape spin by. Freedom to enjoy a pace of life that almost comes to a standstill. Nathan, have you ever really looked at the Italian landscape ... with its architecture so majestically etched into the hillsides, and even when it's decaying it still conveys such grandeur? And Tuscany, and Umbria, and especially Rome. And Florence! Nathan, Florence is wonderful ... and Venice simply takes your breath away. Before I met Nefris, I didn't know how to *really* enjoy all of this. And ... after Greece, I didn't mind being on my own.'

'Nefris?'

Julia nodded, enjoying the feel of Nathan's hands sliding beneath her dress, over her bare skin to her back, and undoing her bra. She sighed as he fondled and kissed her breasts. 'Nefris Patras.'

He slipped the dress off her shoulders, pushing it down to her waist with her bra. Nathan hesitated, feasting his eyes on Julia's partially naked frame. He started to unbutton his own shirt. 'And are there any Italian lovers I should know about?'

'Nope. I told you, in Italy I've been alone. I wanted it that way.

I've liked it that way.' She helped Nathan remove his cuff links and watched as he tossed his shirt on the floor. She lowered her legs and slipped out of her dress.

Nathan ogled her suspender belt and stockings. 'Do you always wear stockings, Julia?' He smiled knowingly. 'Or is it just for me?'

She caught her breath as he ran his hand between her legs. 'Definitely just for you.'

Nathan laughed softly and proceeded to remove his clothes. He gently pulled down Julia's panties and tossed them on to his own heap of clothes.

She pulled him towards her and kissed his mouth. 'I suppose you're going to say I'm too fat now?'

'You're perfect, Julia. You know you are.'

She sighed pleasurably as his fingers set to work. 'Nathan, you've got a really comfortable bed over there.'

He took her hands and moved them on to himself. 'I know. But I'm going to have you here first.'

Julia watched the ecstasy on his face as she stroked him. 'Have me? Is that what this is?'

He didn't hesitate. 'It is with you, Julia. To have and to hold.'

And then he made love to her, and it was like nothing she'd ever experienced before.

75

Julia woke and for a few seconds wondered where she was. She looked at her wristwatch. It was 6 a.m. She turned, enormous relief washing over her because Nathan was still there. But how could he go? She'd made sure of that. Julia swallowed hard, remembering the night before. Had it really happened or had she dreamt it all? She touched his face, very gently. Julia didn't want him to wake, and the love she felt for him was like a nagging pain forever torturing her heart. Would it *ever* go away?

She turned on to her back and looked up at the ceiling, pulling her thoughts together. What would happen now? He'd be different this morning, she just knew he wouldn't be the same. Every time he let her down. First in the nightclub, then at Clare's, and then in her own house in Chelsea. As quick as a flash, she slid out of the bed. Well, he wasn't going to let her down anymore. She'd booked her flight for today, and today she'd go home. He'd asked her to stay and return with him the following day, because he needed to go back to the Trade Fair, he'd got people to see. But what would be the point of following him about like a puppy-dog? Julia was through with all that.

She wandered through to the sitting room and picked up her clothes, still lying as they'd been thrown the night before. She started to dress. Please don't wake, Nathan, please let me leave without you waking, she said to herself over and over again.

She walked back into the bedroom, her handbag over her arm. He was still asleep. Sound asleep. She took a few paces towards the bed and looked down on him, her heart aching. 'God, I love you,' she said out loud. For a second she was tempted to wake him and tell him, just declare her love. But if she did, what had the last five months been about? She would just be stepping back in time.

Julia turned and walked towards the door. She was about to leave when a strong shaft of sunlight filtered into the room. It caught the corner of her eye and the mirror at the end of the bed. Something registered in her head. She hissed, 'Of course!' and bit her lip. '*Of course.*'

Julia looked once more at the bed. She whispered 'I'll *work* for you, Nathan, that's what I'll do. I might not be able to have you, but I can work for you again!' Why had this seemingly obvious thought never entered her head before? Maybe because it was the one thing she wanted too much and dared not think about. But it had to come from him. She rummaged in her handbag, and pulled out the only lipstick she could find. 'Sod it,' she said, beneath her breath. 'Here goes another Lancôme.'

She crept over to the mirror, and in bold letters wrote: '*Buongiorno, N.P. Business: You need me! Sex: 100/10! J.T.*'

And then she left to go home.

76

Nathan woke. He stretched out an arm, expecting to touch Julia. It had been some night. Nathan remembered only one other person who'd made him feel the way Julia just had. In a haze of sleep, he remembered Roberta. *How he'd loved her.* And then his eyes flickered, and opened, because in the end it had been a crippling love. One that had taken him a long time to get over. In fact, he never had got over it. If Roberta walked back into his life tomorrow, Nathan knew he wouldn't be able to resist her.

But she wasn't going to, and he needed adoration from the woman in his life, undivided attention and absolute devotion. And more children. And Roberta's sister would give him all those, he had no doubt. And Julia was clever, and accomplished, and adorably beautiful. And he loved her, as much as he was able.

Nathan stroked her side of the bed, which felt cold and empty. He woke and immediately sat up. Where was she? His eyes ranged around the room, expecting to see her. He clambered out of bed, almost tripping on the bedding half-strewn on the floor after their wild night, and cursed. 'Sod you, Julia, where the hell are you?'

Almost immediately his eyes caught the mirror and he walked towards it, reading her special message. He moved closer, seeing his own naked frame reflected behind Julia's bold words. He'd already decided to offer her a job, but was glad to see she'd thought along the same lines. He did need her. In more ways than one.

He sighed, 'Julia, what a girl you are. In fact . . . what a *lady.*'

77

Julia's first port of call was Chiswick, and Clare. The two women hugged each other, not wanting to let go. Clare kept her arms tightly wrapped round her cousin, practically squeezing the life out of her. 'Oh, Julia, you don't know how I've missed you!' When she did finally stand back and examine her cousin, she beamed her approval. 'You look wonderful, darling! I've never seen you look so well.' She took Julia's arm and led her into the drawing room. 'Now, tell me all about it. I'm dying to hear about this Nefris. You made him sound so adorable, I honestly thought you'd get married. I thought we'd lost you, and you'd stay in Athens for good.'

Julia shook her head. 'He was adorable, Clare, but he wasn't right for me.' She lowered her eyes, remembering Nathan and how *he'd* made her feel. 'And I wanted to come home.'

'Well, this is your home, Julia. You can stay as long as you like.'

'Just two days, Clare, and then I'll go home to Cambridge.'

'Home to Cambridge? But surely you're not going back there to live?'

Julia nodded. 'Yes, I've been thinking about this for a long time.'

'But what sort of career can you make for yourself in bloody Cambridge? Don't be silly, Julia, there are far more opportunities for you here in London.'

'There probably are, Clare, but I want to go home.' She lowered her eyes.

As sharp as ever, she lifted up her cousin's chin. 'Not bloody Nathan again?'

Julia shook her head. 'I don't know. Maybe . . . if he offers me a job. There are so many things I could do for him, Clare. I've got ideas pouring out of my head, and he needs new ideas. We all do.'

'And what if he won't have you back?'

Defiantly, Julia shrugged. 'It'll be his loss.' She walked towards the window, enjoying looking out on to Clare's garden once more. 'I'll set up in opposition, that's what I'll do.'

Clare laughed. 'Atta girl! How about a glass of wine?'

Julia turned quickly and grinned at her cousin. 'Thought you'd never ask.' She followed her through to the kitchen. 'How are the twins? Do you know, Clare, I've missed those girls *so* much.'

Clare took a bottle of Meursault from the fridge and poured two glasses. 'They're fine. Vivien's at last realised that school isn't an option, so she's finally settled down. They loved the postcards you sent them. They've pinned them all around their bedrooms.' She offered Julia some wine. 'Did you know Nick gets married in a couple of weeks' time?'

Julia's face lit up. 'No, really? That's wonderful.' She took the wine and sipped it. 'I shall go and see them tomorrow, before I go home.' Julia looked at her cousin. 'I'm really looking forward to seeing them all . . . the gremlins have now gone.'

Clare squeezed her arm. 'Good. They'd love to see you. Oh, Julia, it's so good to have you home. Life just wasn't the same without you around.'

'And how's your career?'

Clare's face lit up. 'It's going so well. Do you know, I've been on the radio, on *Woman's Hour*?' She gave her tinkling laugh. 'And Dr Clare Purley has even been in a couple of articles in women's magazines.'

'So now you're famous. You deserve it, Clare. What a pity your mother isn't around to see. Wouldn't she be proud? By the way, how's Uncle Peter?'

'He's fine. Already got a lady friend.' Clare shrugged. 'He'll be married again soon, you'll see.'

'Do you mind?'

'No, why should I? It's his life, the same as mine is mine.'

'And Harry? Do you still see her?'

Fleetingly, Clare looked sad. 'Sometimes, but not so often.' She gave a sheepish smile as she sipped her wine. 'Mind you, I do have another rather special friend.'

'Female?'

'Of course.'

'And is she nice?'

Clare shrugged. 'She's more my age, and she's in medicine. In fact, she's a nurse. In fact, I think I'm in love, Julia. Does that sound crazy? I've only known her a couple of months but if I could, I think I'd marry her! Does that sound stupid to you?'

'No, not at all. It sounds exactly right.'

'And the girls simply adore her.'

'Does it worry you – about the girls, I mean? Will you tell them?'

'One day. It's Nathan I worry about the most. He doesn't know, and I'm so afraid he might use it against me.'

'He wouldn't do that.'

'Oh, wouldn't he? I'm not so sure.'

Julia moved closer to her cousin. 'He loves those girls, Clare. Haven't you noticed the way he looks at them, and the way they look at him? It would hurt them deeply if he said anything unkind about you, and confuse them too. Why would he abuse them in that way?'

Clare shrugged. 'I don't know.' She looked up and grinned. 'That's my gremlin, and I just have to live with it, I suppose.'

Later on that evening, Julia rang her mother.

'Oh, Julia! You don't know how good it is to hear your voice in England. When are you coming home?'

'The day after tomorrow. I'm going to see Sarayu, and hopefully Nick tomorrow. Is my flat still reserved, do you know?'

'Reserved and very nearly ready. Top floor, looking out on to the river, with a balcony and three bedrooms, two bathrooms, sitting room, dining room and kitchen. How does that sound?'

'It sounds wonderful, Mum. I can't wait to see it. How's Roberta?'

'She's doing well.'

'And James?'

'Oh he's beside himself with excitement. A pony, and a new baby on the way.'

'And . . . Kit?'

'Kit's fine, Julia. He adores them all.'

Julia looked around Clare's drawing room, wondering for the first time if she'd done the right thing coming home. There were no painful memories abroad. Perhaps she should have stayed in Greece after all. 'And how are you, Mum? I hear Uncle Peter's got a new girlfriend.'

'Has he? I really wouldn't know. I never see him. But I'm fine. Cynthia and I have a jolly old time, I can tell you.'

'I bet you do.' Julia sucked in her breath. 'I'll see you the day after tomorrow, Mum.'

'Oh, Julia, before you go, I almost forgot – Nathan Purley rang. Twice actually. Did you know he's in Milan? Isn't that a coincidence? Anyway, he wants to see you at the warehouse when he gets back and . . .' There was a silence down the phone as Brenda racked her brain to remember the rest of Nathan's message. Julia held her breath. 'Now, what else was it he said? Oh, blimey, I've forgotten. Hang on . . . yes, I remember. He said, "Sorry he missed you, but the mirror said it all."' Brenda laughed. 'Or something like that. Are you going back to Purley's, Julia? I must say, I'm surprised.'

She couldn't speak. The words just wouldn't leave her mouth. *The mirror said it all.* Then her heart plummeted as she thought of the ambiguity of his comment. Why hadn't he simply said, 'Yes, the job's yours!'

'Julia? Are you there?'

'Yes, Mum. I'm still here.'

'So, are you planning to work for Nathan again?'

She gulped. 'Maybe. I'm not sure.'

'Well, I suppose you'll make your own mind up. It's nothing to do with me. Anyway, dear, I shall look forward to seeing you. Are you coming on the train?'

'Yes, but don't worry, I'll get a taxi, Mum. See you soon, take care.'

78

On her return to Newmarket, Julia rang Purley's warehouse and made an appointment to see Nathan the following day. His secretary explained how busy Mr Purley was, how he'd only just returned from Milan, but Julia was insistent upon seeing him soon.

She entered the warehouse not really knowing what to expect. He hadn't rung again although she'd quite expected him to. Julia sighed. The same old Nathan: out of sight, out of mind. But still she'd dressed with care, wearing a close-fitting cream cashmere cowl-necked jumper tucked into the gathered waist of a new calf-length Sarayu suede tan skirt. On her feet were high-heeled leather boots. The sun was shining, and she'd removed her jacket and left it in her mother's car. She wanted to appear casual yet smart.

There were a lot of new faces, in fact she recognised only a few. Everybody looked at her as she strode confidently along to Nathan's office on the mezzanine floor. Julia knocked at the door and went straight in.

He was seated behind his desk, busy on the telephone, and looked up and smiled at her, beckoning for her to sit down. Julia noticed his navy blue jacket, thrown over the back of his chair, and his pale blue shirt with natty striped tie. His hair, slightly shorter now but still flopping over his forehead and covering the tips of his ears, shone with cleanliness. At thirty-three, Nathan Purley hadn't lost any of his good looks; if anything, along with a few character lines, he'd acquired more. Julia slipped into the seat opposite and tried to fasten her mind on work instead of private memories of this man in front of her taking her to incredible sexual heights.

He put down the phone and immediately buzzed through to his secretary. 'No more calls, please.' Nathan got up out of his seat and walked straight round to Julia, taking her hand and pulling her to her feet. He leant back against his desk and gathered her into his arms, guiding her between his legs. Then he hungrily kissed her mouth, and her neck, running his hands round to her back and hugging her tightly. 'I missed you. You shouldn't have left like that.'

She smiled into his eyes. 'At least you noticed I was gone this time.'

'Julia, I always notice when you're gone. I notice everything about you. It's just, in the past, other things have got in the way.'

'Oh, yes. Like Clare? And my sister?'

He nodded contritely. 'I know, and I'm sorry about all that. But to use your words, it's past history.'

Julia pulled away slightly, but Nathan wouldn't let her out of his grip. 'I saw Clare and the girls.' Very softly she laughed. 'I hadn't realised how much I missed them all.'

'How are they?'

'You mean you don't know?'

'Well, I shall see the twins this weekend, but how's Clare?'

Julia looked at him, remembering her conversation with her cousin. 'She has a new friend and she's very happy, Nathan. She even said she'd like to get married.' Julia noticed his raised eyebrows. 'What do you think of that?'

Nathan smiled very wisely. 'I think . . . is her friend marriageable?'

'What do you mean?'

He kissed Julia's nose. 'You know what I mean.'

'Well, she's a woman, if that's what you mean.'

Nathan frowned. 'Look, do we have to talk about Clare? There are so many things you and I have to say.'

Julia was surprised. 'It doesn't bother you then? About Clare, I mean?'

'Why should it bother me? Oh . . . you mean because of the girls?'

Julia smiled and hugged him tightly, admiring his attitude. 'Did you know about her all the time?'

'No. Well, not at first. But when my daughters continually talk about their mummy's girlfriends, Clare's lifestyle starts to make sense.'

Julia giggled. 'Do they? Bless their hearts.'

Nathan tilted Julia's chin and looked into her eyes. 'And in answer to your question, I respect Clare very much as the mother of my daughters. If it wasn't for her, those little girls wouldn't be here now. Because that's another of my wicked deeds – I wanted her to get rid of them! How do you think that makes me feel?'

Julia lowered her eyes and took a deep breath. 'About as bad as me, I should think.'

Again, Nathan frowned and momentarily quizzed her with his eyes. She opened her mouth to speak and he quickly covered it with his forefinger. 'Another time, Julia. Let's talk about happy things today.'

She gulped and bit her lip and Nathan's finger slipped down to her chin. Julia was almost tempted to say, 'I love you.' Instead, she pulled back. 'Have you given any *real* consideration to what I wrote on the mirror?'

He turned and looked at his chair. 'It's all yours, Julia.'

She grinned and sucked in her breath. 'What do you mean?'

'I mean, my job. It's all yours, if you want it?'

'But what are you going to do?'

'Get out and about! Find more business. You can come with me some of the time.' He touched her hair. 'I love your hair like this, Julia. You should keep it this length. It makes you look grown up.'

'I am grown up, Nathan.'

'I know. And that's why I've just offered you my job.'

'And can I use my own ideas, even for the jewellery?'

He kissed her mouth. 'You can do what you like. I shall leave everything to you.'

'God, I . . .' Again, she was tempted to say, 'I love you.'

'I love you too, Julia.'

She froze. 'What did you just say?'

'I said, I love you too, Julia.' He allowed the words to register, then added, 'I realised it for sure when you turned round and looked at me at the Mipel Fair.'

'Nathan. Don't play about with me, please. Don't play about with my heart.'

'I'm not playing about with your heart, Julia. I love you.' He laughed. '*I love you!*'

She wrapped her arms around his neck, smelling the familiar Chanel aftershave, hardly able to believe what he had just said. 'Why didn't you bloody tell me before then?'

'You didn't exactly make it easy for me, Julia.' Briefly, his eyes mocked her. 'I seem to remember you were intent on calling all the shots while we were in Milan . . . and then you ran away!'

'Nathan, I couldn't bear it if I was dreaming. Please don't let me wake up.'

'You're not dreaming, Julia, and I hope you're well and truly awake because I have another proposition for you, and this is very important indeed.' He searched her eyes. 'Next year, I want us to go back to Milan, and stay in the same suite in the same hotel. And I want you to write that same message on that same mirror, but with one slight alteration.'

Julia smiled, not at all getting his drift. 'Yes, yes, yes . . . but what alteration?'

He kissed her mouth and whispered in her ear 'After the J, write P.'

Her heart stopped. She blinked and leant back, appraising this man she adored. 'I'm sorry? What do you mean?'

'Will you marry me, Julia? I would have asked you in Milan, if you hadn't run away.'

'Nathan, are you serious? You want me to marry you?'

He threw back his head. 'I thought a summer wedding.' He looked at her again. 'Let's do this thing in style?'

She put her hands to either side of his face. 'Did you ever doubt I'd say yes?'

'There were times, Julia, when I doubted I'd ever get close to you again. But when we met up again in Milan, I *knew* it was exactly right. I think I've loved you for a long time, it just took me a while to understand it.'

79

April 1977

'James!' Kit, wearing his navy business suit and looking supremely handsome, stood at the bottom of the stairs in Ash Cottage, calling to his step-son. 'James, I won't tell you again, I'll go without you if you're not down here this instant.'

With no make-up, half-brushed hair cascading around her face and down her back, Roberta walked through from the kitchen. She wore a simple white broderie anglaise dressing gown and nothing on her feet. Kit looked at his wife, noting the lustre on her cheeks and the glow in her eyes. Even like this, first thing in the morning, he adored her and would have halted anything just to take her into his arms. 'James?' she called, catching his admiring gaze and giving a half-smile before starting to mount the stairs.

Kit stalled her with his hand. 'No, I'll go.' He pecked Roberta's cheek and swiftly climbed the stairs, two at a time, meeting James at the top. 'Come on, we'll be late for school again.'

James followed him down the stairs. 'Mummy, can I ride Gussie tonight when I get home? You promised last night ... *please*, Mummy?'

Kit tapped him on the shoulder. 'Mummy's supposed to be taking it easy, Jamie, you know that.'

James implored his mother with his eyes. 'But, Mummy, it's *ages* since I rode Gussie.'

She grinned at her son. 'Hmmm ... all of two days.'

'Come on, James, I'll make sure you ride Gussie tonight. I shouldn't be too late. Now, we must be off. Say goodbye to your mum.'

He wrapped his arms around Roberta, as she bent down to kiss his cheek. 'Bye, James. And don't forget Grandma Cynthia's picking you up from school.'

He gave a gleeful smile, nodded, then pulled away and ran towards the front door. Kit watched him go towards the car before turning back to his wife. 'Have a nice lunch with Julia, darling, and you will call in and see me afterwards, won't you?'

'Can I bring her?'

Kit inclined his head towards the front door, before looking back at his wife. He smiled, and Roberta noticed a slight flicker in his grey eyes. 'Why not?'

She put her arms around his neck and kissed his mouth. 'I love you.'

He kissed her back. 'Not at much as I love you. Oh, no, I'm going to be late again. Take care today, Roberta . . . promise?'

'Promise.'

She waved goodbye as they drove off in Kit's car before closing the door and returning to the breakfast disarray in the kitchen. Ash Cottage was very different now. Full of soft greens and creams, yellows and golds, except for the sitting room, which proudly displayed Roberta's oyster pink three-piece suite and matching coloured curtains.

Clutching her back, she strolled rather heavily into the kitchen, with its numerous pots and pans and jolly blind at the window, and walked straight over to the door, opening it and peeking outside. She scanned the garden, then peered further down towards the paddock where James's New Forest bay mare, Gussie, short for Augusta, happily grazed. 'Boris!' Roberta called, and then in rather unladylike fashion put two fingers to her mouth and whistled, something her father had taught her as a child. It wasn't long before her faithful four-legged friend came bounding towards her, rushing into the kitchen to finish off James's breakfast cereal. 'There you are, you little tinker. I bet you've been down there with Gussie again, haven't you?'

Roberta put James's half-eaten cereal on to the floor and Boris lapped it up greedily. She sat down at a smaller version of her original oak kitchen table and poured herself another cup of tea, slumping back in her chair and running a hand through her untidy hair. Roberta's life had changed dramatically over the last seven months. She no longer ran her catering business, although she'd kept the name just in case she wanted to return to it in the future.

But her life was packed with so many other activities. Friends she'd made whilst living in Newmarket continually visited or she visited them, and she regularly had lunch or tea with Brenda and Cynthia, who now lived in her old house. And then there was Boris and Gussie. Roberta spent hours walking her dog, and as many hours lovingly grooming James's pony whilst fondly remembering her father and how he would have cherished being around at this special time. Kit had surprised Roberta by proving to be a fine horseman and giving plenty of time to James and Gussie. It had proved to be a real bonding point for the two of them.

She was happy, and content, and sometimes hardly dared stop to think about her good fortune. And then Roberta would remind herself that, whatever tomorrow brought, nothing could take away today.

80

Le Bistro on Bridge Street, between Portugal Place and the Round Church, was very popular in Cambridge, especially at lunchtimes. It bustled with businessmen and women, ladies who lunched, and maybe the odd student who could afford its delicious French cuisine. Julia and Roberta had eaten their lunch and now sat over coffee at a small round table near the window.

Julia grinned. 'Do you think we'll be like Mum and Auntie Nancy one day? Meeting every month to have a good gossip about our kids?'

Roberta laughed. 'Poor Auntie Nancy. Does Clare miss her?'

Julia gave a very unladylike snort, then chastised herself. 'Oh, I mustn't be unkind. Poor Nancy must have had a hellish life with Uncle Peter, and she was always good to me in her way. And as for Clare, too true she misses her mother, not least because a whirlwind has gone out of her life.' Julia laughed, more kindly now. 'The fuss she made when the twins were born. When I think back, it was an absolute scream! I wouldn't have missed it for the world. She caused almighty havoc, you know, Roberta, all the time. And thank God for Nathan, because any other father might have wrung her neck.'

Roberta allowed her eyes to rest on Julia's sparkling ruby and diamond ring. 'So when exactly in August is the wedding day?'

'The sixth. It's funny, isn't it? Mum was only saying the other day, she would have loved to see Auntie Nancy's face, firstly, when you married Kit and became Mrs Fordham-Clarke, and secondly, when I marry Nathan and become Mrs Purley.' Julia laughed. 'But I'm sure old Nance would have found a few choice words to put us all firmly back in our place.'

Roberta grinned. 'Where we belong.'

'Of course. Let's not forget we're Trees.'

'Well, I'm glad you and Nathan are waiting until August to get married. I don't want to watch you walk down the aisle like this!' Roberta pointed to her protruding belly. 'With a bit of luck, I'll be slim again.'

Julia eyed her sister enviously. 'But you look wonderful, Roberta. If you could just see yourself as others do.'

Roberta took a quick intake of breath, and held her sister's gaze. 'Thank you.'

'It's the truth. And I hope that next year we'll be sitting together like this and I'll look exactly like you.'

Roberta giggled. 'Does Nathan know about this?'

'Do you mind if I smoke?' Roberta shook her head and Julia reached for her cigarettes. 'No, he doesn't know, but I'm sure he won't mind.' She lit her cigarette and blew smoke away from the table. She looked at the cigarette. 'He's even accepted my *filthy* habits!'

Roberta giggled again. 'Well, perhaps he's got a few of his own?'

Julia drew on her cigarette again. 'Oh, is there something I don't know about my future husband?'

Roberta held out her hands. 'I was joking.' She sipped her coffee. 'Are you going to wear white? For the wedding, I mean?'

Julia laughed. 'Well, I thought slightly off-white, you know, more the *shop-soiled* look.'

'Shop-soiled? Don't be silly, Julia, you're not shop-soiled.'

She leant closer to her sister. 'I think perhaps I am but I don't care anymore. The one thing I've learnt about life is that the bad times pass as quickly as the good.'

Roberta surveyed her sister. 'And you're really happy now?'

Julia examined her ring. 'Yes. And you?'

Roberta beamed. Her eyes said it all. 'Like you, I have to pinch myself too, although it hasn't all been plain sailing. We've had a few ups and downs with James. I think Kit thought he could buy his love in the beginning, and strangely enough he did. It was the much coveted pony that really brought the two of them together.' She sat back in her seat. 'And now he wants to adopt James, make us a real family, especially with *Kit Junior* on his way.'

'His?'

Roberta shrugged. 'Or her. I really don't care.'

And what does James think about being adopted?'

'He's all for it, although whether or not he ever calls Kit "Daddy" will remain to be seen. Neither of us will push that. At the moment he's Kit, but James does want to be a Fordham-Clarke. I mean, he is, because I've already changed his name at school, but it would be nice to make it official ... Though I'll never let him forget what a splendid man his real father was. And nor, for that matter, will Kit.'

'I'm sure you won't.'

'And talking about children, what about Clare and her girls? How have they taken your good news?'

Julia drew on her cigarette. 'I think secretly Clare's pleased. I got the usual, "he'll only break your heart again!" stuff, but that's Clare. And, of course, the girls can't wait to be bridesmaids.'

Roberta smiled and looked at her watch. 'I really must be making a move. I'm going to pop in and see Kit. I wondered if you'd like to come with me, Julia? To say hallo?'

Her eyes widened and she bit her bottom lip. 'Is that a good idea?'

'Only if you'd like to?'

'But would Kit like it?'

'Yes. I think he would like to see you, Julia. You are my sister, after all.'

She narrowed her eyes and drew on her cigarette. 'If I come with you, will you come with me?'

'What do you mean?'

'To Chesterton? Nathan's there. Just call in and say hallo.'

Roberta shook her head. 'Oh, I don't think so. Not looking like this.'

'But you look beautiful, Roberta.' Julia stretched out her hand. 'And you are my sister, after all.'

Roberta smiled. 'Okay, if you like.'

Julia tossed back her hair then shifted closer across the table. 'Have you ever thought about it all, Roberta? The four of us ... we're bonded in a way.'

Roberta laughed, 'Yes, I suppose we are.'

Both women made a move, gathering their things together. They said a cheery goodbye to the waiters and left the restaurant, making their way to Portugal Place.

Julia linked her arm through her sister's. 'You and I, Roberta, are special. We're like two sides of the same coin.'

Roberta laughed. 'Oh, are we? And which side am I?'

'You, Roberta, are always the side you want to be. And I, sweet sister, just follow in your wake.'

HITCHED

The bestselling new novel by
Zoë Barnes

Hitch number one ... A quick jaunt to the registry office and off to the pub with a few friends to celebrate. That's all Gemma wants for her wedding to Rory. But then the parents hear the news.

Hitch number two ... Suddenly her little wedding is hijacked and turned into a Hollywood-style extravaganza. Before she knows what's hit her, Gemma is stampeded into yards of frothing tulle, fork buffets for five hundred, kilted page boys and an all-inclusive honeymoon in the Maldives ...

Hitch number three ... And while the dress may be a perfect fit, Gemma and Rory's relationship is coming apart at the seams ...

An irresistible look at wedding fever from the bestselling author of *Bumps*.

"An enjoyable and moving read ... funny and likeable novel"
Maeve Haran, *Daily Mail*

"Funny and eye-opening"   *Sunday Post*

"An entertaining and light-hearted story"   *The Observer*

MISS BUGLE SAW GOD
AMONG THE CABBAGES
Sara Yeomans

Growing up in the small English village of Swain's Chard in the 50's under the auspices of their eccentric headmistress Miss Bugle, Jenny, Phillipa and Ann take her teachings for granted: God is Everywhere: Beauty is Truth, Truth Beauty.

So the "Nothing Matters, Nothing Exists" philosophy of the 60's universities and drama schools they attend is a massive culture shock.

Jenny is crushed by the aftermath of an affair with her moral tutor; Ann has to learn to cope with her dangerous talent for sex; and Phillipa is hampered in her quest for stardom by a less than sylph-like figure.

And now as Miss Bugle's girls return to the redemptive shelter of Swain's Chard they are shocked to find they must fight to preserve their benevolent but threatened corner of England.

"A witty evocation of friendship, class and testing boundaries"
Times Educational Supplement

"Genuinely moving, offbeat, funny novel about two generations of women from childhood to motherhood"
Scotland on Sunday

"Entertaining and witty - Enid Blyton for Bitches"   *19*

The very best of Piatkus fiction is now available in paperback as well as hardcover. Piatkus paperbacks, where *every* book is special.

☐ 0 7499 3083 7	Bonded	Chrissa Mills	£5.99
☐ 0 7499 3030 6	Bumps	Zoë Barnes	£5.99
☐ 0 7499 3072 1	Hitched	Zoë Barnes	£5.99
☐ 0 7499 3098 5	The Count	Helena Dela	£5.99
☐ 0 7499 3087 X	The Long Midnight of Barney Thomson	Douglas Lindsay	£6.99
☐ 0 7499 3052 7	Schrödinger's Baby	H. R. McGregor	£6.99
☐ 0 7499 3080 2	Grace	Carrie Worrall	£6.99

The prices shown above were correct at the time of going to press. However, Piatkus Books reserve the right to show new retail prices on covers which may differ from those previously advertised in the text or elsewhere.

Piatkus Books will be available from your bookshop or newsagent, or can be ordered from the following address:
Piatkus Paperbacks, PO Box 11, Falmouth, TR10 9EN
Alternatively you can fax your order to this address on 01326 374 888 or e-mail us at books @barni.avel.co.uk.

Payments can be made as follows: Sterling cheque, Eurocheque, postal order (payable to Piatkus Books) or by credit card, Visa/Mastercard. Do not send cash or currency. UK and B.F.P.O. customers should allow £1.00 postage and packing for the first book, 50p for the second and 30p for each additional book ordered to a maximum of £3.00 (7 books plus).

Overseas customers, including Eire, allow £2.00 for postage and packing for the first book, plus £1.00 for the second and 50p for each subsequent title ordered.

NAME (block letters) _____

ADDRESS_____

_____

I enclose my remittance for £ _____

I wish to pay by Visa/Mastercard   Expiry Date:_____
